RUSSIA
NMARK
BALTIC SEA
PRUSSIA
K. OF POLAND
BOHEMIA
AUSTRIA
Buda
HUNGARY
TRANSYLVANIA
BLACK SEA
OTTOMAN EMPIRE
Istanbul
Scutari
APLES
Tabriz
Bagdad
CERIGO
RHODES
CRETE
CYPRUS
SEA
Alexandria
EGYPT
Cairo

The Wanderer

Burwell B. Wilkes

ALSO BY MIKA WALTARI

THE EGYPTIAN

THE ADVENTURER

The Wanderer

BY MIKA WALTARI

TRANSLATED BY

NAOMI WALFORD

G. P. Putnam's Sons   New York

Contents

BOOK I.

Michael the Pilgrim

A DECISION once taken brings peace to a man's mind and eases his soul. With my brother Andy and my dog Rael I had turned my back upon Rome and all Christendom and had started on my way to the Holy Land to atone for my sins.

And so when I stood, free as a bird, in the great square of that city of marvels, Venice, I seemed to have risen from the stinking darkness of the grave to a new life. The sights and smells of carnage and the plague in Rome grew fainter in my mind. My body breathed deeply of the sea wind, and my eager eyes gazed their fill at all the Turks, Jews, Moors, and Negroes moving freely about in their varied dress. I seemed to be standing at the gates of the fabled Orient, and I was seized by an irresistible desire to behold strange peoples, and the countries whence those proud vessels, flying the Lion of St. Mark, had sailed into the city.

Neither Andy nor I had anything to fear from the officials of the illustrious Republic, and could settle there or travel as we wished. I had obtained from a shrewd Venetian at an exorbitant price a pass to which was attached a notary's seal. Since I felt confident that no one knew anything of so remote and obscure a country as my native Finland, I gave my true Finnish name of Mikael Karvajalka. This appeared on the document as Michael Carvajal, for which reason I was afterward alleged to be of Spanish birth, although it was expressly stated on the document that I had formerly belonged to the court of the King of Denmark and had rendered useful service to the Signoria of Venice at the sack of Rome in that summer of 1527.

3

I realized that not a whole lifetime would suffice for all that there was to see and admire in Venice, though I would gladly have stayed at least long enough to worship in each of the churches. But the city offered many and powerful temptations, and so I began my search for a ship to carry us to the Holy Land. It was not long before I fell in with a man down by the harbor who had a crooked nose. He greatly applauded my intention and told me that I had come to Venice just at the right time. A large convoy, under the protection of a Venetian war galley, was shortly to sail for Cyprus, and it was more than likely that a pilgrim ship would take advantage of the escort.

"This is the best season of the year for so blessed an enterprise," he assured me. "You will have a following wind and need fear no storms. Powerful galleys mounting many cannon will protect the merchantmen from infidel pirates, who are an ever present menace to single vessels. Moreover, in these disturbed and godless times there are but few who undertake the pilgrimage, so you will not be overcrowded. Good and varied food may be obtained on board for a reasonable price, and there's nothing to prevent travelers from taking their own provisions. Agents in the Holy Land arrange the journey from the coast to Jerusalem in the best and cheapest manner, and the credentials that are to be bought at the Turkish house here safeguard the pilgrim from all molestation."

When I asked him how much he thought the passage would cost, he looked at me with a quivering lip, and stretching forth his hand impulsively he said, "Master Michael, God must have willed our meeting. For if the truth must be told, this lovely city of ours is full of rogues who batten on the guileless foreigner. I'm a devout man, and my dearest wish has been to make the pilgrimage myself one day. But as my poverty prevents me, I've resolved to devote my life to the welfare of others more fortunate than myself, and facilitate their journey to the sacred places where our Lord Jesus Christ lived, suffered, died, and rose from the dead."

He wept bitterly, and I felt great compassion for him. Quickly drying his tears, he looked me frankly in the eye and said, "I ask only a ducat for my services. By this payment you guarantee your sincerity of purpose, and at the same time relieve yourself of all further concern in the matter."

I could do no less than trust him, for as I walked with him along the quayside he greeted many captains, merchants, and customs officers, who smiled and jested good-humoredly when they saw me in his company. I gave him his ducat, therefore, warning him at the same time that I was not a rich man and wished to travel cheaply. He reassured me, and drove a good bargain with the merchant from whom I bought a pilgrim's cloak and a new rosary. Having attended me to my lodging, he promised to call and tell me when our vessel was to sail.

In a fever of impatience I wandered about Venice until at last one afternoon my friend with the crooked nose arrived breathless, and urged us to make all haste to the ship, as the convoy was to sail the following day at dawn. We threw our belongings together and were rowed out to our vessel, which lay at anchor in the harbor. In comparison with the great merchantmen she looked suspiciously small, but my crooked-nosed friend explained this, saying that all the space on board was reserved for pilgrims and that no cargo was carried. The pock-marked captain received us courteously, and when we had counted out eighteen gold ducats each into his outstretched hand, vowed that it was solely out of regard for his crooked-nosed friend that he allowed us so cheap a passage.

The purser showed us to our sleeping places in the hold, which was strewn with clean straw, and pointing to a jar of sour wine, he invited us to make full use of the dipper and refresh ourselves at the owners' expense, as the joyous day of departure was at hand. Our only light came from a couple of feeble lamps, so that despite the uproar all about us we were unable to see much of our fellow passengers.

My friend with the crooked nose left the captain to come and bid us farewell. He embraced me warmly, and with tearful blessings wished us a fortunate journey.

"Master de Carvajal," he said, "I can fancy no happier day than that which brings you back safe and sound. Once more let me earnestly warn you against confiding in strangers, however ingratiating their manner. And should you encounter infidels, remember to say, 'Bismillah—irrahman—irrahim.' This pious Arabic greeting is certain to win you their good will."

Having once more kissed me on both cheeks he climbed over the side, his purse jingling as he did so, and dropped into the rowing boat. But I will say no more of this heartless man, whose very memory is offensive. For no sooner had the patched sails been hoisted, and with timbers creaking and water slapping to and fro in the bilge the vessel stood out to sea, than it was borne in upon us how grievously we had

5

been swindled. The green copper domes of the Venetian churches had not sunk below the horizon before I was forced to look truth in the eye.

Our little craft rolled as sluggishly as a sinking coffin in the wash of the great merchantmen, and lagged farther and farther astern, while from the war galley flew all manner of signals urging us to keep better station. The crew was a tattered, thievish rabble, and from my conversation with other pilgrims I soon perceived that I had paid an excessive sum for our passage, of which the crooked-nosed fellow had no doubt pocketed half. For there were among us some poor wretches who had been allowed to camp on deck, and they had paid no more than a ducat for the whole voyage.

A man lying forward suffered from spasmodic twitches in his limbs. He had an iron band riveted about his waist, and wore heavy shackles on his ankles. An old fellow with burning eyes crawled about on hands and knees and swore that he would make the whole journey from the shores of the Holy Land to Jerusalem in this way. He woke us all one night with fearful screams, and explained that he had seen white angels floating round the ship, and that they had settled to rest on the yards.

But the pock-marked captain was no bad seaman. He never quite lost touch with the convoy, so that every evening as the stars came out we sighted the masthead lights of the other vessels, which had hove to for the night or lay at anchor in some sheltering bay. When we grew alarmed at being left too far astern he readily invited us to man the oars. It would be wholesome exercise, he said. Indeed, we found ourselves obliged to lend the crew a hand at this task several times, although not more than fifteen of the hundred pilgrims were fit for it. The men were for the most part too old, crippled, or sickly, and the women, of course, could not be put to such work.

Among these was one young woman who on the very first day had aroused my curiosity. Both her dress and her graceful bearing distinguished her from the rest. Her silken gown was adorned with silver brocade and pearls, and she wore jewels also, so that I marveled how she could have fallen among such grimy company. An enormously fat serving woman was in constant attendance. The strangest thing about the lady was that she never appeared unveiled. Even her eyes were concealed. At first I fancied that vanity impelled her to protect her complexion from the burning rays of the sun, but I soon found that

6

she retained her veil even after sunset. Yet one could discern enough of her features to be assured that they were neither disfigured nor ugly. As the sun gleams through thin cloud, so did her youthful charm gleam through the filmy veil. I could not imagine what grievous sin had brought her on this pilgrimage and induced her to hide her face.

Seeing her stand alone at the rail one evening, just after sunset, I felt impelled to approach her, but at my coming she quickly turned away her head and dropped the veil over her face, so that I had no time to glimpse more than the curve of her cheek. But her hair fell in fair curls from beneath her round headdress, and as I contemplated this hair I felt a weakness in my knees, and was aware of such attraction as a magnet exercises upon iron filings.

I stood at a seemly distance from her and, like her, surveyed the fading wine color of the sea. But I was keenly conscious of her presence, and after a while she turned her head slightly as if expecting me to speak. I therefore summoned up my courage and said, "We're fellow voyagers, bound for the same goal. In the sight of God and in expiation of sin we are all equal, so don't be offended with me for addressing you. I long to talk to someone of my own age—someone different from all these cripples."

"You interrupt my prayers, Master de Carvajal," she said in a tone of rebuke. Nevertheless, the rosary disappeared between her slender fingers, and she turned toward me readily. I started with pleasure on finding that she knew my name, for it was a sign that she took some interest in me. But in my humility I was frank with her.

"Don't call me that, for I'm not of noble birth. In my own language the name is Karvajalka, and it belonged to my foster mother, who died long ago. She gave it to me out of pity, because I never knew who my father was. But I'm not quite penniless, nor without education, for I have studied at several learned universities. You would give me most pleasure by calling me simply Michael, the pilgrim."

"Very well," she assented cordially. "And you must call me Giulia, without asking about my family or my father's name, or even my birthplace. Such questions would only revive painful memories for me."

"Giulia," I asked her at once, "why do you veil your face, when both the sound of your voice and the gold of your hair hint at its beauty? Is it to prevent the thoughts of us weak men from straying into forbidden paths?"

7

But at these indiscreet words she sighed deeply, as if I had inflicted a mortal wound, turned her back upon me, and began to sob. In deep dismay I stammered apologies and assured her that I would die rather than cause her the least distress.

When she had wiped her eyes under cover of the veil she turned to me again and said, "Pilgrim Michael, just as one man bears a cross upon his back, and another hangs iron fetters upon his limbs, so have I sworn never to show my face to a stranger in the course of this voyage. Never ask me to uncover it, for such a request could only increase the burden God has laid upon me from birth."

She said this so gravely that I was deeply moved. Seizing her hand I kissed it and gave my solemn promise never to tempt her to the breaking of her vow. I then asked her to take a cup of sweet malmsey with me in all propriety, from a cask which I had brought on board. After some modest hesitation she accepted on condition that her old nurse might be of our company, for fear of ill-natured talk. We therefore drank together from my silver goblet, and as we passed this from one to the other, the light touch of her hand sent a thrill through my body. She on her part offered me sweetmeats, wrapped in silk in the Turkish fashion. She would have given some to my dog, but Rael was waging war below against the rats, and so Andy joined us instead and to my satisfaction engaged the serving woman in animated conversation.

When we had been drinking for some time, Giulia's nurse Johanna began to regale Andy with questionable stories of priests and monks, and I too ventured to entertain Giulia with a gallant anecdote or two. She was in no way offended, but laughed her silvery laugh and under cover of darkness let her hand rest more than once on my wrist or knee. So we continued until far into the night, while the dark seas sighed around us, and the heavens, filled with the silver dust of stars, soared in splendor overhead.

Andy took advantage of our new acquaintance by setting Johanna to mending our clothes, and we also pooled our provisions. The garrulous nurse at once took possession of the ship's galley and thenceforth cooked for us, for we should otherwise have fallen sick, as many other pilgrims did, from the wretched fare provided. But Andy was beginning to observe me carefully, and at length he said to me in a tone of warning, "Michael, I'm an ignorant man and simpler minded than yourself, as you have all too often remarked. But what do we know

8

of this Giulia and her companion? Johanna's conversation is better suited to a brothel keeper than to a decent woman, and Giulia hides her face in so sinister a manner that even the crew are uneasy. So be careful, Michael, lest one fine day you should discover a crooked nose behind that veil."

His words cut me to the heart, and I wished to hear no more talk of crooked noses, and so I rebuked him for his suspicions. Next day we sighted the southern point of Morea, now held by the Turks. The weather conditions and the treacherous currents of these waters compelled our convoy to make for the sheltering harbor of the island of Cerigo, which was defended by a Venetian garrison. There we cast anchor, to wait for a favorable wind. No sooner had we done this, however, than our escorting war galley put to sea again in pursuit of a suspect sail or two that had just appeared on the horizon. For in these waters, Dalmatian and African pirate vessels were often known to lurk. Rowing boats swarmed about the pilgrim ship, offering fresh meat, bread, and fruit for sale, and the captain sent our own boat ashore for water, being unable to berth alongside the quay without paying harbor dues.

Brother Jehan, a fanatical monk of our company, told us that the island of Cerigo lay under a curse. It was here, he said, that one of the goddesses of the idolatrous Greeks was born. The pock-marked captain bore him out in this and declared that the ruins of the palace of Menelaus, the unhappy king of Sparta, were still to be seen here. His wife Helen had inherited her disastrous beauty from the goddess who had been born of the foam on the shores of the island. Forgetful of conjugal duty, this Helen had eloped with a divinely handsome youth and thus brought about the terrible Trojan War. I understood from the captain that it was the goddess Aphrodite who had been born off this island, which the ancient Greeks called Cytherea, but I found it hard to understand why the loveliest of all pagan deities had chosen this bleak, rocky, inaccessible isle for her birthplace.

I was therefore filled with a burning desire to go ashore and contemplate the relics of a former age, and discover whether indeed there were any grounds for the tales the ancient Greeks had told. And when I had related to Giulia all I could remember of Aphrodite's birth, Paris's golden apple, and Helen's unlawful love, I found no difficulty in persuading her to accompany me. Her curiosity was, if possible, more intense than my own thirst for knowledge.

Seamen rowed the four of us ashore, and I bought a basket filled with new bread, dried meat, figs, and goat's cheese. I could understand little of the villagers' dialect, but when a goatherd showed me a path, pointed to the top of a hill, and constantly repeated the word *palaiopolis,* I knew that he was showing us the way to an ancient city. We walked uphill beside a stream until we came to a quiet reach where in ancient days many bathing pools had been built. Although the stones were weatherworn and stiff grass grew in the cracks, I could count a dozen of these pools; after a ten days' voyage and a warm climb we could have beheld no pleasanter or more welcome sight. Andy and I plunged in at once, and washed ourselves clean with the fine sand; the two ladies also undressed and bathed in another pool behind a screen of bushes. I heard Giulia splashing and laughing with delight.

With the soft breeze murmuring through shiny green laurel leaves and Giulia's laughter ringing in my ears, my fancy peopled these pools with the nymphs and fauns of legend, and I should have felt no surprise if the goddess Aphrodite herself, in all her glory, had stepped toward me from the thicket.

When we had eaten, Andy remarked that he felt drowsy, and Johanna too, after a hostile glance at the rocky crag and the dense pine forests on its slopes, began to bewail her swollen feet.

So Giulia and I set forth alone together on an arduous climb to the summit. We found there two marble columns whose capitals had fallen to the ground and been buried under sand and grass. Behind them stood the bases of many square pillars and the ruins of a temple doorway. Among the ruins of the temple itself a larger-than-life-size statue of a goddess stood on a marble pedestal. She gazed upon us in regal beauty, her limbs covered by the thinnest of veils. The temple had fallen in ruins about her, but still in her divine loveliness she surveyed us mortals, though one thousand, five hundred and twenty-seven years had passed since our Saviour's birth.

But I was thinking neither of my Saviour nor of the excellent resolutions that had moved me to undertake my long journey. I seemed transported into the golden, pagan age when men knew neither the thorns of doubt nor the anguish of sin; in the face of this potent spell I should have done well to flee. I know I should have fled, but I did not. I did not, and more swiftly than I can write the words we had lain down to rest in the warm grass. I caught Giulia in my arms and besought her to uncover her face, so that no chilling estrangement should linger between us. My boldness was encouraged by the conviction that Giulia would not have been so ready to come with me to this lonely place unless in her heart she had shared my desire. Nor did she resist my lips and hands, but when I would have torn the veil from her face she grasped my wrists with the strength of despair and begged me most movingly to desist.

"Michael, my friend, my beloved, do as I say. I too am young, and we live but once. But I cannot uncover my face for you, for it would part us. Why can you not love me without beholding it, when all my tenderness awaits you?"

But I could not be content. Her resistance made me the more stubborn, so that by force I dragged the veil from her grasp and bared her face. She lay in my embrace with her fair curls over my arm and her dark-lashed eyes tightly closed. Her lips were like cherries, and my caress had brought a warm glow to her cheeks. I was at a loss to imagine why she had so long and so tantalizingly veiled her features from me, for they were beautiful. But she kept her eyes closed, and covered them with her hands; she was unresponsive to my kisses.

Ah, that I had been content with this! But I urged her wildly to open her eyes. She shook her head violently and all her joy had melted away; she lay in my arms like one dead, and not my most daring caresses could revive her. Dismayed I released her and begged her earnestly to open her eyes and look into mine, that she might read there the intensity of my longing.

At length she said sadly, "Then it's over between us, Pilgrim Michael, and may this be the last time that I seek love. You'll soon forget me when our voyage is ended. Let us hope that I shall forget you as easily. For the love of God, Michael, don't look into my eyes. They are evil."

I knew of course that there are people who without any malicious intent can injure others with their gaze. My teacher, Doctor Paracelsus, believed that the evil eye could cause a fruit tree to wither. But it was on account of such beliefs that my wife Barbara was beheaded and burned in a German city, although she was relatively innocent. In my despair I rejected all the evidence that had been heaped against her as malice and superstition, and so incurred the guilt of heresy. Nor did I believe now that Giulia's fair face could be marred by evil eyes, and I laughed. Perhaps my laughter was a little forced, because of her

11

grief, but when I swore that I did not fear her gaze she turned pale and at last withdrew her hands. Her frightened eyes, clear as raindrops, looked into mine.

My blood turned to ice, my heart stopped, and I stared back, as mute and horror stricken as herself.

Her eyes were beautiful indeed, yet they lent a sinister look to her face, for they were of different colors. The left eye was blue as the sea, but the right was nut brown; I had never before seen such a thing—I had never even heard of it—and I sought in vain a natural explanation.

We gazed long at one another, face to face, and instinctively I recoiled and sat a little distance, still gazing, until she too sat up and covered her breast. All warmth had drained from my body and cold shivers ran down my spine; what malignant planets must have presided at my birth! The only woman I had ever loved was beheaded and burned as a witch, and now that another had captured my heart, she too was cursed by God and must veil a face that brought horror and consternation to all beholders. My life was accursed; it might be that within myself there lurked some fatal affinity with what we call witchcraft. I remembered how Giulia's presence, from the time I first beheld her, had attracted me like a magnet, and I could no longer feel that this was merely youth calling to youth. In my heart I suspected some dread mystery.

I was in no condition to express my thoughts to Giulia, and when she had sat for a little while with bowed head, twisting a grass blade about her slender fingers, she rose and said coldly, "Well, Michael, you've had your way and it's time for us to go."

She walked away with her head held high, and I leaped up to rejoin her. Without turning she said in a hard voice, "Master Carvajal, I rely upon your honor not to betray my secret to the ignorant people aboard our ship. Although life is indifferent to me, although it might be better for me and my fellows if I died, yet I long to reach the Holy Land now that I have undertaken the pilgrimage. I want no superstitious seaman to throw me overboard."

I caught her wrists, and turning her to me I said, "Giulia, don't think that my love for you has died; that is not true. Indeed I feel now that fate intended us for each other, for I too am different from other people, though I bear no outward sign of it."

But Giulia said in derision, "You're kind and courteous, Michael, but I don't need your false words; your eyes have clearly spoken your horror. Let it be as if we had never met, for that is the best and kindest thing you can do."

Her bitter words sent a wave of warmth through my heart and I was ashamed. To prove to myself and to her that nothing had changed between us I put my arms about her and kissed her. But she was right, for I no longer felt the same trembling delight. And yet perhaps my embrace held a deeper meaning than before, for now I held a defenseless creature like myself, whom I would comfort if I could in her most dreadful loneliness. Perhaps she understood, for her coldness melted, and pressing her face against my shoulder she broke into silent weeping.

To accustom myself to her strange beauty I begged her, when she had composed herself, to remove her veil and without fear walk with me down the mountainside. The longer I beheld her face and her remarkable eyes the more deeply was I aware of the profound attraction that bound me to her, despite my repugnance; it was as if two people walked beside me, and that in touching one of them I touched both. And so, unknown to me, her evil eyes cast their slow spell upon my soul.

Down by the pools we found Andy and Johanna sleeping heavily, and there was nothing left in the basket but a gnawed bone and the vine leaf that had covered the food. The sun was already sinking; we returned in haste to the port and signaled to the ship to send a boat for us.

At dusk the war galley returned from her vain pursuit, but two days and nights passed before the wind blew freshly from the northwest and we were able to row out of the harbor and hoist sail. I had spent these two days in wholesome reflection, and my proud and chilly demeanor gave place to kindliness. I shared out medicine and bread among my poor fellow passengers and did my best to help them as they lay weeping and praying on the evil-smelling straw. At night I lay awake brooding over Giulia and my own life. For since I had seen her eyes all joy had left me, and I sought oblivion in thinking of others rather than of myself.

But repentance came too late, for the day after our departure from Cerigo the wind freshened, the seas rose, and by evening the sky was filled with flying storm clouds. The ship groaned in all her timbers and began to leak worse than ever, so that all able men were set to the pumps. What with the plunging and creaking of the vessel, the

13

crack of the sails, and the lamentations of the seasick, I confess I trembled in every limb, expecting every moment that we should founder. Yet, rotten and worm eaten though she was, our ship was a sturdy product of the Venetian dockyards, and by daybreak we had suffered no damage. When the sun came out and gilded the foaming crests of the waves we felt we had good reason to give thanks to God and join together in a song of praise.

But to the captain's way of thinking our rejoicing was premature, and when we had ended our thanksgiving he roared at us to take to the oars, for in driving before the wind we had lost touch with the convoy. Neither sail nor land was now in sight, but by hard rowing the captain strove to alter course and so bring us up with the other vessels.

At midday the wind had dropped, although the ship still rolled in heavy seas. A sail was now descried on the horizon, and to avoid an encounter the captain again altered course and we tugged at the oars with the strength of terror. But it was too late, for by the time we could see the low sail, our lofty masts had long been visible to the stranger, who with terrifying speed approached to intercept our flight. On seeing this the captain ranted and swore and consigned all the rapacious ship owners of Venice to the nethermost pit.

"That craft bodes us no good," he said. "If you be brave men, grasp your weapons now and fight beside me. Women and the sick must get below."

My inward parts contracted with fear when I heard his words and watched the narrow enemy ship cleaving the foaming seas toward us, impelled by many pairs of oars. It was not long before two puffs of smoke burst from her bows; one cannon ball had plowed a hissing furrow through the waves and the other had ripped our sail before the wind had even brought us the sound of the shots.

Andy said, "This battle's lost already, as we have no more than fifteen able-bodied men among us. According to all the rules of war—on land, that is; I know nothing of the sea—we should lay down our arms and negotiate for honorable terms of peace."

But the pock-marked captain said, "Let us trust in God and hope that the war galley is not far off, and already searching for us. If I surrender this ship without a blow struck I shall incur black dishonor, and the Signoria of the Republic will move heaven and earth to seize me and string me up at the yardarm. But if I fight bravely and survive, the Signoria will buy me out of slavery. And if I should fall in battle against the infidel, I have good reason to hope that my soul, freed from sin, will fly straight to heaven."

Brother Jehan, hoarse with terror, brandished a copper crucifix and yelled, "He who falls in battle against the followers of the false prophet is worthy of the Kingdom of Heaven! He who while on pilgrimage dies at the hands of infidels wins the glorious crown of the martyrs! And truly that crown has never been nearer to us than now. Let us therefore do battle like brave men, and may the name of Jesus be our war cry!"

Andy scratched his ear dubiously, and thrust his fist into the mouth of our only cannon, which was green with age and neglect. There was nothing in it but bits of old birds' nests. From his cabin the captain threw out an armful of rusty swords, which clattered to the deck, while the crew sullenly picked up their iron pikes. The captain also brought out a big harquebus and I tried to load it, being used to handling such weapons, but the powder was damp. The strange vessel was by now so near that I could distinguish the green and red flags floating from the mast, and we saw also the dread turbans of the crew and the dazzle of many keen scimitars.

At this moment several sharp shots rang out. Two men fell bleeding to the deck and a third seized his wrist with a howl. Then a shower of arrows sang toward us, and many men were hit. When Brother Jehan saw the blood and heard the heart-rending cries of the wounded he was thrown into an ecstasy of sheer terror; he leaped about the deck, tucked the skirts of his habit into the rope girdle, exposing his hairy legs, and shrieked in tones of triumph, "See the blood of the martyrs! This day we shall meet in Paradise, and before God's throne there is no more precious jewel than the martyrs' crown."

Other pilgrims too began madly jumping about the deck and brandishing their weapons, while the invalids gave tongue in a quivering psalm. But Andy drew me into the shelter of the deck house where the captain joined us, shedding tears and crossing himself repeatedly as he said, "May the Virgin and all the saints pity me and may Jesus Christ forgive my sins. I know that ship; she's from the island of Jerba and is commanded by a pirate named Torgut, who shows no mercy to Christians. Let us sell our lives as dearly as we may, since we're bound to lose them."

But any attempt at defense against this seasoned pirate could only

15

result in useless bloodshed, for at a given signal the rowers drew in their oars, leaving their vessel with way enough on her to glide alongside. Numbers of grapnels caught our rail, the two hulls ground together, and we were fast bound to our assailant by countless lines and chains. Our captain, like the honorable man he was, dashed sword in hand to the encounter of the pirates who were now swarming in over the side. But there were few who followed him, and he fell with a cloven skull before he had inflicted a single wound. Seeing his unhappy end his men flung down their pikes and showed their empty hands in token of surrender; in another moment those pilgrims who still showed fight were cut down, and so we won small honor in this unequal struggle.

Andy said, "Our last moment has come. The rules of war require resistance only while the least chance of success remains. Let us not kick against the pricks, but rather die, if need be, like meek Christians."

To the last Brother Jehan assailed the infidels with his copper crucifix, but they never gave themselves the trouble of striking him. One of them simply snatched the crucifix and threw it into the sea, which so enraged the monk that he hurled himself at the man and attacked him with nails and teeth until a kick in the belly sent him rolling and howling on the deck. Andy and I allowed ourselves to be thrust in among the other prisoners, while the pirates poured all over the ship. Their easy victory had put them in a good humor, and at first they showed us no great hostility. But when they discovered that we carried no valuable cargo, they shook their fists at us and uttered threats in every language under the sun. To my amazement I noticed that they were neither Africans nor Turks, and that despite their turbans the greater number were Italians and Spaniards.

These cruel men belabored us with their fists, spat upon us, and tore off our clothes, leaving no more than a rag to cover us. They snapped up our purses and with practiced fingers felt each garment for any jewels or coins that might have been stitched into its lining. But at that moment I cared nothing for my lost possessions, and feared only for my life. Such valuables as they found they threw onto a piece of cloth spread upon the deck.

When they had made an end of this vile work, there appeared among them a dark-skinned man whose large turban was adorned with a bunch of feathers. His silk coat was heavy with silver brocade,

16

and in his hand he carried a curved blade whose hilt was set with dark jewels. Seeing him, our robbed and denuded seamen began eagerly striking their chests and displaying their muscles, but he never so much as glanced at them. His subordinates showed him the negligible spoils, and at a nod from him began to run along our ranks, pinching our muscles and inspecting our teeth, and rapidly weeding out the weak and infirm among us. At this I was even more dismayed, and asked what it could mean, since we had already surrendered. The sailors answered, "Pray that we may find favor in their eyes. They pick out those who are fit to pull an oar, and the rest they kill."

I was seized by such overmastering fear that my tongue swelled in my mouth and I could not even stammer. But just then these cruel men dragged Giulia forward, laughing and shouting because she had my dog Rael in her arms. The dog snarled, showed his teeth, and snapped at them valiantly when they teased him, and they were surprised that so small a dog could display such fury.

The sight and smell of carnage did nothing to soothe Rael, who was a seasoned warrior. He grew anxious on my account and having caught my scent, struggled so violently in Giulia's arms that she was forced to release him. He ran straight up to me, jumped about me and licked my hands to show his delight at finding me still alive.

The infidel captain made a gesture of impatience and at once the chattering and laughter ceased; the wailing captives also fell silent, so that sudden and utter stillness reigned. The leader had Giulia brought before him, tore away her veil and first looked upon her with approval. But when he noticed her eyes he started back with a cry, and his men too made horns with their fingers to avert evil.

Even the men of our own ship forgot their plight and pressed forward past their guards, shaking their fists and crying, "Let us throw the woman overboard, for her eyes have led the ship to disaster."

From this I realized that they had long guessed her secret. But their rage was the best thing that could have befallen her just then, for to show contempt for them the leader of the infidels signed to his men to take Giulia to the round-topped tent on the quarterdeck of the pirate vessel. I felt deeply relieved, although I suspected that only violence and slavery awaited her.

Once more the haughty commander raised his hand, and a gigantic coal-black slave stepped forward, naked to the waist and carrying a flashing scimitar. His master pointed to the aged and feeble, who had

17

already fallen to their knees, and then turned his back. He surveyed the rest of us disdainfully while the black headsman approached the pilgrims and, ignoring their terrified cries, swept their heads from their shoulders.

At the sight of these heads rolling over the deck, and the blood spurting from the bodies, the last of my strength left me and I sank to my knees with my arms about my dog's neck. Andy stood in front of me, feet apart, but when the infidels had patted him on the thigh, impressed by his powerful frame, they smiled at him and bade him step to one side. Thus I lost my only support, and since I had continually hidden behind the backs of others, I was the last to be inspected. They dragged me impatiently to my feet, and pinched me with looks of contempt. I was still emaciated from the plague, and as a scholar I could naturally not compete in bodily strength with seasoned mariners. The commander lifted his hand in dismissal and my guards forced me to my knees, that the Negro might strike off my head, too.

When Andy saw what was about to happen, he stepped coolly forward, unhindered. The terrible Negro paused to wipe the sweat from his forehead, but then as he raised the weapon to behead me he was seized round the body by Andy and flung sword and all into the sea.

So astounding was this spectacle that for a time even the pirates stood gaping. Then their proud leader burst out laughing, and his followers too slapped their knees and howled with delight. No one lifted a finger against Andy. But Andy was not laughing; his face seemed carved from wood as he surveyed me with his round gray eyes and said, "I don't care to be spared, Michael. Let us die together like good Christians. For together we have been through many hard trials. Perhaps, because of our good intentions, God will forgive us our sins. We will hope for the best, for it's all we can do."

Tears rose to my eyes at the greatness and courage of his action, but I said, "Andy, Andy, you're a good brother to me, but you have no sense. And now I see that you're even simpler than I thought. Stop behaving like a fool, and be happy. In heaven I shall pray that your enslavement among the infidels may not be too grievous."

Nevertheless as I spoke I trembled, and my heart was not in my words. Heaven seemed farther from me than ever in my life before, and I would have exchanged my place in it for a moldy crust, so long as I might be allowed to eat it. I wept still more bitterly, and cried

18

aloud, like the holy father of the church, "Lord, I believe; help Thou mine unbelief." It should be accounted to me for merit that I spoke in Latin, and thus did nothing to weaken Andy's simple faith. This was the most anguished prayer that ever rose from my heart, but God in His heaven gave no ear to it. Instead, the frightful Negro clambered over the side, dripping wet, with the scimitar between his teeth. Once firmly on the deck he bellowed like an angry bull, and with rolling eyes charged straight at Andy and would have slain him, had not the pirate captain given a sharp order. His men hastened obediently to Andy's defense and the Negro was forced to halt, quivering with impotent rage. To give vent to this he raised his sword to cut off my defenseless head. But at this most decisive moment of my life there came to me the words which the crooked-nosed man had taught me, and I croaked, *"Bismillah—irrahman—irrahim."*

The cry sounded so convincing that the headsman was astonished, and lowered his blade. I saw nothing funny in this, but the wicked freebooters burst out laughing again while their captain came forward to me smiling, and addressed me in Arabic. I could only shake my head, but my dog was more intelligent, and hurried respectfully forward, wagged his tail, rose and stood unfalteringly on his hind legs, and looked from the captain to me and back again repeatedly. The haughty man bent down, lifted the dog into his arms and began to scratch him in friendly fashion behind the ears.

His men still tittered, but gravely their captain silenced them with the words, *"Allah akbar."* Then turning to me he asked in passable Italian, "Are you a Moslem, that you call upon the name of Allah, the Compassionate?"

I asked, "What is a Moslem?"

He answered, "A Moslem is one who submits to the will of God."

I said, "And should not I submit to the will of God?"

He regarded me mildly. "If you will take the turban and be converted to the true faith Allah is indeed compassionate and I will not have you slain, though as a prisoner of war you will become my slave according to the Law of the Prophet, blessed be his name."

At this I could only repeat, "Blessed be his name," so deep was the relief I felt when I knew I might still draw breath under the open sky, and eat my bread. But Brother Jehan gripped me by the back of the neck, and overwhelming me with frightful curses he struck me and cried, "Viper! Worse than viper if you forsake the Christian faith

19

to save your miserable life. Renegade! Devil's spawn! You will suffer hell fire for this. Your other sins are atoned for by the blood of Christ, but this is a sin against the Holy Ghost, without pardon, and neither in heaven nor earth shall you find grace."

This, and more that was much worse, did that malevolent monk pour out over me, until Captain Torgut—for it was indeed Torgut-reis—had had enough. He nodded. The Negro raised his sword exultantly and at one stroke swept off Brother Jehan's head so that it rolled upon the deck, its mouth yet wide with curses. I could not see in this a very pious death, though no doubt by virtue of his faith he won the glorious martyrs' crown. Be this as it may, I felt profound relief at the sudden cessation of his shrieks, for his atrocious imprecations had set me quaking from head to foot.

When once the merciless Negro had resumed his task, he worked off his fury on the humble pilgrims so rapidly that one head had hardly thudded on the deck before the next was flying to join it. But Captain Torgut took no interest in this melancholy business, and turned his back, still holding my dog in his arms. I followed closely at his heels, but Andy, with a shake of his head, asked, "Have you truly resolved to follow the Prophet, Michael? Have you had time to give the matter serious thought?"

But I would not allow Andy to be my preceptor, and I had had enough unpleasantness from Brother Jehan. So I replied coldly, "In my Father's house are many mansions. Even the holy apostle Peter denied his Lord three times before the cock crew. Don't set yourself up for a better man than he was, but humbly accept our common destiny and take the turban."

But Andy crossed himself devoutly and said, "Far be it from me to deny my good Christian faith and swear allegiance to the false prophet. Or at least not like you, with my eyes shut. Let me first see what we're letting ourselves in for."

His obstinacy annoyed me, but I had no time to argue further, for Captain Torgut turned to me while his men were carrying off the plunder, and once more addressed me in Italian.

"To guide even one unbeliever into the right path would be an act pleasing to God and meritorious to myself. I will therefore answer patiently any questions you may put to me, for I am the Imam aboard my own vessel."

I bowed deeply, putting my hand to my forehead as I had seen

20

his men do, and said, "Before you I stand naked as the day I was born. My own country has long been lost to me, and now that I have lost also my possessions and my Christian faith there is nothing I can call my own. Treat me therefore as a newborn child in matters of religion, and I will do my best to grasp and receive the new faith."

He said, "You speak wisely and sincerely, and may the almighty God account it to you for merit. But you should clearly understand that the Law of the Prophet permits no one to be converted by force or cunning. Do you therefore freely renounce all idolatry and confess that Allah is the one God and that Mohammed is his Prophet?"

I was astounded at his words, and exclaimed, "I don't understand you, for being a Christian I am no idolater."

This greatly incensed him, and he said, "Woe unto you Jews and Christians who received the Scriptures but continued in your unbelief, corrupting the teachings of Abraham and Jesus, and so departing from the one God! We Moslems acknowledge Abraham, and Jesus who was a holy man, and Mary his mother. But we do not worship them as gods, because the omnipotent, omniscient, and eternal God is one and indivisible. Christians therefore sin grievously when they worship images in their churches, for of God no likeness can be made. Further, it is an abominable error—nay, blasphemy—to say that God has a son. Christians see their deity in a threefold form, as a drunken man sees double. But this is not to be wondered at, for Christian priests drink wine at the sacrifice, whereas the Prophet's law forbids the use of wine."

When Andy heard this he started, stared wide-eyed at Captain Torgut, and said, "Perhaps this is a sign, for my worst misdeeds and sins have ever been the result of immoderate wine drinking. I can doubt no longer that God in His inscrutable wisdom has marked me out for slavery among the followers of the Prophet, so that I need never again fall a victim to my besetting sin. I won't quibble over the Trinity, for the matter has always been beyond my feeble understanding, but if Moslems acknowledge the merciful and gracious God, and if your Prophet can really induce you to drink only water, then indeed your faith is worth considering."

Captain Torgut was overjoyed and cried, "Will you too freely take the turban and submit to the will of God?"

Andy crossed himself and answered, "Kill or cure! If it is a great sin,

21

may God forgive me because of my dull wits. Why shouldn't I accept the same fate as my brother Michael, who is more learned than I?"

Captain Torgut said, "Allah is gracious and merciful if we walk in his ways. He will open for you the gates of Paradise with its rippling water brooks. He will give you rare fruits to eat, and virgins await you there. But only God is patient, and I have other things to do than convert my slaves. Repeat quickly what I say and so profess yourselves Moslems."

We repeated after him as well as we could the Arabic words, "Allah is Allah and Mohammed is his Prophet," after which he recited the first sura of the Koran and explained that no agreement between Moslems was binding without it.

While we were wrestling with the difficult Arabic words, the Negro gathered up the lopped-off heads and put them into a leather sack with some handfuls of coarse salt. Then Captain Torgut said to us, "Wind the turban about your heads, and from now on you are under Allah's protection, though you will not be true Moslems until you have learned Arabic and are familiar with the teachings of the Koran. Circumcision is also a custom pleasing to God, which every true Moslem willingly complies with."

Andy said hastily, "Not a word has been said about this until now, and the step I've taken fills me with misgivings."

But I silenced him for fear of vexing the haughty captain, and whispered, "A wise man chooses the lesser of two evils. However unpleasant circumcision may be, it is at least preferable to beheading. Remember that all holy men in the Bible were circumcised, from the patriarch Abraham to the apostle Paul."

Andy admitted that he had never thought of this.

"But," he went on, "my manhood revolts against it, and I doubt whether afterward I could look a decent woman in the face."

By now the ship was sinking beneath our feet, and so we went aboard the narrow Moslem craft which, being built only for speed and combat, was very far from roomy. Four of our sailors whose lives had been spared were at once chained to the rowers' benches, but Torgut-reis allowed us to remain near him while he sat himself down with crossed legs on a cushion before his tent. His good will emboldened me to ask what was to become of us.

"How do I know?" he replied placidly. "Man's fate is in the hands of Allah, and the days of birth and of death are predestined. You're

22

too frail for rowing and too old to be made a eunuch, and so no doubt you'll be sold to the highest bidder in the Jerba market. Your brother, though, is a brawny fellow, and I would willingly have him in my crew."

Andy said gravely, "Noble captain, don't separate me from my brother, for he is weak and defenseless and without my protection would soon be devoured by wolves. Sell us like two sparrows, for the same farthing. Also I'm in no hurry to fight my Christian brothers, having seen how cruelly they're treated."

Captain Torgut's face darkened.

"Don't dare to speak of cruelty, for Christians treat Moslems far more savagely. From sheer bloodlust they slay them all, irrespective of age and sex, while I kill only from necessity and carefully spare all who can be useful as slaves."

To lead the conversation into smoother channels I asked, "Exalted captain, do I rightly understand you to serve the great Sultan? How is it then that you attack Venetian vessels, although a state of peace and friendship is said to prevail between Venice and the High Porte?"

Captain Torgut answered, "You have much to learn. The Ottoman Sultan rules over more lands and peoples than I can count. And yet more numerous are the countries, cities, and islands that pay him tax and enjoy his protection. As Caliph, the Sultan is the radiant sun to all Moslems, with the exception of the redheaded Persian heretics, God's curse be upon them. The Sultan is for true Moslems what the Pope is for Christians, and as the Pope rules in Rome, so does Suleiman rule in the city of Istanbul, which Christians call Constantinople. Thus the Sultan is lord of both halves of the world and is Allah's shadow on earth. But to what extent I serve him and obey his commands I hardly know. I obey only Sinan the Jew, Governor of Jerba, and he has his orders from the great Khaireddin, whom Christian seafarers have confused with his dead brother Baba Aroush and whom in their terror they have named Barbarossa. In Sultan Selim's day, Baba Aroush captured Algiers, and the Sultan sent two war galleys full of janissaries to his relief."

"Then you are the Sultan's subject?" I persisted, for all these names were so much Hebrew to me.

"Don't pester me with difficult questions. My master Sinan the Jew pays tribute to the Sultan of Tunis; nevertheless Sultan Suleiman's name is mentioned every Friday in the prayers of all the mosques in

23

Khaireddin's domain. But after his brother's death Khaireddin lost Algiers and the Spaniards have built a stout fortress on the island, blocking the entrance to the harbor. Well, the High Porte is far away, and at sea we wage war on all Christians without distinction."

He rose impatiently and gazed out across the sea. The galley slaves pulled till the timbers creaked and the water foamed at the bows, for we were still in pursuit of our convoy. But the sun was setting, and still no sail was to be seen. Torgut cursed savagely, and cried, "Where are my other ships? My sword thirsts for Christian blood!"

He glared at Andy and me so ferociously that I felt it wisest to hide at once among all the bales and boxes that cluttered the hold, and Andy kept me company. But as the crimson sun sank below the horizon Captain Torgut became more composed and sent a devout man aloft to call the faithful to prayer. In a harsh voice this man shouted the name of Allah to all four quarters. Silence fell upon the ship, the sail was furled and the oars drawn inboard. Captain Torgut washed his feet, hands, and face in sea water, and his example was followed by the Italian renegades and most of the rowers. Then Torgut caused a mat to be spread before his tent and having laid his spear on the deck in the direction of Mecca he began as Imam to recite the prayers aloud. He grasped his right wrist with the left hand, fell upon his knees, and pressed his forehead down on the mat; this he did several times and his men did the same so far as the cramped space permitted.

With the outlandish words ringing in my ears I felt wretched and defenseless and forsaken; I pressed my forehead on the deck and dared not pray even in my heart as I had learned to pray in childhood. Nor could I pray to the god of Arabs, Africans, and Turks—that god whom they declared to be so merciful and gracious to the faithful.

Night fell, but after the fear and suspense that I had undergone I could not sleep; I lay listening to the light seas washing along the hull by my ear, under a starry sky. Brother Jehan's frightful curses thundered in my head still, and in my horror I repeated them all. Not one of them had I forgotten, for terror had etched them into my heart forever.

That very morning I had been rich and in full enjoyment of life's blessings. I believed that in Giulia I had found a friend who like myself was alone, and I longed for her, even while I strove to overcome my repugnance. The pilgrimage I had undertaken had freed me from

24

the nightmares of memory. But now I was the poorest of the poor, a slave owning nothing but the rag round my loins, a slave whom a purchaser could dispose of as he pleased. Also I had lost Giulia, and I dared not think what would befall her in Torgut's tent. The pain of losing her was torment enough.

But all this was nothing compared with the betrayal of my faith and my refusal to suffer martyrdom, to which the other pilgrims had so humbly submitted. For the first time in my life, at the age of twenty-five, having escaped many mortal perils, I had been confronted with a clear-cut choice which allowed no evasion. I had made my decision and, most shameful of all, I had made it without doubt or hesitation. For once I stood face to face with myself and examined my heart. "Michael, of Åbo town in faraway Finland! Who are you? Should I not abhor you, shun you, hate you with a bitter hatred—you who throughout your life have never been or done anything completely, but have always faltered and stopped halfway? You may have meant well, but you never had strength enough to work for good. And whatever your intentions you have done much that was bad; worst of all was what you did today, for which there is no forgiveness."

I sobbed as I sought to defend myself, "I never wanted to deny my faith—truly, I did not want to, but I was forced."

But my relentless accuser answered me, "The same fate awaited the others, but they chose death rather than betrayal. Was your plight worse than theirs? Think, Michael, and look truth in the eye."

My terrors were increased; drenched with sweat I stared into the darkness, and asked, "Who are you? Which of us is the true Michael: you who accuse me, or I who breathe and live and, despite my anguish, secretly rejoice in every breath I draw—rejoice even in the sweat that pours from me and proves that I'm alive? But I confess it: my most heartfelt penitence, my deepest sorrows and my bitterest trials, disappointments, and hard-won lessons have poured like water off a duck's back. When the storms passed I shook myself, and was as dry as before. I donned the pilgrim's cloak in a desire to believe that all riddles would be answered beside our Saviour's tomb, in the land where He was born, where He lived and died. I wanted to believe it, because it was pleasant. But now that I look you in the eye, you unknown Michael, I see that it was from you I fled."

I had never made a truer confession than this. I faced myself honestly, to be stricken at what I saw, for it was a void. But my accuser was not yet satisfied.

"And what of your faith, Michael? What do you believe? What was it you denied when you denied your faith, though others were ready to die for theirs?"

This was the bitterest cup of all, but the unknown Michael saw through me and I could only mourn, "You are right. I lost nothing when I denied my faith, for in me there was not faith equal to a grain of mustard seed. If there had been I would have died for it. My pilgrim's cloak was a brazen lie. Until today my whole life has been a lie. But I would rather bite my tongue off than admit this even to myself. For what is left of me then?"

When I had said these words I felt for the first time a hint of peace in my soul. The stern judge within me said more gently, "Now at last we have reached the kernel of the matter, my poor boy. But let us go yet a step further, if we can bear to do it. Perhaps after all we can be friends. Look into yourself, Michael, and confess. In your heart, are you really as unhappy as you make out?"

When he had said this I looked again into that inner emptiness and marveled to feel a dim, uncertain yet most glorious happiness dawning in the void. It was a happiness of the soul, because I had searched myself, cleansed myself, and was preparing now to begin again from the beginning. And so I answered meekly, "You are right, unknown man within me. Now that you have crushed and ground me to powder I am no longer so very unhappy. In fact I have never known such spiritual joy before, or even thought it possible. But now, destitute as I am, renegade to my faith, with nothing to look forward to but the fetters of slavery, I am reconciled with you and therefore I am happy. But whether you are of God or of Satan I dare not guess."

The unseen judge was wroth at this, and demanded, "Michael, Michael, what do you know of God or Satan?"

To preserve my new-found peace I confessed hurriedly, "Nothing, truly, nothing, incorruptible Michael. But who are you?"

He answered, "I am. This you know, and it is enough."

The words bowed me to the earth and filled me with such overwhelming happiness that I thought my heart would burst. Tears of joy rose to my eyes and I said, "You are within me. This I know, and it is enough. Be it so; the one incorruptible judge of all I am and do has his dwelling in my own heart, and stands above all understanding and all knowledge. For swift as thought you answer my questions with a voice that cannot be stifled; nor will I seek to stifle it, although hitherto I have so consistently turned a deaf ear."

Still happier was I to feel my dog softly creeping into my arms. He had gnawed through the thong with which Torgut had tethered him, and having found me he licked my ear, pressed his nose to my cheek, and curled up comfortably with a long sigh of content. I too sighed deeply and fell asleep.

We cruised all next day, combing the coastal waters until we sighted a sail similar to our own. On approaching we beheld a vessel whose hull and rigging had been badly damaged by roundshot. We could hear the cries of the wounded while yet at some distance; there was little life left among the rowers, and of the rest of the crew hardly more than half were fit for combat. The captain had been killed and his body thrown into the sea, and a terrified renegade had taken command. This man now touched his forehead, bowed low before Torgut and said, "By the favor of Allah you had three ships under your command, Torgut-reis."

"*Allah akbar,*" returned Torgut impatiently, and although he guessed what had happened and his limbs trembled with rage, he controlled himself. "So it was written. Speak!"

It appeared that when the gale had separated Torgut from his other two ships, these found each other, and together attacked a merchantman of the convoy. But the roar of her guns brought the war galley speeding to her assistance, and one of the pirate vessels, which had not had time to cast off from her, had been crushed between the two hulls.

"And you? What did you do to help?" inquired Torgut with deceptive gentleness.

"Lord," answered the renegade frankly. "I freed the grapnels and we made off as quickly as the oars could take us. Under Allah you have only me and my presence of mind to thank for saving even one ship, for the war galley followed in pursuit and fired its frightful guns at us. Judge from our condition how hard we fought. We fled not to avoid battle but to find you and confer as to what had best be done."

Torgut was no fool. He put a good face on it, and repeated several times, "Allah is great," after which he embraced the frightened renegade and spoke to him kindly. And although he would clearly have preferred to kick him overboard he praised his resourcefulness in the

27

hearing of all. Then, having bestowed upon him many beautiful presents, and distributed silver coin among the crew, he caused both vessels to set a course for the island of Jerba, off the African coast. After this he retired to his tent and for two days and nights he never showed his face, even at the hours of prayer.

During this time the crew also were dejected, no doubt dreading their return; for they had lost one of three ships and suffered severe damage to another, while the spoils they brought were not worth mentioning. Soon they must meet Sinan the Jew, the Governor of Jerba, and render an account to him of all they had done.

In his melancholy, Torgut drove Giulia from the tent, and I asked her anxiously, "How are you, Giulia, and what dreadful things have happened? Has that repulsive Torgut offended you?"

Giulia withdrew her hand from mine and answered, "No. When he had assured himself as to whether or not I was a virgin he never molested me; on the contrary he has behaved to me like any well-mannered captain and even allows me the same food as himself."

I only half believed her, and asked yet again, "Is that true? Has he really not molested you?"

Giulia wept, and said, "I was ready to plunge a dagger into my breast—or so I fancy, but I was very much confused when I was led into his tent. He conquered my fears however, and was afterward careful not to insult me; from this I see that even infidels shun me for my eyes' sake, although I had hoped, when once beyond the borders of Christendom, that I should no longer have to suffer for what I cannot help."

Despite my relief that no evil had befallen her, I was shocked, and said reproachfully as I took her hand again, "Giulia, Giulia, what are you thinking of, to mourn and complain because this ruthless man spared your virtue?"

She snatched away her hand to dry her tears, and her eyes of different colors blazed with rage as she retorted, "Like all men you're denser than you look. If he'd touched me I would have stabbed myself—I think. I weep because he never even tried, but withdrew at once and began mumbling his prayers. I can only suppose that he feared my eyes, and his revulsion wounds me deeply. It seems I am unfit even for heathens."

I could make nothing of this, except that she was out of her mind with horror at having fallen into slavery, and I consoled her as best I

28

could, saying that to me she was lovely and desirable and that her eyes did not repel me at all; that on the contrary I bitterly regretted my stupidity in drawing back from her at so auspicious a moment. She grew calmer and at last said hopefully, "Captain Torgut expects to get a good price for me in Jerba, and he told me that was why he spared my virtue. But it must have been mere politeness, for if he had really liked me he would have kept me for himself."

I was enraged at her unreasonable attitude, and more maddened still to think that I must lose her and perhaps never see her again. The blue and brown brilliance of her eyes was so enchanting that I could not imagine how I had ever feared her.

"Giulia, Giulia! Only old men are rich, and some repulsive graybeard will buy you. Why didn't I take you while I could, so that at least we could have shared the memory? Now there will never be anything for us to share."

But at this she stared at me in amazement.

"You take too much for granted. If you'd tried to do any such thing I would have scratched your face."

"Then why did you come with me to that lonely place, and why were you so angry when your eyes aroused in me the feelings rather of a brother than of a lover?"

Giulia shook her head slightly and sighed.

"If I talked till doomsday you'd never understand. Of course I hoped that you would try, and perhaps you might have succeeded, as the place was deserted and you are stronger than I. But you did not try, Michael, and that is what I can never forgive you. I hope you will come to suffer bitterly for my sake. My dearest wish is that you may see others pay sacks of gold for what you might have had for nothing. This may give you something to think about for a long time to come."

I perceived that I understood little of feminine logic. She veiled her face once more and left me alone, a prey to exceedingly confused ideas. In her present mood I hardly recognized the modest, straightforward woman I had known.

That night I beheld such a shower of falling stars that for a moment the dark sky seemed strewn with sparks. The man at the steering oar murmured Arabic words, and when I asked him what they meant he answered, "I trust in God and not the devil stoned." He explained that Allah used the lower stars to throw at the devil, and so it was a good omen that Allah should be doing this as we neared the isle of Jerba.

The explanation seemed to me childish, but I said nothing—only sighed and thought of the slavery awaiting me.

Next day we entered Jerba harbor. Torgut appeared on deck to lead the prayers and the whole crew donned their finest clothes. They avoided blue, I soon learned, because it was the Christian color, and also yellow, which was the color of the Jews. Both Andy and I were given a clean strip of stuff to bind in a turban round our heads. As I could do no more for my own adornment, I washed the dog, despite vigorous opposition, and combed his curly coat with my fingers.

The low, sandy isle beneath a burning sun presented no very cheering prospect. As we drew level with the beacon at the mouth of the harbor, Torgut ordered a shot to be fired from his light harquebus only, to show that this time his spoils were little to boast of. I saw the low cupola and white minaret of the mosque, a swarm of mud huts and, on a green mound, the walled residence of Sinan the Jew. But the governor did not ride down in state to meet us, as no doubt he would have ridden if we had arrived firing a salute of cannon and flying the flags of victory. Only a gang of ragamuffins had collected on the beach, and the harbor felt like a glowing oven as we entered it from the cool sea.

Despite our fine clothes and flashing weapons we looked a pitiful little group as we set off along the dusty bridle track to Sinan's kasbah. At our head walked the Negro with the scimitar, carrying on his back the sack full of Christian heads. After him, their hands bound behind them, came the four seamen who had been found suitable for the galleys. Andy and I walked with a chain about our necks although we had accepted the one God and therefore ought not to have been bound. In happy ignorance of our slavery and the Law of the Prophet my dog followed close at heel sniffing avidly at all the new smells, which were indeed plentiful in this squalid haunt. Next came the galley slaves carrying the plunder, which had been divided up into many bundles and boxes to make it seem more than it was. Lastly followed Captain Torgut and his men, who strove to utter cries of triumph. The townspeople hurried after us too, politely screaming out their blessings in the name of Allah. Only the merchants, gathered in front of their booths, pointed contemptuously at us with their thumbs. Giulia had been arrayed in her best clothes and now rode heavily veiled upon a donkey immediately behind Torgut, attended by four men armed with scimitars.

30

The gates of the kasbah were opened wide, and on either side of them we saw sun-dried human heads, impaled on hooks fixed to the wall. In the middle of the great courtyard was a basin of hewn stone surrounded by grass. Prisoners and slaves who lay dozing in the shade sat up and gazed at us dully. Torgut, having sent his men in with the booty, left them to wait by the well. Andy and I were also left alone and Giulia dismounted from her donkey to join us. To show compassion in the name of Allah, Torgut's men loosed the seamen's bonds and let them drink from the fountain. I drank, too, for a beautifully wrought copper cup was chained to the rim, and I marveled at the excellence of the water, having yet to learn that by the commandment of the Koran there must always and in every place be fresh water available to the thirsty.

Sinan the Jew was in no hurry to see us, and Torgut's men squatted patiently down upon the ground to wait. Andy was astonished, and remarked, "The customs of sea warfare are evidently different from those on land, for if these lads had been Germans or Spaniards they'd have had a good fire going by now and a roast and casks of ale, and the wine jar would be passing from hand to hand; there'd be swearing and brawling and dicing, with the camp drabs busy in the shade of the wall. We've come a long way from Christendom."

While Andy was yet speaking, Captain Torgut's savage Negro stepped up to him, bringing an Italian as interpreter, who said, "Mussuf the Negro is angry because you treacherously seized him from behind and threw him into the sea. He could not be revenged at that time, since the Law of the Prophet forbids dispute among the faithful in time of battle. But now he would measure his strength with you."

Andy could hardly believe his ears.

"Dares that poor wretch really challenge me? Tell him I'm too strong to fight with him, and let him go in peace."

The Negro jumped up and down, rolled his eyes, and insulted Andy, beating himself on the chest and tensing his muscles. Andy, to give friendly warning of his own strength, rose from the millstone he had been sitting on, bent down to grasp it and lifted it smoothly above his head. Not content with this he put his left hand behind him and held the huge stone on his right hand alone. When Torgut's men saw this, many of them rose and gathered about him, until he let the stone fall to the ground with a mighty thud.

The Negro in his turn bent down and with enormous effort raised

31

the stone in his arms; but twist and struggle as he might he could not lift it above his head. His legs began to tremble; he dropped the stone and if Andy had not skipped aside his toes would have been crushed. He admonished the Negro mildly, but the man rolled his eyes worse than ever, and the Italian said, "Be on your guard, for Mussuf threatens to throw you over the wall. But if you'll try an honest fall with him he'll not be too rough with you."

Andy put both hands to his head.

"One of us three is mad. But I've warned the fellow; now he shall get what he asks for."

He took off the garment that he had been given to protect his back from the sun, and stepped up to the Negro. After that all I could see was a whirling tangle of arms and legs, until suddenly Andy flew into the air, to land on his back with such a crash that he lay there astounded and unable to believe his senses. The Negro burst into joyous laughter, so that his teeth gleamed white in his black face, but it was clear that he bore Andy no ill will.

Seeing him lie there motionless I hurried over to him, but he thrust me aside, sat up and asked where he was and what had happened. I fancied that he was play-acting and that he had let the Negro win, to flatter him. But Andy felt his limbs and back and said, "There must have been some mistake, and I can't for the life of me make out how I come to be sitting on the ground while that black fellow's on his legs, sniggering."

He got to his feet again, flushing darkly, and hurled himself with a roar at his adversary, so that for a while nothing was to be heard but the fearsome cracking of bones and sinews. Then as if by magic Andy was lifted once more into the air, and the Negro tossed him backward over his shoulder, without even turning to see what became of him. The sight so horrified me that from force of habit I crossed myself. Andy staggered up on trembling legs and said, "Turn away your head, Michael; don't look at me. I don't understand what's happening to me, unless I've fallen foul of Satan himself. But the third time's lucky, and I'll get a grip of this oily devil somehow, if I have to break his bones to do it."

Once more he made a violent rush, the dust swirling about his feet. But the Negro handled him seemingly without effort, and at length grasping him by wrist and leg he began whirling him madly round and round. Then he let go, so that Andy thudded to the ground and

32

rolled some distance in a cloud of dust. When I reached him I saw that his shoulders had been cut by the stones and that blood was pouring from his nose.

"Easy, Michael, easy," he panted, with a face like thunder. "I tackled him carelessly, and he got the better of me by some trick."

He would have charged in again, but the Italian renegade came soothingly toward him and said, "Let that be enough, now, and pray harbor no ill feelings. Mussuf has none. You needn't be ashamed to acknowledge him the victor, for he's a renowned *guresh,* or wrestler. He has thrown you three times running. Come, then, admit yourself fairly beaten. He owns that you're the most powerful man he's ever met."

Andy was unappeased. His eyes were bloodshot as he thrust the renegade aside, and he was on the point of hurling himself yet again at the Negro when Captain Torgut appeared at the entrance to the palace and ordered us sharply to make an end of our sport. Andy was compelled to choke back his rage, wipe the blood from his face, and cover his flayed back, while the Negro threw out his chest like a fighting cock and strolled over to the group of renegades to receive their praise.

I was crestfallen on Andy's account, and strove to comfort myself with the thought that the sea voyage had not suited him and that he had been weakened by poor food. But I had little time to brood over our disgrace, for Captain Torgut ordered us abruptly to enter the palace and present ourselves before his lord, Sinan the Jew. We were led through the building into an inner courtyard bounded on all sides by a cool colonnade and made beautiful by many varied fruit trees. Beneath a roof supported by pillars sat Sinan the Jew. He had one eye, a thin nose, and a sparse beard, and wore a plume in his turban. He was not long past middle age and his lean face was that of a warrior, though for the moment he was content to sit cross legged on a cushion.

He began by surveying the four poor seamen, but found little to interest him there, and he dismissed them with a disdainful jerk of his thumb. Then fixing his eye on Andy and me he said in Italian, "So you have taken the turban, in the name of Allah the Compassionate. You have well chosen, and if you prove diligent in the faith it will be accounted to you for merit and you will be admitted to Paradise with its rippling water brooks. But," he went on with a malicious smile, "here on earth you are slaves, and don't imagine that the Law of the

33

Prophet will ameliorate your lot in any way. If you try to escape, your bodies will be cut in pieces limb by limb and hung upon hooks on either side of the gate. Now tell me, you, what can you do, if anything, that would be of use to your owner?"

I answered quickly, "By your favor, Prince and Lord of Jerba, I am a physician. When I have learned Arabic and acquired knowledge of the remedies used in this country, I will gladly practice healing to the profit of my lord. And I may add without boasting that I'm familiar with many medicines and methods that will certainly be unknown here."

At this Sinan the Jew stroked his beard, and his eye flashed as he asked, "Is it really true, then, that you won't try to escape, but will submit yourself as a Moslem?"

I answered, "Try me, Prince. It is needless to threaten me with quartering, for having taken the turban I should suffer a still more hideous death at the hands of Christians. This is your best guarantee for my sincerity."

He turned thoughtfully to Andy and ordered him to take off his cloak. At the sight of the fearful bruises that had begun to appear on Andy's body he asked who had treated him so roughly. Andy answered, "No one has ill treated me, great lord. Mussuf and I had a little innocent sport together in the outer court. We matched our strength in a friendly bout of wrestling."

"*Bismillah—irrahman—irrahim,*" exclaimed Sinan piously. "An excellent idea. If he has a good instructor and is not too thick witted he can earn great sums for his master as a wrestler. Tell me, what is necessary to man?"

"Good and abundant food," answered Andy readily. "May the gracious God send me a master who is liberal with that, and I will serve and obey him faithfully."

Sinan the Jew sighed, scratched his head and said, "This man is certainly very simple. He doesn't even know that prayer and profession of faith are the most important things. Tell me, what are seven and seven?"

"Twenty-five," answered Andy, with a candid look.

Sinan the Jew tore his beard, called upon Allah, and demanded of Captain Torgut, "Are you making game of me, that you bring me such a fellow? He will eat his master out of house and home and bring disaster upon him through his stupidity. Best to trade him for

34

a bunch of onions, if anyone is fool enough to make so bad a bargain."

Nevertheless he was amused, and asked Andy another question.

"How far is it from earth to heaven?"

Andy brightened, and said, "I thank you, sir, for contenting yourself with easier problems. It takes no longer to travel from earth to heaven than it takes a man to crook his finger."

"Do you dare to trifle with me, miserable clod?"

Andy regarded him with docility, and said, "How could I dare to trifle with you, Lord and Prince? You have only to crook your finger and in a flash the head is off my shoulders. Therefore I say that it takes no longer to get to heaven than to crook one's finger. But I was thinking of myself, not of you, for you have certainly farther to go to reach heaven. Aye, infinitely farther, one might say."

His words brought a smile to Sinan's lips. He ceased his attack.

"And the dog?"

When Rael felt Sinan's gaze upon him, he wagged his tail and stood gaily on his hind legs, so that Sinan was astonished.

"To Allah be the praise! Take the dog to my harem. If my wives like it I will give it to them."

But Rael growled and showed his teeth when a wizened little eunuch came forward to take him, and only at my order would the dog follow, lured by a juicy mutton bone. But he gave me a last reproachful glance, and I could not restrain my tears.

My distress dulled the agony of seeing Giulia led forward and bidden to remove her veil. Captain Torgut, alarmed, said hastily, "Why begin with her face? Keep the best till the last, and examine first her other charms. You will see that I spoke the truth about her. She is as fair as the moon, her breasts are roses, her belly a silver cushion, and her knees seem carved from ivory."

To explain how it was I so well understood their conversation, I should mention that these African pirates were one in religion only, and came from every country, with every country's speech upon their lips. Sinan was by birth a Jew from Smyrna, and Captain Torgut was the son of poor Turks in Anatolia, while their men were for the most part Italians, Sardinians, and men of Provence, Moorish fugitives from Spain, and renegades from Portugal. They conversed together in a queer jargon made up of every sort of language, and known as lingua franca. (They called Christians Franks.) I had learned to understand

35

this mongrel tongue while aboard ship, and as I have always had great facility for languages it gave me no trouble.

Sinan the Jew looked suspiciously at Captain Torgut and said, "Why save her face to the last if she is truly as fair as the moon? I see by your look that there's something fishy here, and I must get to the bottom of it."

He stroked his beard with his slender fingers and ordered Giulia to undress. After modest hesitation she obeyed and uncovered all but her face. Sinan told her to turn, and surveyed her both from the front and from the back. At length he said reluctantly, "She's too thin. She might set a boy on fire, but a mature man needs a broader, deeper cushion than does a youth whose limbs are still firm and wiry, and who can therefore be at ease even on a narrow plank."

"In the name of the Compassionate!" cried Captain Torgut, his face dark with wrath. "Do you call this girl a narrow plank? If so it is from avarice, to lower her value and beat down the price. But you have not seen everything."

"Pray don't excite yourself, Torgut. I freely admit that the girl will not lack merit when regularly and lavishly fed with good kukurrush, so that her breasts swell up to look like ripe gourds. But it will be for the buyer to see to her diet. She doesn't interest me."

At this Giulia lost all patience; she tore the veil from her face and stamped upon it, crimson with fury, as she cried, "Sinan the Jew, you're a spiteful man and I won't endure your insolence. Look me in the eyes if you dare, and see something you have never seen before!"

Sinan the Jew bent forward and stared, so that his one eye almost started from its socket. His jaw dropped, revealing his rotten teeth, and he gazed unwinkingly into Giulia's eyes until at last he hid his face in his hands and cried hoarsely, "Is she a specter, a witch, a jinni? Or am I dreaming? For her eyes are of different colors: the one blue and sinister, the other brown and false."

Torgut seemed put out at his words but defended himself stubbornly, saying, "Your eyes do not deceive you. Did I not say that I had brought you a treasure whose like had never before been seen? One eye is a sapphire and the other a topaz, and her teeth are faultless pearls."

"Did you say a treasure?" exclaimed Sinan incredulously. "What wonder that you lost one of your good ships, for this girl if anyone has the evil eye, and I tremble at the very thought of the misfortune you may have brought upon my house. Allah! The costly rosewater

36

I must sacrifice to purify the floor and the doorposts! And you call her a treasure!"

When Torgut saw his last hope vanishing, his lips trembled and his eyes moistened as he said resolutely, "So be it. I will put out one of her eyes, and no one can then be offended, though I doubt whether I shall get a good price for a one-eyed woman."

My anxiety for Giulia was keener than ever, but at that instant I had what seemed to me an inspiration. I stepped forward boldly and having obtained permission to speak, I said, *"Bismillah—irrahman—irrahim.* I have often heard it said that nothing happens contrary to the will of Allah, and that all is predestined. Why then do you so stubbornly oppose his will? for he clearly intended that Captain Torgut should bring all three of us before you. Therefore instead of putting out her eye, you should seek the hidden meaning in her coming."

These words made a deep impression on Sinan. He stroked his thin beard slowly and reflectively, but found it unbefitting his dignity to reply. After a while he ordered the holy book to be brought. It was a large volume, ornamented with gold and silver, and it lay open on an ebony stand so that he could turn the pages without altering his position. Having bent his head and murmured a few verses, he said, "I will follow the guidance of the holy book." He drew out of it a long gold pin which he handed to Giulia. "Unbeliever though you are, take this golden pin and thrust it between the pages, and I will read the lines to which it points. May those lines be my guide, and determine the fate of you and your companions. I take you all to witness that I will submit to the judgment of Allah, the Almighty."

Giulia held the pin as if she would rather have driven it into Sinan's body, but she obeyed and thrust it defiantly and at random between the leaves of the Koran. Sinan opened the volume reverently, read the passage indicated by the needle's point, and exclaimed in wonder, "Allah indeed is great, and marvelous are his ways. This is the sixth sura, called Alanam—cattle—which is plain enough, for what are you three slaves but cattle? The needle stopped at the seventy-first verse, which reads:

"'Say, shall we call upon that, besides God, which can neither profit nor hurt us? and shall we turn back on our heels, after that God hath directed us; like him whom the devils have infatuated, wandering amazedly in the earth, and yet having companions who call him to the true direction, saying "Come unto us"? Say, the direction of God

37

is the true direction: we are commanded to resign ourselves unto the Lord of all creatures.' "

He looked up amazed, and surveyed Giulia, Andy, and myself in turn. Torgut too was impressed and said, "Truly Allah is Allah and I made no error in bringing this girl to your house."

I cannot say whether Sinan the Jew was really pleased with the Koran's decree, but he said, "I take back all I said in my foolishness. Who am I to doubt the judgment of Allah? Yet I cannot tell what to do with these slaves. I'll take them, Torgut, but only at a fair price. In the presence of witnesses I will give you thirty-six ducats which, with the horse you've already had from me, is a good sum for these useless, ignorant creatures."

But Torgut was incensed, and cried, "Cursed be you, Sinan the Jew, for seeking to swindle me! The girl is almost a virgin, the gray-eyed Frank is a powerful fellow, and the third has the same name as the angel who rules the night and the day. Furthermore he is a skilled physician and a learned man, speaking all the Frankish languages, and Latin, too. Ten times that sum would leave me the poorer, and I should never even consider so bad a bargain were you not my father and my friend."

Sinan the Jew became annoyed in his turn, and said, "The sun has dried your brains. A moment ago you were ready to kill the girl, or at least to put out one of her eyes; now you exaggerate her non-existent charms in order to rob me. If you reject a fair offer, sell these slaves in the open market, and I'm ready to make the highest bid, so long as you swear by the Koran not to bribe anyone to force up the price."

Torgut scowled.

"As if anyone in the bazaar would dare to outbid you! And you would certainly spread slander about these wretched slaves and so lower their price. The Koran has revealed their true value to you, and I submit to its ruling, though I lose by it. Was it not the seventy-first verse of the sixth sura? Together that amounts to seventy-seven gold ducats—an auspicious number which in itself emphasizes Allah's intention. Or would you prefer us to add the numerical values of the letters?"

By this time Sinan was tearing his beard, and now he cried out, "No, no—perish the thought! It would be waste of time, as not even

38

scholars are agreed on those values. In any case there was no mention of gold in the sura."

"It is unbecoming in you to struggle against the will of Allah. Were I a more learned man I could point out plenty of characters signifying gold; but it is enough for me that the Koran is more precious than gold and that each letter contains ten benedictions. Therefore let us dispute no longer. I will be content with seventy-seven gold ducats."

The end of it was that Sinan the Jew counted out the ducats, sent Giulia to the harem, and ordered Andy and me out of his sight. We returned to the outer court, where huge dishes of mutton and rice cooked in fat had been brought out for Torgut's men. These had squatted down in order of rank round the dishes, and were picking morsels of meat from them, and pressing the rice into neat balls which they put in their mouths. But the slaves and prisoners had gathered behind them, and with famished looks followed every mouthful as it disappeared. The sight depressed me very much, but as we drew near Mussuf at once made room for us beside him, and offered Andy a fine piece of meat, dripping with fat. I urged Andy to accept this as a peace offering.

The food in the dish now began to dwindle rapidly, and I had difficulty in keeping up. The others, seeing Andy's prowess, looked askance at us and called on Allah, and when the dish was empty one of the renegades remarked, "He's no true Moslem. See what manners —to sit on his bottom and stuff his mouth with both hands!"

Andy was offended by these words, but I said to the speaker, "We have but now found the right road, and stumble along it like blind men, having no one to lead us. Explain to us the points of good behavior."

Sinan the Jew must after all have been well disposed toward us; I cannot otherwise account for the fact that the wrinkled eunuch appeared in the courtyard in response to Andy's roars for more to eat, and ordered the servants to refill our dishes. I bade Andy hold his tongue while the Moslems taught us proper table manners and good behavior. Delightedly and all talking at once they began their instruction. We must always wash our hands before eating, they said, and bless the food in the name of Allah. We must sit cross legged before the dish, on the left haunch, using only three fingers of the right hand to take food. No knife was to be used, as all was cut beforehand into pieces of suitable size, and no more was to be put in the mouth than

39

it would comfortably hold. The rice was to be kneaded together in small lumps, and not shoveled into the mouth like porridge. A well-bred man did not stare at his companions but looked straight before him and was content with what he had. Finally they recited a phrase or two from the Koran and said, "Ye who believe, eat the good things which God hath given you, and offer your thanks to Him."

When the food was nearly all gone, they pointed out that no believer quite finished what was on the dish, but charitably left some to be distributed among the poor. Now also they left many good pieces of meat and some rice, and handed it to the slaves and prisoners, who fought savagely over it, for although they were Christians they displayed little of the Christian spirit.

The Moslems' explanation gave me much to think about. They went on to tell me of the fast of Ramadan and of the pilgrimage to Mecca that every believer ought to make at least once in his life. But if prevented by poverty or some other cause his omission was not accounted to him for sin. I asked them their views on wine drinking, at which they all sighed deeply and answered, "It is written: 'Ye who believe: wine, games of chance, worshiping of stones, and dicing are abominations of the devil. Shun them, that ye may be blessed.'"

But others among them said, "It is also written: 'Wine drinking is a great sin, albeit man may have some good of it. But the sin is greater than the good.'"

The eunuch, who had stood behind us listening, could contain himself no longer. "There's much to be said for wine, and many poets—especially the Persians—have celebrated its best qualities. Persian is the language of poets, as Arabic is the Prophet's, whereas Turkish is spoken only by the dogs of the big cities. And in praising wine the poets have used it as a symbol of the true faith. Yet even apart from its symbolic aspect, wine is beneficial to health. It stimulates the kidneys, strengthens the bowels, eases care, and renders a man magnanimous and noble. Truly, had not Allah in his inscrutable wisdom forbidden the faithful to drink it, it would have no equal on earth."

Hearing this song of praise Andy regarded the eunuch with displeasure, and said, "Gelding! Are you trying to annoy me? I have taken the turban with the sole purpose of avoiding the curse of wine. Wine runs away with good sense and good money, infects a man with diseases, and causes him to see creatures that are not there. Allah preserve me from allowing the filth to pass my lips."

But the eunuch squatted down beside me and said, "Your questions are sincere, and you show willingness to learn first what is forbidden. But Allah is not minded to enslave his faithful or make life hard for them. Repeat the prescribed prayers, and give what alms you can afford; for the rest put your trust in Allah the ever compassionate. You may spend your life studying the Koran and the interpretations of scholars, and be no wiser at the end of it."

I listened to what he said, understanding that there was something he wished to tell me. But Andy broke in, "If this is true, I confess that the teaching of the Prophet, blessed be his name, is as it were a flowing cloak that nowhere chafes the wearer. Yet I cannot believe what you say, for all the priests, monks, and teachers I've met or heard of have always been the first to forbid pleasant things, such as the lusts of eye and flesh; they insist that the way to heaven is narrow and stony, while all broad, smooth roads lead straight to hell."

Mardshan the eunuch smiled all over his wrinkled face and said, "Though much is pleasing to God—more than I can remember—yet all is not necessary. There is a tradition that the Prophet, blessed be his name, once said, 'If, upon the last day, there comes before Allah a soul to whom can be credited not a single good action, and he is judged worthy of the fires of hell, this soul may appeal and say, *Lord, you have called yourself merciful and compassionate; how then can you punish me with hell fire?* Then shall Allah in all his glory say, *Truly I have called myself merciful and compassionate; lead therefore this servant of mine to Paradise, for my mercy's sake; for I am the most merciful of all who show mercy.*'"

Andy was greatly astonished at this, and said, "Allah's teaching is plainly a good and merciful teaching, and if I had not seen salted heads stuffed into a sack in his name I should even be misled into believing it to be the best of all religions. But a doctrine which commands a man to slay innocent people because of their beliefs is anything but merciful; for who can be converted by having his head struck off?"

But I wondered why this Mardshan was so eager to make his faith acceptable to us, and I said to him, "That was a pious and beautiful story. But what is in your mind? What is it you want of us?"

He raised his hand as if in wonder and exclaimed, "I? I am only a poor eunuch. But the task has been laid upon me to teach you Arabic, if you're quick at learning. Your brother shall be trained as a *guresh* if the Negro Mussuf consents to teach him, for at the moment my master has no other employment for him."

Sinan the Jew and Captain Torgut now appeared at the doors of the palace, and the noise in the courtyard died away. Sinan spoke with the pirates and caused garments of honor and also small sums of money to be distributed among them. Thus the day ended. Mardshan the eunuch led us to remoter parts of the building, and showed us very pleasant quarters in the barracks where Sinan's slaves and bodyguard were housed.

Mardshan taught me Arabic, and showed me how to read and write its strange characters. The Koran was my lesson book. As Mussuf had gone to sea again with Captain Torgut, Sinan the Jew found another wrestling instructor for Andy. My dog was given back to me, and I hardly know which of us was happiest. So I found nothing to complain of in my bondage. And yet as the days passed the oppressive sensation grew within me that I was being watched and that my smallest action was recorded, so that I began to speculate upon the fate in store for me. Sinan the Jew was not one to show favor to anyone without good reason.

One day when I was scrubbing the bathroom floor Giulia approached me, unseen by anyone, and said, "The slave does slave's work!"

I was so glad to see her that I ignored her words and exclaimed, "Giulia! Are you well, and well treated? Can I do anything for you?"

She said, "Scrub your floor and keep your eyes lowered in my presence, for I'm a lady of distinction, and have no need to work or do more than eat rose leaves in honey, and good kukurrush, so that I am as you see noticeably plumper than before."

I was seized by terrible jealousy, and asked, "Has Sinan the Jew found delight in you, then? And doesn't time thus idly spent hang heavy on your hands? Idleness is the mother of vice, and I would not see you sink into vice, Giulia."

Giulia drew aside her veil a little absently, stroked my cheek, and said, "I've every reason to think that my lord has found delight in me, for he often summons me to gaze into a copper dish filled with sand, in which I draw lines with my finger."

"Allah!" I cried, even more surprised at Sinan's behavior. "Why does he want you to draw lines in the sand?"

"How should I know?" returned Giulia frankly. "I believe he is in

42

his second childhood, and likes to have an excuse to send for me and admire my beauty. For I am indeed fair as the moon and my eyes are like jewels of different colors."

There was a roar of laughter from behind me, and Sinan the Jew, drawing aside a curtain, stepped forward unable any longer to contain his mirth. Mardshan the eunuch followed close at his heels, distractedly wringing his hands, and I thought my last hour had come, for I had presumed to speak to Giulia, and she had uncovered her face before me, which among Mussulmans is a great sin.

Panic stricken though I was, I yet sought to save Giulia and raising my scrubbing brush I said, "Lord, punish me, for she is innocent and I addressed her first. But we have uttered nothing but praise of your gentleness and wisdom."

Sinan laughed still more and answered, "I heard how warmly you praised me. Rise up out of the dirt, Michael, and fear nothing. You're a physician, as you assured me, and before such men a woman may unveil without sin. But come, it is time I talked to you seriously. I want to present you to your future master, to whom you owe obedience."

He went, and my heart turned to ice. But Mardshan said, "Sinan has given you away and you must follow Abu el-Kasim, your new master. He is a drug merchant of ill repute from the town of Algiers, the curse of Allah be upon him."

My heart was in my mouth and I was a prey to great anguish, but Mardshan ordered me to hasten, and as I had no choice I hurried after Sinan the Jew.

With lowered eyes I entered the room; Sinan spoke to me kindly, bidding me be seated on a cushion and look about me fearlessly. On obeying I was surprised to behold a small, apelike man wearing a ragged cloak. He looked a very shady character and as I submitted to his keen gaze I felt I need expect no good from him. I turned beseechingly to Sinan, who said smiling, "Behold your new master, Abu el-Kasim. He is a poor man and makes a bare living by diluting rose water, and selling imitation ambergris and inferior eye black. He has promised to send you every day to the madrasseh of the mosque in Algiers, where you may hear the best teachers and so most rapidly learn Arabic and acquire knowledge of the pillars of the faith—of law, tradition, and the true path."

I dared not utter a word of protest, and bowed my head submissively. Abu el-Kasim stared at me and said, "I'm told you're a physician and familiar with Christian remedies. Now, I have undergone an arduous journey and am sick at the stomach. Can you cure me?"

He leered unpleasantly and I found him so repellent that I had no wish to examine him. But my duty compelled me, and I said, "Show me your tongue. Have your bowels moved today? Let me feel your pulse. When I have also felt your stomach I will tell you what medicine you need."

Abu el-Kasim held his belly and moaned.

"I see that you know your business according to Frankish practice. But the best remedy for these pains of mine would be a good wine. Were it prescribed by a physician I could drink it without sin."

I wondered at first whether he were testing me. But now Sinan the Jew also rubbed his belly and with loud lamentation said, "Oh, accursed! Abu el-Kasim, you have brought an infectious sickness into my house, and I too am afflicted. Hell is loose within me, and only the good remedy you speak of can bring relief. By the boundless favor of Allah I happen to possess a sealed jar of wine, given me by a sea captain who knew no better; I could not have declined the gift without offense. We trust you, Michael. Break the seal, smell and taste the wine, and tell us whether it will be of benefit. If so we may drink it without sin."

The sanctimonious old frauds sat and looked at me as if I had been their master instead of their slave, and I had no choice but to break the seal and pour the wine into three finely ornamented cups which Sinan readily handed me.

"Taste the medicine," he said, "and tell us whether it is suited to our disorder."

But it was not the quality of the wine he doubted; he wanted first to assure himself that it had not been poisoned, and then to incriminate me, so that I could not afterward inform against him. However, I needed no second bidding. I tasted the dark, sweet, fragrant wine with relish and said quickly, "Drink in the name of Allah, for this is a good wine and will certainly cure all ills of mind and body."

When we had drunk, and refilled our cups and drunk again, Abu el-Kasim said to me, "I am told that you're familiar with Christian methods of warfare, that you know the qualities of the Christian leaders, that you have yourself served in the wars, that you speak many Christian languages and have in general deeper knowledge of all these

44

matters than one could expect in a man of your age. Even Mardshan the eunuch has often wondered at it."

I made no answer, but with burning cheeks drank more wine; for the words came strangely from such an old ragbag as he was.

He then asked, "If, besides adulterating drugs and pursuing useless studies at the mosque school, you had the chance to serve the world's mightiest ruler, what would you say?"

I answered bitterly, "I served him long enough, and ingratitude was my only wage. I've had more than enough of the Emperor; he even wanted to send me across the western ocean, to conquer new kingdoms for him, under the command of a one-time swineherd."

Abu el-Kasim said eagerly, "You speak of things new to me. But it was not the Emperor of the unbelievers that I meant—the ruler of the German and Spanish dominions—but the great Sultan Suleiman, who justly and liberally rewards his servants."

"Blessed be his name," added Sinan the Jew. "The Sultan has captured the Christian strongholds of Belgrade and Rhodes; he has conquered Hungary and, according to prediction, he is to subdue all the Christian peoples. As High Porte he is the refuge of all kings. He makes the rich poor and the poor rich and lays no undue burdens on any, so that within his dominions the nations live without fear and in brotherly concord."

"These are dreams born of wine," I said. "You speak of a realm that may perhaps exist in heaven, but never on earth."

But Abu el-Kasim warmly concurred in what Sinan said.

"This is no drunken dream. In Sultan Suleiman's empire justice is incorruptible; judges pronounce sentence according to the law, without respect of persons. Nor are any forced to renounce their faith, for Christians and Jews enjoy equal rights; so that for example the Greek Patriarch holds the rank of vizier and is a member of the Divan, or council. Thus it is that the oppressed and persecuted of all lands take refuge with the High Porte, and there find protection. Blessed be Sultan Suleiman, the people's sun, the Lord of both halves of the world!"

"Hosannah!" cried Sinan the Jew with tears in his eyes, forgetful of his turban.

I concluded that they must both be very drunk, for I could not believe more than half they said. But Sinan unfolded a great map and pointed to the coasts of Spain, Italy, and Greece, and opposite to them

45

the coast of Africa. He showed me where the island of Jerba lay, and the sultanate of Tunisia, the town of Algiers, and the island of Zerjeli, where Khaireddin was mustering his fleet.

Then he said, "The Hafsids have ruled these coasts for three hundred years—too long a time. Sultan Muhammed of the Hafsid dynasty is a lecherous old man who governs Tunis and is an ally of the Christian Emperor. His family were also lords of Algiers until the great Khaireddin and his brother drove them out and placed themselves under the protection of the Porte. But the faithless Hafsids sought help from the Emperor and both Khaireddin's brothers fell in battle against the Spaniards and Berbers, so that once more Algiers came under Hafsid sway. In recognition of their help, the Spaniards built a strong fortress at the mouth of the harbor, which is a great stumbling block to us in our naval warfare against the Christians. In this way the bloodthirsty Hafsids have set themselves up against the Sultan and now omit his name from their intercessory prayers in the mosques on Fridays. But by forming an alliance with unbelievers and allowing the Spaniards to dig themselves in at the harbor mouth, Selim ben-Hafs has squandered the period of grace allowed him."

"But," said I, "in Christian lands the story went that the King of France had formed an alliance with the Sultan against the Emperor. How can the great Sultan accept an unbeliever as his ally, if such alliances are to be condemned?"

They looked askance at one another, and Sinan answered, "We know nothing of that, but Sultan Suleiman can of course help the King of France, if the King humbly requests it. For the object there is to weaken the power of the Emperor, whereas the ruler of Algiers and Tunis seeks the aid of unbelievers against Khaireddin and the Sultan, which is a different thing altogether."

"Maybe," I said. "But surely you don't expect me to set off with my two empty hands to win back Algiers for the Sultan, whom I've never even seen?"

They burst out laughing and slapped one another delightedly on the shoulder. Their faces were aglow with wine and they cried together, "This is a most excellent *hakim,* and his hawk's eyes discern hidden things. That is indeed what we expect of you. With empty hands you shall win back Algiers and proclaim the great admiral Khaireddin as its governor, so that he may drive out the Spaniards

46

and obtain peace for those unhappy coasts. After that the malevolent Spaniards can no longer obstruct our naval enterprises."

"Then, if as you say I am a *hakim,* a physician, I forbid you to drink any more wine, for already your wits are clouded. Is not Algiers a great and mighty city, surrounded by impregnable walls?"

"It is indeed," they cried in chorus. "It is a shining city on the shores of this blue sea, a flashing jewel which our commander Khaireddin desires to set beside the crescent on Sultan Suleiman's turban, so to deserve his favor. And the whole of this city is guarded by the island fortress of the Spaniards, which blocks the entrance to the harbor and obstructs sea traffic."

I tore the turban from my head and cried aloud, "What curse is on me, that I must ever fall among maniacs who either cheat me or demand the impossible from me?"

But Abu el-Kasim spoke soothingly, saying, "You are here offered the opportunity for great deeds which will bring you honor. The Hafsid rule has been marked by so many crimes, fratricides, and feuds, and such licentiousness, that its overthrow will be an act pleasing to God. Baba Aroush fell in the attempt, as also his brothers Elias and Ishak, so that now only the youngest brother Khisr, called Khaireddin, remains alive."

"You've set too many names whirling in my head at once," I told them. "Nor do I see how you, a trafficker in cheap perfumes, can talk of this admiral as if he were your brother."

Sinan interposed here, to say, "The wise man hides his treasure. Never judge a man by his clothes or his seeming poverty. Even I, poor wretch, am a Jew by birth, so that I was compelled to turn Christian before I was allowed to take the turban and acknowledge the Prophet, blessed be his name." Mastering his tears he went on, "We, who drag our bare living from the sea, are feeble enough taken singly. Storm clouds are piling up, especially in the west, and we must unite our strength and lay the foundations of solid sea power, with the support of the Sultan, so that he recognizes Khaireddin as beylerbey in Algiers and sends him a kaftan of honor and a horsetail switch. That is the simple core of the matter. We must first get Algiers into our hands, then build an arsenal and a base for operations at sea."

Thus it was that Sinan the Jew disclosed to me the pirates' secret plans. There was no fault to be found with them; indeed I was bound to admit to myself that the time was ripe for their realization, now that the Emperor was waging bitter war against the French King, the Pope, and Venice. Moreover the Emperor had split his forces by frivolously sending good ships to the new countries beyond the western ocean. For my own part I cherished no very friendly feelings toward His Imperial Majesty, although I had taken part in the sack of Rome on his behalf. But neither had I any wish to lose my head for Khaireddin. I said therefore, "Muster your fleet, attack Algiers like brave men, and win it for the Sultan! The time is favorable, and I make no doubt that the Sultan will have the greatest pleasure in sending you kaftans of honor, and no doubt horses' tails as well."

Both talking at once, they said, "No, no, that will never do. The inhabitants must overthrow their own ruler and summon Khaireddin to be their governor. Our forces are too weak to take the place by storm, especially with the hostile Berber tribes at our heels. We know; we have tried."

Abu el-Kasim said, "You shall come with me to Algiers, where you will gain a reputation as a physician. You shall also study at the mosque school and be circumcised, that you may gain the confidence of your teachers. Your brother shall earn his living as a wrestler in the market place near the mosque. If he's as strong as we hope and believe, his fame will soon reach the ears of Selim ben-Hafs and he will be called to display his art before that bloodthirsty Sultan. Lastly the girl whose eyes resemble jewels of different colors shall gaze into sand, drawing lines in it with her finger, and make many useful and apposite predictions."

I could not believe my ears and said, "Do you really mean that you won't separate me from my brother, that you're taking Giulia as well, and that I needn't be parted from my dog?"

Sinan the Jew nodded, and mellowed by good wine he said, "Such was the guidance I received from the holy book. If we succeed, further tasks may await you, beside which this will appear a mere test of your loyalty."

I gave a jeering laugh.

"Those last words of yours in no way increase my interest in your schemes, for were I successful I should only be burdened with ever more difficult tasks until I sank beneath the load. And what can you know of my loyalty? What should hinder me from going straight to

48

Selim ben-Hafs as soon as we reach Algiers, and betraying your plans to him?"

Sinan's one eye was stony as he said, "Slave, you might win brief happiness by so doing, but it would be followed by a misery far greater; for sooner or later Khaireddin's hand would reach you, and he would have you flayed alive and roasted on a spit."

But Abu el-Kasim raised his hand and said with a smile, "Don't excite yourself, Sinan; it is my business to weigh the hearts of men, and I tell you that Michael Hakim will not betray you. How I know this I cannot tell you. I believe not even Michael himself knows it."

His trust went to my heart, for I thought of my former life and knew that neither he nor anyone else had any very good grounds for faith in me, although my intentions had always been sincere.

"I'm but a slave," I said. "I'm not free to act of my own will. But if Abu el-Kasim trusts me, I will try to be worthy of his trust. Answer me one more question—can a slave own slaves?"

My question surprised them very much, but Sinan the Jew at once replied, "Of course a slave may own slaves once he has attained an honorable position. But such slaves still belong to his master."

This greatly cheered me, and I said, "Then I submit to the will of Allah, and if my loyalty should result in death, the matter is predestined and I can do nothing to prevent it. Show yourself noble and open handed, my lord Sinan, and promise me your slave Giulia if I should succeed in my task, which I very gravely doubt."

Sinan the Jew stroked his beard with his slender fingers and said, "Slave, who are you to bargain with me?"

"There's no bargain about it," I said in surprise. "Such a promise would not increase my loyalty or my eagerness to serve you by a hair's breadth. I'm not even convinced that your consent would prove a blessing to me. Nevertheless I humbly entreat you—promise her to me!"

Sinan turned the wine jar sadly upside down and said, "My own liberality brings tears to my eyes. Michael, my dear slave, I promise that on the day Khaireddin marches in triumph through the open gates of Algiers, the girl shall be yours, and I will make over my right to her in the presence of witnesses. May the devil devour me if I break my promise."

He shed tears of emotion and embraced me, and Abu el-Kasim also put his arms about me. Then Sinan kicked aside the rich carpet, seized

49

a copper ring that was bolted to one of the marble slabs, and with a great effort hauled this up. Forgetful of his dignity he lay down at full length on the floor, put his arm into the hole beneath and drew up a fresh wine jar.

I have only an indistinct memory of what happened then, but when I opened my eyes next morning I was lying with Sinan's beard in my hand and Abu el-Kasim's toes in my mouth, and I must confess that the awakening was far from pleasant.

After a Turkish bath and massage I was so much recovered and so well pleased with life that I half thought I had dreamed the events of the previous day. But after the noon prayer, Sinan ordered me to prepare for the journey.

At dusk Abu el-Kasim led us to a little vessel moored in the harbor. Giulia came too, heavily veiled and too haughty to speak a word to us. We were soon heading out to sea with a fair wind. Thus Abu el-Kasim left the island of Jerba as quietly and inconspicuously as he had come. I stared out into the darkness and put my hand to my neck; this seemed to me thinner than ever, and I reflected anxiously upon the dangers among which, despite all my good intentions, my unlucky star had plunged me.

BOOK 2.

The Deliverer Comes from the Sea

WE DID not sail direct to Algiers, for Abu el-Kasim explained that the Spaniards who held the island fort at the mouth of the harbor were in the habit of stopping and searching any vessels that sought to enter. For this reason we landed some distance along the coast, and we were not the only people to bring wares by devious routes into the city. In the sheltered bay where we anchored we found a great number of small craft whose owners were voluble in cursing Selim ben-Hafs and the Spaniards for obstructing honest trade. These vessels were discharging cargoes of captured Christians, and plunder rolled up in mats; instead of customs seals, patches of fresh blood were to be seen, so that my heart sank as I beheld the work.

We spent the night in the hut of a swarthy peasant, who was a friend of Abu's and a man of few words. Next day Abu hired a donkey, loaded it with two great baskets and bade Giulia mount upon its back. After much argument he persuaded some peasants who were also bound for the city to conceal among their baggage a great many of the bundles and jars that he had unloaded from his ship. And truly I have never seen a more ·woeful creature than Abu el-Kasim as he wrung his hands, rent his dirty clothes, and besought both black and white Berbers to pity a poor wretch and save his goods from the rapacity of Selim ben-Hafs.

This was of course the purest humbug, for as we approached Algiers he told me, "Ours is a dangerous trade, Michael my son, and we cannot long ply it without attracting attention. Too much secrecy would defeat itself, and it's better to expose oneself to scorn and mockery than

53

to lose one's head. And so I make as much commotion as possible, and I'm already notorious in Algiers, so that children run after me, pointing. Countless times I've been punished for my shifts and expedients and my clumsy attempts to fool Selim ben-Hafs's customs officials. This time I shall no doubt get caught again, and some of my goods will be confiscated amid general gaiety. But all this is perfectly in order. My best wares will arrive safely; I know the rules of the game. By the way, it would do no harm for your brawny brother to jeer at me now and again. For who takes notice of a man who's mocked by his own slaves?"

I noticed that the country round Algiers was beautiful, rich with gardens and fruit trees, while numerous windmills on the hillsides bore witness to the wealth of the city. We forded a river on whose banks I saw a crowd of women, both black-skinned and brown and wearing only brightly colored cloths wrapped about their loins, who were washing clothes.

The city lay on a slope by the blue, hazy sea, and gleamed dazzling white in the sunshine. It was surrounded by a sturdy wall and a ditch, and at its highest point there rose from an angle in the wall a round keep, which dominated town and harbor. At the eastern gate we joined a great throng; the guards were sorting sheep from goats with blows of their sticks, letting the peasants through and detaining all strangers to examine their baggage. Abu el-Kasim urged us to follow close at his heels, then, drawing the corner of his cloak over his face and murmuring numerous blessings and quotations from the Koran, he attempted to slink past the guards. But they seized him and uncovered his face, and I have never seen a more crestfallen figure than Abu el-Kasim at that moment. He cursed his birth and whined, "Why do you so relentlessly persecute me—me, the poorest of the poor? You'll soon cause me to lose faith in the mercy of Allah the Almighty."

The guards laughed and said, "We know you, Abu el-Kasim, and you can't deceive us. Tell us what you have to declare, or you'll lose all."

Abu el-Kasim pointed to Andy and me and Giulia on her donkey, and wept bitterly, saying, "Do you not see, you hard-hearted men, that I bring but four eggs and a nest to hatch them in?"

But the men ignored his jest and took us to the guardroom. Abu el-Kasim buffeted us on before him, and I turned, smacked his face, and said, "Is this how you treat valuable slaves, fellow?"

Abu el-Kasim raised his hand as if to chastise me but seeing the look on my face he quailed, and mourned, "See how even my slave behaves to me! What can I think but that Allah has cast me out, when he burdens me with such a creature as this?"

The guards handed him over to their chief, to whom Abu el-Kasim mentioned the wares for which he was willing to pay, and these were noted down by the clerk. He then declared, "As truly as I'm a blameless man who never in his life tried to cheat anyone, I bring nothing else on which I should pay duty. For guarantee, and in token of my good will, I make you a present of these three gold pieces, which are my last."

The men were content with this, and laughingly accepted the money, from which I concluded that the city was less well ordered than it might have been, since its officials allowed themselves to be bribed so openly. But as Abu el-Kasim was on his way out, a piece of costly ambergris the size of his fist slipped from under his arm where it had grown warm, and now filled the whole room with its fragrance.

Abu el-Kasim's face turned ashen gray, and I could not think how he was able thus to control his features, unless it was that he so lived his part that he had come to believe in it himself. He stammered, "Hassan ben-Ismail, I had indeed forgotten that little piece of ambergris. Also a camel follows, blind of one eye, bearing a basket of grain in which are hidden five jars of good wine. Let the camel through and come and see me tomorrow evening, when we can discuss the matter rationally in all its aspects. In the meantime as a token of my good will you may keep that piece of ambergris, and Allah will reward you on the Last Day."

The official laughed scornfully but agreed, and even gave back the ambergris, saying that its perfume made the place unbearable. As soon as Abu el-Kasim had come out into the narrow street he climbed nimbly onto Andy's shoulders and shrieked, "Make way for Abu el-Kasim, the almsgiver, the friend of the poor, now returned from a journey which Allah has blessed!"

Thus was Andy compelled to carry his vociferous burden, and we attracted much attention as we trudged through the streets toward Abu's hovel, which was near the harbor. From behind latticed windows curious glances followed us, and soon we had a flock of joyously screeching urchins at our heels. Abu el-Kasim threw a copper coin among them from time to time, calling God and all the faithful to witness his liberality.

Abu el-Kasim's dwelling was a sagging mud hut, and his little shop, bolted and barred, was full of stinking jars. In the yard a feeble-minded wretch of a slave kept watch. He had been deaf and dumb from birth, and it was with grunts and flickering fingers that he began to relate what had passed during his master's absence, repeatedly kissing the hem of Abu's grimy cloak. I was at a loss to understand how a man like Abu el-Kasim had been able to inspire such devotion in this slave, who had not even a name, a name being useless to one who cannot hear it called. But although he was clumsy and constantly broke things, and cooked miserable meals, Abu el-Kasim treated him kindly. I was surprised at his forbearance, but he said, "He suits me admirably, for he hears nothing of what is said in this house, and can't mention what he has seen. Moreover he gives me daily occasion to practice patience and self-control, and these qualities are essential in my dangerous vocation."

When we had entered the miserable den and surveyed its two rooms with their beaten-earth floors and tattered paillasses, Giulia drew aside her veil and mourned, "Have I endured the pangs of seasickness and the burning glare of the sun, only to land in such a place as this—I who have eaten good kukurrush and won the favor of Sinan the Jew? How could he give me to so contemptible a man?"

She could not conceal her disappointment, but vented it in loud lamentation. Abu el-Kasim laid his hand comfortingly upon her shoulder, and the deaf-mute, alarmed at her weeping, fell on his knees before her and pressed his forehead to the ground. But Giulia kicked him with her red slipper, shook off Abu el-Kasim's hand and screamed, "Sell me in the market to whomsoever you please, but don't come near me, or I will plunge a dagger into your throat."

Abu el-Kasim wrung his hands, but his eyes gleamed as he said, "Alas, queen of my heart, how can you treat me so harshly? I fear I made a bad bargain in buying you from Sinan the Jew for the sake of your radiant beauty and the glorious diversity of your eyes. Perhaps the wretched Jew deceived me when he praised your amenable nature and swore that you could foretell the future by tracing characters in the sand."

Giulia was so astounded that she forgot her wailing and said, "Cer-

56

tainly he taught me to draw lines in the sand and to speak of what I see there; but of fortunetelling and prediction he said not a word!"

Abu el-Kasim answered, "Yes, and for me too you shall draw in the sand and speak of what you see, for you are fairer than the moon and your speech in sweeter than honey, and I see I must disclose to you all my secrets. Follow me, but never breathe a word of what I shall show you."

From one of his hiding places he took out a key wrapped in a rag and led us to his dark storeroom. Here, having rolled aside barrels and jars, he revealed a narrow door, which he unlocked, and then led us through into a room hung and carpeted with costly rugs and containing a quantity of brass and copper vessels of beautiful workmanship. Next, drawing aside a mat that hung on the wall, he showed us a wrought-iron gate and behind this an alcove with a wide divan in it, and a Koran on its stand. He opened the gate with a special key and kindled a small cone of myrrh, which soon spread its blue smoke through the room. Then he raised the lid of an iron chest and took out lengths of velvet and brocade, silver vessels and a number of heavy gold goblets. I could only suppose that he was seeking to gratify Giulia's vanity by this display.

And Giulia became indeed somewhat reconciled, and admitted that in time she might feel at home in the place, hardened as she now was by so many privations.

"But you must give me the key of the grille," she said, "so that I can retire when I please. I permit no one to disturb me while I'm engaged in meditation, or in tending my beauty, or in sleep, and if you fancy you're ever going to share that bed with me, Abu el-Kasim, you're greatly mistaken."

But Abu el-Kasim turned a deaf ear and, spitting on a golden goblet which had lost its luster, began carefully polishing it with a corner of his cloak. At a sign from him the deaf-mute brought drinking water, and into this he dropped aromatic herbs which gave it a refreshing and thirst-quenching taste. When we had drunk he invited us to sit down on the cushions, while he fetched a large copper dish and filled it with fine sand.

"Have compassion on your servant, cruel Delilah," he said. "Since the day Sinan the Jew told me of your strange gift I've been impatient for this moment. Gaze with your wonderful eyes at the sand, stir it with your finger and tell me what you see."

Incense caressed my nostrils, the drink glowed in my belly, and sitting there cross legged on the low cushion I felt strangely drowsy. Even my little dog had laid its nose between its paws and sighed contentedly in that twilit room. Giulia, too, no doubt felt the prevailing languor, for without argument she bent forward and drew lines abstractedly in the sand. She said, "I see roads, cities, and the boundless sea. I see also three men. One of these is thin and ugly as a monkey. The second is sturdy as a tower, but his head's no bigger than a pigeon's egg. The third looks like a goat with little horns—very little horns, but sharp."

I thought Giulia was saying all this to make fun of us, but gradually her voice altered, she stared seemingly bewitched into the sand, and her finger moved as if she were unaware of the figures she was tracing. Abu el-Kasim swung the bowl of myrrh and said in a low voice, "Delilah, Delilah—Christian Giulia, tell me what you see in the sand!"

Giulia's smooth brow was now furrowed. She groaned, and a harsh, alien voice spoke through her mouth. "The sand is red as if with blood—I see a seething cauldron, and in it people—warriors, ships, banners. I see a turban fall from a puffy head—I see a harbor—many ships entering the harbor in a roar of cannon."

"The Deliverer comes from the sea," said Abu el-Kasim in a low voice. "The Deliverer comes from the sea before the figs have ripened. That is important, Delilah. You see the usurper on his throne, the blasphemer who neglects the commandments of Allah. But you see also the turban falling from his head, and you see the Deliverer coming from the sea before the figs are ripe."

Giulia stirred the sand intently, and suddenly the alien voice broke out in derision, "Abu el-Kasim in your donkey's hide! Why do your bleeding feet tread a thousand paths when only one is needful? You're but a fish in God's net, and the more stubbornly you thrust against it, the more hopelessly are you entangled in its meshes. Your life is but a reflection in a pool whose calm surface is quickly shattered by the hand of a child at play. Why are you ever your own dupe, when you gain no peace by it, however feverishly you flee from yourself and change your form?"

Abu el-Kasim was thunderstruck, and cried out, "In the name of Allah the Compassionate! A wicked spirit speaks through this woman, and her eyes must indeed be evil."

He wrenched the copper dish from Giulia's grasp, though she clung

58

to it convulsively with both hands. Her eyes shone like jewels in her white face and she did not wake from her trance until Abu el-Kasim shook her and bent her head repeatedly from side to side. Then her glance came alive again and rising abruptly she boxed his ears, saying, "Don't touch me, you filthy ape! Don't dare to take advantage of me when I dream like this. It often happens. It used to happen long ago when I looked into a pool or a well. And I like it, for it seems to free me from the curse of my eyes. But that's no excuse for shameless assault. Let me rest, for I'm very tired. Go away, all of you, and leave me in peace."

She drove us from the room.

Abu el-Kasim gave us blankets and bade us find sleeping places for the night. Then he went out. The deaf-mute brought clean straw and did his poor best for us. Toward evening he began cooking broth, and cut up a few small pieces of mutton for grilling. Andy, seeing this, shook his head sadly and remarked, "The poor fellow can never have had a square meal in his life. To look at him you'd think he was going to feed a couple of hens and a blind puppy. That may do for skinny old Abu, but not for me."

He pushed the slave gently aside, built up a good fire, hung the cauldron over it, and flung in all the bits of meat and fat he could find. The unhappy deaf-mute, seeing Andy pile on the fire all the twigs and dried dung that had been so slowly and painfully collected, was appalled; but when Andy began cutting up half a sheep to fill the pot the man grasped his wrist, and his eyes swam in tears.

Just then I heard my dog yelping outside in the yard, and I found him running madly round and round, pursued by two black hens. Rael took refuge between my feet and I saw that his muzzle was bleeding. Greatly incensed—for Rael was a peaceable creature, and never chased fowls—I seized a stake and wrathfully attacked the aggressors. The dog helped me as well as he could, and Andy appeared in the doorway, to encourage us with joyous shouts until at last I was able to catch the birds and wring their necks.

The commotion had brought a crowd of neighbors to the gate, but Andy quickly snatched up the fowls and threw them to the slave for him to pluck. The poor wretch, being now out of his wits, meekly obeyed and his tears fell among the feathers. I pitied him, but felt that he might as well accustom himself to the new circumstances without delay.

59

When the sun was setting and the melancholy cry of the muezzin reached us from the minaret of the mosque, Abu el-Kasim dipped his fingers into a bowl of water and splashed a few drops over his feet, wrists, and face. He then unrolled a mat and recited the prayers, while I knelt too and pressed my forehead to the ground in time with him. When our prayer was ended Abu el-Kasim sniffed the air and said, "Let us bless the food in the name of Allah, and eat!"

We sat down in a ring on the floor. Here Giulia joined us, rubbing the sleep from her eyes and stretching her slender limbs. But when Andy carried in the great cooking pot, Abu el-Kasim grimaced as if he had bitten into a sour fruit, and said, "I don't intend to feed all the poor of the quarter, nor are we a platoon of janissaries. Who's to blame for this terrible mistake? Let it be the last. Were it not that I wish our first evening to be harmonious I could fly into a passion."

Dipping his hand into the pot he drew forth the leg of a fowl, which he gazed at in wonder, shifting it from hand to hand and blowing on his fingers.

"Allah is indeed great," he said. "Here is a miracle. A piece of mutton seems to have turned into a drumstick."

The deaf-mute began waving his arms, opening his mouth and pointing at Andy, me, and the dog, which sat meekly awaiting its scraps. And when at last Abu el-Kasim grasped what had happened he quite lost his appetite, and wept.

"The curse of Allah upon you for killing both my hens, Mirmah and Fatima. Alas, my hens, my little hens, that laid me such round, brown eggs!"

Tears poured down his cheeks and his sparse beard, and Andy looked uncomfortable. But I flared up, "Don't swear at us, Abu el-Kasim, but at your wicked hens that tore my dog's nose. It was I who wrung their necks, and if you don't want to eat, you can fast."

Abu el-Kasim continued to sigh and wipe the tears from his beard, but when he saw how the food was disappearing he forgot his sorrow and helped himself. Afterward he patted his stomach contentedly, but warned us that at this rate we should eat him out of house and home.

Andy retorted, "Of what use are starving servants? I'm content with plain food so long as there's plenty of it. Give us half a sheep and a bag of meal daily, and neither you nor I need complain."

Abu el-Kasim's only response was to tear his beard, and shortly afterward we retired to rest.

60

Next day, after the morning prayer, Abu el-Kasim took us out and showed us objects of interest in the town. Many close-packed buildings stood within its walls, and in the narrow alleys it was difficult to push past those whom we met. Here were representatives of every Christian and Moslem nation, as well as Jews and Greeks. I saw also desert horsemen, who kept their faces covered.

There were many fine houses surrounded by walls, and public bathhouses open to all, irrespective of faith, color, or means. The rich paid most for their baths, while the poorest might bathe for nothing, in the name of the Compassionate. At the highest point of the town stood the kasbah of Selim ben-Hafs, with its countless buildings, and on either side of its main entrance iron hooks were to be seen, on which were impaled human heads and limbs. The finest building of all, however, was the great mosque by the harbor. The Spanish island fortress commanded the harbor mouth, and Spaniards armed with swords and harquebuses rowed freely to and fro, or stalked haughtily among the populace, whom they compelled to make way for them. This offended many a devout Moslem, for by the law of the Koran no believer ought to step aside for an unbeliever, but should crowd him and jostle him out into the street.

On our way about the city, Abu el-Kasim gathered together with many blessings the jars which, hidden in peasants' grain baskets, had arrived at the houses of his merchant friends, and we carried them back to his house. The city was divided in a very sensible and practical manner into different quarters, in which each kind of merchandise and craft had its own street. Thus the coppersmiths kept to one alley, while tailors, tanners, dyers, and all other artisans each had theirs. Our own house was in the street of the spice merchants and dealers in drugs. It was one of the more respectable thoroughfares, since wealthy merchants as well as poor ones lived there, as could be seen by the crowd of beggars and cripples who squatted all day at rich men's doors in the hope of alms.

At noon Abu el-Kasim took us to the mosque, in whose forecourt was a marble basin supplied with fresh running water. We performed the prescribed ablutions and entered the mosque, carrying our slippers in our hands. There were costly carpets on the floor, many lamps hung from the roof by copper and silver chains, and columns of different colors supported the great dome. We murmured our purpose in coming and imitated the actions of the reader, kneeling when he knelt

61

and bowing down as he did. After the prayers Abu el-Kasim took us to the madrasseh, or mosque school, where youths under the direction of gray-bearded teachers were studying the Koran, the duty of man, the traditions, and the law. Abu el-Kasim had given us clean clothes, and he now presented us to an elderly man with a white beard, saying, "Venerable Ibrahim ben Adam el-Mausili! In the name of the Compassionate I bring you two men who have found the faith and desire to follow the true path."

From that day forward, after the evening prayer, we attended the school for converts, to learn Arabic and the seven pillars, roots, and branches of Islam. Not even Fridays were excepted; for although Moslems leave their labor or their business to attend the noon service on that day, yet they count no day as a day of rest. In their opinion the Christian and Jewish manner of honoring the Sabbath is blasphemous, because it is based on the idea that God, after creating heaven and earth, rested upon the seventh day. Moslems acknowledge that God created heaven and earth, but being omnipotent He must have done it without effort; the very notion that He could be in need of rest is blasphemy to them.

When the old teacher Ibrahim ben-Adam observed my genuine desire for knowledge he conceived a liking for me and expounded the Koran to the best of his ability, and often I stayed on after the others had left until late in the evening. He was very devout and never wearied of reading the sacred writings. It was from him I learned that Islam has room in it for many paths whose followers dispute among themselves. But these questions did not disturb my peace of mind, for I studied the Koran with intellectual detachment, and solely from a desire for knowledge. I soon perceived that Christians had little to be proud of in their supposedly superior religion, for dogmatic disputes, sanctimoniousness, hypocrisy, and the nonobservance of fasts were features common to both persuasions.

During the day I helped Abu el-Kasim to mix drugs and grind kohl to a fine powder for eye black. I also prepared a dye of indigo and henna, which gives a blue-black tinge to women's hair. By kneading indigo leaves to a stiff dough we obtained a substance that women used to color their eyebrows dark blue; and Abu el-Kasim told me that the fine ladies of Baghdad often shaved off the eyebrows that Allah had given them, to replace them by penciled blue lines.

But the most important of Abu el-Kasim's wares were the leaves of henna that he obtained from Morocco, where they were gathered three times a year. Women moistened these and kneaded them to a greenish paste which they rubbed into their faces to freshen and rejuvenate their complexions; elderly women could not live without it. Henna was also used in the preparation of a dye for nails, hands, and feet. Abu el-Kasim had his own methods of making this, which enabled him to sell it at prices that varied according to the means of the customer.

He taught me to knead a little lemon juice and alum into the henna paste, and so produce an orange-colored mixture for coloring the nails. He would mix some of it with rose water or essence of violets, put it into different pots under different names and price it according to the lure of those names. In this way he could charge many times the price of the original commodity. Vain men dyed their beards with henna, and fair-haired women could use it to turn their hair fiery red in the Venetian manner.

Other preparations he made entirely himself, including the burning "paradise ointment," which he declared could restore virginity to a prostitute, though she had visited all the ports of Africa and reached the age of forty. When I rebuked Abu for his heartlessness in robbing the poor by selling them worthless goods he looked at me with his monkey eyes and answered gravely, "Michael el-Hakim, you mustn't blame me, for in selling these things I sell much more than their ingredients. I sell dreams, and the poor have greater need of dreams than the rich and fortunate. To aging women I sell youth and self-confidence. Besides, you'll have noticed that I sometimes give away henna and rose water for some poor girl's wedding, and so acquire merit. Don't reproach me for selling dreams to others, though I've lost my own."

I give no opinion as to the rights or wrongs of this, and as to whether it is better to live unhappy in the truth or happy in a lie. However it may be, I helped Abu el-Kasim in every way I could and was flattered when he began to call me el-Hakim, the physician. It came about when he was seeking an Arabic name for me. Rearranging the letters of "Michael" or "Mikhael," he produced to his own surprise the words "el-Hakim."

"There's an omen indeed!" he cried. "As Michael the angel you did Sinan a service by inducing him to seek guidance in the holy book;

63

now as el-Hakim the physician you shall serve me. May the conjunction be a fortunate one for both of us."

I first saw Sultan Selim ben-Hafs one Friday as he came riding down the steep street from the kasbah to the noon service in the mosque. He was attended by a flock of richly dressed slaves, and by a company of bowmen who, with arrows ready fitted to the bowstrings, closely scrutinized the lattice windows and flat roofs of the houses. In the forecourt of the mosque Selim made a disdainful gesture, and a sackful of square silver coins was flung to the poor. Within, having carelessly rattled off the prayers, he sat cross legged on his throne and dozed while passages from the Koran were read aloud. Thus I had a fair opportunity of watching him and studying his face, and I cannot say that I was attracted, for it was ravaged by vice and his drooling mouth hung open. He was middle aged; his face and his dark beard gleamed with rare ointments, and his bloodshot eyes framed in heavy, puffy lids were as lifeless as his mouth. Abu el-Kasim told me he ate opium. Afterward, on his return to the palace, Selim paused at the entrance to witness two executions and the flogging of some young boys who were bound to posts on either side of the gate. He let the whipping continue until blood was pouring down their backs, while he sat slumped in his saddle with a hanging lip, dully looking on. If the Hafsids had ruled Algiers for three hundred years, I thought, it was at least one hundred years too long.

I soon came to love Algiers—the street where I lived, and the people who talked to me. This foreign city, with the strange smells and colors, the charcoal braziers, the fruit trees, and the many ships in the harbor, was like a city from some story book. Each day I ate mutton and rich broth; often Abu el-Kasim with a sigh would loosen his purse strings and give me a few square silver coins, and I would go to the market to buy plump ptarmigan, which Giulia afterward dressed with lavish seasoning.

For Giulia had gradually become reconciled to her lot. Abu el-Kasim pleased her by taking her to the bazaar and buying her beautifully wrought bracelets and anklets of silver. To my annoyance she dyed her fair hair red. Her nails, the palms of her hands, and her feet up to the anklebones were always orange-red, and she also painted her eyelids and eyebrows after the fashion of Algerian women. To her credit be it said that she soon wearied of our housekeeping and took it into her own hands, inducing Abu el-Kasim to repair the house and

64

even demanding a covered pool in the courtyard, so that he was forced to pay a large sum for the right to pipe water from the city water tower. Giulia in short claimed the same amenities as our neighbors, until Abu el-Kasim tore his beard and wrung his hands, and in moments of desperation ran out into the street to call everyone to witness how the abominable soothsayer was plunging him into ruin.

The neighbors stroked their beards and gloated. Some said, "Abu el-Kasim has grown rich," and others said, "What a joyful day it will be when next Selim ben-Hafs's taxgatherer visits our street!" Only the most compassionate remarked, "Abu el-Kasim has clearly gone out of his mind. It would be a kindness to him and pleasing to Allah to carry him to the madhouse and have the evil spirit whipped from his body."

I was not at all surprised at these remarks, for now and then Andy in a howling fury would chase the agile Abu round the court, until he fled over the wall and hid in the cess pit. For Abu el-Kasim purposely teased and goaded Andy every time he was beaten on the wrestling ground behind the mosque. On such days Andy would be in a surly humor, and if on top of this Abu waved a wine flask in front of his nose, inviting him to take a pull at it and gain a little vigor, it was enough, and I was often afraid that Andy would knock Abu to pieces. But when enough interested onlookers had gathered in the yard and Andy's fury had somewhat abated, Abu el-Kasim would creep out of the drain, smelling very evilly, and approach Andy with an ingratiating air, to feel his calf muscles and assure the neighbors that Andy would yet bring him in a fortune by wrestling.

When I expostulated with Abu for teasing Andy he looked at me in wonder, and said, "Why deny my neighbors a little innocent fun? Besides, it's good for your brother, for otherwise he'd only sit and sulk after a defeat, until he got cramps in the stomach. As it is, he can work off his fury on me and so regain his good fighting humor."

This was true, for after such outbreaks Andy quickly cooled, and laughed at Abu for a silly old fool.

Abu el-Kasim then persuaded him to lie full length on a bench, and massaged his arms and legs, oiled his massive body and rubbed healing salves into his bruises. Now that Andy had adopted the Moslem faith he had to have a new name, and Abu el-Kasim called him Antar, after the great hero of the Arabian tales. In the bazaar he so loudly praised his strength and skill as to arouse curiosity and many people

65

gathered behind the mosque to watch him wrestle. At least once a week Abu el-Kasim mounted on Andy's shoulders and rode thus to the market place, issuing loud challenges to all and sundry to try a fall with the invincible Antar. There Andy stood up naked save for a pair of leather breeches reaching to the knee, while Abu rubbed him with oil and loudly eulogized his muscles. Among the loiterers on the shady side of the market place, and under the colonnade of the mosque, there were always some disengaged *gureshes,* each of whom had a patron or master who fed him and wagered money on him. Such wagers were not held to be gambling, which is forbidden by the Koran, since the result was determined not by chance but by the strength and skill of the wrestlers.

These patrons were the idle sons of rich merchants and shipowners, whose forebears had built up their fortunes by piracy. But since Selim ben-Hafs, through fear of the great Sultan, had allied himself with the Spaniards, piracy had ceased, and so these young men were without an occupation. They passed their days at the baths and their nights in secret wine drinking in company with dancing girls. They sought to stimulate their jaded senses by patronizing this sport. Many of the wrestlers were rough fellows who had chosen this way of life from laziness. At times, when they found themselves outmatched, they were apt to sink their teeth in an opponent's ear and tear it off. Therefore Andy had to be on his guard, and despite his lamentations and references to Samson's disastrous fate, Abu shaved his head so that no adversary could grasp him by the hair.

When first I went with Andy and Abu el-Kasim to the market place I was horrified at the sight of these fearful wrestlers, half naked and gleaming with sweat, as they made themselves supple by trying holds on one another, and forcing one another to the ground. They were big, fat men with bulging muscles, and I fancy any one of them could have cracked my ribs with a poke of his forefinger.

But Abu el-Kasim made a great commotion, chattering like a monkey and screaming, "Is there anyone here who dares wrestle with the invincible Antar? His knees are as the pillars in the mosque and his trunk is a very tower. He was bred among idolaters in a land far to the north, and is hardened by the snow and ice that covers the country all the year round—ice, which you idlers know only as fragments in your sherbet."

After continuing thus for some time he climbed down from Andy's shoulders, spread a piece of cloth upon the ground and threw a square silver coin upon it as a reward to the winner, crying aloud to Allah to witness his liberality. This provoked a roar of laughter which brought others running to the scene, while the wealthy patrons held their sides and cried, "You seem to have little faith in your Antar—and no wonder. He looks as lumbering as an ox."

But the curious began throwing coins onto the cloth until a little heap of silver lay there, and even a small gold coin or two. The wrestlers looked critically from the pile of money to Andy and back again, gathered in a ring with their hands on one another's shoulders and chattered, until one of them undertook a "good" bout with Andy. In "good" wrestling, the opponents were not to inflict willful and lasting injury on one another, whereas in "hard" wrestling everything was allowed. In "hard" bouts men were apt to lose an eye or an ear, and professional wrestlers did not willingly engage in them.

Andy and his adversary now tackled one another, and Andy, putting into practice the holds that Mussuf the Negro had taught him, flung his man over his shoulder to the ground with a resounding thud. To encourage the victim the bystanders flung more money onto the cloth, but Andy succeeded in throwing three men in succession—no mean feat for a beginner. But with the fourth he had the worst of it, for after a prolonged struggle his foot slipped and he fell, so that his opponent could get an arm under his shoulder and over the back of his neck and force him down.

Abu el-Kasim uttered shrieks of anguish and wept as if he had lost a great sum of money instead of the one silver coin he had thrown onto the cloth. But Andy rubbed his aching neck and said, "I only hope Mussuf taught me right; I can't stand up to these slippery fellows, though I'm certainly stronger than they are."

He sat with a colored cloth over his shoulders, carefully observing the matches that followed. I believe he learned a great deal from them, for encouraged by the considerable sum now amassed on the cloth the wrestlers fought their best. The final victor was one Iskender, who looked no more formidable than the rest, though his shoulders were as broad as a bread oven, and a lighter man could not move him from the spot. Andy surveyed him wide eyed, and said, "That Iskender's no fool, and he'll be an opponent after my own heart when I get so far. But I've seen enough today to know that I've much to learn."

He did not let his first defeat discourage him, and indeed it proved

67

an advantage, for the other *gureshes* were all the readier to accept him as one of themselves. Iskender gave him four silver pieces from the heap he had won and declared that Andy had fully earned them; for custom required the victor to share his winnings with the other competitors.

The stake money was however the least of the sums to change hands on such occasions, for large amounts were wagered among the onlookers, whether on individual bouts or on the final result; this last was by no means a foregone conclusion. Even the most eminent wrestler, having come triumphantly through ten or fifteen successive encounters with powerful adversaries, could never be confident of wresting the final victory from perhaps a weaker man who came fresh to the attack. Wrestlers and their patrons followed a set system for determining the order of competitors on different days, which evened out the chances and made the final result very uncertain. If therefore a novice wagered solely on the appearance of the men without knowing anything of the order in which they were to fight, he might make very bad mistakes.

Spectators and patrons began to pay greater attention to Andy, and soon it was his turn to gather up the pile of money. On that day Abu el-Kasim's joy knew no bounds. He jumped up and down, then flew open armed at Andy and planted a smacking kiss on his mouth, so that Andy yelled, spat, and hurled him back among the onlookers who, in an ecstasy of mirth, caught him on their outstretched arms. Abu el-Kasim at once bestowed the prescribed proportion of his winnings in alms, displaying deep emotion at his own munificence. But the rest of the money he quickly knotted into a bundle and clasped to his breast, wondering aloud where he could lay hands on an iron chest in which to secure it.

The sum was negligible in comparison with his real fortune, but he liked to feign poverty and entertain the public with his dread of the taxgatherer. And indeed, it was not long before a fat, breathless man arrived at our dwelling. He leaned on his staff of office and looked about him greedily from under a big, bulging turban, and at the sight of him Abu el-Kasim cringed, wrung his hands and said, "O taxgatherer Ali ben-Ismail, why do you persecute me? Not three moons have passed since your last visit, and I'm a poor man."

He hastened forward to support Ali ben-Ismail; I took the visitor's other arm and between us we helped him to a seat on the broadest cushion in the house. When he had settled himself and got his breath back, he smiled sadly and said, "Abu el-Kasim! The ruler of Algiers and of the sea, king of countless Berber tribes, Allah's representative and commander in this city—in short, Sultan Selim ben-Hafs—has been pleased to turn his eyes upon you. You've become rich; you've brought water to your courtyard and refurnished your rooms. Costly rugs have been seen here and even silver cups, which are forbidden by the Koran. You have bought three new slaves: one brings you in enormous sums as a wrestler, another is an indescribably lovely woman with eyes of different colors, who sees strange things in sand, so that even the women of the harem have taken to visiting the public bathhouse to hear her foretell the future. The third earns substantial sums for you as a quacksalver—he's no doubt this goatlike man beside you, who now stands and goggles at me. I'm also told that people come to you from remote villages to bring something which you call 'cheap ambergris.' By such false terminology do you swindle your customers."

Abu el-Kasim warmly denied the charge, but the taxgatherer smote him on the head with his staff and said irascibly, "That's what I'm told, and I should pay little attention if the matter had reached no other ears than mine. I'm a good-natured man and because of my bulk I dislike trudging the streets. But Sultan Selim ben-Hafs has also heard of it, which has put me in a questionable light. I'm vexed with you, Abu el-Kasim; hitherto I've been content with ten gold pieces a year and you've vilely cheated me, setting at nought my friendship and protection. Now we're both in trouble, for the Sultan has laid an extra tax upon you of a thousand gold pieces."

"A thousand!" yelped Abu el-Kasim. Throwing off turban and cloak he began to jump about half-naked, knocking over jars and baskets in his frenzy. "A thousand! The whole street isn't worth that sum, and Allah has plainly deprived Selim ben-Hafs of the remainder of his wits. By the time I'd collected even the tenth part of it I should be toothless with age."

"Did you say the tenth part?" exclaimed the taxgatherer in amazement. "A hundred gold pieces? Then Allah is indeed great and I've found for my lord a goose that lays golden eggs all unsuspected. You astonish me; for I was only joking, being inquisitive about your growing fortunes."

Abu el-Kasim had abruptly ceased his capering, and now said with a malicious glint in his eye, "So. You were making game of me. Then

I'll give your wife such an ointment of paradise that after embracing her you'll die in agony, foaming at the mouth."

Taxgatherer Ali ben-Ismail sweated slightly, and his eyes were cold as he said in a harsh tone, "Don't take the jest to heart, my dear Abu. It's all part of my duty. I've been ordered to make closer scrutiny of your household because Selim ben-Hafs, blessed be his name, needs money to buy another couple of boys. So let us come to some friendly arrangement, as usual. You'd gain nothing if I were dismissed and replaced by a leaner, hungrier man whom you would have to make fat."

Abu felt grave misgivings on hearing that his fortune was the talk of the town. But all he said was, "Cursed be Selim ben-Hafs. He has already thirty young boys in his harem and at least as many women. Am I, poor wretch, to pay for his lascivious amusements? Hear now a remarkable dream that I've had. A Deliverer came from the sea, and at his coming the taxgatherers were led in bonds through the city and flogged at every street corner."

The fat official sweated more than ever, and raised a finger to silence Abu.

"Such dreams are dangerous," he said, "and I cannot think how it is that so many others have been plagued with them. In the name of the Compassionate, dear Abu, refrain from trumpeting your dreams abroad! Remember that even we, the taxgatherers, are poor men."

After prolonged haggling Ali ben-Ismail agreed to take fifty pieces of gold, and said, "I know that you'll feel the loss of this great sum, and I advise you to make up its value in silver coins and cups, and in your slave woman's bracelets. Carry all this to the treasury to be weighed, so that everyone may see how I've denuded you."

No suggestion could have been more welcome to Abu. He gathered up vessels and coins to the value of fifty pieces of gold and having helped Ali to his feet they set off. The taxgatherer walked first, leaning on his staff and panting, while sweat poured down his fat cheeks. After him scuttled Abu el-Kasim wearing only a dirty turban and a loincloth, with the bundle on his back. As he went he shrieked, lamented, and uttered heart-rending appeals to Allah, so that even the neighbors were moved. For once his tears were genuine, for fifty gold pieces was a great deal of money, even for him.

However, before the hour of evening prayer, Abu el-Kasim returned well satisfied from the treasury. He washed, put on clean clothes, performed his devotions, and said, "The money fell in good soil, for even the clerks pitied me when they saw me compelled to surrender my slave woman's bangles, and this evening the whole city's in an uproar over Selim's rapacity. Lamps will burn late tonight in all wealthy houses while the owners bury their treasure beneath the flagstones."

Nevertheless the treasury had wrought a marvel in extorting fifty gold pieces from Abu el-Kasim, and not many days later my white-bearded teacher said to me,

"I have praised your aptitude for learning, and the Faqih himself wishes to behold your face."

This was the greatest honor that could have been done me, for the Faqih was the most learned man in the school, and deeply versed in the branches of *fiqh,* or jurisprudence. As mufti he was competent, in all matters relating to the law in which there was uncertainty or ambiguity, to issue a decree called a *fatwa.* He stood in high favor with the ruler, for he had profited by his knowledge of the Koran, Sunna, and *fiqh* to make pronouncements favorable to the Sultan in troublesome affairs. Compared with him my teacher was but a poor man whose only merit was to know the Koran by heart and be competent to instruct the newly converted.

I was alarmed at the thought of meeting this great man, for only gradually had I come to appreciate the wealth of the Arabic language and to learn how many ways there were of reading the Koran, how many words could be made to express one idea and how many interpretations could be put upon one word. My teacher counted fifty words for "camel" and as many as a hundred for "sword," to denote all the varieties of that weapon.

The Faqih was sitting with his writing materials before him, in a room containing many books and reading desks. He had a jar of dates by him and from time to time he took one out, sucked it, and spat the stone onto the floor before me, then licked his fingers and took a sip of water from a goblet. Seeing that he was enjoying a period of rest and refreshment, I took courage and greeted him reverently.

"I have heard," said he gently, "that you're a skilled physician from the Frankish countries, and are zealously striving to become a good Moslem. Tell me, therefore, of your Lord, your Prophet, and your rule."

These things were well known to me and I answered, "Allah the one God is my Lord and Mohammed is his Prophet, blessed be his name. The Koran is my rule, virtue the way of my spirit, Sunna my path."

He nodded in approval, and stroking the beard which reached to his belt he asked, "What is the key to prayer?"

This question too was easy, and I answered readily, "The key to prayer is devout purification; the key to purification is the profession of the name of God; the key to profession is steadfast faith; the key to faith is trust; the key to trust is hope; the key to hope is obedience; and the key to obedience is: *Allah most high is the one God and him do I profess.*"

Again he nodded, and asked, "How do you perform the purification when preparing yourself for prayer?"

"I have been taught that there are six requirements for the partial ablution: announcement of intention, the washing of the face, hands, and arms to the elbows; the drying of the head and the washing of the feet to the ankle bones, all in the proper order. But the following ten actions are meritorious—to wash the hands before dipping them in the bowl; to rinse the mouth; to rinse the nose by sniffing up water; to wash the whole head and cleanse the ears inside and out; to comb the beard with the fingers; to spread out fingers and toes when washing them; to wash the right hand and right foot before the left hand and left foot and to repeat all this thrice in succession."

The Faqih sucked dates, his eyes half closed.

"What do you repeat after the ablution?"

"After the ablution I say, 'I bear witness that there is no God but Allah. He is one and indivisible and Mohammed is his servant and Prophet. O Lord, grant me to be among the penitent, grant me to be of the company of the pure. Praise be to Allah! To his glory I declare that there is no other God than he. Before his face I plead for mercy and repent of my evil deeds.' According to the sacred tradition, the Prophet with his own mouth has proclaimed, 'For him who pronounces these words after every ablution the eight gates of Paradise stand open, and he may enter through which one he pleases.'"

So I ended, feeling well satisfied with myself for having been able to recite these important prayers. But the Faqih suddenly opened his eyes, spat out a date stone and said angrily, "You speak the holy words like a parrot, and prate of Paradise when you're not even circumcised."

72

I choked. Many renegades submitted to circumcision after only an hour or two of instruction, to be done with it, but I had hesitated to undergo this unpleasing ordeal, and hoped I might succeed in evading it altogether.

Having thus thoroughly frightened me, the Faqih went on in triumph, "If you'd been speaking from the heart instead of from the lips you would long since have become united to Islam through the outward token of circumcision. Islam does not ask after a man's nation, nor after the color of his skin, for all races and colors are united by that sign. But you're only a slave, and perhaps your master is to blame for the omission. I hear that he's a wealthy dealer in drugs, named Abu el-Kasim, and that he owns a Christian woman. Her eyes are said to be of different colors, and therefore she is able to see coming events in a bowl of sand. And I am told that the women of the harem run to the public bathhouse to meet her, and reward her richly for foretelling the future for them. Is this true?"

"Venerable and learned Faqih," I exclaimed, "may Allah of his grace preserve me from spying in the bathhouse during women's bathing hours!"

"Don't prevaricate! I've heard that it is so. But whether the gift is from Allah or the devil, or whether she's a charlatan, your master must have a *fatwa* for her, or else lock her up."

I was shocked at his greed, and losing all veneration for him I looked up and said, "My master may have forgotten, but he'll no doubt offer you a gift proportionate to his means, on receiving from you the necessary *fatwa*. But the taxgatherer has squeezed him dry, and not even by force could you extort from him more than a couple of gold pieces."

Tears of indignation rose to my eyes as I reflected what vile cheats there were in the world. But the Faqih raised his head and said, "Before issuing this *fatwa* I must see the slave woman, but she must not give scandal by coming here. After the evening prayer on Friday I will visit Abu el-Kasim's house and he is not to receive me with the honor befitting my rank. I shall come secretly, with my face hidden. Take this message to Abu el-Kasim. Perhaps I will be content with fifty pieces of gold, for Allah is merciful and gracious."

I wondered what was really in his mind, for I had grown accustomed to the habit common to the people of Islam of never speaking out. But Abu el-Kasim was delighted at the message, and said, "Things are going better than I could have hoped, and Sinan the Jew was

73

indeed wise to provide me with such good bait for my hooks. For this day's work I'll give you a new turban and a white robe, and so acquire merit."

I asked in surprise, "How can you rejoice that this greedy Faqih comes to rob you?"

Abu el-Kasim answered, "Of course he wants money. He's no more than human. But his curiosity is as strong as his greed. He must surely have heard the nature of the visions that our Delilah sees in the sand, and now wishes to observe for himself which way the wind blows, so as to gather all safely in before the storm."

When Friday came, Abu el-Kasim bade Giulia roast some ptarmigan, and not stint pepper, cloves, or nutmeg. I bought sugar cakes from the pastry cook and filled a bowl with fruit and sweetmeats, sprinkling over these a white powder that gave them a fiery taste and induced thirst. Abu chilled the drinking water and flavored it with stimulating spices. Then—most important preparation of all—he told Giulia what to say, warning her against giving herself into the power of evil spirits and seeing profitless visions.

After the evening prayer the Faqih arrived, his face hidden by a corner of his cloak, and knocked on the door with his staff. On entering he sniffed the good smells with pleasure, and drawing forth his beard which he had tucked under his belt he stroked it and said reproachfully, "Prayer is better than savory food, and I would be loath to cause you any trouble, Abu el-Kasim. A fig or two and a bowl of water are enough for me."

Nevertheless, after much voluble protest he allowed us to set the dishes before him, and ate slowly and purposefully until they were empty. Abu el-Kasim served him and poured water over his hands. Then he proffered a beautifully embroidered silken bag, saying, "This purse contains twenty pieces of gold which I hope you'll accept as a present. Believe me, they're all I possess, but I won't forget to make you further free-will offerings when I have more. Now I have a slave woman about whom I would ask your advice, to ensure against any infringement of the law. Her eyes are of different colors and she can see strange things in sand."

The Faqih nodded, weighed the bag in his hand, and tucked it thoughtfully under his girdle. Abu el-Kasim led in Giulia by the hand, drew aside her veil and held up a lamp that the Faqih might see better.

"Allah is great!" said the Faqih in wonder. "Never have I seen anything of the kind. But with God all things are possible—and indeed it would amount to a Persian heresy to say that evil spirits were more powerful than Allah, and could bring about such a miracle against the divine will."

Careless of cost, Abu el-Kasim threw a pinch of genuine ambergris onto the brazier; then he poured fine sand into a large copper dish and ordered Giulia to stir it with her finger. And as she gazed down into the dish she fell into a trance and began to speak in an altered voice. But I was now used to this, and neither believed nor feared.

"I see turbulent waters—out of the sea rises the banner of the Prophet. Indeed, the banner of the Prophet rises from the waves, and the Deliverer comes from the sea."

"Do you speak to me, heathen woman?" demanded the Faqih in astonishment. "I don't understand you, for the banner of the Prophet is kept in the Seraglio of the Great Sultan."

Ignoring this, Giulia went on quickly and earnestly, "Out of the sea come ten asses with silver bits and silver bells. Ten camels follow —the camels have golden saddles and are laden with gifts for you, O Faqih. I see the waters full of ships. They are laden with plunder and sail into the harbor, and from their plunder generous alms are brought to you in the mosque; the hunters of the sea offer liberally of their booty and build splendid mosques and fountains. The king of the sea founds schools and hospitals and endows them richly, and the teacher shall not suffer want under his rule. But Faqih, Faqih! Before all this comes to pass, there is blood."

The Faqih had been eagerly listening, but now he fingered his beard uneasily and said, "Blood? Foolish woman, do you indeed see blood? If so I suspect that an evil spirit speaks through your lips."

"I see blood," she went on. "A little pool of black, evil blood that doesn't even soil the hem of your cloak—it sticks to your shoes. And so you change your shoes—you throw the old ones away and put on new ones—new shoes of red, scented leather. They're adorned with precious stones—after that day there is no richer Faqih than yourself. Your name flies over the seas and the banner of the Prophet shields you from the wrath of the unbelievers. All this I see in the sand, old man, but no more—unless it be a cedarwood coffin with a turban upon it, to which pilgrims, remembering the great Faqih, come and pray from far distant lands and so acquire merit."

Giulia covered her eyes with both hands and moaned as if she had

75

had a bad dream. But the Faqih was in no way dismayed by the talk of a coffin; on the contrary the prophecy flattered him, and he said, "These predictions are remarkable, but I hardly think we need put much faith in them. They may have more to do with you, Abu el-Kasim, than with me, and I hardly know what to think; for a poor drug merchant would hardly pay twenty gold pieces just for advice. Let's have no more beating about the bush; dismiss your slaves that we may talk alone together with none but Allah to hear us."

Abu el-Kasim sent us away at once and locked the door, setting Andy to guard the outer gate. The learned Faqih remained until late that night, and when at last he departed as secretly as he had come, Abu el-Kasim sent Giulia to bed and summoned me.

"The plans are taking shape," he said. "Have no fear, Michael el-Hakim; whatever happens the Faqih won't betray us. True, he won't risk burning his fingers by making out a *fatwa* for Delilah, but neither will he interfere, and she may continue plying her trade in the bath-house."

Thus Abu el-Kasim drew cautiously at first one thread and then another, knotting them together in a net in whose meshes Selim ben-Hafs would one day be entangled.

But the Faqih's threats concerning circumcision had filled me with dread and I asked Abu el-Kasim whether Andy and I must indeed submit to so unpleasant an operation. He looked at us scornfully, and having rehearsed the many advantages to be gained by it he ended, "Why oppose it, when by such a trifle you may win the respect of all true believers? On that joyful day you may ride round the city on a white donkey and all devout believers will bring you presents and rejoice at your conversion."

I replied crossly that I had not the least wish to ride round the city on a white donkey, to be made a public laughingstock, and reminded him that Andy's progress as a wrestler would be seriously hindered if at this stage he were compelled to lie up with a slow-healing wound in his tenderest part. And I would never consider undergoing it without him, for we were brothers; we hoped to enter Paradise side by side and together enjoy the shade of its fruit trees.

Abu el-Kasim was not deceived by my pious words, and said, "Well! There's a time for everything, and I shall eagerly await the day when, in accordance with the will of Allah, your brother justifies the high hopes I have of him."

76

Nor did he have to wait long. Some days later he climbed on Andy's shoulders and rode to the market place, and hardly had the wrestlers gathered in a ring with their arms about each other's shoulders to determine the order of the bouts when a big black fellow appeared, attended by a party of soldiers. He threw out his chest and thumped it with his fists as he challenged, "Iskender, Iskender! Come here and have your ears torn off! After that I'll attend to Antar, of whom I've heard so much."

The wrestlers muttered uneasily among themselves, and warned Andy, saying, "That is Selim ben-Hafs's master wrestler. Don't anger him; let him win and take the money, for then perhaps he'll leave us in peace and not hurt us. But if you win you'll be summoned to wrestle before the Sultan, and although at first you may get the better of all his wrestlers, the day will come when you find yourself lying in the sand with a broken neck."

Andy answered warmly, "Your faith seems weak; you forget that Allah has preordained all things. Go, Iskender, and let him beat you! Then I will tackle him and you shall behold such a match as you've never seen before. If it be the will of Allah, this shall be my last bout in the market place; after that I shall appear only before the Sultan and his court."

At this, great excitement arose among the wrestlers' patrons, and silver and gold pieces showered onto the cloth. The soldiers formed a circle and thrust back the onlookers, while the Sultan's master wrestler, ugly and gleaming with oil, jumped up and down in the middle and roared his challenge. Iskender, adjuring him in the name of Allah to observe the rules of "good" wrestling, ran in at him, but it was not long before he was tossed into the air, and fell with a crash. He lay moaning for some time, feeling his arms and legs, but I think he was little harmed by the fall, and behaved thus to flatter his ferocious opponent. Two other men stepped forward and the master wrestler threw them without difficulty. But when he noticed that he was beginning to sweat and pant, he became suspicious and cried, "Where's that Antar skulking? He's the man I came for, and I shan't stay all day for him. My bath awaits me."

Ignoring the warnings of the rest Andy at once stepped forward. It was clear that the black man held him in great respect, for he circled watchfully about him for some time before suddenly charging in like a bull with his head lowered, meaning to butt Andy in the stomach

77

and wind him. But Andy stepped nimbly aside and getting a mighty grip of the other's waist flung him high in the air. Like the adept he was, however, he landed on his feet, but at once Andy struck them from under him and he came headlong to the ground with Andy uppermost. Andy took firm hold of the back of his neck and pressing his face to the ground, he cried, "Which of us is biting the dust?"

The other wrestlers uttered warning yells, for in his extremity the brutal black took to "hard" wrestling, and getting his arms round one of Andy's legs he set his teeth in the calf muscles. If Andy had been able to maintain his grip he would certainly have broken the fellow's neck, but now pain forced him to loosen it. Soon they were rolling over and over each other on the ground, and I have never in my life seen such a struggle. Now Andy's head thrust up, now he was down again while the blackamoor jumped on his chest, and would have broken all his ribs but for Andy's massive build. Bleeding and with torn ears they at last broke loose from each other, and Selim ben-Hafs's champion had evidently had enough. He was breathless, and letting his arms fall to his sides he spat some blood from his mouth and tried to laugh as he said sourly, "You live up to your reputation, Antar, and know something of 'hard' wrestling too; but I've no right to expose myself to danger in the absence of my master the Sultan. Nor did I fail to notice your underhand stratagem in tempting me to waste my strength before I started on you. So let us continue our match tomorrow, in the presence of the Sultan. I don't doubt that he will richly reward whichever one of us survives."

Casting an embarrassed glance around him he wiped the blood from his ears to gain time for recovery. But the crowd uttered wild cheers and their hatred of Selim ben-Hafs found vent in savage abuse of his wrestler.

Andy, breathing hard, yelled, "You bit me in the calf, you swine. Tomorrow my leg will be swollen and I shan't be at all surprised if your poisonous teeth cause me to run about barking and foaming at the mouth and avoiding water. And it was for the sake of water that I became a follower of the Prophet. But you shall learn tomorrow that I too have teeth—and teeth that can crack marrow bones!"

When the black wrestler had gone, followed by his guards, Abu el-Kasim burst out into wild lamentations as usual, and smote Andy over the head with his staff. For if Andy were beaten next day, what was Abu to do with a cripple? And if he won it would be worse, for then Selim ben-Hafs would buy him and Abu would have lost him for good.

But the other wrestlers snatched the stick from his hand and attended us in triumph to our house, where I washed and dressed Andy's leg wound and anointed his bruises, a task to which I was already well-accustomed.

Seeing what good will the other wrestlers bore to Andy, Abu el-Kasim resigned himself to the will of Allah. A sheep was roasted in the forecourt and a cauldron of millet was set boiling, and when all was ready Abu filled several dishes with this good food and carried it to the wrestlers with his own hand.

After the meal, when at sunset the muezzin called the faithful to prayer, the wrestlers washed themselves, performed their devotions, and recited three or four—some of them even ten—verses from the Koran, for Andy's success. "We have every confidence in Allah," they said, "but it must be easier, even for him, to help a man who helps himself." And so they stayed until late at night to teach Andy all they could about "hard" wrestling. As I listened to them, and saw the tricks they demonstrated, the hair rose upon my head in horror.

Abu el-Kasim took me aside and said, "This is the will of Allah, and never will you get a better chance to learn your way about in Selim ben-Hafs's kasbah. You may even be able to make useful acquaintances, and it'll do no harm if I give you a few coins to knot into your girdle. If you should happen to drop one or two of them, don't stoop to pick them up again; remember that miserly behavior is unbecoming in the mansions of the great."

At about midnight, Abu drove out the wrestlers and we put Andy to sleep on the softest pillows in the house. He tossed and turned and sighed half the night, then with a curse he took his cloak, wrapped it round his head and curled himself up on the floor. Immediately his snores resounded through the house. We did not wake him for the morning prayer, and Abu prayed on his behalf. Later we took Andy to the baths and had him rubbed by a powerful masseur to drive the stiffness out of him. Next we shaved his head, oiled him with the slipperiest oil we had in the house, and strengthened his leather breeches at waist and knee, lest they be stripped off during the fight.

After the noon prayer all the wrestlers of the market assembled, and noisily carried Andy up the steep street to the kasbah, to spare his wounded leg. At first he resisted, but they forced him to lie in the litter which they took turns to carry on their shoulders. And so he resigned himself, and lay with one hand supporting his chin and the other waving greetings to the faithful, who showered him with blessings and urged him to tear the ears from Selim ben-Hafs's master wrestler and not to spare even his more intimate parts.

The uproarious crowd followed us to the place of punishment outside the great gateway of the kasbah, but when they saw the guards parading in line and the remnants of executed persons impaled on the iron hooks, a sudden silence fell upon them, and many remembered important business awaiting them at home. Nevertheless the sons of many rich merchants, as well as money changers, backers, and other followers of the sport followed us through the gates. Under the archway we were all thoroughly searched by the guards, who made us remove our cloaks and then felt along all seams and hems; much cunning would have been necessary to smuggle in even the smallest knife.

On either side of the forecourt were the barracks and kitchens of the guard. A gateway in the inner wall led to a second courtyard, where our clothes were searched again. Before us rose a wall in which a fine wrought-iron gate allowed us a glimpse of a fountain and a number of evergreen trees. In our own court also there was a pool, and under a roof supported by most lovely columns stood the throne. The guard gathered about this and showed the spectators to their places.

The ring was not large, but was strewn with soft sand in which one sank to the ankles. Andy was amazed at this, having seen nothing like it before; here, he said, one could fall on one's head without breaking one's neck. But on the other hand it prevented quick moves and evasions. Brute strength counted for more than skill here; one could not even dash the adversary's head against a stone, but had to vanquish him with one's bare hands.

A large number of chamberlains, eunuchs, mamelukes, Negroes, and boys with painted faces gathered in the courtyard and took up their positions in front of those who had come in from the city. At the latticed window above the Sultan's throne appeared a group of veiled women, who ordered the concealing slatted blinds to be removed, that they might have a better view and be themselves more visible to the spectators.

At last the gate in the third wall was opened, and Selim ben-Hafs, attended by the most distinguished members of his suite, staggered down the steps. His eyes were almost closed up by the quantities of opium he consumed, and his oiled face showed him to be in an evil humor.

The savage-looking wrestlers stepped at once into the arena, and dashed at one another till the sand flew; yet they were careful not to hurt one another, and their performance was largely make-believe. Selim ben-Hafs soon wearied of them and in a shrill, furious voice degraded them to hewers of wood, which seemed rather to please than to dismay these peaceable men.

Meanwhile I had been edging forward among the spectators, looking here and there as if in search of a better vantage point. I thus contrived to move about the courtyard and peep behind curtains, and no one stopped me, even when I entered the empty palace. I crept in and out of the cellars and even looked into the kitchens, where I was surprised by a cook who asked me in amazement what I wanted. I said, "I'm the brother of Antar, the famous wrestler, and a slave like yourself. Being very anxious on my brother's account I find myself in need of the privy."

The cook kindly showed me to the servants' privy, which had brick supports for the feet and troughs which could be sluiced with water. Having relieved myself I conversed politely with the cook, and he invoked many blessings upon me, so that I gave him two square silver coins. He was delighted and showed me the great kitchen; he told me how many different dishes were prepared there daily for the Sultan, and how they were carried in and tasted three or four times before being set before him.

I asked him about the women of the harem, of whom Giulia had had so much to say after meeting them at the public bathhouse. The cook smiled slyly and replied, "Our ruler despises and neglects his wives, and therefore allows them a quite unseemly freedom. He delights more in boys. If you should happen to have another couple of silver coins on you I could show you a little secret which might amuse you, since you seem an inquisitive man."

As I fumbled with my girdle I let fall a gold coin as if by accident, but did not stoop to pick it up. The cook was overjoyed, and said, "I see that you've had a good upbringing, slave though you are; and you're a good Moslem too, for in the eyes of Allah avarice is the most detestable of sins."

81

He picked up the coin, and having looked about him carefully, he led me up a narrow stair and along a passage that ended at an iron door.

"I've been told," he said, "that this door is often used by those who for one reason or another do not wish to be seen at the golden gateway to the Court of Bliss. The door opens silently. If anyone comes out this way, all slaves and servants turn their backs. If anyone enters it, he blinds the eyes of the curious with a shower of gold and silver."

At this point we heard a vigorous clanging of bells from the courtyard. The cook was eager to see the greatest match of the day, and I followed him into the open air. But, as in Sinan's house, I had had the impression, throughout my rambles in this palace, of being watched. I felt that invisible eyes had followed my every step. Therefore I rejoined Abu el-Kasim and stayed beside him to watch the wrestling, as if I had had indeed no other object in my wanderings than to find the privy.

Andy and the Sultan's black master wrestler had now stepped into the ring. Amid the ringing of bells they greeted Sultan Selim ben-Hafs, who responded merely with a gesture of impatience, as a sign that the fight might begin. At the same instant the black charged at Andy with lowered head, snatching up a handful of sand as he ran and throwing it in Andy's face to blind him. But Andy turned aside in time and shut his eyes, their two powerful bodies collided, and each got a sturdy grasp of the other. The black man had a body like a hundred-year oak, and his limbs were as knotted as its branches; it was a magnificent sight to see these two herculean men squeezing one another, each striving to break the other's hold.

In honest wrestling Andy was clearly the better man, and when his black adversary saw that he lacked the strength to overcome him fairly, he sank his teeth into Andy's shoulder. He had aimed at his ear, but Andy was too quick for him, and now panted wrathfully.

"A man must follow the customs of the country"—and in his turn Andy bit deep into the Negro's shoulder, so that the fellow howled and Selim ben-Hafs burst out laughing.

Andy was already forcing the black to his knees, but the oily body slipped from his grasp and the next moment the Negro drove his head violently against Andy's chest, which resounded like a drum. Undeterred, Andy stooped like lightning and seized the fellow's ankles, threw him down and began whirling him round at such speed that the

82

onlookers cried out aghast, and Selim ben-Hafs recoiled and clutched his head with both hands. But Andy did no more than hurl his opponent headlong onto the sand. Unhurt, the man leaped to his feet and charged again.

The struggle continued, with Andy holding his own, and the backers, forgetful of the Sultan's presence, shouted and raised their bids. But Selim ben-Hafs scowled and showered insults upon his champion. From now on the rabble knew that this man's life was at stake. Once more he gained firm hold of Andy, twisted and turned and tried with all his might to get his thumb into his eyes or kick him in the groin. He would not give in though Andy threw him several times so that by rights he should have confessed himself beaten. But each time he rose, and with foaming lips and bloodshot eyes dashed in mad fury at Andy, to kill him at the first opportunity. At last he got a thumb into Andy's eye, and it was Andy's turn to yell with pain. But at that moment came a snap as the champion's arm was broken, and in a flash Andy was pressing the man's face into the sand.

He thought the sport was at an end, but Selim ben-Hafs had wearied of his own wrestler, who had shamed him before all the people, and he signed to Andy to continue. Andy rose bewildered, not understanding what he meant, and at once the Negro, careless of his agony, threw his sound arm round Andy's legs and brought him to the ground; then knelt upon his tenderest parts and tried to get his teeth into his throat. Nothing was left for Andy to do but lock the fellow's arms and break his neck. Selim ben-Hafs burst into noisy laughter and applause.

A bundle containing money was now given to Andy; Selim ben-Hafs also bestowed a purse upon him and Abu el-Kasim received a kaftan of honor, in recognition of the great pleasure the contest had afforded the Sultan. But the body of the champion Selim ordered to be taken away and thrown into the sewers, since in his opinion the fellow deserved no better burial. When the spectators began to leave we were detained by the Sultan's servants, and we wondered uneasily what more he required of us.

Abu el-Kasim was first brought before him, to kneel and kiss the ground before the throne.

"What is the price of your slave?" asked Selim ben-Hafs.

Abu would not have been Abu if he had not instantly burst into tears and vowed that he was a poor man, and so on incessantly, until

83

Selim ben-Hafs raised his hands and commanded him in the name of Allah to cut short his lamentations.

"What is the price of your slave?" he repeated, signing meanwhile to one of his attendants, who in a significant manner began fingering a supple cane.

Abu el-Kasim broke from the grasp of the two men who held him, carefully removed the kaftan of honor that the Sultan had presented to him, and then rent his garments, calling Allah to witness that never in Algiers or indeed anywhere in the world had such another wrestler been seen. Such a marvel of nature only appeared once in a hundred years, just as Allah sent to mankind every century a new interpreter of the Koran, to invigorate the ancient wisdom.

But Selim ben-Hafs turned a deaf ear and yawned, "Send him to my palace tomorrow. Allah will surely recompense and reward you with his favors."

The attendants hastened to raise the Sultan from his throne, and we were conducted through the archway into the forecourt. There an old woman approached me, held out a dirty bundle and whispered rapidly, "My name is Fatima. The eunuchs know me, if you inquire for me and give them a trifle. Open this bundle in private and read the letter in it to the one to whom it's addressed."

I hid the bundle under my cloak and we returned to Abu el-Kasim's house, in the street of the spice dealers, where a crowd of wrestlers and others were waiting to acclaim us. They gave presents to Andy and invoked many blessings upon him; but when, with a bad grace, Abu el-Kasim had served them food, he sent them all away and locked the doors. We then attended Andy's hurts. I feared most for his eye, which was badly swollen, but found that its sight was uninjured.

Remembering the bundle I had been given, I opened it and stared in amazement. Hidden in the dirty rag was a beautiful purse embroidered with silver thread, containing six gold pieces and a scrap of paper. I unfolded this and read a poem in Arabic, written in a graceful hand and, so far as I could understand, having as its theme Andy's bodily attractions. Abu took it from me and having read it, said, "This was written by a woman, who's no very eminent poet. But her meaning's clear. I won't trouble about the first verses, for they'd only make a simpleton like Andy vainer than he is. But she goes on, 'Do not repulse a woman sick for love of you, who can but bewail, in her anguish, her inability to conceal the passion that tears her heart. As a token of her good will she sends you these six gold pieces. You have only to consult your guide secretly to learn the time and place for bringing her your answer.' "

This was by no means the first time that Andy had received a delicate hint of some woman's favor. The poem aroused pleasant hopes in him and he seemed not altogether sad when next day Abu el-Kasim took him to the palace and handed him over to the Sultan's attendants.

I saw nothing more of him for a week, and then one day he kicked open our door and swaggered in singing. I thought he had forgotten his good resolutions and was drunk. He was wearing baggy trousers and a kaftan of the very finest cloth. On his head was the tall felt cap of a soldier and at his belt hung a scimitar in a silver scabbard. At first he pretended not to recognize us, and demanded, "What is this hovel, and who are you miserable wretches, slaving here in the sweat of your brow? Do you not see that I'm a man of rank?"

He smelled of musk and looked so unfamiliar in his splendor that even my dog sniffed nervously at his red leather shoes. Abu el-Kasim raised his hands to heaven, crying, "Praise be to Allah! Surely you have brought me presents from Selim ben-Hafs to whom I gave you."

Andy forgot his play-acting and answered, "Don't speak to me of that nauseous beast. His memory is shorter than a hen's; for years he has neglected even his wives, and the poor women complain bitterly, and await the Deliverer's coming. He sends you no gifts, Abu el-Kasim, having long since forgotten you. He eats so much opium that at times he hardly knows whether he's awake or dreaming. But I share liberally with my friends, so take this purse as a present from me, Abu el-Kasim."

He threw into Abu's arms a purse so heavy that the poor man's knees sagged beneath it. Then Andy embraced me, and took my dog into his arms; I was horrified to notice that his breath smelled of wine.

"Andy, Andy!" I said. "Have you forgotten all your good resolutions and broken the Prophet's law?"

He regarded me with shining eyes and replied, "The Prophet's law is not binding on me so long as I wear the felt cap on my head and the warrior's sword at my belt. It's written plainly in the Koran that no one may join in prayer among the faithful when drunk, and may the devil devour me if anyone can get drunk without drinking. This was explained to me by a shrewd and cultured woman, whom I fully rely upon. It was she who persuaded me to drink wine and so over-

85

come my natural bashfulness in her presence. So let's have no more nonsense, my boy. And Abu el-Kasim! Open a jar of your best, and don't imagine I don't know what you have in all those vessels."

He paid not the smallest attention to my remonstrances. Success had so gone to his head that he forgot his own unhappy experiences of the mischief caused by wine drinking. I was obliged to take a cup myself for consolation. And at last when Abu el-Kasim noted how the wine was disappearing he went and locked the door, after which he too filled a goblet, saying, "Since fate has decreed that my valuable wine be wasted, let me at least mitigate the loss by enjoying some of it myself. And since we're alone within these four walls where none can see us, it can hardly be accounted to us for sin, for we give no scandal."

The strong wine soon dispelled his regret for its loss, and when I urged Andy to tell us what had happened to him, he began thus: "When Abu el-Kasim had left me at the mercy of the servants, I sat alone for a long time, bewailing my fate like a young raven fallen from its nest. No one asked my name or gave me anything to eat. Only the shameless boys blinked their painted eyelids at me, and pointed and put out their tongues, and pinched me each in turn. Then an old woman called Fatima came in; she comforted me and assured me that all would turn out for the best if I would only have patience and wait. The Court of Bliss must of course remain closed to me, but she told me to walk up and down before the gate and gaze at the latticed windows, and assured me that benevolent glances would follow me from behind the reed blinds. At dusk she returned and led me to an iron door, which opened silently, and we stepped into a sweet-smelling room where she left me. The walls and floor were covered with valuable rugs, and strange to say when the woman had gone I couldn't find the door, search as I would.

"As nothing further happened I grew hungry and tired; I stretched myself out on a bed that was there and fell asleep. When I awoke, the room was lit by many perfumed lamps and beside me sat a veiled woman who held my fist in her plump hands, and sighed. She addressed me in a language I didn't know. I answered by reciting a poem with great difficulty, which Abu here had taught me. After that we exchanged a few words in the Frankish talk they use in the city— which must be the oldest in the world, since it evidently dates from the great confusion of Babel. For something to do, I pulled the veil from her face. She tried to prevent me—but not very hard. I must admit that she was beautiful and quite to my taste, though not exactly a chicken. Presently Fatima entered and set before us a number of delectable dishes—which reminds me that I'm hungry, and long for a good solid meal after all those delicacies."

I brought him food, and at the sight of the familiar cooking pot Andy uttered joyful exclamations, and then continued, "When we had eaten I took this understanding lady's hand, to show my good will. She sighed deeply, and so did I, for I saw that such was the custom. At this Fatima took pity on us and brought a jug of wine and a cup, after which the lady read to me from the Kòran and expounded it more competently than many a scholar, so that I soon overcame my misgivings and distaste, and drank cautiously. Besides, I was confused at finding myself in such company, and hoped that the wine would help me to vanquish my bashfulness. I can't speak of all that happened, but this I can say: we soon found that we had much in common. We were obliged to rise and wash ourselves, in compliance with the Koran, and refresh ourselves with reviving perfumes. This happened many times, until the obliging Fatima became impatient. She had never a wink of sleep and was constantly running up and down the steep stairs with buckets of water. She urged us in the name of Allah to make an end of our incautious behavior, as the cocks were crowing and the hour of the morning prayer was near. She was sent to fetch these clothes for me, for my own rags had long ago been flung into a corner."

Andy lowered his eyes modestly, and having fished up a piece of mutton from the pot he went on, "Fatima took my hand, opened the iron door, and led me out, calling down the blessing of Allah upon me. And the blessings bore fruit, for in my new clothes I found a purse, into which my delicate-minded lady had slipped a gold coin each time I washed myself. I felt I could well spare two out of the seventeen gold pieces for the faithful Fatima who had so zealously served us. I wandered about the courtyard for a time, but felt just the least bit tired—and perhaps also a little muzzy, not having tasted wine for a good half-year. As I now wore a sword, and supposed that the men in the barracks would pay little attention to a slight deviation from the true path, I went and found an empty bed in the barracks. No one was surprised to see me; on the contrary they made me welcome with deep salaams, and the other inmates hastened to clear their belongings out of my way. There's no more to tell."

Abu el-Kasim passed the wine jar round again. Lifting the purse in his hands he said doubtfully, "Allah is great. You spoke of seventeen gold pieces, but if I'm not mistaken this purse contains at least a hundred."

Andy turned very red and avoided my eye. Then he said somewhat hesitantly, "Well, that first evening in barracks I'd hardly risen from the prayer mat when Fatima appeared again, pulled at my sleeve, and with many tender expressions summoned me to the same agreeable occupation. At daybreak I was much richer than I had been on the previous evening. But Fatima is a frail old thing, and being wearied by the continual water carrying she invited me to come that evening straight to the Sultan's bathroom. With a bundle of firewood on my back I passed straight through the Gateway of Bliss, and the eunuchs readily showed me the way. I spent an agreeable night in that warm place, and lacked neither food nor drink. When day dawned, the understanding lady raised her hands to heaven and said, 'Allah is great. I have a good and trustworthy woman friend who won't believe what I say of you. Allow me, therefore, my dear Antar—' these were her very words—'allow me therefore to bring this skeptical woman with me to the bath.' "

"Andy!" I exclaimed, much shaken. "You shock me unspeakably. To comfort one lonely and open-handed woman is one thing, but to lure another into your shamelessness is another. You go too far."

"Exactly what I said," agreed Andy hastily. "But this devout woman recited so many verses from the Koran and expounded them so fully that my head was in a whirl; moreover she was a woman of education, and I could hardly set myself up to know more than she did."

"Great Allah!" exclaimed Abu el-Kasim. But Andy continued, the back of his neck growing ever redder, "The lady appeared that evening with her friend; and I didn't regret it, for this woman was if possible even more luscious than Amina. And I think that neither of them was dissatisfied with me. The other lady also, with equal delicacy, put a gold piece in my purse each time I washed. But—" and here Andy groaned—"how could I guess on the following night no fewer than three woman would preen themselves before me, each lovelier and more blooming than the other! It was hard not to offend any of them, and favor one at the expense of the rest. But when on the night after

88

that, four came, I was annoyed, and told them that there was a limit to everything."

"And you were quite right," assented Abu el-Kasim in alarm. "The pitcher can go once too often to the well, and I feel really anxious on your account."

Andy swallowed another cupful of wine and continued, "In the morning Amina said, 'You have four devoted wives, Antar, and you've neglected none of them, but have observed the injunctions of the Koran concerning behavior to a woman. But my moon is waning, and I wish no one to have pleasure of you in my absence. I shall love you to my last hour. Eat and drink diligently that you may be at the height of your powers when next I summon you.' "

I was struck dumb by his story and could not utter a word. Abu el-Kasim finished counting the money and locked it up carefully in his strongbox. At last I stammered in the greatest agitation, "Is this the thanks I get for having tried to set you a good example all these years? Never could I have believed that the poetic art could cause so much harm, for all this began with a scrap of verse that according to Abu was not even good. Now I understand why the Prophet, blessed be his name, laid his curse upon poets."

I was so angry with Andy that I could have struck him—most of all because he had won the favor of four distinguished ladies and, as a reward for his sin, a bag of gold—while I knew not a single friendly disposed woman who desired my company, even for nothing. But Andy was unmoved. He rose and left us, his baggy trousers flapping in the spring breeze. Abu el-Kasim gazed after him and said with a shake of his monkey head, "His foolishness and audacity may be very useful to us, but I daren't whisper any of our plans to him, for those women would have it out of him in no time. Michael el-Hakim, the time is nearly ripe, the spring winds are blowing, and the Deliverer comes from the sea. So let's leave ointments and eye black and think of graver matters. We will capture the city of Algiers with our bare hands as we promised Sinan the Jew."

Next day Abu el-Kasim summoned some of the wealthiest merchants, entertained them on a princely scale, and let Giulia gaze into the sand for them. When they had heard her these respectable men tore their beards and said, "If it were true! If the holy banner of the Prophet should really rise from the sea to free us from the greed of

Selim ben-Hafs! But his soldiers have keen swords, and his executioners stout ropes at their disposal."

Abu el-Kasim tore his own beard and said, "I'm a merchant like yourselves and make many journeys. At such times I hear much that remains unknown to the rich and mighty. Last autumn it was already said that the great Khaireddin was fitting out his fleet to recapture Algiers for the High Porte before the figs were ripe. I'm anxious on your account, as you're wealthier than myself, and have more to lose. For if the great Khaireddin should meet with opposition, the last state will be worse than the first. Personally I fail to understand why anyone should risk his business and his property for these infernal Hafsids."

The merchants said hopefully, "Let us send him secret word that we won't oppose his coming, but greet him with palm branches, if only he will drive out Selim's people and bow the tyrant's head to the dust."

But Abu el-Kasim shook his head with a worried air and said, "I hear he wishes to ride in through open gates and be met by you carrying Selim ben-Hafs's head on a golden platter. And further, you're to proclaim him in the mosque as governor of Algiers and so atone for your former treachery. On these conditions he promises to drive out the Spaniards and destroy their fortress at the harbor mouth. And he will certainly reward those who proclaim him governor."

The merchants raised their hands in deprecation and cried with one voice, "Alas, this is wild and dangerous talk. How are we, with our bare hands, to vanquish Selim ben-Hafs and his thousand stern soldiers, with their cannon and their swords?"

Abu el-Kasim answered, "I saw in a dream ten wily men who between them collected ten thousand gold pieces and placed them in the hands of a trustworthy friend. Hassan, the officer commanding at the eastern gate, shut his eyes; camels brought arms into the city, hidden in the grain baskets, and the merchants concealed these weapons in their warehouses. I saw also ten bold men, each of whom chose and spoke to ten other bold men, and these in their turn did the same. They remained undiscovered, for each man knew only the nine others in his group, and his chief. In my dream this happened very quickly. I saw arms hidden in the sand of the seashore and a great fleet lay off the coast awaiting the signal to anchor and land its forces on either side of the city, so that they might march in through the open gates.

In this strange dream of mine it was all as simple as cracking an egg. But no man is answerable for his dreams."

By this time many of the merchants were holding their hands over their ears so as not to hear such dangerous talk. Others were dubious, but the oldest among them stroked his beard and said, "Were a *fatwa* to be issued, the duty of every true Moslem would be to rise against Selim ben-Hafs and crush him. We should merely proclaim the *fatwa* at some suitable moment, and distribute the weapons. The Faqih has the fullest knowledge of the Koran and the sacred tradition. Selim ben-Hafs betrayed the faith when he allied himself with the Spaniards. As soon as the Faqih has prepared his *fatwa* he can set forth on a pilgrimage; should the enterprise fail, Khaireddin would certainly secure his old age. I'm willing to speak to the Faqih; being an old man and tired of life I have little to lose. The only question remaining is where to find a trustworthy man to hold the ten thousand gold pieces."

"He sits before you," said Abu el-Kasim, with simple dignity. But the eldest merchant paid no attention. He stroked his beard and said, "The man must be entirely trustworthy, for if he's discovered and is asked whence this money came, we shall deny everything and swear on the Koran that he's a liar. It will be no sin if we have a *fatwa* to appeal to. But if all goes well we can present ourselves before Khaireddin and say, 'Behold, we did this thing; do not forget us.' There remains only the problem—where to find the right man?"

Abu el-Kasim swore by Allah, the Koran, and his own beard that he was working in the cause of freedom and demanded nothing for himself. Having no other proposal the merchants found themselves compelled to trust him. At dusk one evening an iron chest appeared in our courtyard. In it lay ten leather bags within each of which were ten smaller ones, containing one hundred gold coins apiece. With some difficulty we carried this chest indoors. Abu el-Kasim locked the door and closed the shutters, and when Giulia had retired for the night he carefully counted the money. I had never seen so much gold in a single heap before, and I said, "Abu, my dear master, let us quickly put the money back in the bags, hire a sturdy camel, and leave the city while there's yet time."

But Abu el-Kasim sighed, "Lead me not into temptation, Michael el-Hakim. Khaireddin's weapons are ready, but it will take much to induce the rapacious Hassan to look the other way when they're

91

brought to the city. There are also Selim's troops to be bribed. We can be thankful if even half this sum remains for us."

All went smoothly. At the caravansary strangers with lean faces and burning eyes appeared, fumbling for the swords they did not carry. Poor tradesmen and artisans quaked and spent sleepless nights when in compliance with the *fatwa* they concealed weapons in their warehouses and granaries. But the Faqih set forth upon a long pilgrimage, and the eldest sons of the merchants kept him company; for so it was ordained in a marvelous dream that he had had.

Fruit trees blossomed and braziers were no longer necessary indoors. My heart was in my mouth all that time, though Abu el-Kasim cheered me, saying, "Ah, Michael, danger is the spice of life! How soon we weary of a quiet, comfortable existence. Nothing in the world gives a man so good an appetite or such sound sleep as approaching danger. Only then does a man fully appreciate the days remaining to him."

No doubt he spoke in mockery, for I continually cried out in my sleep, and an unpleasant sensation in my throat had bereft me of all desire for food. But when the soft spring wind brought the scent of blossom to my nostrils I could find comfort from time to time in thinking of all the poor and oppressed people whom we should now be able to liberate from tyranny. And ever more eagerly I awaited the hour when Giulia would become my slave.

I was working outside the shop one warm spring day when I saw a strange youth approaching our house. As he walked one heard a pleasant jingling sound, for he wore a short tunic with a silken, tasseled girdle to which silver bells were fastened. Below his knees he had bound silken ribbons with similar bells, and over his shoulders hung a lion skin, its forepaws crossed upon his breast. His well-kept, curly hair waved over his shoulders, he wore nothing on his head, and his black beard gleamed like silk. He carried a book bound in soft leather and as he paced along the street he opened it now and again and read, seemingly oblivous of all that went on around him, twirling the tassels of his girdle abstractedly, so that the bells jingled in time with his steps.

He was indeed the handsomest youth I had ever seen. When he drew nearer and I noted his beauty and his graceful, dignified bearing, I was filled with envy. He paused before me and addressed me in carefully articulated Arabic, "I have been told that Abu el-Kasim the drug merchant dwells here. If you are his son, Allah has indeed blessed him!"

My clothes were dirty and my hands stained with dye, and feeling exceedingly inferior in the presence of the stranger I replied abruptly, "This is Abu el-Kasim's shop, but I'm only a slave. My name is Michael el-Hakim and I can't invite you into the house as my master is out."

The stranger surveyed me with his brilliant eyes and exclaimed, "Are you Michael el-Hakim? I've heard of you. Never have I beheld such beautiful eyes, such rosy cheeks, and such admirable hands as yours."

He bent to take me in his arms and kissed me on both cheeks, so that I had difficulty in disengaging myself and began to have grave suspicions of him. When my dog saw me in this fair youth's embrace he began barking and sniffing at the hairless legs. So the stranger released me, but whistling softly he bent to stroke Rael and spoke to him kindly in Arabic, Persian, and Turkish, thus revealing himself to be a man of education. So friendly was he to my dog that my hostility melted away, and I asked what he wanted of me. He answered, "I'm a wanderer for my faith, Michael el-Hakim, and I belong to a brotherhood of wanderers, a Sufi sect known by some Mussulmans as Love's Beggars. My name is Mustafa ben-Nakir and I'm not of humble origin, though I call myself son of the angel of death. My lot is to wander from country to country and from town to town; as I go I read Persian poems to rejoice my heart."

He opened his book, jingled his bells, and in a musical voice read aloud to me a few verses of Persian poetry, which were certainly very pleasing to the ear, though they meant as much to me as pearls mean to a swine. He evidently belonged to some sort of sacred brotherhood within Islam, but in contrast to most dervishes he glorified the pleasures of this life by the studied perfection of his appearance. I could not resist his attraction, and said, "Mustafa ben-Nakir, son of the angel of death, I've given much thought to death and your coming is timely. Yet you must be a great liar, for what should you know of me, a slave? Come in, however, and let us see if we can find a piece of bread and some dried figs. When my master returns you must vanish, for he's an irascible man and won't tolerate strangers in his house."

Mustafa ben-Nakir needed no second bidding, but stepped indoors and looked so keenly about him that I hid the jar of small change. I

93

took him into the inner room and there poured water over his hands, and he told me he would now perform his devotions. His clear eyes and beautiful voice enchanted me during the prayer, and I could have believed him to be a real angel had he not been carrying that book of Persian poems. As I set food before him I asked him about his faith, and he said, "I was born in Istanbul, that most lovely city where the two halves of the world meet. My father was a wealthy merchant and my mother a Greek slave. They hired a wise Arabian tutor to instruct me in the true interpretation of the Koran, and a Persian poet to teach me versification. I listened to the most eminent teachers in the mosque school, but when I was seventeen I received a divine revelation. The forms of prayer and the letters of the Koran became as an empty husk. Nor was I the only one to be thus awakened; many another rich man's son wearied of the luxurious life we led, and of the empty letter of the law. And so we joined this mendicant brotherhood, to sing and dance in the streets to the music of our bells, until we wearied also of this, and set forth on journeys to foreign lands to observe all the forms and customs with which men fence in their lives. I've seen Bagdad, Jerusalem, and Cairo, and have never repented my impulse to exchange a life of luxury for one of danger and hardship. I live in poverty, gaining the necessities of life from the liberality of devout women. Never yet have I had to go hungry."

His story enchanted me, though I suspected that pious imams and faqihs could hardly approve his doctrine. I asked him further questions, but regarding me with his limpid, angelic eyes he said, "The profoundest element of my belief is complete freedom, admitting neither law nor formula. The dictates of the heart form the only rule for one of my fraternity. All I possess I carry upon me, so that when I see a caravan move off I can join it, should the whim take me. But then, if a strange bird flies across my path, I can turn aside and follow it, and in the wilderness devote myself to solitude and meditation. If in some port the sail of a vessel is hoisted I may take it as a sign and go aboard. And when a white hand appears behind a lattice to throw a flower at my feet, I follow that sign too, without misgivings."

Mustafa ben-Nakir went on to speak at great length of his singular doctrine, until I came to feel that nothing in the world was so essential to a man as sitting idly and passing the noon hours in lofty conversation. Abu el-Kasim's arrival took us altogether by surprise, therefore, and he exclaimed aloud in his wrath. But Mustafa ben-Nakir

94

rose and greeted him with the deepest respect, touching forehead and ground with his hand. To my amazement he added, "I'm told that the Deliverer comes from the sea at the next new moon, and will land his forces when he sees the signal fires. Under cover of darkness they will approach the city and march through the open gates at dawn."

"*Bismillah,* and so forth!" said Abu el-Kasim. "Why didn't you say so at once? Two sheds on the hillside near the palace are filled with fuel; when they're alight and the guards hurry out to extinguish them, a few bold men may force their way into the kasbah. And so we shall kill two birds with one stone. But what is your task, fair youth?"

Mustafa looked at him in bewilderment and replied, "I have brought you the message, and have no more to do than to follow my own will. I leave you therefore to the protection of Allah, and will go to some hospitable house where poetry is understood."

He prepared to depart, but Abu el-Kasim restrained him, saying, "Don't leave us, bringer of good tidings. Let us rather converse together confidentially, for you are certainly more than you seem. Advise me, for many difficulties remain."

"Allah, Allah!" said Mustafa. "All happens in conformity with his will, and he has chosen a most auspicious time for action. The Spanish Emperor's armies are shut up in Naples, besieged by the superior forces of the French King. The imperial navy is defeated, and Doria, who's in the French King's service, has blocked the harbor. And so the Emperor has other things to think of than Algiers."

I could hardly believe my ears, and cried, "How is this possible? Less than a year ago I was with the Emperor's army at the sack of Rome, and all Italy was then in his hands."

Abu el-Kasim silenced me and said, "Let us put our faith in the Deliverer. If he chooses to hasten matters he must have good reason. The new moon is the day after tomorrow, so you had better say your prayers, Michael el-Hakim, and prepare yourself for your task."

I was astonished at his words, and said, "Have I not carried out your orders to the best of my ability? What more do you require of me, dear master Abu?"

Abu el-Kasim surveyed me coldly.

"At cockcrow the day after tomorrow," he said, "we must carry Selim ben-Hafs's head to the Deliverer on a golden platter. It's only fair that we should divide this work between us. You, therefore, will get his head, and I on my part will provide a most magnificent dish."

My heart flew into my mouth and despite the heat my teeth chattered. Mustafa ben-Nakir, son of the angel of death, regarded me with sympathy and said, "Drink a little water, Michael el-Hakim. And have no fear, for I've been told that a *fatwa* has been issued for the purpose and so your deed will not be sinful; on the contrary you'll be performing a most meritorious action in cutting off Selim's head. If the knife is sharp, and doesn't jam between the vertebrae, you will have no difficulty."

To avoid their gaze I withdrew against the wall, but Abu el-Kasim, noting my fear, cursed me and said, "Have you no confidence in me? Patiently, sparing neither time nor trouble, I have woven my net to make all easy for you. In the palace you have your brother Antar, whom you can trust. The chief eunuch I have bribed. Delilah will go with you to the palace, to gaze into the sand, and I've already prepared a Cretan potion to be given to Selim instead of opium to send him into a deep sleep."

Mustafa ben-Nakir touched my shoulder with his shapely hand and said, "Ah, Michael el-Hakim, you please me and my heart urges me to go with you to the kasbah, to encourage you with my advice; above all to see that you carry out your task and at the proper time. Have no fear, for a stone can fall and crush your head as well here as in the Courtyard of Bliss."

But the whole thing had come upon me as too much of a surprise, and I cried in a fury, "In the Courtyard of Bliss it'll be a sword and nothing else that will fall on me. Truly I was born under an evil planet. But I'm a slave and have no choice. May the *fatwa* protect me. I hear and I obey."

Just then Abu el-Kasim raised his head, listening attentively, and said, "Allah! What can that mean?"

I too heard it. It was the rumble of distant gunfire. We ran all three into the street, and so did the neighbors, their hands uplifted in astonishment. There was no doubt that the noise came from Selim ben-Hafs's kasbah on the hillside; the wind brought us the sound of shrieks and clashing weapons, and then a cannon roared, echoed by another from the Spanish fortress at the harbor mouth.

"Allah is great," said Abu el-Kasim, and now it was his turn to weep. "All is lost, but I take refuge in Allah and not in the devil whom he stoned."

Uproar broke loose in the city; many people dashed along the streets and up the hill; merchants closed their shops and locked their doors. But Mustafa ben-Nakir surveyed his painted nails and said, "Allah is great, and nothing happens contrary to his will. Let us go and see what has happened."

We hastened up the steep street to the kasbah. An uneasy crowd had already gathered at the place of execution, but nothing else was to be seen save a couple of irate soldiers, who with muskets at the present stood blowing their smoldering matches and angrily ordering the crowd to keep its distance.

Within the kasbah the clash of weapons died away and only the yelling of the soldiers was to be heard; we could not tell if they yelled with delight or wrath. It was rumored among the crowd that some wood carriers and cooks had climbed the walls of the palace and fled; they dashed down the slopes crying out that Selim ben-Hafs was running about the Courtyard of Bliss, stark naked and with sword in hand, slaying everyone he saw. But no one could say whether this was true.

Presently we saw over fifty Spaniards armed with harquebuses marching up from the harbor toward the kasbah. The Spanish consul walked at their head, gesticulating violently. The party came to a halt before the shut gates; their commander inquired loudly of the guard as to the meaning of the shots they had heard, and ordered the gates to be opened.

In the loopholes of the wall there now appeared a number of Spanish and Italian renegades, who jeered at the troops and bade them return to their fortress, as they had no business here. The bystanders, egged on by this defiance, began throwing stones and camel dung at the Spaniards, who threatened to open fire upon them regardless of their agitated consul. The commanding officer ordered his men to train their light fieldpiece on the gate, and threatened to discharge it unless Selim ben-Hafs showed himself without delay.

The gate swung open on grating hinges and the Spaniards started to march in; but their cries of triumph died away at the sight of two cannon trained upon them in the archway, and beyond them a troop of horsemen who had the greatest difficulty in controlling their mounts. The Spanish commander at once ordered his men to retire,

97

and in much milder tones asked to speak to someone in authority who could tell him what had happened in the kasbah. And now in boundless astonishment I beheld Andy standing between the two guns, linstock in hand. He turned to speak to the horsemen with so careless a movement that one of his pieces went off and hurled its ball into the closed Spanish ranks, felling many men to the ground. At this the troopers could no longer rein back their horses, and they charged through the gateway with drawn swords.

Abu el-Kasim seized his head in both hands and cried, "Am I awake or dreaming?"

Nevertheless he played his part by tugging a holy Marabout by the sleeve and bidding him proclaim the *fatwa*. Then, like the cautious man he was, he ran for shelter behind a ruinous hovel and set fire to it. But I had seen Andy knocked down by the charging horses, and forgetful of danger I hurried to help him. He staggered up, wiped the dust from his face, and asked in amazement, "What has happened? Where have you sprung from, Michael? Go away at once, for we seem to have a war on our hands. The gun went off accidentally. Fortunately, everything is preordained; but I never meant to start fresh trouble now that we've restored order in the kasbah. Go away, now. I've caused mischief enough and I don't want to drag you into it."

He smelled strongly of wine, and may well have been kicked on the head by one of the horses. At any rate he picked me up and slung me far out of the archway and there was nothing for me to do but seek cover, for the Spaniards were shooting and slashing, the crowds were proclaiming the holy war, and the sheds which Abu el-Kasim had set alight were now blazing to the sky.

I ran this way and that like a distracted hen until Abu el-Kasim and Mustafa ben-Nakir seized my arms, shook me and asked why Selim ben-Hafs's mamelukes had attacked the Spaniards. I answered frankly that I had not the remotest idea, but besought them to rescue Andy as the Spaniards were certain to hang him.

For the moment, however, the Spaniards seemed indisposed to hang anyone, having trouble enough in regaining the harbor. Many of them lay in their own blood, while down in the city the fleeing remainder were met by an armed mob. From the roofs showered stones, boiling water, and balks of timber. Selim's mamelukes, however, imbued by now with a healthy respect for the murderous Spanish harquebuses, withdrew again into the kasbah, leaving pursuit to the townsfolk.

Dervishes and other holy men proclaimed through foaming lips that the gates of Paradise stood open to all who fell at the hands of Spaniards.

Abu el-Kasim was not greatly tempted, and Mustafa declared that we had more important things to think of than the houris of Paradise. When the uproar had somewhat subsided we summoned up courage to address the guards at the gate of the kasbah, blessing them in the name of Allah. I begged them to call my brother Andy, and when Abu had thrown some silver among them they did as we asked.

Shortly afterward Andy appeared in the gateway, his hands thrust into his sash with a swaggering air. He surveyed us in surprise, and said, "In the name of Allah! What are you standing out there for? Come and share in our joy!"

He had quite forgotten having seen me just a few moments before. We dared not accept his cordial invitation, and I said, "Andy, you can't be drunk? Come out to us and we'll hide you from Selim's wrath."

He looked at me blankly.

"Are you raving, Michael? Selim ben-Hafs is dead and I serve his son Mohammed ben-Hafs, blessed be the dear boy's name."

Abu el-Kasim uttered a loud cry, and demanded, "How is this possible?"

Andy avoided our eyes, and rubbing the palms of his hands together in embarrassment he replied, "Most people believe that he slipped in the bath and broke his neck. But the sad truth is that it was I who broke it for him. It was quite a mistake, and in self-defense—and perhaps I was a trifle fuddled."

"Good God in heaven!" I gasped. "Have you slain Selim ben-Hafs, and so ruined all my excellent plans? I begin to wonder why the Creator gave you a head at all, unless it was just to keep your ears apart."

Andy flared up, being still fiery with wine.

"Why bewail Selim's fate? Mourn rather for the two other sultans who have reigned here this day, for if the truth must be told, Mohammed is Selim's third successor."

Just then four or five soldiers in felt caps ran up to tell Andy that the Aga was calling for him. Andy followed them unsteadily across the courtyard, leaving us under the protection of the sentries. Abu el-Kasim and I sat down in the shade with heavy hearts, but Mustafa ben-Nakir took out his Persian book and began to read poems, glancing complacently from time to time at his painted nails.

Presently we sprang to our feet, for from the Aga's house came the sudden sound of screams and shots. I thought never to see Andy again, but I should have known him better. He came staggering across the courtyard toward us with a troop of yelling soldiers at his heels. On his head was the Aga's turban, adorned by a plume held in a jeweled socket. He sighed, "May Allah forgive my many sins. I must certainly be drunk. I was forced to slay the Aga, though I knew that assault upon a superior officer is the worst crime a soldier can commit. But he was plotting little Mohammed's downfall, and if he had been successful no one would have remained to inherit Selim's throne; so to avoid confusion I slew the Aga and took his turban. But help me now, Michael, and Abu my dear master, for I need a dromedary."

I was now convinced that he had lost the last remnant of his wits, until it dawned upon Abu that Andy meant a dragoman, to interpret. But I exclaimed, "In the name of Allah! My brother is not answerable for his actions. Give him the powerful sleeping draught prepared for Selim, and when he has slept himself sober we can talk some sense into him."

Just then an irate eunuch, attended by soldiers, approached from the inner court bearing the Sultan's signet ring in his hand. After him came servants dragging a heavy iron chest. The soldiers shouted that they were bringing the Sultan's money, to be shared out among his loyal troops. If it had been noisy before, the tumult now increased to that of some gigantic dogfight, and with my hands to my face I took refuge behind a buttress of the wall. Soldiers swarmed up on all sides, hacking at one another and trampling the weaker underfoot as they ran, until the eunuch, having vainly brandished the signet ring, threw himself over the chest and commended his soul to Allah's protection.

Andy now bade us a confused farewell and fought his way through to the chest. He thrust the eunuch aside and commanded all the scribes to keep strict account, so that each and every man might receive his fair share. Strange to say, these savage fellows obeyed him promptly, and paraded in order of rank to await their turn. They felt honored when Andy cuffed them over the head and called them drunken swine. The trembling scribes sat on the ground with the regimental rolls before them; the eunuch threw out his arms despairingly, unlocked the chest, and withdrew. Andy peered into the chest and cried aghast, "Cursed be the name of Selim ben-Hafs, who swindles us even when dead! He perished not a moment too soon."

The sergeants pressed forward and stared into the chest, and were in their turn astonished, for what they saw there was not enough to provide one gold coin for each man. But they soon recovered from their surprise and said, "We are poor men, but the city is rich. Let us hasten down and take what we can before the Spaniards get their claws into it."

Andy scratched his head. "Who am I to gainsay you? A hundred heads must be better than one. Yet we should think twice before pillaging a city which the Sultan placed under our protection."

Abu el-Kasim burst into tears, and said, "All things are preordained, and now is our last chance to save what can be saved. Go, Mustafa ben-Nakir, and reason with these men, while I and my slave Michael hasten home for the gold which was to be the comfort of my declining years. It will amount to four gold pieces for each man, and may enable them to possess their souls in patience until the Deliverer reaches the city."

Mustafa walked forward to Andy with his usual dignity, while Abu and I hurried out of the gate and down into the city. We saw the last of the Spaniards rowing back to their fortress and a crowd of people standing on the quay, shouting and brandishing their weapons. But we had hardly reached our house when the guns of the fortress began to roar; a roundshot whistled through the air and knocked a hole in the house next to ours. Hastily we dug up the treasure hidden beneath the floor, stowed the money bags in a chest, and loaded this onto a stray donkey that fate had sent to our very door. The firing had terrified it, but reassured by the feel of its weighty burden it plodded readily up the steep street.

When we arrived with our load at the forecourt of the kasbah, we found the soldiers sitting on the ground and listening quietly to Mustafa ben-Nakir's inspired description of the joys of Paradise. Now and then he read Persian poems to them from his book. Andy was dozing and nodding on the lid of the chest. Mustafa ben-Nakir sent us a reproachful glance as we arrived sweating and shouting with our donkey, disturbing his mellifluous recital. But Andy sprang up and greeted us with blessings.

"We must now consult Amina and her son, whom I've made sultan because she swore to me that he is Selim ben-Hafs's lawful heir. It's true that this charming lady had often bitterly complained of Selim's neglect at the material period; but we've no other sultans to choose from, now that she has strangled both Selim's elder sons."

Mustafa ben-Nakir closed his book of poems and said with a sigh, "Let us seek out the boy, Michael, for the paying of these men will take a long time, and I've already prepared them for the Deliverer's coming."

Andy ordered the soldiers to obey Abu el-Kasim and the scribes, that no disputes might arise over their pay; then he came with us into the inner courtyard where we saw many corpses, and a number of shot holes in the marble colonnade. But Andy took us straight through the golden Gateway of Bliss, shoving the startled eunuchs aside, then muttered thickly, "Let's go to the baths, for I fancy I have two unopened wine jars there."

With the assurance of a sleepwalker he led us along many labyrinthine corridors to the baths, and there kneeling at the brink he fished a jar from the water, broke its seal, and drank greedily. I glanced round the place and beheld Selim ben-Hafs's body lying on a marble slab—no lovely sight, for it was more swollen and livid than ever. The eunuchs who had been attending to it melted away like shadows at our approach. Mustafa ben-Nakir seated himself cross legged on the bench at the dead man's feet and said, "We must all die, and each moment of our lives is preordained. It is also the will of Allah that we should sit in this bathhouse and that you should cleanse your conscience so that afterward we may order all things for the best. Speak, therefore, wrestler Antar!"

Andy stared, hiccupped, felt the feathers in his turban and said in hurt tones, "I'm no wrestler, but the Sultan's Aga—if only I could lay hands on the Sultan. And all that happened was that evil tongues spread slander about me, persuading Selim ben-Hafs that I'd spat in his bed—which is a black lie as I've never so much as seen his bed. This morning Selim came stark naked to the bathhouse to sweat away the opium, and a whole crowd of painted boys came too, to wash him. When he saw me he began to screech for his scimitar. His wife Amina, who was wearing no more than was once customary in Paradise, tried to calm him and at least gain time for me to get my breeches on. But at the sight of her the licentious old man was more rabid than ever. Luckily his pretty boys took to their heels when they saw Amina, so I was able to bar the door and consider what was next to be done. She said I had no choice but to bring the Selim to a better frame of mind by force, so I just took him by the neck with the tips of my fingers, and it broke. My dear Amina was as frightened as myself."

Andy wiped the tears from his eyes with his thumb, but Mustafa ben-Nakir, contemplating his nails, asked, "And then?"

"Then?" Andy rubbed his temples to refresh his memory. "Yes. Well, then the lady Amina said it was the will of Allah, but that for our own good it would be best to say that Selim had slipped on the smooth floor and broken his neck. She then told me that other more important duties awaited her and quickly left the room, promising to send the Aga and the eunuchs as witnesses to what had occurred. The eunuchs laid Selim on the bench, tied his toes together and proclaimed the new sultan, while I took the Aga by the arm and returned with him to the barracks, as it seemed to me I had no business in the house of mourning. I thought him a pleasant fellow, yet in that I must have been mistaken, since so far as I can remember I've just killed him."

He fingered his headdress thoughtfully for a little, then started and said, "Where was I? Ah, yes. There was trouble over the new sultan, for Selim ben-Hafs had two sons besides Amina's, and these two were proclaimed sultan simultaneously. The uproar and fighting went on until it was found that Amina had had both the elder boys strangled, and their mother, too, for safety's sake. When I reproached her for this she asked if I would have preferred to see her and her son strangled; for it seems it is the custom here for the ruler to leave no rival alive. She then hinted broadly that she meant to marry me, so that I might protect her son till he grew up. I've nothing whatever against Amina—fine woman—but she's handier with the noose than I should like any wife of mine to be."

He began angrily calling for Amina, and was almost too drunk to stand, but Mustafa ben-Nakir had heard enough and rose, saying, "Antar, you've done your part, and need rest. There is no sultan but Suleiman, the Sultan of Sultans, and in his name I take possession of this kasbah until the Deliverer comes to reward and punish each man according to his deserts. Slave Michael, take your brother's sword which he's not in a condition to wield and strike off Selim's head, that it may be set on the top of a pillar in a golden dish in the sight of everyone. With him the Hafsid dynasty is at an end; no intriguing women shall rule in this city, and the throne shall remain vacant until the coming of the Deliverer."

Mustafa spoke in a voice of such authority that I dared not disobey, and grasping Andy's sword I struck off Selim's head, disagreeable though the task was. But as I was handing back the weapon a crowd of splendidly dressed eunuchs and black slaves entered the room. In their midst was a boy in a gorgeous kaftan and with far too large a turban on his head. He tripped over the long kaftan as he walked, and held his mother by the hand.

Andy, looking much ashamed, greeted this woman by the name of Amina. When she saw the state he was in she forgot to veil herself, stamped, and screamed, "I ought never to have trusted one of the uncircumcised! Where is the treasure chest? Why don't the soldiers proclaim my son sultan? And how could you allow my lord's body to be thus desecrated? The best thing I could do would be to have your throat cut, since you use it only to defile it in defiance of the Prophet's law."

"B-blessed be his name," stammered Andy, swaying and hiccupping, while I stood nonplussed with Selim's head still in my hand; the infuriated woman snatched off her red slipper and began beating Andy over the head with it, until the Aga's turban fell off. I hardly know how it would have ended had not Mustafa ben-Nakir stepped forward, jingling the bells at his girdle, and cried, "Veil your face, shameless woman, and take your bastard back to the harem! We have nothing to say to you, and Allah will punish you for thus treating a man who has done you and your son far greater service than you deserve."

His demeanor was so proud and commanding that the woman recoiled and said, "Who are you, fair youth, and how dare you use that tone to me, the mother of the ruling sultan?"

"I am Mustafa ben-Nakir, son of the angel of death. My task is to see that each is rewarded after his deserts." Turning to the eunuchs he said, "Take the woman back to the harem, and let this drunken swine sleep it off in some obscure corner. Then fetch a kaftan befitting my rank, so that I may take command of the city until the coming of the Deliverer. And do all this more swiftly than I can find an appropriate gazel, or many of you will find yourselves a head shorter."

He turned his back on Amina, opened his book, and began reading aloud to himself in his musical voice, so impressively that none dared to question or disturb him, but obeyed his orders. I was greatly relieved to find amid the general confusion at least one man who knew his own mind. But my great natural curiosity got the better of me, and I asked, "What manner of man are you, Mustafa ben-Nakir, that all obey you?"

He smiled and bent his head.

"I but follow the impulses of my heart, which tomorrow may lead me out into the wilderness. Perhaps men obey me because I'm freer than others—so free that I care not whether they obey me or not."

The eunuchs soon returned with splendid clothes, which they helped Mustafa ben-Nakir to put on. They shod him with jeweled slippers and girded a bright sword about his waist; lastly he set upon his well-groomed locks the Aga's turban. He bade me put Selim ben-Hafs's head on the golden dish, which the eunuchs brought at his order, and then with his hand to his mouth he yawned slightly and said, "The money will soon have been distributed among the men, and it will be wise to keep them occupied. I fancy nothing will answer the purpose so well as attacking the Spaniards. I must therefore send a Latin-speaking envoy to their fortress to demand compensation for all the damage they've done. If they refuse, they must be told that the new sultan will not tolerate their behavior, and must summon Khaireddin to his support. This will give us time to take the guns down to the harbor. But if you have a better plan, Michael, speak freely."

"Whom do you mean by the sultan?" I objected. "Is little Mohammed ben-Hafs the lawful sultan of Algiers?"

"Ah," he replied, suppressing another yawn, "we believe in Allah though we haven't seen him; why should the Spaniards doubt the existence of a sultan whom they've never beheld? Speak to them of this invisible sultan, and let that suffice them."

"Allah, Allah!" I gasped. "You can't mean to send *me?* Spaniards are cruel men, and even if they leave the head on my shoulders they're likely to remove my nose and ears."

Mustafa ben-Nakir gently shook his head. "I would gladly go myself, for I like to visit new places and people. But I lack proficiency in Latin, and have also other things to do. You had better stay at the fortress for a time. Now you must not disturb me, for I'm composing a Turkish poem in the Persian manner and must count the syllables."

To comfort me, he ordered the eunuchs to provide me with an exceedingly fine kaftan, and I had then no choice but to take Selim's head on the golden charger and follow Mustafa ben-Nakir. The armed

Negroes attended us and we paced in solemn procession to the fore-court amid the astonished shouts of the soldiers. Abu el-Kasim dashed up to us and fell on his knees before Mustafa to kiss his slipper. Seeing this, the eunuch also knelt; Mustafa took the Sultan's signet ring from his hand and fingered it reflectively. Soon the whole court was full of bowing soldiers, who touched forehead and ground with their finger tips.

Mustafa ben-Nakir summoned the sergeants and arranged for some men to guard the gates and others to quench the fires down by the harbor. But the greater number he ordered to drag the cannon to the shore. No vessel was to put out for the fortress without his permission, and anyone approaching from that direction was to be arrested and brought before him.

When he had finished speaking he contemplated his nails and asked whether there was anything further the men wished to know. They murmured among themselves until one took courage and yelled, "Driveling fop! Who are you to give orders?"

This was greeted by expectant laughter, but Mustafa ben-Nakir coolly took a broad scimitar from a Negro's hand, advanced to the speaker and looked him steadily in the face. The other soldiers made way, and Mustafa with a lightning stroke took off the man's head before he could lift a finger. Without so much as a glance at the head-less body Mustafa returned to his place, handed the sword back to the Negro, and asked if anyone else had anything to say. But the smile had frozen on the lips of the curious, and those standing next the dead man contented themselves with stooping to empty his purse. After this the different detachments marched off in good order to the duties assigned them.

Abu el-Kasim rubbed his hands and said, "We've brought the business to a happy conclusion, though at considerable expense. But I have no doubt that the Deliverer will fully reimburse me. We must now decide what to say to him, and how to say it, so that we may not contradict one another when the time comes."

Mustafa ben-Nakir graciously assented, adding, "And it would be well for your slave Michael to go at once to the fortress and begin negotiations with the Spaniards." He turned to me. "If you can induce them to leave, so much the better. If not, there's no harm done."

Having given orders for two soldiers to attend me, he returned to the Courtyard of Bliss. There was nothing for it but to curse my fate

106

and betake myself to the harbor, where troops were putting out fires, building breastworks, and dragging ordnance into position.

The boatman had not far to take me, but the round keep and massive walls of the fortress seemed to grow ever darker and more menacing as we approached. When we had covered half the distance a shot was fired from a little cannon on the wall, and the ball fell so near my boat that the splash of it drenched me. In my alarm I began to jump up and down waving the skirts of my kaftan and shrieking in my best Latin that I was the Sultan's messenger. We should certainly have capsized had not the boatman pulled me down again on to my seat. But there was no more firing, and as soon as I was within earshot a monk in a black habit appeared on the jetty and addressed me in Latin, asking in God's name what had happened, and blessing my arrival, since great anxiety prevailed in the fortress.

We drew alongside the jetty, and I demanded in the name of the Sultan to speak with the garrison commander. While this officer was changing into clothes worthy of the Sultan's envoy, the monk set wine before me, and would have offered me food had supplies allowed. But these were dwindling now that purchases in the city had become impracticable. So guileless was this good man that he asked me to send my boatman back to fetch meat and greenstuff, for the wounded especially were suffering from the lack of these victuals.

I soon gathered that no one in the fortress had the least idea of what had happened in the town. For ten years the garrison had led a lazy, peaceful life, and it was thought that I had come to beg forgiveness on the Sultan's behalf. Selim ben-Hafs had always regarded these Spaniards as his only protection against Khaireddin.

This situation only increased my dread of the wrath which my errand might arouse in Captain de Varga, the Spanish commander, and I sought to stiffen my courage with deep draughts of wine.

At last Captain de Varga appeared, in shining armor, attended by the Spanish consul who had fled from the town with the soldiers. The consul had a bump on his forehead and was in a state of intense excitement because his house had been looted. Captain de Varga spoke a little Latin, and was a proud, resolute man; yet in consequence of his inactive life he had put on weight, so that the costly armor pinched him here and there: a circumstance in no way tending to increase his good will toward me.

First he asked what had happened in the city, and why the Sultan's troops as well as the townspeople had so treacherously attacked his own almost unarmed men and caused such damage to property. At this point the consul, the veins swelling at his temples, shouted that the losses he had sustained far exceeded in value the lives of a few blockheads of soldiers. He demanded full compensation and a new and better house, for which he had already chosen the site.

When at last I had a chance to speak I chose my words with care: "Noble Captain, most excellent Consul, and Reverend Father! Sultan Selim ben-Hafs, blessed be his name, died this morning by accident. He slipped and fell in the baths, breaking his neck. After much discussion among his fatherless sons, the seven-year-old Mohammed has assumed the kaftan and ascended the throne. He has secured his position by distributing money among his loyal troops, and beside him as counselor stands his wise mother Amina. His elder brothers will not oppose him, for in the course of a meal a datestone lodged in each of their throats and choked them. No doubt the hand of fate thus intervened to prevent disputes over the succession.

"But," I went on with a quaking heart, though still looking Captain de Varga steadfastly in the eye, "while all this was taking place in accordance with the time-honored customs of this city, a horde of pillaging Spaniards arrived, bringing artillery with them. I hold you in no way to blame, noble Captain, for this gross infringement of national rights. The lawless rabble must have left the fortress without your permission, and profited by the ruler's death to bring disorder to the town. Nevertheless they desecrated the mosque, willfully defiled the holy Marabout's tomb, and then opened fire on the kasbah, no doubt with the object of seizing the treasury. The Aga was compelled to dispatch a few cavalrymen to drive them forth with as little violence as possible. The Spaniards then overran the city, looting the homes of the faithful and ravishing their good wives. To prevent further disorders, the Sultan has been graciously pleased to sever communications between fortress and city, lest the people, enraged at the pollution of the mosque and tomb, should return evil for evil and attack the fort. The Sultan has also ordered the digging of trenches about the harbor, where he has set up his artillery, as you may see for yourself. But these measures have been adopted solely to protect the fortress and to prevent fresh violence, which might prejudice the friendly relations now happily existing between the Emperor of Spain and the Sultan of Algiers."

108

Wine had so loosened my tongue that I was moved by my own eloquence. The consul listened open mouthed, but the Dominican crossed himself repeatedly and said in tones of satisfaction, "It's only proper that our Christian soldiers should have desecrated the mosque and tomb of the infidels, and I cannot sufficiently praise them. All too often have we seen Moslems trample the Cross underfoot, to enrage us."

Captain de Varga bade him hold his tongue, and looking at me darkly he said, "You lie. I sent the patrol ashore to discover the reason for the shooting in the kasbah, entirely in the interests of Selim ben-Hafs; but my men fell into the trap prepared, and only their good discipline saved them from utter annihilation. If there has been looting and arson the Moslems themselves have committed it, to cover their own misdeeds."

I bowed low and said, "I have heard you, noble Captain. All that remains for me to do is to return to the Sultan and inform him that you distort the truth, harden your heart, and do your utmost to cloud the cordial relations that have hitherto existed between the Hafsids and the Emperor, your master."

"Wait!" said Captain de Varga hastily. Taking a paper from the consul he read it through and went on, "I ask nothing better than to see those happy relations restored, and I'm willing to forget the whole incident in return for indemnification for damaged property and weapons, and for the suffering caused—and also the customary compensation to the families of the fallen. I will accept in all the sum of twenty-eight thousand Spanish gold pieces, half to be paid before the infidels' sunset prayer, and the other half within three months, as I realize the young Sultan will have other expenses to meet at the beginning of his reign."

I exclaimed at the very thought of so fabulous a sum, but Captain de Varga raised his hand and continued, "To prevent future misunderstandings I claim the right to build an artillery tower in the harbor, near the mosque. Further, the Sultan shall have a Spaniard for his vizier who must be allowed an armed bodyguard, to be maintained at the expense of the treasury."

I perceived from these terms that he was a farsighted man who served the Emperor well, and was in all respects a worthy foe. Genuine tears came to my eyes as I knelt before him and begged him to strike off my head rather than send me back to the Sultan with such a message, for the Sultan would certainly not spare me. In so doing I relied on his honor as a nobleman and was not disappointed, for he bade me rise, and said, "Serve me faithfully, persuade the Sultan that I'm in earnest, and I'll allow no harm to come to you. Tell him that my gunners stand with smoldering matches, that I mean to bombard the city with red-hot shot and that I shall occupy the harbor unless I receive a favorable answer by the hour of morning prayer tomorrow."

"Allah is great," said I. "Since you trust me, let me give you some good advice. Don't threaten too much, or the Sultan—moved by wicked counselors and by the angry populace—may send word to the great Khaireddin, to make a treaty with him, and with his help expel you from your island."

He laughed. "Renegade, you're a wily fellow! But even a seven-year-old boy would hardly be so foolish as to saw off the bough he sits on. If he called Khaireddin he'd get more than he bargained for. But I'll listen to any proposals the Sultan may make when he has heard my terms."

Notwithstanding his laughter I could see that the very name of Khaireddin had startled him; and so I said, "My lord and protector! You need not send me away, for I bring you the Sultan's proposals. He demands nothing but fair compensation for the damage done by the Spaniards' raid, and a thousand gold pieces to buy rose water for the purification of the mosque and the Marabout's tomb. He is willing even to reconsider the question of compensation, provided you block up all loopholes commanding the city under supervision of his officials. If you reject these proposals the Sultan will be compelled to assume an intention on your part to interfere in internal affairs, and will then seek help wherever it may be found, to prevent further conspiracy."

"God save us!" said Captain de Varga, crossing himself. "The terms are harder than I expected, but I know how suspicious these infidels are; because they plot incessantly they fancy others do the same. But I'm a Castilian; I will die rather than surrender—for surrender it would be. My last word is this: let us talk no more of compensation on either side. We're all human; we're all liable to err. I'll even punish the culprits who have desecrated the holy places—if indeed that tale is true. But I cannot afford rose water."

The consul wailed and the monk deplored the punishment of Christian men who had deserved reward. But Captain de Varga said, "As you see my aims are conciliatory, and in that respect diametrically opposed to those of my advisers. Further I cannot go. If your lord won't listen, my guns must speak. Warn him above all against Khaireddin, for the least approach to that godless pirate will be regarded by me as an act of hostility toward my lord the Emperor."

He handed me a worn leather purse containing ten gold pieces, and I concealed my amazement that the Emperor should allow this loyal young officer to languish in such poverty. I was then honorably escorted to the jetty and at my desire—perhaps also to persuade me that he had plenty of gunpowder—he ordered a salute to be fired as we shoved off. His proud credulity astonished me and caused me to reflect that in all negotiation the honest man is bound to come off worst, while bluff wins every point.

The whole affair had gone better than I could have hoped, and my conscience was clear, for I had given him plainly to understand that he had Khaireddin to reckon with as an adversary. I stepped ashore well satisfied, and observed that the fires in the harbor quarter had been put out and that many of the gun emplacements were completed. These works would have been gravely impeded by bombardment from the fortress; my negotiations had therefore fulfilled their purpose.

On my return to the kasbah I was taken at once to the garden of the Courtyard of Bliss where Mustafa ben-Nakir, reclining at ease on a down pillow beneath a canopy, was reading Persian poems to my master Abu el-Kasim. They mentioned discreetly that Amina was no more, and while I felt no great regret I thought anxiously of Andy's despair when he woke from his drunken stupor and learned of his beloved's death. Mustafa divined my thoughts and said, "Allah is swift in judgment. We spoke with the woman and know that she exploited your brother's simplicity for her own wicked ends. She bribed the eunuchs to leave Selim ben-Hafs alone with your brother in the bathhouse. So, Michael, you needn't wonder that in righteous indignation at such treachery we arranged for her to be strangled by the eunuchs. We had your brother's best interests at heart."

"Yes, indeed," put in Abu el-Kasim. "But, reflecting that the fruit never falls far from the tree, we had Amina's son removed at the same time. This makes matters simpler for Khaireddin, who might have been inconvenienced if the boy had lived and gone over to the Spaniards, thus giving them a pretext to interfere in the succession."

I now perceived that Mustafa ben-Nakir had deliberately sent me out of the way lest I should hinder these shady doings, and I pitied the little boy who had held his mother's hand and stumbled over the long kaftan, and who had now perished in so sorrowful a manner.

I went back then to Abu el-Kasim's house. The stars were already glittering in the heavens. Many people were awake upon the house-tops, and in the still night I heard the sound of laughter, of stringed instruments, and of dovelike cooings. My heart was gentle as I stepped into the house and called out that I had come home. My dog ran up in the darkness to lick my hand, while Giulia lit the lamp and said, "Is that you, Michael, and alone? Where have you been all this time, and where is Abu? I've lain awake wondering if something terrible had happened. There's been fighting in the town and they say the Deliverer will soon be here. And when I came home I found a great hole in the floor and feared that robbers had broken in."

Her affectionate anxiety melted my heart still further and I said, "Nothing terrible has happened. Everything indeed is going better than I could have hoped. The Deliverer will come tomorrow at cock-crow, and for you great things—happier things than you can imagine —are in store. So let us make much of one another, for spring is here and we're alone in the house with none to see us save the dog, who need not make us bashful."

Giulia clapped her hands for joy and cried, "How I long to see the great Deliverer who rules the seas! Surely he'll reward me very generously for having so diligently foretold the future on his behalf, and prepared the way for his coming. Perhaps he will allow me to look into the sand alone with him. They say his beard is soft, and chestnut brown. He has certainly all the wives the law allows him, and the mother of his son is a direct descendant of the Prophet. Still, he may incline to me and keep me beside him."

Her prattle oppressed me, and when I sought to fold her in my arms she quickly veiled her face, stamped on my toes and said, "Are you out of your mind, Michael, to behave thus in the absence of our master? Control yourself. And where did you get that fine kaftan? If you would give it to me I could make a charming jacket out of it."

She began eagerly feeling the material; in the dim light of the lamp she was so marvelously beautiful that I could not resist her, and reluctantly I let her remove the kaftan, which indeed was the most splendid garment I had ever worn. She crushed it in her bare arms, greedily breathing in its pleasant scent of musk, and cried, "Will you

really give it to me, Michael? If so you may kiss me, but in all innocence. I'm a fiery woman and have trouble enough as it is to protect
my virtue."

She allowed me to kiss her cheek and even offered me her lips, but
when I would have taken her in my arms she struggled and threatened to scream and stamped on my toes until I had to let her go.
As soon as she was free she fled with the kaftan to her alcove, slam-
ming and locking the grille and deriding my prayers and tears. As I
stood there half-naked shaking the wrought-iron gate I remembered
for the first time that I had left my slave clothes in the kasbah, and
so had nothing to put on to greet the Deliverer in the morning.

Tossing sleepless on my bed that night I was yet comforted by the
thought that tomorrow Giulia would be my slave and my lawful
property. I resolved to exact full requital for her torment of me, and
hoped that she was not quite indifferent, since she had shown such
anxiety for me and had accepted my kaftan as a present. Comforted
I fell asleep and did not wake until the cocks of the city began to
crow, and the joyful voice of the muezzin proclaimed that prayer was
better than sleep. I looked up and saw to my astonishment that the
muezzin was leaping and dancing on the balcony of the minaret; now
he was proclaiming the coming of the Deliverer. Rising hastily, I
flung on what garments I could find, grasped Giulia's hand and sped
with her up the steep street leading to the palace. The dog followed
us with joyous barks, trying to tug at the cloak I had thrown over my
shoulders.

The whole populace was on its feet, some running to the palace, but
most hastening to the western gates to meet the Deliverer beyond the
walls and follow him into the city. They laughed and pointed at me
and the dog, but I took no notice, reflecting that he laughs best who
laughs last. We had a setback at the palace gates, however, for the
guards flatly refused us admission, but fortunately a scared eunuch
appeared, who recognized me. Stammering with fear he promised to
take me to Abu el-Kasim, and begged me in return to say a good
word for him. In my extremity I promised all he asked, and he led
me through the Courtyard of Bliss to a small room where Abu el-
Kasim, with red-rimmed eyes and clearly in a bad humor, was just
finishing his breakfast. A flock of slave women were in attendance,
but although they held up one magnificent kaftan after another and
besought him to make haste and dress since Mustafa ben-Nakir and

113

his suite had long since ridden to meet the Deliverer, he cut them over the shins with a cane and said, "No! I'm a poor man and dislike strutting in borrowed plumage. Bring my plain spice merchant's cloak whose smells are familiar to me and whose fleas know me. In that garment I have served the Deliverer and in that garment I will meet him, that with his own eyes he may behold my poverty."

The slaves wrung their hands and with lamentations brought out the ragged old cloak. Abu smelt it joyfully, combed out hair and beard with his fingers and allowed the terrified eunuch to help him on with the dreadful garment. Then only did he turn his eyes to me and say angrily, "Where in Allah's name have you been, Michael? I hope you haven't lost the golden dish and the Sultan's head? We should have been in the mosque long ago, to meet the Deliverer."

I had in fact not the remotest idea what had become of these things, and I hastened off on a frantic search through the various courtyards. Luckily the friendly eunuch came to my help; he had taken care of both head and dish and set them on the top of a pillar. No harm was done, therefore, except that Selim's head had begun to take on a most hideous appearance, and that the dish seemed much smaller than before.

With these objects under my arm I returned to Abu el-Kasim, and was distressed to behold Giulia embracing and kissing and coaxing that remarkably unhandsome man. He wept, but was prevailed upon at last to send the slave women to the store chamber of the harem, and they returned with such a wealth of veils and slippers that Giulia was hard put to it to decide what pleased her best.

To me Abu el-Kasim gave Mustafa ben-Nakir's mendicant dress, which after some hesitation I put on. Being used to garments reaching to the ground, I had the uneasy sensation of nakedness from the waist down. But the tunic was of the finest and softest stuff, and with every step I took the bells rang so sweetly that Giulia surveyed me wide eyed and assured me that I need not be ashamed of my bare knees and shapely calves. She sent for the necessary ointments and rapidly painted my hands and feet orange color, and then, since no headdress was worn with this costume, she oiled my hair with fine oils and applied blue beneath my eyes so that I hardly recognized myself when I looked in the mirror.

Before we set forth for the mosque, Abu wanted to see how Andy was faring. He took me to the cellars of the palace, moved aside an iron trap door and pointed to Andy, who lay sprawled on the hard stone floor below us, moaning in his sleep. His narrow cell was lit by a small window with bars across it as thick as my wrist. He was quite naked, and beside him stood a water jar, which was already empty. The compassionate Abu ordered the guards to refill it, and to lower a great quantity of bread. I pitied Andy deeply, but saw that he must be kept in that bear pit until he had quite recovered, or he would seek to combat the effects of his drinking bout with a fresh one, and his last state would be worse than the first. Lest he should feel lonely when he woke, I left my dog with him in his cell.

When we had left the evil-smelling cellars and our eyes had become accustomed to the sunlight on the high terrace, we saw the Deliverer just riding through the western gate of the city, followed by a large troop of cavalry. Weapons flashed in the sun, and the vast crowds, which had come to meet him, waved palm branches and shouted and cheered until their voices came to our ears like the boom of a distant sea. Through the quivering heat we could see also a number of vessels riding at anchor in the farther bay. We counted nearly twenty of them, all bedecked with flags and pennants.

We hastened down into the city, and with difficulty elbowed our way into the packed mosque. We could never have managed it if I had not jingled my bells to make the people believe I was a holy man. They would have made way for us readily enough if I had displayed what I carried under my arm, but I had covered the golden dish with a cloth, for who could tell whether there might not lurk among them some adherent of Selim ben-Hafs?

Within the mosque an indescribable din prevailed, which reached its climax when with drawn swords Khaireddin's janissaries and renegades appeared in the doorway and began to clear a path for their lord. Khaireddin himself advanced among his warriors, sending greetings to right and left, and waving his hand. Before him marched a number of standard bearers, and immediately after him the white-bearded Faqih and the eldest sons of the merchants who had already returned, it seemed, from their important pilgrimage. Mustafa ben-Nakir was also of the suite, clad in a splendid kaftan and the Aga's turban; from time to time he surveyed his well-kept nails.

I was disappointed at my first sight of Khaireddin, of whom I had heard so much. He was a man of little majesty, being indeed short and rather fat. As a mark of dignity he wore a tall felt cap bound with a turban of white muslin. Strangely enough the turban was not even clean, though it was adorned in front by a crescent of sparkling stones. He went empty handed and had not even a dagger in his girdle. His beard was dyed and there was a smile on his round, catlike face as he walked with short steps across the floor.

When he reached the reader's place he made a sign to show that he was going to pray. He uncovered his head, rolled up his sleeves, and in the sight of everyone performed the prescribed ablutions. The Faqih poured water over his hands and the eldest sons of the merchants dried his hands, head, and feet. He then replaced the turban on his head, recited the prayers and three suras of the Koran, while the assembled people listened attentively. The Faqih then sat in the reader's place and intoned certain verses. He read very beautifully; without difficulty he found passages appropriate to the coming of the Deliverer, and others enjoining mercy, justice, and liberality.

When the Faqih had read for so long that the people began to grow restless, he at last resigned his place to Khaireddin, who mounted the high seat, crossed his legs under him, and with a slight stammer began to expound the sacred texts in so easy and entertaining a manner that now and then laughter could be heard among his audience. At last he raised his hand gently and said, "My dear children, I have come back to you, impelled by an auspicious dream, and I will never abandon you again. Henceforth I will protect you as a good father should, and you shall endure no more wrongs, for in this city justice shall ever prevail."

Emotion threatened to stifle his voice, but wiping tears from his beard he went on, "I would not sadden your hearts by recalling unpleasantness, yet in the name of truth I must admit that it was with a sentiment of profound disgust that I left this place, after my brother Baba Aroush had fallen in the unhappy war with the Sultan of Telmesan. Honesty compels me to add that I was very greatly cast down by the ingratitude and deceit with which the inhabitants rewarded my efforts to defend them against the unbelievers. A rancorous man in my position might requite evil with evil. But I seek only justice, and have often repaid a wrong with a good action, as I do today in returning to protect you from the enemy. But I note that no one answers me, and not the meanest present has been brought before me

116

in token of your good intentions. Indeed, I fear that I shall again be overcome by repugnance for this town, and find it desirable to depart more swiftly than I came."

The people in alarm began loudly beseeching him not to abandon them to the Spaniards' wrath; many fell upon their knees, strong men wept, and old men tore their beards to demonstrate their loyalty. Gifts proportionate to the means and standing of the givers were hurriedly brought forward, each man being careful to mention his name and his offering, that both might be recorded in the books. And now before the raised seat of the reader there rose a mighty mound of bales, chests, gold and silver vessels, jewels, baskets of fruit, and a quantity of money; even the poorest made shift to offer at least one silver coin. But Khaireddin surveyed the growing heap without enthusiasm; indeed his face darkened, and at last he raised his hand and said, "I knew that the town of Algiers was poor, but I could not have believed it to be as poor as this. In all the heap before me I cannot see one present of the sort that would appeal to me. Not that I made such a present a condition for my return; nevertheless I believed that you would so far have considered my wishes as to remember it."

The congregation were crestfallen indeed at his words, but Abu el-Kasim pinched my arm and together we pushed our way forward to Khaireddin's throne. Abu el-Kasim addressed him, saying, "Poor though I am, I have awaited your coming with eager impatience, O lord of the sea! See, I bring you a good gift which I am persuaded will find favor in your eyes. Nor do I doubt that you will reward me in a fashion worthy of yourself."

The people were accustomed to look upon Abu as a clown; they wondered what this present prank of his might be, and put their hands to their mouths to suppress the burst of laughter they had in readiness. But the smile froze on their lips when, at a sign from Abu, I uncovered the golden dish and he seized Selim's swollen head by the hair, holding it up for Khaireddin and all the rest to see.

Now Selim ben-Hafs had in his time sorely injured Khaireddin, so it was no wonder that he laughed arrogantly at the sight of his enemy's head, and clapping his hands together cried, "You've divined my innermost thoughts, good merchant, and your gift outweighs all the injuries done me in this city, which henceforth shall be my capital. Tell me your name."

117

Abu, grimacing in his excitement, gave his name, and Khaireddin contemplated his enemy's head with rapture. With a sweeping gesture he cried, "Take all this rubbish, Abu el-Kasim my loyal servant, and share as much of it with your slave as you think fit. The givers of these things shall carry them to your house and so appreciate the regard I have for you."

For once Abu el-Kasim stood speechless amid the awed murmur of the throng. Then Khaireddin awoke from his rapture and, with a sideways glance at the great heap, added quickly, "Naturally a tenth must be paid into my treasury, as in the case of prizes captured at sea. And further—"

As by magic Abu el-Kasim regained his speech and sought to drown further retractions by loud cries and the invocation of countless blessings upon the head of Khaireddin, wherein I seconded him with all my might. The ruler began to relent, and stroked his dyed beard. But the Faqih hastily interposed, saying, "Allah blesses the open-handed, and you, Abu el-Kasim, shall carry nothing away until the mosque has received its fifth of the gold and silver and its tenth of all other wares. That the valuation may be fair and impartial, I call upon the foremost merchants of the city to effect it."

Abu's jaw dropped. Looking up reproachfully at Khaireddin he said, "Alas, why did you act with such ostentation, O lord of the sea? You might as easily have given me these things when we were alone together, without witnesses. I could then have decided for myself, according to my own conscience, what my obligations were."

Delight in the misfortunes of others is of all delights the keenest, and Abu el-Kasim's despairing face aroused exultation in the hearts of everyone. He hurled himself madly upon the merchandise and behaved in so eccentric a fashion that not even the great Khaireddin could keep a straight face.

But at length he wearied of it all, and mindful of his dignity he rose and left the mosque attended by his officers, amid the benedictions of the crowd. Outside he distributed liberal alms. Moved by the general rejoicing, the Turkish janissaries began firing salvos with their muskets, while down in the harbor the artillerymen joined in and discharged their cannon until we were deafened, and market place and mosque were enveloped in smoke. Captain de Varga, the Spanish commander, could hardly be blamed for answering the fire, since the guns in the harbor were trained on the fortress and their shot tore holes in the wall of the keep.

I fancied the noise was all salutes and salvos until something crashed into the wall of the mosque. I ran out in a fright, to see the great minaret toppling in a cloud of lime dust. Nothing more fortunate for Khaireddin's purpose could have occurred, for the crowds, filled with righteous indignation, accused the Spaniards with shrieks of deliberately firing upon the mosque.

Captain de Varga himself must have been appalled at what he had done, for the firing soon ceased. But Khaireddin proclaimed in a voice of thunder that this sacrilege should be the last crime committed by Christians in Algiers. For Abu el-Kasim the incident was a gift from heaven, since the merchants were in a hurry to get home, and the Faqih suddenly remembered that it was his hour for solitary meditation. The valuation of the goods was therefore very summarily performed and much to the advantage of Abu el-Kasim, who professed willingness to remain in the mosque all day for the sake of a fair and equitable assessment.

Our house in the street of the spice merchants stood at a relatively sheltered corner, and Abu el-Kasim hastened, not without difficulty, to convey his new possessions home. With the help of a few courageous donkey drivers we at last had everything secured behind bolts and bars.

I began to feel great anxiety about my brother Andy, and wanted to visit the palace and help him in any way I could. At first Abu refused on any account to let me go, saying that the deaf-mute could not be left to guard the treasure alone. But when I mocked him for becoming a slave to his own greed, instead of trusting to Allah as the best watchman, he cursed and swore indeed. Yet he sought out the deaf-mute and, thrusting a cudgel into his hand, ordered him in violent pantomime to stay behind the door and club anyone on the head who tried to enter.

Abu el-Kasim and I then hastened to the palace, and as we went Abu observed, "Great men have short memories. We must put in a word for your brother and try to get in touch with Sinan the Jew. And if we achieve nothing else, we shall at least be invited to a meal at the palace."

We encountered many merchants and sheiks belonging to the most distinguished families in the city. They were coming away from an audience with Khaireddin, and gesticulated excitedly as they discussed what had been said.

On our arrival we were warmly welcomed by Khaireddin, who sat beneath a canopy on Selim's red velvet cushion, surrounded by his most eminent officers, of whom I already knew Sinan the Jew and proud Captain Torgut. A map of Algiers harbor lay outspread at Khaireddin's feet. Pointing to the Spanish fortress and the sandbanks near it he said, "Allah is with us, and I could not have chosen a better moment for the capture of that fortress. It lacks both provisions and powder, the guns are worn, and I have some of my own men there who will do as much damage as they can, and try to convince the Spaniards of the uselessness of resistance. We must waste no time over this little enterprise, for our anchorage is exposed, and the spring victualing flotilla from Cartagena may already have sailed with necessities for the garrison. You shall have eight days in which to effect the capture."

Khaireddin explained to each officer what he had to do, and gave orders for the ships to weigh anchor next morning and bombard the fortress from the sea. The shore battery he put under Torgut's command, since this proud man had risen to his present position from the rank of ordinary gunner. He then commended his officers to Allah's protection and dismissed them, keeping only Sinan at his side. Mustafa ben-Nakir also remained, being too deeply engrossed in the scansion of a new Persian poem to notice that the others had withdrawn. But now he raised his eyes and stared at me with the veiled look of a sleepwalker, then rose and despite my protests undressed me and gave me in exchange the fine kaftan and the Aga's turban that he had been wearing. He resumed his own mendicant dress, and the music of its little bells so greatly inspired him that he was soon deep in composition once more.

I put on the kaftan, but having set the turban upon my head also I quickly removed it and said, "I'm but a slave and have certainly no right to the Aga's turban. By your favor, O lord of the sea, I lay it at your feet. Bestow it upon some worthier man whom your warriors will obey."

Though it was a bitter thing to renounce the plumed and jeweled turban, I thought of the forthcoming siege, and the flaunting of so noticeable and perilous a headdress tempted me not at all. The folds of the kaftan, however, felt unusually thick. As if fate would reward me for my unselfishness, I found two pockets, in each of which was a heavy purse. But I would not expose anyone to temptation by taking them out to examine them. To cap this, Mustafa ben-Nakir contemptuously threw at me my own purse, which I had left in the girdle pocket of his dress, for men of his sect despise money beyond everything.

While I was putting on the kaftan, Sinan the Jew suddenly spoke. "What do I see? Is this not the angel Michael, my slave, whom I lent to Abu el-Kasim, to help him prepare the way for the Deliverer?"

He rose and embraced me warmly, taking care at the same time to feel the stuff of my kaftan; for it was indeed a superb garment, embroidered all over with gold and having gold buttons set with green stones. Abu el-Kasim was pale with envy, but Sinan the Jew turned to Khaireddin and said, "Believe me, Khaireddin, this man who has chosen the right path brings good fortune with him, for he has a singular gift for creeping in and out through the smallest keyhole, and whatever happens to him he falls on his feet, like a cat. With all this he bears ill will to no one, and would have everyone be happy in his own fashion."

Abu el-Kasim broke in hotly, "Don't listen to him, lord of the sea! Michael is the laziest, greediest, most ungrateful man on earth. If he had any sense of what is fitting he would change kaftans with me, for what is he but my slave?"

Khaireddin replied, "That kaftan becomes him better than it would you, and he needs such a one, so I'm told, to win the heart of a certain vain woman. Your secrets I have already learned from Mustafa ben-Nakir here, when he appeared before me as the ear and eye of the High Porte. This, of course, I ought not to have mentioned, and I can't think how it came to slip over my tongue."

Abu el-Kasim was thrown into a great fright by this, and made haste to kiss the ground before Mustafa ben-Nakir, and would have kissed his feet too, if the poet had not kicked him. But I said, "Lord, may your slave address you? While laughter wrinkles are yet radiant about your eyes, let me put in a word for my brother, lying now in fear of death in the dungeon beneath our feet. Let him be fetched and let me speak on his behalf, for he's a foolish, simple man, incapable of arranging words in a seemly manner."

Khaireddin replied, "Not so, let us go ourselves to fetch the notable Antar, of whose strength I have heard such tales. But don't betray me. Let me stand by unknown, and hear what he says when he wakes."

We left Mustafa ben-Nakir to finish his poem and descended to the cellar floor—Khaireddin, Sinan, Abu el-Kasim, and myself. The jailer shoved aside the iron trap door, and each of us in turn was lowered into the cell, where my dog Rael at once greeted me with joyful barks. Andy woke and sat up, holding his head in both hands and staring at us bleary eyed. The water jar was empty and all the bread eaten, and he had indescribably befouled the floor all about him. After glaring at us for some time he asked in a feeble voice, "What's happened? Where am I? Why weren't you with me, Michael, in the hour of my degradation? Only this brute beast witnessed my awakening, and licked my aching head in pity."

He put his hand to his stomach and groaned.

"You may remember," I said hesitantly, "that Sultan Selim ben-Hafs is dead?"

Andy looked blank. Then a spark of intelligence appeared in his round eyes. He looked wildly about and whispered, "I remember it very well. But didn't we agree that it was an accident? Don't tell me the truth has been discovered? Where is the wise Amina? She will explain everything. How could she let them throw me into this cess pit and leave me here stripped and beaten, after all I did for her and the other women?"

"Andy," I said gently, "bear this like a man. I have to tell you that by the will of Allah Amina and her son are dead."

Andy pressed himself against the stone wall, wide-eyed with horror, and exclaimed, "You can't mean that in my drunkenness I was so rough as to kill her? Never, never have I offered violence to any woman." He rocked to and fro with his head in his hands and mourned. "It can't be true, unless the devil bewitched me—for certainly he dwells in the sealed wine jars of this country."

I felt pity for Andy in his anguish, and did my best to console him.

"You never laid a finger on her. She perished otherwise, for her evil-doing, and it will be best to speak no more about it. One thing only you must know. She was a designing woman who deliberately entangled you, and it was she, remember, who tempted you to drink wine and forget your pious resolutions."

He gave a deep sigh of relief, squeezed a few tears from his swollen eyes, and said, "So I'm left a widower. Poor creature! She was in the prime of life, a faithful wife and a fond mother. And we shouldn't speak ill of the dead, though truth to tell she was not altogether free from evil desires. Well, I hope you and all good people may feel for me in my sorrow, and not judge me overstrictly, even though I've sought to drown my troubles in wine and so committed a great deal of foolishness."

He regarded us hopefully, but Abu el-Kasim said with a sigh, "Alas, Antar my slave, you slew the Sultan's Aga and stole his turban. If you've anything to say in your defense, say it now. Otherwise you must be taken before the cadi, and then hanged, quartered, burned, and thrown to the dogs."

Andy flung out his hand and said, "Do with me as you will. I've deserved all these penalties, and should feel the better for losing this aching head. Though indeed I deserve punishment only for the first draught of wine; everything else followed of itself. I killed the Aga as a result of a brawl—a common thing among soldiers—but it was no punishable offense, for we were not then at war, and the articles of war had not been read. I know more about these things than you. Therefore I shall appear before my judge with a clear conscience, and yours will be the shame and not mine if I am sentenced to flogging for such a trifle."

Andy regarded us with an air of great assurance, and seemed persuaded of the justice of his cause. When I had translated his words—for he had spoken in Finnish—Khaireddin could no longer contain himself. Bursting into a shout of laughter he went up and clapped Andy on the shoulder, saying, "You're a man after my own heart, and because of your astute defense I forgive you your crime."

Andy shook off Khaireddin's hand angrily and asked me, "Who's this fellow and what's he doing here? I've had enough of their unseemly pawings."

Aghast at his indiscretion I told him who his visitor was. But Khaireddin took it in good part and said, "I will give you new clothes and a saber. You shall serve me, and I fancy you'll be useful in many ways."

But Andy answered bitterly, "I've been led by the nose long enough, and care nothing for your saber. I shall go out into the wilderness and end my days as a holy hermit. Indeed, if you give me clean clothes and a crust or two to gnaw, you may leave me alone in this hole with a good conscience."

Nevertheless we persuaded him to climb up out of his cell, and while he washed himself in preparation for his long-neglected prayers, Khaireddin sent him fine clothes and so splendid a scimitar that Andy could not resist testing its edge on his nail, after which he buckled it round him with a contented sigh. I then told him all that had happened during his absence, and ended, "You can see for yourself that for once mercy has prevailed over justice. Khaireddin might well have been angry with you for upsetting all the plans that Abu el-Kasim and I had laid with such care during the winter."

But Andy retorted, "If my head didn't ache so damnably I might begin to suspect that I've been basely swindled. By marrying Amina I should have become the most powerful man in Algiers. With luck I might have had a son by her, who would have been sultan here. But you in your blue-eyed innocence have let Khaireddin reap where I have sown, and I'm not at all surprised that he should seek to appease me with a fine saber and an expensive kaftan."

But now I longed more than ever for my own reward, and after we had eaten I asked Abu where Giulia might be. He exchanged glances with Sinan the Jew and sighed, "Allah forgive me if I've done wrong, but the great Khaireddin wanted her to gaze into the sand for him, and so I left them alone together. But that was some time ago, and I begin to wonder what they can be doing."

These words filled me with foreboding, and with a black look at Abu el-Kasim I said, "If anything has happened to Giulia I shall strangle you with my own hands, and I think no one will blame me."

Ignoring the protesting eunuchs we passed through the golden door into the harem, and there we found Khaireddin seated on a mat with a dish of sand before him and beside him, gazing into it, was Giulia. Khaireddin's eyes bulged in amazement, and on seeing us he exclaimed, "This Christian woman has seen the strangest things in the sand. If I told you all, you'd think I was out of my mind; but so much I can say: she beheld the waves of the sea softly kissing my tomb in the city of the great Sultan, on the shores of the Bosphorus. And she vowed that this tomb shall be revered and honored by all, so long as the name of Ottoman survives on earth."

While he was speaking Giulia forgot her feminine modesty and

124

pressed herself against him. But the lord of the sea surveyed her with indifference, and I flared up and said, "Giulia, Giulia! Remember your behavior. And know that from now on you belong to me, as my slave. But if you do your best to please me I may one day take you for my wife."

I could contain myself no. longer, but caught her hands and drew her eagerly toward me to embrace and kiss her to my heart's content. But she struggled like a wildcat until I was forced to release her. Her eyes glittered with fury as she burst out, "Take away this lunatic slave and send him to the mosque hospital, to be thrown in chains and have the madness whipped out of him. Sinan the Jew gave me to the Deliverer, to gaze into the sand for him; I will gladly obey *him* in everything, as soon as he has grown used to my unfortunate eyes."

So intense was her rage that the smile faded from Sinan's face and he mumbled hesitantly, "Allah forgive me, but Michael el-Hakim is right. I swore by the Koran and by my beard that you should be his slave, and I can't break such an oath. You're now his slave, beautiful Delilah, and are bound to obey him in everything. This I declare here and now in the presence of the necessary witnesses."

He repeated the first sura rapidly, to clinch the matter, but when he would have laid Giulia's hand in mine she recoiled, thrust her hands behind her, and gasped in a stifled voice, "Never! Tell me, you black-guards who bargain away a woman's honor behind her back, why is this miserable slave allowed to insult me? Is this the love you swore you felt for me, Abu el-Kasim, with such sighs and lamentations?"

Sinan the Jew and Abu el-Kasim raised their hands with one accord and pointed at me, saying, "No, no, we're innocent! It was Michael who plagued and tormented us into it. And anyhow we were sure that he would fall into the hands of Selim ben-Hafs, and perish long before the Deliverer arrived in the city."

Giulia stared at me incredulously. She came forward and brought her face close to mine and said, pale with fury, "Is this true, Michael? Then I'll give you a foretaste of the joys awaiting you!"

With that she dealt me a resounding box on the ear, which deafened me and brought tears to my eyes. Then she broke into violent weeping, and sobbed, "I can never forgive you for this, Michael. You're like a vicious boy who bites his mother's hand. And what service did *you* render the Deliverer that can merit reward? I, by foretelling the future to the women of the harem, have done more than anyone. Indeed it was I and no one else who by this means slew Selim ben-Hafs as certainly as if I had done it with my own hands."

Thinking that rage had bereft Giulia of reason, I strove to calm her, and begged the others to pay no attention to what she said. But she stamped her foot. Blue and yellow lightnings flashed from her eyes, and she screamed, "*I* chose Amina for the work, because she was the most wanton of all in the harem, and the most ambitious. It was at her orders that the black wrestler came down to the market place to challenge Antar. Everything went as planned and Antar won the match, as I had foretold in my sand gazing. It was through my soothsaying alone that he was enrolled in the palace guard. Then I saw in the sand that Amina's son would be sultan, as indeed it was, though for a very short time. If there's to be a reward for removing Selim ben-Hafs, I am indeed the only one who can fairly claim it."

I listened to her open mouthed, marveling at the skill with which she had played the part of an innocent, while in reality fully aware of the secret plot. She stormed and raved, Abu exclaimed, Andy expostulated, and she sank her teeth in his hand until at length he quelled her with a sharp slap on the hinder parts. By this time Khaireddin was weary of the scene, and ordered me to remove my property and trouble him no longer.

"You've made your bed," he said. "Now lie on it. You have no one to blame but yourself."

There was nothing for it but to go. Hesitantly I held out my hand to Giulia and said, "Don't you understand that I love you, Giulia? It was to win you that I toiled and strove so long, and risked my life."

But Giulia's shoulders were like lead beneath my hand, and she answered sourly, "Don't touch me, Michael, or I won't answer for the consequences. You've wounded me deeply."

We set off for home, the dog slinking behind us with his nose to the ground. When we came to the door of our house I put the key into the lock, but it jammed, and struggle as I would I could not turn it. At last in a rage I forced the door and tumbled inside. The dog yelped with fright and a cudgel came down on my head with such violence that all went black and I knew no more until next morning. Giulia and the deaf-mute carried me to bed; it was this blockhead, faithful to his charge, who had dealt the blow. He had felt me tugging and rattling at the door, and in the darkness mistook me for a thief.

Such was my bridal night, and I have no more to say of it. I will therefore begin a new book to tell of how I captured the Spanish fortress, and how a notion of Mustafa ben-Nakir's led to my entering the service of the ruler of all the faithful—the great Sultan in Constantinople.

BOOK 3.

Giulia

I CAME to my senses in a soft bed, and was aware of a continuous din as of thunder that shook the room and caused cups and dishes to rattle together. At first I thought the noise came from my own aching head, and I wondered where I was. I seemed to see two angels, a white one on my right hand and a black one on my left, both engaged in recording my good and evil deeds in their books. But the white angel had seemingly little to write, while the black one was so busy that his head wagged with the exertion. I besought them in piteous tones to bring water that I might wash myself and say my prayers. The room vibrated to renewed thunder, but just then my dear dog jumped up onto my chest and licked my face. With tears in my eyes I said, *"Bismillah* and *inshallah!* Allah is merciful indeed to allow my dog to keep me company in hell. Rael is many times more deserving of Paradise than I am, but I know he would turn his back upon it to follow me into the abyss."

The white angel lifted my head, causing such acute pain that the scales fell from my eyes and I saw that I lay in Giulia's bed. Giulia herself was anxiously bending over me. To my left sat the deaf-mute, mixing eggs and honey together into a paste. Ashamed of my distracted fancies I said sharply, "Leave my head alone, Giulia. If it has not already split it soon will." I pushed away the dog pettishly and asked what the noise was, and whether Giulia had hit me on the head the night before. Giulia wept and stroked my cheek.

"Ah, Michael, are you really alive? Although I was angry with you I don't want you to die. The noise you hear is gunfire; the Moslems

131

are besieging the Spanish fortress. And it was not I who struck you, but this faithful slave."

I felt my head cautiously and found it still upon my shoulders, though because of the many bandages it felt twice its usual size. I sighed feebly and whispered, "Giulia, send at once for a cadi and four witnesses. Take the purse from my kaftan and pay them, and keep the remainder for yourself. My intentions weren't so base as you supposed; I never wanted you as a slave, though I said so to tease you. I meant to send for a cadi and the necessary witnesses and give you your freedom; that was why I claimed you in reward for my services. It seemed the only way to set you free."

I hardly know whether this was the truth. Perhaps it only came into my head when I regained consciousness. Yet I had toyed with the idea before, so it seemed natural to me. But Giulia, thunderstruck, stared at me blankly and stammered, "I don't understand you, Michael. If you give me my freedom you can no longer force me to obey you. I thought you wanted to possess me, but now I'm at a loss to know what it is you do want."

I was already repenting of my excessive benevolence, and retorted angrily, "Nonsense, Giulia! If I set you free, it's to be rid of your incessant nagging. I always meant to let you choose whether to stay with me or go. I'm not such a fool as to try and force you to love me. And just now you seem to me about as seductive as an old shoe. Praise be to Allah, my love is quenched!"

Giulia stood weighing the purse in her hand and staring, shaken now and then by a sob. The deaf-mute made desperate attempts to feed me with the mixture of eggs and honey, and though it revolted me I forced myself to swallow it. In a gentler tone I said, "Why so doubtful, Giulia? Why are you sniveling? Aren't you glad to be rid of me so easily? It has always been your dearest wish."

She answered crossly, "I am not sniveling. My nose tickles." But next moment she burst into wild weeping and cried, "You must still be delirious and I'm not so base as to take advantage of that, though you seem always to expect the worst from me. Where should I go in this heathen country, and who would protect my innocence? No, Michael, you may think to revenge yourself in this way, but you shan't be rid of me so easily."

I threw out my hands helplessly and said, "Whatever I propose seems wrong and I shall never please you. At least leave me alone now,

132

for my head's going round and round and this egg mess has made me queasy. Stay if you want to; go if it suits you better. I care nothing either way while my head aches so atrociously."

With this Giulia was content, and to her credit be it said that she nursed me well and silently, and moved about the room as quietly as she could. Yet it was of little help to me, for the guns roared incessantly, sand sifted through the cracks in the roof into my eyes, and the whole room shook. After the noon prayer Abu el-Kasim and Sinan the Jew could no longer master their curiosity and they paid me a visit, bringing wedding presents with them. When Abu el-Kasim saw me lying pallid and bandaged in Giulia's bed he struck his hands together and exclaimed, "What is this, Michael el-Hakim? Was it so hard to tame the woman? I could never have believed that one night in her company could reduce you to so pitiful a condition."

Sinan the Jew remarked that with so fiery a creature beside me I should need no other wives, and life would be cheap for me. I had no strength to reply to their sallies, but lay there silent. When Abu el-Kasim learned what had really happened he was genuinely concerned. He examined me and mixed me a strengthening medicine, and I soon fell into a pleasant sleep, to awake later much refreshed.

My first thought was for Andy, and when I asked after him, Abu el-Kasim tore his beard and cried, "The curse of Allah on your stupidity, Michael el-Hakim! Why did you never so much as hint that your brother's a trained artilleryman and can even cast cannon? This important fact was discovered quite by chance; for today when he heard the sound of firing he went down to the shore to cure his headache—so he said—with the wholesome smell of gunpowder. There Khaireddin saw him thrust aside our men and lay the guns himself, soon displaying his skill by shooting the Castilian flag from the tower, to the fury of the Spaniards. Khaireddin gave him the turban of a master gunner and ten gold pieces, and I fancy he'll soon have sweated the poisons from his wine-sodden body."

I was horrified to hear of Andy firing on his Christian brothers. Later, when the bombardment ceased for the noon prayer, he came to see me and his face was blackened with powder. I rebuked him for what he was doing, but he answered, "Guns are my music, and I ought never to have left them. You mustn't scold me for returning to my proper trade like the shoemaker to his last, as they used to say in Rome."

"But my dear Andy, how can you bring yourself to fire on men redeemed by the blood of Christ—men who are doing their utmost under extreme difficulties to serve the Emperor under whose colors you yourself have fought?"

Andy replied, "Remember I bear a grudge against the Spaniards. In Rome they behaved more like wild beasts than men, and I needn't remind you of their treatment of women. Not even Moslems would do as they did."

"But they're Christians! How can you bear arms against them with Mussulmans, when in your heart you're not a Moslem at all?"

Andy glared at me angrily and said, "I'm as good a Moslem as you are, Michael, even if I don't know as much of the Koran by heart. But the whole matter was clear to me when I discovered that Islam means submission to the will of God, and that the God called Allah is the same as the Frenchmen's *sang dieu,* the Germans' *Herrgott* or *Donnerwetter* and the Latins' *Deus* or *Dominus.*"

My reproaches rolled off him like water off a duck's back. He insisted that guns were his music and that pay was pay whether the coins bore the Emperor's head or an Arabic flourish. He sat in thought for a time with his head on his hand, and when he spoke again it was on a note of tenderness.

"I never knew how fond I was of guns until I smelled the hot metal again, and the stinging smoke. I couldn't help stroking them—and believe me, not the most opulent woman can compare with the burning touch of a cannon after the fifth shot. When Mustafa ben-Nakir saw my eagerness he told me that the Sultan of Turkey had found a new way of transporting even the heaviest pieces; where the roads are bad he loads gun metal onto camels, so that the cannon can be cast at the place where they're to be used. No one has ever thought of doing that before, and I should like to see for myself how they manage it. Mustafa couldn't tell me, but his account made me long to visit Istanbul, the Sultan's capital. And he has promised to recommend me to the artillery commander there."

I was staggered by these wild projects, but he continued eagerly, "First we have to build a breakwater for Khaireddin, so that his ships can find shelter in the harbor. His only reason for attacking the fortress is to get ready-hewn stone for the breakwater, and cheap labor. Prisoners of war get no pay, and crusts and water suffice to feed them."

So he babbled on until he became aware of his own garrulity and bent to stroke my dog in embarrassment.

After a few days my strength was fully restored, though I was prompt in taking to my bed again when I saw anyone coming. I felt not the smallest desire to become involved in the siege and perhaps be brought face to face with Captain de Varga, who would certainly have a bone to pick with me. Abu el-Kasim told me that immediately after my visit, de Varga had sent a fast-sailing sloop to Cartagena; therefore Khaireddin was making ready to storm the fortress at once, taking into his service all who could stand on their feet and who desired to win Paradise without delay by falling in battle against the unbeliever.

Nevertheless Khaireddin's plans had been impeded by Captain de Varga who, despite the Dominican's protests, hanged the two young Moors whom Khaireddin had smuggled in as spies. We learned this from a Spanish traitor who had had enough of the siege and came swimming across the bay one dark night to join Khaireddin's men. He told us that there were many wounded in the fortress, that the walls were badly cracked, that the Spaniards lacked food, water, and powder, and that all except de Varga were willing to negotiate for permission to leave unmolested. But de Varga would not hear of this and when the Castilian standard was shot away he himself stood as a living flagstaff at the top of the tower, with the flag wound about his left arm, and proclaimed that anyone daring to whisper of submission should instantly be put in irons.

A few days later, however, a promising breach was made in the walls, and Khaireddin ordered his men to lash boats together into rafts, with gabions at their bows for cover. He then retired to pass the night in solitary prayer and fasting, in preparation for the decisive assault.

After the evening prayer, Andy, Abu el-Kasim, and Mustafa ben-Nakir assembled at my bedside. When we had conversed for a time on general topics they gently but firmly dragged me out of bed, set me on my feet, felt my head and limbs, and praised Allah for favoring me with so speedy a recovery. Mustafa ben-Nakir said, "Ah, Michael, how glad I am, for now you can take part in the attack and with us make yourself worthy of Paradise!"

My knees failed me and I should have fallen had it not been for Andy's powerful arms.

135

"Alas!" I cried, "I'm dizzy—I can't stand. But with the remnant of my strength I will crawl to the shore and tend the wounded. It would be deplorable indeed were the faithful to bleed to death because of Abu el-Kasim's ineptitude. I won't even claim a fee for my labor of mercy, but will content myself with what is offered me."

Mustafa ben-Nakir looked at me with shining eyes and said, "You're surely not afraid? Your brother Antar and I have resolved to board the leading craft; we shall be the first to scale the walls and tear the Castilian flag from Captain de Varga's hands. For friendship's sake we'll take you with us, to share the glory and the reward of our exploit."

I retorted testily, "Afraid? And what is that? An empty word. I'm a peaceable man, and a sick one, with no ambition to be hailed as a hero."

Giulia had been standing behind a curtain, listening to the conversation in silence. Seeing me sway upon my feet, she stepped forward and helped me to lie down again upon the bed.

"Why do you pester him?" she demanded. "I'll never let him go to that terrible island. He has been too weak even for love. I'd take a sword in my own hand rather than see him do it."

This speech offended me for some reason, and I snapped, "Hold your tongue; you weren't consulted. It's easier to inflict wounds than to heal them, and perhaps after all I'll join you tomorrow."

Mustafa ben-Nakir's jaw dropped and I saw he had only been teasing me, as his habit was, because he thought me a weakling. Nothing could have annoyed me more than such a notion. Caution is not cowardice and in the course of my life I had shown often enough that I could take as many and as desperate risks as anyone. But Giulia's behavior had irritated me, and the blow on my head so clouded my judgment that in stubborn idiocy I vowed that I was quite recovered and fit to go into battle. When the others had gone it was evident that she wanted to make it up with me, but I hardened my heart to punish her, and once and for all to subdue her vanity. I feigned indifference to her pleading, so that at last she gave up the attempt and vented her anger on the pots and pans, assuring me that I was the greatest liar she had ever met and that she believed not one word I told her.

Yet she was frightened enough next morning when long before dawn I rose, washed myself in the courtyard, and with my face to the east recited the prescribed prayers. In further token of my valor I grasped a sturdy cudgel before staggering on trembling legs into the street. Only then did she see that I was in earnest; she rushed after me, seized my sleeve and cried, "Ah, Michael! Perhaps I've been unkind, and proud, but I had reasons that my modesty forbade me to mention. If by a miracle you return from the battle I'll tell you my secret, and you shall decide how to act. But if we should meet only in heaven—and even that seems unlikely, since you're a Moslem and I'm a Christian—the secret will have little importance. So I won't cry it aloud in the street for all to hear; it would only distress you at such a moment as this."

I believed she had no such secret and was merely trying to arouse my curiosity and so detain me until I was too late to take part in the attack. So I tore myself free and hurried down to the harbor. But Giulia was not the only woman to beg her man to stay at home that day, and with sighs and sobs assure him that an honest, profitable trade was greatly to be preferred to the joys of Paradise.

I reached the harbor at sunrise when Khaireddin, surrounded by his officers, was giving his final orders.

"Today is Friday, a lucky day. May it bring joy and profit to Islam. Today the hundred gates of Paradise stand wide open; never has there been a better opportunity to enter those glorious realms where dark-eyed virgins wait upon the faithful amid rippling water brooks. Gird on my sword, for I mean as usual to be in the forefront, and by example encourage even the fearful to follow me boldly through the breach."

As if by order his officers began to exclaim and wring their hands, among the most animated being Sinan the Jew and Abu el-Kasim. They strongly opposed Khaireddin in his resolve to expose himself to danger, reminding him of the irreparable loss his death would mean to Islam. But he stamped with fury and cried, "O disobedient and unnatural children! Would you deny me this honor? Why should I alone be forced to abstain from Paradise, which now stands open to the poorest Moslem?"

He rushed back and forth shouting for his sword, and the captains had to catch and hold him by the arms lest he tumble headlong into the water. By this time the enthusiasm among the people knew no bounds; they shouted his name and praised his valor, exhorting him at the same time not to imperil his priceless life. At length he was compelled to resign himself, and said with a deep sigh, "Well, I will stay here among you, since you beg me so importunately. But I shall

137

watch the assault, and will afterward reward the valiant and punish the cowardly. It remains only to choose a leader. No doubt you will race one another to the island, yet custom requires that one shall be chosen beforehand to lead the force into the breach."

The officers at once fell silent and looked askance at the fortress that rose from the water a bowshot from land; their eyes rested with distaste on the gap in the wall, black as the mouth of hell. They turned pale and whispered among themselves, saying, "The offer is indeed tempting, but I'm unfit for such an honor. You're older than I am and I resign in your favor."

While they were yet busied with these affectations, Andy stepped forward and said, "My lord Khaireddin, let me lead the assault and bring you back the Castilian flag!"

I limped forward to protest, but before I could explain to our commander that Andy must be out of his mind, Khaireddin stretched out his hand toward me and shouted, "See, good people! Take these men as your pattern! It is but a little time since they found the true path, yet all the keener is their longing for Paradise. I cannot deny you the honor you beg of me, el-Hakim; go with your brother. You shall be the first to set foot on the rock of Penjon, and I shall know how to reward you."

I tried to tell him that he had quite misunderstood me, but my terrified stammer was drowned in the acclamations of the officers.

Meanwhile Khaireddin's fleet had sailed from its anchorage further along the coast, and now began a bombardment to distract the garrison's attention from what was happening on land. Soon the shore batteries also opened fire, and the thoughtful Andy urged me to put on armor. I reflected for a little and then said, "Nothing happens save by the will of Allah. A good sword is enough for me. Go first, Andy my brother; I will follow at your heels and do my best to protect you in the rear."

Mustafa ben-Nakir looked at me dubiously and said, "You're right, Michael el-Hakim; if we were to fall overboard in full armor we should sink like stones. I shall take off my lion skin lest I lose it in the struggle, and be the third man of your party, trusting that your brother's massive body will protect us from the worst unpleasantness."

We then stepped aboard the leading raft and took cover behind gabions stuffed with earth and wool. A crowd of stouthearted men followed us, and the rowers dipped their oars and began pulling for

138

dear life toward the fortress, loudly invoking Allah's help and cursing the Spaniards.

All went well, and few shots greeted us from the scarred embrasures of the fortress. Should I ever be suspected of exaggeration or boastfulness, let me say here and now that no better opportunity than the present ever occurred; nevertheless I shall confine myself to relating what really happened, and must therefore admit that the capture of Penjon cannot be numbered among the heroic deeds of history. On this occasion virtue was its own reward, and I won a reputation for valor and audacity without being exposed to any particular danger.

A few roundshot sang over our heads and threw up fountains of water as they fell into the sea astern. Shortly afterward our bows grounded on the shore with a jar that knocked me backward. Andy hauled me up by the scruff of the neck and dragged me ashore, with Mustafa ben-Nakir close behind, and we made a mad dash for the breach. I had little time for reflection, and when at last I looked up we were already halfway through the gap; before us in bright armor and with the Castilian flag wound about his left arm stood Captain de Varga, brandishing a sword and ready to give the last drop of his blood in defense of the stronghold. He stood alone, for his men, to their undying shame, had deserted him. Hunger and despair cannot excuse them, though for my own part I had no complaint to make of their prudent behavior.

Captain de Varga, then, stood before us alone, a haggard, swarthy figure. He glared at us with burning eyes, and there was froth at his lips. Andy, astonished, lowered his sword and called to him to surrender. But Captain de Varga laughed and shouted back, "I won't rehearse my lineage to you, for a de Varga does not boast; but I'll show you what is meant by loyalty to God, king, and country."

In our rear more boats and rafts were being beached, and when the brave Moslems saw that one man alone was defending the breach they rushed up in a dense mob and swept me along with them, so that I lost my footing. I believe it was Andy who struck the sword from de Varga's hand, and the next moment the Captain was lying on his back with me on top of him. Notwithstanding his noble lineage, notwithstanding the protection my body afforded him against the wild Moslems who lay over me in a kicking, struggling heap, he so far forgot himself as to sink his long teeth in my cheek.

De Varga would certainly have lost his life then and there if he had not been clad from head to foot in iron, for pain and fury so maddened me that I would have seized the first opportunity to drive my sword into his throat. But gradually the pressure lightened; the Captain let go of my cheek, and we both sat up to see the Moslems pour in a howling flood through the breach. Andy braced himself with feet apart in front of de Varga, and Mustafa ben-Nakir also helped us to defend him. Blood was streaming down my cheek and I bitterly reproached the Captain for conduct so unbecoming to a nobleman, pointing out that I should most probably carry a disfiguring scar to my life's end.

Seeing that further resistance was useless he collapsed in tears and begged me to bear no malice. In return I asked him to surrender the Castilian flag, for which he could have no further use. Sighing deeply he unwound it from his arm and laid it in my hands. To me, therefore, fell the honor for the capture of Penjon.

Meanwhile the Moslems had been streaming past us through the breach in such numbers that the courtyard was soon crammed, and in their frenzy they slew a number of Spaniards before Khaireddin's officers and janissaries could intervene. Khaireddin had given strict orders that as many Spaniards as possible should be spared, for he stood in great need of labor for demolition and building works, and for repairs to buildings damaged in the street fighting and bombardment. The savage bloodlust of the Mussulmans so revolted me that I longed to get away, and Andy too was fidgeting. We therefore resolved to embark and bring Captain de Varga before Khaireddin.

Khaireddin, attended by a numerous suite, was waiting on the shore. Many foolish Moslems had hastened up to him and thrown the heads of unbelievers at his feet. At last he lost his temper and shouted, "A hundred lashes to the next man who dares bring me a Christian head. Spaniards are sturdy fellows and every head leaves me the poorer."

But he soon forgot his wrath when Andy, Mustafa ben-Nakir, and I approached him, thrusting Captain de Varga before us. Blood was still running from the wound in my cheek as I threw the Castilian standard at the feet of Khaireddin. He trod it eagerly underfoot, exclaiming piously, "Allah is great, and marvelous is the might of Islam, that transforms a lamb into a ravening lion."

Turning to Captain de Varga he said curtly, "Wicked and obstinate man, where is your king and the help you were expecting from Spain? Will you confess now, idolater, that Allah alone is mighty?"

Captain de Varga answered, "You have only my men's treachery to thank for victory. Given the smallest support I would have driven you from the city and occupied the harbor."

Khaireddin surveyed him for a time, stroking his beard. He could not but admire the inflexible spirit of his enemy, and said, "Ah, Captain de Varga! Had I such men as you beside me, I could certainly drive the Emperor from his throne. Tell me what I can do for you, for I desire your friendship."

Captain de Varga replied, "Brave men always understand one another, and that is something that cowards can never grasp."

"There are many mussel shells in the world," remarked Khaireddin, "but few contain pearls. Even rarer is a truly brave man. Therefore I'm willing to bestow riches on you and even place you in command, on one condition—that you take the turban and acknowledge that the one God and his Prophet are worth more than Christian idolatry. You'd not be the first Spaniard to take this step, as you may see for yourself by glancing at my officers."

Captain de Varga was outraged, and stared at his adversary for some time; his beard quivered and his eyes glowed when at last he replied, "Were I false to my faith I should be worse than the worst of my betrayers. Do not insult me with such proposals, and remember that I am a Spaniard and a gentleman."

Khaireddin sighed. "I have no wish to coerce you, for Islam forbids forcible conversion. But you're too dangerous a man to let loose among the other prisoners, and I shall be unhappily compelled to behead you if you refuse the turban."

Captain de Varga crossed himself meekly and said, "I'm a de Varga; may my ancestors never have cause to be ashamed of their kinsman. Strike quickly, then, that I may show myself worthy of my God, my king, and my country."

He said a few prayers, crossed himself, and knelt down upon the sand. The executioner took off his head at one stroke, and expressed admiration for his noble behavior. He then threaded a leather thong through the ears and suspended the head from the bridle of Khaireddin's horse.

Thus the siege of Penjon was accomplished, long before the muezzin had called the faithful to the noon prayer. For my own part I could not sufficiently thank my lucky star for protecting me from all danger and covering me with glory.

Later, when I started to walk home, Mustafa ben-Nakir came with me, absently twirling the bells of his girdle. The deaf-mute was preparing food when we arrived, while Giulia sat on the bed painting her toenails. She paid us little attention, from which I concluded that she had been down to the harbor to spy upon us and had seen me there unhurt in Khaireddin's company.

"Oh, is it you, Michael?" she exclaimed in feigned surprise. "I hardly expected you so soon. And where can you have been, I wonder? While the faithful were waging their holy war you were no doubt dallying in some harem, for you appear to have been somewhat passionately kissed."

Mustafa ben-Nakir said, "Delilah, I appreciate that with a veil you couldn't perform your present important task. But remember that I find the temptation of your eyes very hard to withstand. I beg you to leave us. My friend Michael and I have much to talk of; if you have a spark of pity in your cruel heart, don't allow that mad slave to poison us with the garbage he's preparing, but cook something for us with your own fair hands."

So he flattered Giulia and at the same time taught me how one should speak to women when one wants something from them. When Giulia had put away her toilet box and left us, Mustafa ben-Nakir drew forth his Persian book and began to read aloud. But I was weary of his whimsical ways and busied myself with dressing the wound in my cheek. At last he laid aside his book and said, "You surprise me, Michael el-Hakim. I hardly know what to make of you. I wonder whether after all you're a little simple? I can find no other explanation of your foolhardy behavior."

"Perhaps like you, Mustafa, I allow myself to be ruled by impulse at times. Ask me no questions about today's doings. Truth to tell I hardly know why I acted as I did, unless it was to show Giulia that I take no orders from her."

Mustafa ben-Nakir nodded. "We'll talk of Giulia later. You need not part with her: she shall go with you. Perhaps you know that for years Khaireddin has been out of favor with the High Porte. He and his brother are thought to have made illicit use of the ships and janissaries sent by the Sultan to Baba Aroush. There may be some truth in this, but since then Khaireddin has thought better of it. This summer he means to strengthen and consolidate his power; but in the autumn his ambassador is to sail for Istanbul with rich presents for the Sultan, to claim confirmation of Khaireddin's appointment as beylerbey of Algeria. After this Khaireddin will again place himself under the protection of the High Porte. Besides gifts, the envoy will take many slaves to the Sultan, including yourself, Michael el-Hakim, your brother Antar, and your own slave, Delilah, whom you call Giulia."

"Allah is great," I said bitterly. "Is this the recompense for all I have done—to be led once more by the nose into the unknown, like a ringed ox?"

Mustafa ben-Nakir was shocked. "How ungrateful you are, Michael el-Hakim! Another man would fall and kiss the ground at my feet in thankfulness. You cannot know that the most powerful men in the Ottoman Empire, from the Grand Vizier downward, are all slaves of the Sultan. Most of them were brought up in the Seraglio and have advanced, each according to his talents, to the most responsible positions. The very highest officials are subordinate to one or other of the Sultan's slaves. To be a slave of his is therefore an aim worthy of the most ambitious; if he succeeds there is no limit to what he can do."

"Many thanks!" I said with irony, though I had listened attentively to what he told me. "But I'm not in the least ambitious, and I feel that the higher a slave may climb toward the pinnacles of power, the more terrible will be his fall."

"You're right, Michael," Mustafa admitted. "Yet even on a level floor a man may stumble. And climbing is difficult; it demands experience and practice. There's more to it than merely scrambling upward. One must also shake off and kick away those who climb after—those who tug at one's cloak and try in every way to drag one down. But climbing strengthens a man and forms part of that wise statecraft which the sultans inherited from the emperors of Byzantium. Remember that the Ottomans have always been ready to adopt whatever is useful and practical, from any nation. Only the shrewdest and most resourceful man can attain the heights of power in the Seraglio, where everyone spies on his neighbor and tries to trip him up. Yet the disadvantages of the system are outweighed by the element of chance. All advancement depends ultimately on the Sultan's favor, which may be won as easily by the humblest woodcutter as by the most powerful vizier."

A chill stole over me.

"Who and what are you, Mustafa ben-Nakir?" I asked.

His brilliant dark eyes rested upon me as he answered, "Haven't I told you many times that I'm just a wandering mendicant? But my brotherhood has powerful patrons. We see much in the course of our journeys and it's easier for us to feel pulses and search hearts than it is for the green-clad agents of the High Porte. Thus in following my own whims I serve my lord the Sultan—or rather his Grand Vizier Ibrahim Pasha, who in our brotherhood holds the same position as does the Grand Master in the Christian Order of the Knights Templars. This is a closely guarded secret which I impart to show my trust in you and to explain why I send you to the Seraglio as the Sultan's slave."

He rose, stepped noiselessly to the doorway, and, quickly drawing aside the curtain, seized Giulia by the hair so that she fell forward into the room. Smoothing her hair again she said in injured tones, "That was very vulgar of you. I was simply coming to find out whether you would like Italian vegetable sauce with your chicken. But you're on no account to drag Michael into your intrigues, for he's very credulous and would soon become hopelessly entangled. The matter concerns me too. Do you mean to send me to the Sultan's harem? I hear he's a morose man who seldom seeks the society of women. You'd better let me know your plans, or I might put a spoke in your wheel when I enter the Seraglio."

Mustafa ben-Nakir had no doubt guessed that Giulia was eavesdropping, for he now went on as if nothing had happened, "Sultan Suleiman, whose empire comprises all races and tongues, is indeed a morose, brooding man, who favors justice rather than violence and lawlessness. But as a counterweight to his somber nature he likes to have smiling faces about him, and people who can lighten his mood. The Grand Vizier is about the same age; he's the son of a Greek sailor, and as a boy was taken from his home and sold to a Turkish widow. She soon discovered his talents and gave him a good education. He's versed in law, speaks many languages, has studied history and geography, and is an excellent performer on that Italian instrument, the violin. Above all, he has won the Sultan's friendship and favor to such an extent that Suleiman cannot be without him for a day, and often spends the night too in the Grand Vizier's bedchamber. The Sultan met him when he was still a young man, in a provincial town whither the stern Selim had sent his son as governor, away from the intrigues of the Seraglio. When Suleiman ascended the throne he set Ibrahim in command of the palace falconers. Four years later he appointed him grand vizier and arranged his marriage with a Turkish princess, whom he elevated, after the death of her parents, to the rank and dignity of his own sister."

Giulia broke in, "Such exaggerated friendship between men is strange indeed. Even if they spend their days together they ought at least to be parted at night, and I should have thought that of all people the Sultan had ample opportunity to find a more natural bedfellow."

Mustafa ben-Nakir smiled, and looking at Giulia with his shining eyes he said, "In friendship between men there's much that women cannot understand or approve. But in this case you need harbor no ugly suspicions, for Sultan Suleiman is a great admirer of lovely women and has several sons, of whom the eldest, Kaiman Mustafa, was born of a marvelously beautiful Circassian known as the Rose of Spring. But she was a tiresome creature and her place has long been taken by a Russian girl whom the Tartars of Crim sent to Istanbul. Her gaiety won her the name of Khurrem, the Laughing One. She has borne sons to Suleiman, and her merry laughter dispels his melancholy whenever Ibrahim is engaged with affairs of state. The Sultan's happiness, therefore, is complete, since he has a good friend and a loving wife; and I see no reason to send you to the harem to compete with Khurrem for his favor. Khurrem is an excitable, ill-bred woman, and you might not emerge unscathed from the encounter. But the harem will certainly have room for a good soothsayer, and by your arts you could agreeably entertain its jaded inmates."

Giulia was satisfied, and Mustafa ben-Nakir continued, "I forgot to mention that with this embassy will travel also a rich drug merchant named Abu el-Kasim. No doubt he'll open a shop in Istanbul, and if you work for him your fame may well penetrate the walls of the harem. Michael el-Hakim can't begin to compete with the celebrated court physicians until his beard has grown longer. But his knowledge of languages and of the states and kingdoms of Christendom may be of great service to the cartographers, whose task is to gather information about Christian countries."

"But why all this?" I asked. "You still have not explained."

"No? Well, I might use fine phrases and say that it is for the good of Islam and the Ottoman Empire. The Turks are not mariners, but Ibrahim, the son of a sailor, grew up among ships and hopes to see the Sultan lord of oceans as well as lands. In these plans Khaireddin plays

145

an important part. The Grand Vizier has lost faith in the Sultan's sea pashas; Khaireddin is the only true seaman. So the way is to be made smooth for him and only good is to be spoken of him in the Seraglio; his name and reputation must be exalted there, his victories painted in glowing colors, and any defeats explained away. Most important of all, Khaireddin must owe promotion solely to the Grand Vizier. You too must remember that in furthering Khaireddin's cause with the cartographers, you serve Ibrahim. To him and to him only must you show gratitude, if ever you attain to a post of honor."

"What you say is strange and disquieting," I remarked. "Shall I not also be serving the Sultan?"

"Of course, of course," returned Mustafa impatiently. "The Grand Vizier's power derives from the Sultan, and anything that serves to strengthen Ibrahim's position must ultimately be of profit to the Sultan. But the Grand Vizier can't fill the Seraglio with slaves of his own choosing, as this might give rise to base suspicions. Whereas if Khaireddin sends you and your brother and other useful slaves to the Seraglio, no one can suspect them of being secretly at Ibrahim's orders. His power exposes him to envy, as you can understand, and for his own sake he must weave a stout net to catch him were he to fall, and toss him up again to even greater eminence."

Mustafa ben-Nakir was silent for a little before continuing, "We're weavers, Michael el-Hakim, weaving a huge carpet. Each of us has his own thread and his own part in the great pattern. The whole pattern—the world-picture—we do not see; but it is there. Single threads may snap, colors may be clouded, and the individual weaver may fail in his task; yet the great overseer has the great pattern ever before his eyes and corrects the petty errors. You, too, Michael, shall be a weaver; then all your thoughts and actions will have purpose. You'll be fulfilling your task within the great framework, and your life, hitherto so empty, will be filled with meaning."

"If you allude to Allah's carpet of eternity," I said, "then I'm already a weaver, whether I like it or not. But if you mean Grand Vizier Ibrahim's carpet, woven on the Sultan's behalf, then I fear it's too bloodstained to appeal to a sensitive heart. I also fear that it will be very clumsily cobbled together, and prove useless."

"Allah's will be done," returned Mustafa suavely. "Remember you're a slave, Michael el-Hakim, and *must* weave, with or without your good will. Life is a game—a strange one—and once we realize this our task is easier to fulfill; for all games come to an end. The fairest flowers fade, the most melodious song must sooner or later die away. What matter, my friend, whether your beard grows long in the service of the Seraglio, or whether in the flower of youth you're gathered into the arms of eternal night?"

Giulia who had been listening patiently, now rose and said, "At the baths I've heard women all shrieking at once until I couldn't hear myself speak, but even their cackle had more sense in it than the big, empty words of men. Here you sit spinning phrases about weavers and rulers and Michael's beard, while all the time the fowls are stewing to rags in the pot."

She brought us the good food and filled Abu el-Kasim's most valuable goblet with spiced wine, saying, "Your religion of course forbids you to drink, but after all the soul-shaking talk I need something reviving."

The sight of her white arms made me quite limp, and the wound in my cheek was very painful, and so I begged her earnestly to pour wine for me, too, as I was not yet circumcised and therefore not wholly bound by the law. Mustafa ben-Nakir smiled mysteriously and declared that his sect also was untrammeled by the letter of the Koran.

When we had finished the sweetmeats and fruit that brought the meal to an end, we went on drinking until Giulia became slightly affected. A deeper red colored her cheeks, and as if by chance she laid an arm about my neck and stroked me with her soft finger tips.

"Mustafa ben-Nakir," she said. "You know the art of poetry and perhaps also the secrets of women's hearts better than Michael does. Tell me what I must do, for Michael has long desired me and I'm his defenseless slave. Hitherto I've resisted him because of a secret which I would not divulge. But wine has softened my heart and I beg you, Mustafa ben-Nakir, not to leave us alone together, but tell me what I must do to protect my innocence."

Mustafa ben-Nakir replied, "I've not the least regard for your virtue, false Delilah, and feel only pity for poor, sick Michael; for you would never ask my advice unless you'd already made up your mind."

He rose to leave us, but Giulia, genuinely troubled, caught him by the girdle and said, "Don't go, Mustafa ben-Nakir! Help us to a reconciliation. My purpose was to make Michael too drunk even to see me, far less discover my secret. But it would have been better if he'd whipped me long ago, for then I might have given way to him even though I bore him ill will."

With this she threw herself at my feet, crying aloud and weeping and imploring forgiveness. I suspected mischief, but I tried to lift her up and calm her. She wept the more bitterly until Mustafa ben-Nakir said impatiently, "Cease your howling, Delilah, for you have nothing in your heart but falsehood and deceit. What is more painful and pointless than these intimate revelations? The relationship between men and women would be incomparably happier if each party kept his own mistakes and secrets to himself."

Giulia dried her eyes, raised her tear-stained face, and said, "Michael prefers it so, though perhaps he won't admit it. And for some unknown reason I can't lie to him with my body. Perhaps it is that I really love him; if so I love for the first time in my life, and so passionately that I'm afraid. What devil's spell is it that has bound me to this foolish, credulous man, so that even to look into his trusting face makes me loathe myself? It's like snatching a pretty toy from a child."

I could hardly believe my ears; yet of all her words I heeded only those which told of her love for me, and I could not understand why she had always treated me so badly. I cried out to her to hold her peace. Ah, would that she had! But wine had clouded her judgment, and she said, "Michael, beloved Michael! Forgive me, but I'm not the innocent you suppose and I cannot think how you got such an idea into your head."

"Oh, God help me! How came you to lose your virtue? Haven't I always tried to shield you from assaults upon it?"

I felt as if I had been kicked on the jaw. Giulia twisted her slender fingers together and went on, "I'm not even as young as you think me; I was twenty-five some time ago—nearly as old as you. I've been married twice, though each time to an old man. The first time was by my mother's wish; I was only fourteen, but my eyes so horrified my husband that he died of a stroke on our wedding night. My second husband also died so suddenly that I was compelled to sail for the Holy Land, meaning to take refuge with a distant relative in Acre and escape from the foul suspicions that were cast upon me. It was on that voyage that you met me, for I had bribed the captain to take me aboard without the knowledge of the Venetian authorities."

All this came upon me so suddenly that I could not at first grasp the full implications of what she said, and I stammered, "But when we

148

met you gave me to understand that you were still innocent. Why?"

"Never, never did I claim to be a virgin. But when on the island of Cerigo you first saw my eyes you were so shocked that you dared not touch me. No deeper insult can be offered to a woman than this, and I tried to persuade my wounded vanity that you were only sparing my virtue. And so I began to see myself with your eyes, Michael, and since then I've been as chaste as a virgin—" Here she faltered, looked away, and added, "Almost."

Enraged I seized her by the hair, shook her head and hissed, "Why do you stammer and look away? Have you deceived me with Moslems, too, you false and shameless woman?"

She raised her hands and declared, "As God sees me, no Moslem has touched me save Captain Torgut and Sinan the Jew, into whose hands I fell as a helpless slave. But here in Algiers I've lived almost chastely for your sake, dearest Michael. If a few wanton women have caressed me a little at the baths, it was only to please them and comply with the customs of the country. I took no pleasure in it myself."

As it dawned upon me how shamelessly she had deceived me my grasp slackened and tears ran down my cheeks. She put out her hand as if to wipe them away, but she dared not touch me, and looked appealingly at Mustafa ben-Nakir for help. But even Mustafa, who paid little heed to moral laws, had been startled by her confession. It was some time before he hit upon the right words.

"Remember that Allah is merciful and gracious, Michael el-Hakim! This woman undoubtedly loves you with a strong and passionate love, or she would never have laid bare to you her worthlessness. For your peace of mind it would have been better if she'd made you drunk, so that next morning you would have had no notion of what had taken place. But Allah willed it otherwise. All you can do now is to resign yourself and look upon Giulia as a young and undeniably beautiful widow; the main thing is that at last she surrenders herself to you."

His clear thinking helped me to recover my own scattered wits and I realized that it would be petty to make too much of Giulia's former life. I myself had committed the most grievous sin in denying my Christian faith and taking the turban. Giulia, whatever her faults, had at least remained a Christian and so was less guilty than I. The consciousness of this caused me bitter pangs and I had not felt so contemptible since the day when in mortal terror I first called upon the name of Allah the Compassionate. My own rottenness forbade me to condemn Giulia, and it was but just that for my sins I should be saddled with this false and depraved woman. I said, "Be it so, then. I am not without sin; how should I cast a stone? But I still cannot understand why you feigned innocence."

Giulia, seeing my rage melt into resigned dejection, summoned fresh courage and her eyes glistened with tears as she replied, "It was for your own sake, beloved Michael. And then people believed in my fortunetelling only because I was, as they thought, a virgin. If I'd betrayed my secret earlier you would have seduced me and then wearied of me, as others have done. I wanted to make sure; and now that you've grown accustomed to my eyes you must admit that from now on you could find no delight in ordinary women and their cheap love. Henceforth we will trust one another and have no secrets. And God help you if you so much as glance at another woman, now that I've consented to be yours."

Mustafa ben-Nakir burst into loud laughter, though I could not imagine why, for Giulia's eyes rested tenderly on me. I had never hoped that she could look upon me with such desire. And so I humbled my heart and said, "I forgive you, Giulia, and I shall strive to see you as you really are. It's true that for me you've been transformed from a golden chalice to a cracked earthenware pot, but the hard crust of truth is more wholesome than the freshest wheaten loaf. Let us share this crust together."

Giulia answered readily, "Ah, Michael, how deeply I love you when you speak and feel like this! But you have yet to learn how sweet a drink may be contained in a cracked earthenware pot. I think we need no further help from Mustafa ben-Nakir, who must have a great deal to attend to at the palace, so let us detain him no longer."

She tried to thrust him forth, but he drew out his Persian book with the intention, no doubt, of declaiming an edifying nuptial poem. But Giulia drove him out at last, slammed the grille, locked it, and drew the heavy curtain. Her face glowed with passion as she turned to me, her eyes shone like contrasting jewels, and she was so breathtaking in her beauty that I could not but recall the disappointments she had caused me. I clenched my teeth and slapped her hard upon the cheek. She was so staggered at my action that she sank down powerless at my feet. Overwhelmed, I caught her head in my hands and kissed her —kissed her passionately and without ceasing—and we lay and loved all night.

When at length I lay resting, my swollen cheek on her breast, reason awoke and I said, "Giulia, we must think of the future. If you want me as I want you, it will be best for me to free you from slavery and marry you according to the law of Islam. Thereafter you'll be a free woman and at no one's orders, even should I become the Sultan's slave."

Giulia sighed deeply, and this sigh was even more enchanting to my ears than the quick, passionate breaths of approaching ecstasy. She kissed my cheek with her soft lips and said, "Ah, Michael, in my heart I always meant to make you marry me, at least according to the law of Islam. But you can't know what joy you give me by saying this of your own free will. Beloved Michael, my whole heart flows out to you. Yes, I will be your wife—as good a wife as I can, though I'm a deceitful woman with a poisonous tongue at times. Let us be married early tomorrow, before anyone can stop us."

She went on talking, but I slept, with her soft hair over my face. Next morning all went as planned. In the presence of the cadi and four approved witnesses I first gave Giulia her freedom and then declared that I took her to wife, repeating the first sura to confirm both acts. Cadi and witnesses received lavish gifts, and Abu el-Kasim gave a banquet to which both known and unknown guests were bidden—as many as could find room in house and courtyard.

"Eat till you choke," was Abu's constant exhortation. "Eat till you burst, and take no thought for a poor old man without even a child to care for him in his old age."

I ignored this customary lamentation, knowing that he could well afford the entertainment and spare something for the poor as well, and in my overflowing joy I sent some of the good food to the Spanish prisoners toiling at the demolition of Penjon fortress. Giulia received many presents; Khaireddin himself sent her a golden comb with ivory teeth and Andy gave her ten gold pieces. Looking at me doubtfully with his round gray eyes he said, "I wonder whether you've been wise in marrying this wayward woman? Her eyes alone are a warning, and I should be afraid lest my son inherit them."

I thought he was envious of my happiness and perhaps even jealous of Giulia, so I clapped him on the shoulder and said, "Have no fear, my dear brother Andy. I've made my bed and will lie on it, and you mustn't think that my marriage will part us. We shall be brothers as before. My house shall be your home always and I shall never be ashamed of having a simple fellow like yourself for a friend, even should my intelligence and learning raise me to a loftier position than you can ever reach."

In my present gentle mood I was moved to tears by my own speech, and putting my arms about his broad shoulders I assured him of my friendship, until Giulia found me and caught me by the elbow. To the sound of drums and tambourines we walked together into the bridal chamber. But when I would have caught her in my arms she pushed me away telling me not to crush her lovely wedding dress. She then began to finger all the presents and count the givers until I was thoroughly weary, and only then did she let me kiss her and help her to undress. But her body was now known to me and could no longer give me the same joy. My head ached from the heavy incense, and once we were in bed I was content to lie with my hand on her breast and listen silently to her endless chatter.

It seemed to me that all this had happened before, and half in a dream I began wondering who she really was, and what it was that linked me to her. She came of an alien race whose language and way of thinking were different from mine. So immersed was I in my somber mood that I failed to notice when she ceased talking. But suddenly she raised herself in bed and stared at me with a look of fear.

"What are you thinking of, Michael?" she asked in a low voice. "Something unpleasant about me, no doubt."

I could not lie to her, and answered with a shudder, "Giulia, I was remembering my first wife, Barbara—remembering how even dead stones came to life when we were together. And then she was burned as a witch, and so I feel very lonely in the world in spite of lying here beside you with your lovely breast under my hand."

Giulia was not angry as I had expected; she stared at me curiously and her face took on an unfamiliar look. With a faint sigh she said, "Look into my eyes, Michael!"

If I had wanted to I could not have freed myself from those eyes, gazing at me under their lowered lids. She spoke in a low voice, and although I hardly listened to her I knew what she said, "You've doubted my ability to see things in sand, Michael, but as a child I could do the same with water. Perhaps I hardly know myself how much of it is genuine and how much pretense and imagination. But now look deep into my eyes as if into a bottomless well. Then answer me. Which lives in you now, your dead wife or I?"

152

I gazed and could no longer turn away my head. Giulia's strange eyes seemed to grow to the size and depth of pools; I could feel my inner self open out and flow into their darkness. Time seemed to halt and then roll backward until all was one engulfing vortex. I seemed to be looking into the green eyes of my wife Barbara and to see her face full of ineffable, mournful tenderness. So real did she appear that I felt I might have touched her cheek. But I would not try.

I stared long at this face, while yet aware that Barbara had been dead many years and that her body had been burned to ashes in the market place of a German city. I was aware of pain—a pain so intense as to seem an ecstasy surpassing any bodily joy. For in seeing again one who had been reft from me by force and whom I had long mourned and missed, I perceived with agonized clarity that her face had nothing more to say to me—that it belonged to another world and another existence—and that I was no longer the man who had shared those two short years with her. My experiences and mistakes, my good and evil actions had raised an insurmountable wall between us, and she would not even have recognized me now. It was useless to recall her among the living. In my heart I had lost her, and forever.

I neither spoke her name nor put out my hand to touch her, and after a little time her yearning face faded into the grave countenance of Giulia. At this singular point in time something happened in my heart that made me feel I understood Giulia better than before, and I believed I really knew her. Then the mist faded; I lay once more in the familiar room and raised my hand to stroke her face. She closed her eyes and drew her brows together with a sigh.

"Where were you, Michael?" she whispered, but I could not answer her. Without a word I took her in my arms and in the warmth of her I knew the boundless solitude of the human heart. My anguish of soul was too keen for me to feel tenderness or desire. I shivered, comfortless. Passing my hand over that lovely body I thought how one day it would grow old, how the soft smooth skin would wither, the round neck shrivel, and the perfumed hair turn dull and gray. So also my desire would fade and dissolve into nothingness. If I loved her, I must love her simply for being the only creature in the world who was near to me, though even this might be a cruel illusion.

As summer neared its end, Khaireddin was satisfied that he had at last consolidated his position in Algeria, and he began to prepare the long-planned embassy to Sultan Suleiman. For as long as confirmation from the High Porte was lacking, the title of beylerbey, which he had already assumed, was worthless; he was shrewd enough to see that he could not found a kingdom of his own on the Algerian coast without becoming the Sultan's vassal.

When the ships were taking the last of the cargo aboard, Khaireddin ordered me and the other slaves to make ready. He presented me with a kaftan of honor and a copper pen case, and explained to me the maps, charts, and notes that I was to offer as a gift from him to the cartographers of the Seraglio. He gave me also two hundred and fifty gold pieces to distribute among minor court officials who, though without great influence, were able from time to time to gain the ear of their masters. He advised me to squander rather than hoard this money, and promised to replenish my funds should the seed I sowed fall on good soil. But if I stole more than fifty gold pieces of it, he vowed, he would flay me alive with his own hands.

Not more than a fortnight after our wedding I began to notice that Giulia could not bear my dog Rael. She forbade him to sleep by me and chased him into the courtyard, saying that he had fleas and left hairs on the rugs. I was astonished at her fickleness, for before our marriage she enjoyed feeding the dog and talking to him, and never drove him out. Rael, however, had always treated her with reserve, and on her approach would withdraw to a corner with his hackles up, ready to snap, though he never attacked anyone else.

After our marriage he began to grow thin and his coat became rusty. Often he would sit whining softly in the yard, and I noticed his un- willingness to eat the good food which Giulia threw so impatiently into his bowl, though from my hand he eagerly took the hardest bone or the driest crust. I was really sad on poor Rael's account and took to feeding him myself in secret, and keeping him company in the yard. I continued to confide my troubles to him as of old, but now I had no joys to share.

Giulia's behavior to Andy too was very arrogant. She respected his physical strength and his skill in the casting of cannon, but for the rest she regarded him as a simpleton with a bad influence on me, for she had noticed that when in his company I was often irritable with her. She did all she could to bring about a rift between us.

Her loveliness and our shared delights could always dispel my ill humor and my doubts, however, and I had only to gaze into her strange eyes, shining like blue and brown jewels in her beautifully painted face, to forget all else; I would think myself a fool to trouble about a poor soulless wretch of a dog, or the simple Andy. At other times as I sat dejectedly in the courtyard with my faithful Rael's head in my arms, I saw with startling clarity the emptiness of sensual pleasure, and was aware of Giulia as a stranger doing her utmost to part me from my one true friend.

It was already October when, with straining oars and spread sails, we glided upstream through the fortified straits leading into the Sea of Marmara. The hazy yellow heights to the eastward rose fom the Asiatic mainland, while to the west lay that part of Europe which in bygone days had belonged to Greece, but which the Ottomans afterward conquered. Somewhere in this region lay the ruins of Troy, the city of which Homer sang, and here, too, Alexander the Great was buried. I stood on deck and surveyed the gliding shores, thinking of old tales and of the many peoples who had sailed through this channel between the two halves of the world, in search of fortune.

Giulia complained of the hardships of the voyage, and expressed a longing for fresh water and fruit and a proper bath. And indeed after our long period at sea a most abominable stench prevailed aboard our handsomely painted vessel. We put in at a little place near the mouth of the straits and lay there for two days and nights, while we cleansed ourselves and our ship. Long pennants floated in the wind and rich carpets hung over the rail as, to the sound of drums and tambourines, we weighed anchor and with long oar strokes headed toward Turkish Istanbul—once Constantinople, the fabled city of Byzantium.

The weather next day was glorious. The blue hills of the Prince's Islands rose from the embrace of the sea, while far in the distance the city of the emperors shone toward us like a dream of white and gold. As oars and sails brought us ever nearer to our goal, more prosaic details emerged. We saw the high, gray walls lining the shore, and the colorful houses seemingly fused together in masses on the slopes. When we had passed the Fort of the Seven Towers our eyes fell upon the Sophia mosque, once the most wonderful church in Christendom, whose mighty dome and minarets still dominated the great city. Behind it on the point, surrounded by the lush green of gardens, lay the numberless dazzling buildings of the Seraglio, marked by the towers that flanked the Gateway of Peace. Opposite the Seraglio, on the other side of the Golden Horn, were the slopes of Pera and the foreigners'

155

quarter beneath the tower of Galata, with its floating standard—the Lion of St. Mark.

As we glided past Seraglio Point and the Sultan's marble quay we fired a salute, but the din of it was borne away by the wind. We had sent word of our coming, however, and our salvo was acknowledged by three shots from the cannon on the point. A French vessel anchored in the roads also fired hastily in reply, from which we concluded that King Francis must indeed be in trouble, or his ships would not have deigned to salute a vessel belonging to the pirate king Khaireddin. Our reception was nevertheless devoid of ceremony, and I think that all of us, whatever our rank, were oppressed by a sense of our own insignificance here in the Sultan's capital.

The turbaned dock laborers cursed and swore at their toil. Only very slowly could we ease our way through the dense shipping to our own berth, where we hove out the anchor astern and made fast by the bows. Before us rose countless warehouses, and beyond them the high, crenelated walls of the harbor quarter. No one heeded us or bade us welcome, and I felt like a rustic come to town for the first time. Captain Torgut evidently felt as I did, for when he had donned his best clothes and a jeweled sword, and had waited for a long time on the quarterdeck, his face darkened and without a word he retired into his cabin.

To my regret Khaireddin had chosen Torgut-reis as his emissary to the High Porte, for Torgut was the youngest and handsomest of his officers; his proud manhood and his taciturnity made a strong impression on those who met him for the first time and knew nothing of his limitations. He was the son of an Anatolian robber and therefore of purely Turkish origin. Khaireddin knew he could trust him, for there was no room in his head for anything but ships and seafaring, fighting and fine clothes. To advise him in matters connected with court intrigue Khaireddin had sent with him an experienced eunuch who had belonged to Selim-ben-Hafs. The fellow was corrupt and untrustworthy, but Torgut had been authorized to behead him if necessary, and in these circumstances Khaireddin considered he might be useful; he hoped he might gather information from the eunuchs of the Seraglio, since these persons readily make one another's acquaintance and confide in one another more freely than they do in uncastrated men.

We had been waiting impatiently all day when one of the white slaves of the Seraglio suddenly appeared, riding a mule and attended by a large party of janissaries. He bade us welcome, promised to leave us some janissaries as guards, and told us that the Divan might attend to Khaireddin's letters within the next few weeks, if Allah so permitted.

Torgut-reis was incensed by the messenger's discourtesy and replied sharply that if such were the case he would cast off at once and return with all the rich presents to Algeria. His face crimsoned with anger as he cried that Khaireddin owed the Sultan nothing, and that on the contrary the Sultan was greatly in Khaireddin's debt for the conquest of a new province and the harassing of the Emperor. Torgut did not mean to wait like a beggar at the rich man's door, and nothing need prevent Khaireddin from omitting the Sultan's name from the Friday prayers in the mosques.

The eunuch no doubt marveled in his own mind at Torgut's uncontrolled behavior. However, he bowed repeatedly, declaring that it was a great honor to appear before the Divan at all, and that ambassadors from the Emperor and from the Emperor's brother, the King of Vienna, had sometimes to wait for months before gaining an audience. They might even be locked up and have to spend their time of waiting in the cells of the Fort of the Seven Towers. But as for us, the eunuch promised—rubbing finger and thumb together abstractedly—he would put at our disposal a house befitting our dignity and a grant for our maintenance while in Istanbul.

There was nothing for it but to give him a little foretaste of the treasure that Khaireddin had sent. When he had gone, the janissaries settled down on deck and on the quay. Taking off their tall felt caps they began to plait their lock of hair, keeping a sharp lookout to see that no unauthorized person came aboard and that none of us went ashore. These blue-clad warriors, with their long mustaches and sharp chins, kept their heads shaven save for one long lock on top of their heads, so that if the worst befell them their victors need not pierce their ears but could conveniently carry their severed heads by the hair. We realized that we were prisoners, and Torgut perceived too late the mistake he had made in not sending a trustworthy man to call secretly on the Grand Vizier. To prevent bloodshed in the Sultan's capital, the carrying of arms was forbidden, and the janissaries were armed only with rods of Indian bamboo; nevertheless Torgut believed our situation would hardly be improved by offering violence to the people of the Seraglio.

When from the balconies of the minarets the muezzins proclaimed the hour of evening prayer, we were sitting together dejectedly in Torgut's cabin and did not even raise our heads from our hands. Dusk erased the yellow, red, gray, and purple colors of the buildings in which countless tiny flames were kindled so that one could appreciate even more clearly the vast extent of this city. Beyond the Golden Horn blazed the foundry fires in the Sultan's arsenal, whence came the ceaseless sound of hammering. The eunuch told us that this noise usually boded war, and it might therefore be surmised that the Sultan had more important matters to think of than ourselves and our gifts.

But Abu el-Kasim said, "Even though the Mohammedan part of the city is closed to us, the Venetian quarter is open and there should be no difficulty in finding a boatman willing to ferry us across. From what I know of the Venetians they keep late hours, and an astute man could gather useful information about the customs of this city by searching the taverns for a sufficiently exalted—and inebriated—personage. Michael el-Hakim can still pass for a Christian, and if Antar will only promise to keep sober he may go with him as bodyguard."

Hardly had he finished speaking when we felt the slight shock of a rowing boat against our hull and heard a man whining for alms. For two aspers this fellow promised to row anyone to the opposite shore and its wonderful pleasure haunts, where the commandments of the Koran did not obtain and where women, kinder than the houris of Paradise, entertained the guests so long as their money lasted. Night in the harbor quarter was not made for sleep, the eloquent boatman assured us in a whisper. It was not long before Andy and I found ourselves gliding over the dim waters of the Golden Horn, unable in the darkness to make out the features of our ferryman.

As we approached the farther shore the waters reflected the glow of torches and we heard the gay music of stringed instruments. We drew alongside a stone quay and I gave the ragged boatman the fee he demanded, though it was an extortionate one for so short a journey. The watchman paid us no heed and we passed straight through the harbor gates into the brightly lit street, where unveiled women addressed us without embarrassment in a number of different languages. Suddenly Andy opened his eyes wide, seized me by the arm, and exclaimed, "As I live, there's a cask of honest ale standing by that door, with a bundle of straw above it!"

He carried me through the doorway as if I had been a feather and when our eyes had grown accustomed to the light we beheld a number of rough fellows sitting at tables and drinking. A fat, gray-haired man was busy at a cask, filling tankard after tankard with foaming ale, and on seeing us he said, "By Allah, you're not the first Moslems to enter this respectable tavern, for the Prophet never forbade his followers to drink ale. The holy book mentions only wine, and so with a clear conscience you may drain a tankard here."

As he spoke he surveyed us suspiciously, as if wondering where he had seen us before. I stared back, and suddenly recognizing those bristly eyebrows and that purple nose I exclaimed in astonishment, "Jesus, Mary! Is it not Master Eimer? How in the world did you get here?"

The man turned deadly pale and crossed himself repeatedly. Then, snatching up a carving knife, he hurled himself upon me and shrieked, "And you're that accursed Michael Pelzfuss, Madame Geneviève's confederate! Now at last I can make mincemeat of you."

But Andy snatched away the knife and hugged him to his breast to stifle his wrath; as he struggled and stormed in Andy's arms I thumped him heartily on the back and Andy spoke kindly to him, saying, "How pleasant to meet an old friend on our first evening in the Sultan's capital! May it prove a good omen for our task here. Don't abuse Michael, dear Master Eimer; was it not you who lured Madame Geneviève from him and so found yourself supping with the devil? It's no fault of his that Madame Geneviève cheated you of your money and then sold you to the galleys. It's the result of your own sins. Madame Geneviève is now proprietress of a highly esteemed brothel in Lyons, founded with your money."

Master Eimar was purple in the face.

"Burn me if I'll bandy words with curs like you! You both helped to rob me and I was mad to trust such devil-ridden heretics. That you should have trodden the Cross underfoot and taken the turban is no more than I might have expected. It's but a step from Luther's abominable heresies to the Prophet and his teaching."

But when Andy seized him by the throat and threatened to pull the house down about his ears, Master Eimer's tone grew milder; he asked us to pardon him for losing his wits in the surprise of meeting us, and to give him our opinion of his ale, as he was not altogether satisfied with the Hungarian hops of which it was brewed. Andy at once swallowed a mugful, licked his lips, and agreed that there was something a little strange about the taste, though it was long since he had so much as seen a drop of honest ale. After a further draught he nodded and said, "Now I taste it. It's as it used to be, and tickles the nose pleasantly. Surely no better ale is brewed this side of Vienna."

By the time we had drunk a few stoups of this really excellent strong ale, the three of us were friends and it was cheering to meet with a good Christian again after all these Moslems. I begged Master Eimer to tell me his adventures, but he was unwilling to say anything of his sufferings as a galley slave aboard the Venetian warship. Yet, after some further drinking, he displayed to us his fat back with its network of scars—a perpetual reminder of the overseer's whip. He held himself askew when walking and believed he would never lose this habit, which resulted from two years spent chained to the same oar. Master Eimer was over fifty and he thought he must have perished but for the powerful brewer's heart he inherited from his father and grandfather, further strengthened by good ale of his own drinking.

In the course of a battle with the Imperial fleet, the Venetian war galley had been so badly damaged that in the confusion Master Eimer was able to hammer out the bolt to which he was fettered and swim ashore. Soon afterward he was taken prisoner by Moslems and sold in the Cairo slave market. A compassionate Jew who had embraced the faith of Islam bought him his freedom; then took him to Istanbul and financed a brewery for him. The tavern had paid well, for ale was rare enough among Mussulmans for the price to be kept high. (This last was to our address, for he had noted how smoothly the good drink was slipping down our throats.) With a jingle of my purse I asked coldly what we owed him, and he named a figure that made my hair stand on end. After that I could not wonder that he had laid the foundations of a substantial fortune is so short a time.

I asked him to advise me how an insignificant person like myself could obtain audience of the Grand Vizier, as I had matters of great weight to impart. To my boundless amazement Master Eimer answered, "Nothing easier! All you need do is go up the hill here and have a word with Master Aloisio Gritti. You can be sure he'll further your business if it's of real importance. Try him. At the worst, his servants can only throw you out."

I asked who Master Aloisio Gritti might be. Eimer replied, "In all the Pera quarter there's no one with a worse reputation. But he's rich—a natural son of the Doge of Venice and a Greek slave woman.

They say he's a close friend of the Grand Vizier and directs the secret negotiations between the Christian states and the High Porte."

I doubted very much whether I should be doing Khaireddin a service by dragging the Venetians into his affairs. But these misgivings came too late, for just then a man in the dress of a Christian clerk rose and approached me to ask if I sought Master Aloisio Gritti. He declared himself willing to guide me to his house as he was bound thither himself. I was averse from keeping company with strangers in a seaport town such as this, but Master Eimer rebuked me for my suspicions, saying, "The Sultan's city is the safest and most peaceable of all cities in the world, especially at night, for the Sultan allows no brawling or thieving. During the hours of darkness his janissaries patrol the streets, maintaining good order everywhere. You may accompany this man with an easy mind, Michael Pelzfuss, for I know his face and believe him to be one of Master Gritti's servants."

We took cordial leave of Master Eimer and went out with the clerk. As soon as we were in the street he said, "You're two of the pirate king's party and arrived today from Algeria. But I didn't want to disturb you until you had emptied your tankards."

I asked him how in Allah's name he could know who we were, and he replied smoothly, "When Master Gritti learned that janissaries were guarding your vessel he sent a boatman to fetch you. He's already waiting to learn whether you have anything of importance to tell him."

I was struck dumb with amazement, but Andy said, "We are indeed sheep, led hither and thither at the bidding of the shepherd. But perhaps this too is the will of Allah, and if so there's nothing to be done."

Stumbling over heaps of garbage in the narrow, twisting street we made our way toward the top of the hill; then as we walked up some broad, easy steps, I saw the mighty Galata tower outlined like a dark shadow against the starry sky. The young moon gave little light, but the crescent is the symbol of Ottoman power, and as I now beheld it I was filled with a strange conviction that a turning point in my fate had come.

At last we reached a wall in which was a small door. Our companion unlocked this and we passed through. The house beyond lay in darkness and I began to suspect that we had fallen into a trap. But as soon as we stepped into the entrance hall we saw light issuing from the inner rooms, by which we could see that the house was gorgeously furnished in the Venetian style. I could hear also the notes of a gay air played on a violin.

Our companion passed along a dark corridor and into a lighted room to announce our arrival. When out of curiosity I began to follow him, a black hand shot from the shadows and seized me so hard by the arm that I cried aloud in fear. Two Negroes stepped silently forward out of the darkness and barred the way with crossed scimitars. I now had no doubt but that the Venetians for some reason wanted to kidnap me. We had left our vessel without permission and no one would investigate our disappearance. But Andy said in his usual blunt fashion, "Think nothing of it, Michael. We'll manage these two, if I can get a proper grip of one and kick the other where it hurts most."

He smiled engagingly at the Negroes and began to tease them by pinching their arms, so that it was all I could do to control him. Fortunately the clerk returned and bade us step into the lighted room at once, whereupon he disappeared behind a curtain.

We stepped boldly in and bowed low, touching forehead and floor with our finger tips, for politeness could not come amiss in the presence of so important a man as Master Gritti. When I looked up I saw a table resplendent with gold and silver and lit by numberless candles in a candelabrum of Venetian glass. Two men had recently finished their meal; one, wearing the gorgeous dress of a Venetian nobleman, was lying back in his chair. Raising his goblet he bade me welcome in the Italian tongue. Only from the many fine wrinkles in his face could it be seen that he was considerably older than myself, for his figure was as slender as mine. I also observed that his eyes were red and swollen with drink. Beside him stood a man dressed in a Turkish kaftan of silk and a plumed and jeweled turban, holding a violin in his hand. He was the most magnificent-looking man I had ever seen, and gave forth a sort of radiance which made it difficult to take one's eyes from him. His skin was smooth and milk white as a boy's, though he was certainly more than thirty. His bright dark eyes rested on Andy and me with a mocking smile, as if he were conscious that no one could look upon him unmoved; yet his assurance had nothing in it of conceit. He was not even very splendidly dressed, and except for the jeweled buttons of his kaftan and the fine diamonds on his fingers and in his ears, his attire was of so quiet a distinction that an inexperienced eye might have found it plain. But when I looked into his eyes I trembled; I fell on my knees before him and pressed my forehead to the ground. Andy hesitated for a moment and then followed my example. Master Gritti burst into forced laughter and said as he spun the wine cup between his fingers, "Why do you show such veneration for a common fiddler, rather than for me who am master in this house?"

I answered humbly, "Fiddler he may be, yet the whole world is his violin and the nations of the earth are the strings. His proud gaze speaks the prince, whereas your puffy eyes, Master Gritti, tell of one lost to decency through gluttony and drink. While he stands you loll in your chair, nor do you treat me with fitting respect, though as Khaireddin's representative I consider myself in every way your equal."

Master Gritti, offended, demanded scornfully, "How can you, the slave of a pirate, consider yourself equal to a distinguished Venetian? If you want anything from me you must adopt a humbler tone."

Knowledge of his illegitimate birth gave me courage, for in that respect at least we were equals. And so I replied, "*I* want anything from *you?* You're mistaken. You wouldn't have sent for me in this clandestine fashion unless you hoped to gain something by it. You may represent the most illustrious Republic, but I am the envoy extraordinary of Khaireddin, lord of the sea. Which of us, do you think, takes precedence before the Divan—you, an idolatrous Christian, or I who am of the Faith?"

The violinist laid aside his instrument, sat down, and addressed me in faultless Italian, "So you are Michael el-Hakim and this is your brother Antar, the wrestler and gun founder. I've heard of you and you do right to defend your master's honor. But you must not quarrel with this man, who is my personal friend and an excellent musician. Tell me rather why you showed me such marked deference. Did you know who I was? If so, Master Gritti has performed his task imperfectly."

I looked at him in unfeigned admiration, for he was indeed more worthy of it than any man I had seen. And I answered, "I don't know who you are, but I suspect that the wanderer Mustafa ben-Nakir, whom I met in Algeria, has often spoken of you. If you are that man, then indeed reality surpasses his account as the sun surpasses the moon in splendor, and I can only praise the bright star that brought me to your presence. Praise be to you, most fortunate Ibrahim, pillar of the

Ottoman Empire—you on whom the Sultan has bestowed greater power than ever subject held before!"

He inclined his proud head and answered with easy modesty, "I am but my lord's slave."

Then his animated mood prevailed again and he went on, "As you may realize, I arranged this meeting so as to gain certain necessary information from you regarding Khaireddin's intentions. If you're surprised that the meeting should take place in the foreigners' quarter and in the house of a Venetian, you must understand that it's to our advantage to let the illustrious Republic know what may be expected from your master. Venice also is at war with the Emperor. If Khaireddin receives the horsetail switch of a beylerbey he must obey the Sultan only, and cease harrying the vessels of our French and Venetian allies. Do you think he can control his pillaging officers, and one day join the allied fleets of France and Venice in a great naval attack on the Emperor?"

I replied, "Khaireddin is an unusual man, and very shrewd. Since his brother's death he has encountered difficulties enough to show him that in the long run he can't hold his kingdom without the Sultan's powerful support. His ambition is limitless, his officers trust him implicitly, and he calls them his children. The richness of the presents he has now sent best proves his sincerity, and I know he venerates you and the Sultan so highly as to feel like a humble disciple beside you. It would flatter his vanity to receive the horsetail, a kaftan of honor, and a personal letter from the Sultan. And to my mind such a mark of favor would be a modest price to pay for Khaireddin's mighty fleet and fine seamen."

Beneath Ibrahim's dark gaze I felt no wish to resort to fulsome flattery or exaggeration, and believed I could best serve Khaireddin's cause by giving my honest opinion of him. Yet with my whole heart I longed to win the Grand Vizier's confidence. So strong was his charm that I desired his favor for its own sake, without thought of the advantages it could bring me. He questioned me very thoroughly, and with practical knowledge, on the subject of Khaireddin's building works and other activities, until Master Gritti interrupted him, and turning to me asked, "Can this Khaireddin sail oceans as well as seas, to crush the Portuguese spice trade and hinder Spanish traffic with the New World?"

Ibrahim said, "The Sultan of sultans and lord of all peoples is no

164

spice dealer. In furthering the interests of the illustrious Republic, Aloisio Gritti, you see no further than your own nose and your immediate advantage. The shortest way to the control of the spice trade is over the Red Sea and the Persian Gulf. When once we have conquered Persia, the Ottoman fleet can sail unmolested to destroy the Portuguese trading posts in India. Nothing can then prevent us from digging a canal between the Mediterranean and the Red Sea, thus rendering pointless the Portuguese discovery of the passage round the southern tip of Africa. But there's a time for everything, and first the Emperor must be defeated."

Master Gritti, discomfited, was silent. The Grand Vizier turned to me and went on, "No, we're not spice dealers, and the Sultan has no real enemy but the Emperor, Charles V, for we're now allied with Venice and the French King, and even to some extent with the Pope. The King of France is once more in difficulties, and to relieve him the Sultan must oppose the Emperor, or at least obtain from him fair terms of peace for France. It will be for Khaireddin to block the Imperial sea power when our army opens its campaign in the spring. If Allah wills we shall defeat Ferdinand, the Emperor's brother, and take possession of his domains, for so long as the war with France continues Charles can send him no help. It's true that the Emperor is negotiating secretly with Tahmasp, the Shah of Persia, and sooner or later the Sultan must fight the Emperor on Persian soil as well, at the same time liberating the holy tombs of Islam from the hands of the red-haired Shiites. But the cornerstone of Ottoman policy is neither more nor less than the blocking of Imperial world dominion which, were it to continue, would destroy the freedom of all peoples. Anything therefore which harms the Emperor helps the Sultan, and vice versa. Grasp this and you grasp all."

Master Gritti, who was evidently bored, emptied another cup of wine and said, "Master Michael Carvajal—you'll allow me to address you thus, for I happen to know that Master Venier of Venice made out your pass in that name. Well, Master Michael, the Ottoman emblem is the bald-necked vulture that appeared to Osman in a dream. Clearly, in order to survey wider expanses than come within the range of ordinary mortals, the vulture must mount high in the heavens. I, poor earthbound man, am more interested in the spice trade and the best way to protect Venetian merchant shipping against the pirates of Islam. For these are matter-of-fact, everyday problems, and their solution will bring many benefits. Our violinist should content himself with capturing Vienna and bestowing the crown of Hungary on my friend Zapolya, who has humbly sought the aid of the High Porte. For he is the lawfully elected king of the downtrodden Hungarian people, whose arrogant lords have accepted King Ferdinand as their ruler. By law, only a native of Hungary may wear the sacred crown of St. Stephen, yet the Viennese King's German men-at-arms are still roistering in Buda. The forces of the Crescent ought to have freed Hungary from the German yoke as long ago as last summer."

The Grand Vizier only smiled and drew a few pleasing notes from his violin.

"Last summer Allah sent heavy rains and floods in our path," he said, "but next summer Vienna shall be captured and the faithful Zapolya shall receive his well-earned reward. For as you may know, the Sultan has sworn by the Prophet and by his sword to be Zapolya's true friend and shield him from all his enemies."

Aloisio Gritti made a wry face and said, "And King Zapolya swore, too, through his ambassador. He swore by the living God and Jesus our Saviour, who is God also, that he would ever remain a friend to the friends of Sultan Suleiman and an enemy to his enemies. But while you were playing your fiddle the greedy landowners and the Germans oppressed the people and left them destitute."

"Allah's will be done," returned the Grand Vizier. To me he said, "You may apply with full confidence to Master Gritti for any information regarding the Christian states. Through him we learn not only the secrets of the illustrious Republic, but also news from King Zapolya of matters great and small in Germany and the Viennese court."

His face darkened, and springing up he cried, "Crowns and coronations are but a mirage to delude the foolish. Not the crown but the sword confers sovereignty. Lands trodden by the Sultan's chargers are forever united with his realms. Therefore I, too, burn with impatience to open the greatest campaign in the history of the Ottoman Empire. If afterward Zapolya reigns as king of Hungary, it will be by the Sultan's favor, to ensure free passage through his domains at all times."

Although I well understood that these preparations for a campaign which indirectly threatened the whole of Christendom greatly exceeded in importance the affairs I had on hand, yet I strove like Master Gritti to keep my feet firmly on the ground; I asked what reception was to be given to Khaireddin's envoy. The Grand Vizier replied,

166

"The Sultan still regards Khaireddin as a common pirate who, with his brother, betrayed the trust placed in him by the Sultan's father, Selim. Khaireddin also has the second and third viziers against him, and I advise you to provide handsome presents for these men. But foremost among his opponents are the Sultan's sea pashas who fear and envy him. He has a trustworthy supporter in the Chief Pilot, the learned navigator Piri-reis. Piri-reis has drawn a chart by whose help anyone may sail the Mediterranean with safety; when you meet him, praise this work. Since a few copies of it fell into the hands of Christians it has ceased to be a secret. Piri-reis is an elderly man who lives among papers and feels no resentment for Khaireddin. The only gifts that please him are Christian charts which he likes to compare with his own. Tomorrow I intend to take up the question of Khaireddin with the Divan; I shall mention the magnificent gifts he has sent, and stress his firm intention of turning Algiers into an impregnable naval base. If Allah wills it, the Sultan himself shall receive the deputation in person, and the other viziers must accept the position with what grace they may."

After giving me further instructions and addressing a kind word or two to Andy, he dismissed us. Master Gritti escorted us past the Negro guards to a side door, and before we left him he said, "If you're indeed a man of education, Master Michael, and find time hanging heavily on your hands, come and visit me without fear of intruding; I enjoy listening to Seraglio gossip. The Seraglio is if possible a worse hotbed of gossip and intrigue than even the Vatican or the Emperor's Court. I can offer you some unusual enjoyments, too, and acquaint you with vices with which because of your youth you're perhaps still unfamiliar. I regret that this evening I was unable to offer you some young slave girl, for I have a number of these in my service, of different races and color and all expert in the erotic arts of their own countries. Indeed, I believe you'll be astonished."

I thanked him politely for his great kindness and promised to call upon him as soon as I had news from the West, when we could exchange useful information. But in my heart I resolved to keep as far as possible from this false man whose masterly intrigues made him dangerous company for me, while for Giulia's sake I dared not even consider his hospitable offers. The silent clerk escorted us back to the shore, spoke to the guards and led us onto the quay where our boatman was dozing, half-naked though the autumn night was chilly.

The crescent moon shone like a drawn scimitar above the great dome of the mosque as we glided over the Golden Horn to our ship. We were unmolested, though a couple of janissaries on the shore stared at us as we climbed aboard.

Next morning I told Torgut-reis and the eunuch all that had happened and urged them to await the summons to the Seraglio in all confidence, since by diplomacy I had succeeded in winning over the Grand Vizier to Khaireddin's cause. At first the eunuch would not believe that I had met the Grand Vizier in person, but while we were yet talking a horseman arrived to bid us make ready to appear before the Sultan. Soon afterward cooks and scullions arrived in great numbers, bearing with them in Chinese bowls an abundant meal from the Divan kitchen. After the noon prayer a hundred mounted spahis clad in purple suddenly appeared. Their jeweled weapons flashed in the sun, and their saddle cloths were adorned with heavy turquoises. Their Aga presented Torgut with a gift from the Sultan—a magnificent horse whose bridle and saddle were ornamented with silver, pearls, and precious stones.

Overjoyed at this splendid present, Torgut-reis gave me thirty ducats and the eunuch added a somewhat smaller sum. We then set forth in ceremonial procession to the Seraglio. Huge crowds hailed us as we passed, and called down blessings upon our heads. Slaves, black and white, carried Khaireddin's presents, of which the most gorgeous had been uncovered for all the people to behold. Ten beautiful girls and boys carried coins and gold dust in baskets of plaited palm leaves, so that we felt deeply thankful for the protection of our mounted escort. In my arms I held a white-cheeked monkey that had grown so much attached to me on the voyage that it allowed no one else to carry it. It put its arms about my neck, chattering and grimacing at the bystanders until I had a flock of laughing, shouting children at my heels.

We were led past the great mosque and through the Gate of Happiness to the forecourt of the Seraglio, which was surrounded by the barracks of the janissaries, the Sultan's stables, the library, and the soldiers' bathhouse. In the forked branches of ancient plane trees hung numberless iron cooking pots, and on the lawns groups of janissaries were taking their ease. The Aga of our escort handed us over to the guards at the Gateway of Peace, and here the merchandise, slaves, and seamen were left while Torgut-reis, the eunuch, and myself were shown into a waiting room within the archway. We sat down on hard and dirty cushions, whence we could see into another room on the opposite side of the arch. Broad-bladed headsman's axes hung there on iron hooks fixed to the wall, and on the floor was a pyramid of some thirty human heads. The stench was unbearable, for many of the heads were no longer quite fresh, having been brought from different parts of the Ottoman Empire for the viziers to see, as conclusive proof that sentence had been carried out.

The sight did not tend to raise our spirits, but since I was always eager to learn, I engaged the guard in conversation. In return for a ducat he showed me his bloodstained apron and also the pit into which the bodies were thrown, to make their slow way along an underground drain into the Sea of Marmara. He told me that even the most eminent ambassadors had to wait on the same cushions as ourselves, as this gave them opportunity for wholesome meditation upon the Sultan's limitless power, the vanity of existence, and the incalculable twists and turns of fortune. I learned that only about fifty heads a day were thrown into the vaults, which testified to the mild rule of the Sultan and the good order prevailing in his dominions. Suleiman would not even allow torture at interrogations. Besides the deaf-mutes there remained a few skilled executioners, both black and white, who had been in the service of Selim the implacable, also a Chinese and an Indian specialist in methods of torture peculiar to those distant lands.

"But," added the friendly guard, "should our lord the Sultan wish to rid himself of some slave who has fallen out of favor, after being honored with his friendship and a high appointment, such a slave is not made to kneel at the block. Instead the Sultan sends him a black kaftan and a strong silken cord. No one has ever abused this mark of favor; all have gladly ended their days by their own hand and received honorable burial. The Sultan then takes back house, slaves, and all that the deceased used and enjoyed while the sun of fortune and favor stood at the zenith. Especially during the reign of the beloved Sultan Selim were sudden changes of fortune seen, and he was not sparing in the item of black kaftans. Great activity prevailed always in the tailors' workshops, and in those days we would curse our enemies with the words, 'May you become Selim's Vizier!'"

Hardly had he ended when two gigantic men stepped up to me, grasped me firmly by the arms and led me between them into the

169

Courtyard of Peace. Torgut-reis and the eunuch were treated in the same manner. I struggled and protested loudly that I had done no wrong, but one of the chamberlains hastened forward to me with his staff of office in his hand, and exhorted me in a whisper to hold my tongue.

I became aware of the breathless stillness that hung over the Courtyard of Peace, so brilliant in its white and gold, and fell silent. They led me unresistingly into the great chamber of the Divan where a number of the most eminent dignitaries of the Seraglio were assembled, wearing ceremonial kaftans. I had no time to look at them more closely, for we were taken straight across the room to a low throne. I at once fell to my knees and pressed my forehead to the floor, remaining in this position like Torgut-reis and the eunuch until by a gentle pressure on my arms my escort signed to me that I might now lift my eyes to behold the lord of the two halves of the world, the Sultan of sultans, Allah's shadow on earth.

The moment is fitting to bring this book to an end and begin the next, in which I shall tell of Sultan Suleiman and of my own new dignities in the Seraglio.

BOOK 4.

Piri-reis and Prince Jehangir

THE Sultan of the Ottomans, Allah's Deputy, Ruler of Rulers, Commander of Believers and Unbelievers, Emperor of East and West, Shah of Shahs, Great Khan of Khans, Gate of Victory, Refuge of all Peoples, and the Shadow of the Eternal—in short, Sultan Suleiman, the son of a slave girl—was at this time thirty-four years old. Sitting cross legged on the cushions of his low throne he was more breath taking in the fantastic splendor of his dress than any jeweled idol. From a canopy blazing with rubies and sapphires a tassel of giant pearls hung down over his head. A damascened and jewel-hilted blade lay within his reach, while on his head he wore the turban of the sultans, ringed with a triple diamond tiara. The backward-sweeping plume was held in place by a diamond crescent; his dress flashed with myriads of precious stones and must have been heavier to wear than iron chains. At every movement, at every breath, he sparkled with all the colors of the rainbow. Yet it was the man behind the glory who held my attention.

His rather thin face and slender neck appeared pale against the glittering gems; he had the smoke-colored complexion often seen in those of melancholy temperament. The keen, aquiline nose reminded me that the symbol of Ottoman sovereignty was the vulture. The lips under the narrow mustache were thin, and the cold sternness of his gaze was such as to inspire the profoundest awe in those of his subjects who had the supreme privilege of pressing their foreheads to the ground before him. But when I scrutinized this face to read its secret, there seemed to flow from it a fathomless, hopeless woe, telling

173

me that he of all men best understood the futility of power and knew himself to be as mortal as the meanest of his subjects. Perhaps he too harbored within him an incorruptible judge.

At his right hand stood Ibrahim, the Grand Vizier, as splendidly arrayed as the Sultan himself, though without a tiara. On his left stood the second and third viziers, Mustafa-pasha and Ajas-pasha, whose long beards and air of covert suspicion threw into yet stronger relief the open, noble bearing of Ibrahim. I contemplated this most remarkable man with even greater interest than I felt for the Sultan, seeing personified in him the glorious future standing guard over the Ottoman throne; the two old men were but the vanquished past.

Ibrahim addressed Torgut-reis on behalf of the Sultan and received from him Khaireddin's letters in a silken bag. Seraglio attendants then brought forward some of Khaireddin's most princely gifts, which Sultan Suleiman was graciously pleased to survey. In token of his favor he extended his hand for Torgut to kiss; no doubt Torgut's proud warrior face appealed to him. With this the audience was at an end. We were led back into the courtyard, where our escort took their hands from our arms and held them out for reward.

While we yet lingered in the forecourt by the Gateway of Peace, dazed by the honor conferred upon us, a languid little assistant of the Defterdar approached and ordered his clerks to make a list of the presents Khaireddin had sent. Andy and I were included in the roll of slaves, and but for Torgut-reis and the eunuch we should have been sent off at once with the Italian boys for a medical inspection. But Torgut spoke so warmly on our behalf that the assistant set us down for special duties. For his part, he said, we might go where we pleased; he couldn't find a crib for every donkey they sent him.

We rewarded him for his good will and returned to our vessel, where servants of the second and third viziers presently arrived to acquaint us with their masters' willingness to receive gifts from Khaireddin, as a mark of favor to us. We sent our eunuch to the Old Seraglio with an assortment of costly stuffs and ornaments for the Sultan's mother, receiving in return a Koran bound in gold and silver, which she hoped might stimulate Khaireddin to strenuous and unceasing warfare against the unbeliever.

Meanwhile Abu el-Kasim wandered about the great bazaar negotiating for the purchase of a shop. Near the shore he found a dilapidated house and invited Giulia and me to live there with him, if we would bear our share of household expenses. But for the present I thought it well to remain in the house that had been put at Torgut's disposal, at least until I received orders as to my future.

I soon began to suspect, however, that my future depended upon chance alone, for my first impression of the Seraglio was one of utter confusion and disorder. Its functionaries shuffled off duties and responsibilities upon one another or neglected them altogether, for fear of making a mistake. And while a most irksome and finicking exactitude was observed in all matters of routine, any novelty was the source of infinite worry to the officials. From woodcutter to baker, from groom to kennelman, each slave had his minutely prescribed duties which might not be exceeded by a hair's breadth. Whether he held a high or low position, his task, rank, and payment were fixed by statute. So there was nothing for Andy and me to do but wait patiently for suitable vacancies to occur, through either death or disgrace. Only by an order from the very highest level could a special appointment be created for us, and as I learned afterward, respect for the Sultan entailed the continuance of such appointment after our death and forever, whether necessary or not.

Thus I came gradually to see that it was not so very easy to run a household of several thousand people, and I was assured that the most rigid order was needful if friction was to be avoided. For example, a special sum was set aside for the maintenance of a slave girl whose sole duty was to appear silently before the Sultan wearing a flame-colored dress, whenever a great fire broke out in the city. With the exception of the mosques, the buildings were of wood and such a conflagration might cause untold destruction. As I wandered about the capital I came upon huge ravaged areas where goats and donkeys grazed among the ruins. The superstitious Moslems did not willingly build new houses on land that had been swept by fire.

My anxiety proved groundless. Difficult as it had seemed for an outsider to gain a footing in the Seraglio, all went smoothly as soon as the necessary order was issued from above. When we carried Khaireddin's gifts to the Grand Vizier's gleaming palace, beyond the janissaries' training ground, Ibrahim gave me no sign of recognition. But on the following day the Chief Pilot of the Cartographer's Office, Piri-reis, sent a servant to bring me to his house, while almost at the same moment an artilleryman in leather breeches came for Andy.

I followed the barefoot slave, who guided me past the Seraglio to the shores of the Marmara. Here on a slope near the sea wall, stood the house of Piri-reis, surrounded by a wooden fence and a number of acacia trees whose leaves were already turning yellow. Round the usual stone basin lounged a group of retired or invalided sea janissaries. Many were maimed or scarred, and had evidently been given these light guard duties in return for a lifetime of service at sea. Yet they were not idle, but with great skill carved models of ships and furnished them with oars and sails. They bowed respectfully as I greeted them in the name of the Compassionate.

The house was low and shabby, but unexpectedly spacious. I was taken to a meagerly carpeted room, where models of many types of ships hung from the ceiling. The Chief Pilot sat on a dirty cushion, turning the pages of a great atlas on a stand before him. To my surprise I noted that he was wearing a rich kaftan and a ceremonial turban in honor of my coming. I threw myself on the ground before him to kiss his slipper and greet him as Light of the Sea, who had turned night into day for those who sailed remote and unknown waters.

My humility so won his heart that he cordially invited me to rise and sit beside him. He was nearly sixty years old, his beard was silver gray, and wrinkles without number surrounded his short-sighted eyes. I found him a delightful old man.

"You have been commended to me as a man of learning," he began, speaking in Italian. "It seems you have command of many Christian languages and know the kings of Christendom and their statecraft. You now wish to extend your knowledge of seafaring and map reading so as to be of service to the Refuge of all Peoples. I shall not name your patron, for you know well enough who he is. Of him may be said in the words of the Prophet, 'Allah makes easy the fulfillment of his desires.' So you've only to command me, Michael el-Hakim, and I will obey, placing my skill at the service of your benefactor. Mention this to him, if at any time he is pleased to hear you."

I saw that this distinguished old man actually feared me and fancied me to be in special favor with the Grand Vizier. So I at once assured him that I had no other object than to serve him faithfully to the best of my poor ability and that no task was too humble for me, though I should prefer to be given work connected with map making. I hoped soon to become proficient enough in the Turkish language to be of use as dragoman to the Cartographer's Office.

176

Piri-reis said with a sweeping gesture, "The Cartographer's Office, in the service of the Abode of Bliss, you see before you. I beg you not to take offense when I tell you that many a learned Christian navigator has visited me, boasting loudly and making very impudent claims. Some of them took the turban to please the High Porte while in their hearts they remained idolaters, and aroused scandal and indignation by their manner of living. They stole and dirtied my charts, arrived drunk and broke my models, annoyed my slave girls with indecencies, and even molested married women. I had more trouble than help from them, and therefore dislike having ex-Christians living in my house. Pray do not ask to lodge here, at least until I know you better; don't be angry with me for what I've said, for I'm an old man and love peace and quietness."

His words alarmed me, for I thought he wanted to be rid of me altogether. I said, "I have a wife, and prefer to live with her in the city. But don't send me away, for I must feed and clothe myself and my wife as befits our rank, and for that a steady income is essential."

With lifted hand he invoked Allah and said, "Don't misunderstand me. In accordance with the wishes of your exalted patron you will of course receive the highest possible salary—and with all my heart, for I've taken a liking to you. But I beg you not to roar and yell like other Christians, or stamp and tear the turban from your head when I assure you that I can give you no more than twelve aspers a day and a new suit of clothes once a year."

He looked at me appealingly while I rapidly calculated that twelve aspers a day came to about six gold ducats a month—no mean sum for a man who could at most distinguish an oar from a sail. I therefore kissed his veined hand and blessed him in the name of the Compassionate for his generous treatment of a renegade exile. My sincere gratitude delighted him, and he added, "Believe me, this modest fee will secure your future better than the weightiest purse, provided you truly desire knowledge and are as fond of maps and charts as I am. No one will envy you and you'll make no enemies to plot against you, slander you, and profit by your mistakes to overthrow you. You may come and go daily as you please. You may speak with my slaves, clerks, and map makers, and ask me for what you want as if you were my son. One thing only I beg. Never come to my house in a drunken state, but send word that you're ill in bed."

It was clear that his experience of renegades had been most unfortunate. But I would not show that he had hurt my feelings. Instead, I resolved to prove by my behavior that where I was concerned his suspicions were unjustified. I spoke to him as to my father, and followed Grand Vizier Ibrahim's advice by saying, "Noble Chief Pilot Piri-reis ben-Mohammed. If I have not already troubled you too much, I should like above all things to see your celebrated manual of navigation, named Bahrije. Its fame has spread to Christian lands and by its help the seafarers of Islam can safely navigate Greek waters as well by night as by day, in fair weather or foul."

Nothing could have been more acceptable to him than this; his brown, wrinkled face lit up as he pushed the reading desk toward me and said, "Here is my own copy of this modest work, which nevertheless I have sought to make as complete as possible. Besides my own observations I have consulted ancient Mohammedan and Christian charts, maps, and books, and in the course of years have made continual revisions and additions. But I have to beware of ignorant seafarers who from conceit and boastfulness seek to impose much nonsense on me. Just now I was examining the pages relating to Algeria, having heard that Khaireddin, that light of Islam, has torn down the Spanish fortress there and built a breakwater. As his intentions were no doubt of the best, I forgive him the trouble he has caused me by necessitating the alteration to my map."

He opened the book at the passage concerning Algeria, and in a singsong voice read aloud the description of the town of Algiers and its harbor. I clapped my hands with delight, assuring him of its accuracy in every detail, though it seemed almost beyond belief that such perfection could be attained. Then I handed him drawings by the master builders and map makers in Khaireddin's service, showing the alterations in the harbor, also a plan of the arsenal. I said, "Compared with you Khaireddin is an ignorant man, though able enough in the pursuit of Christian ships. It was with great diffidence that he bade me present you with these plans and he humbly begs forgiveness for having been compelled to demolish the fort and build the breakwater without your permission, thus doing violence to the perfections of your work. To regain your favor he sends you all the maps and charts found aboard the Spanish vessels and also these finely wrought sextants from Nürnberg, which were taken from the Spanish admiral's stateroom after the great victory off Algiers. You will no doubt understand their use, though he does not, despite the efforts of the Spanish

178

prisoners to curry favor with him by explaining it. He further bids me hand you this silken purse containing a hundred gold ducats, in part compensation for the expense of altering your most excellent atlas."

Piri-reis rejoiced over the sextants like a child with a new toy, and stroking them tenderly he said, "I well know these new nautical instruments; it's with their aid that Spaniards and Portuguese sail the vast Western ocean. And I gladly accept the maps and charts for my collection, which is the largest in the Ottoman Empire and possibly in the world. If the Divan should ask my opinion of Khaireddin I shall most certainly speak in his favor. Take ten gold pieces from the purse for yourself, for you have given me very great pleasure. And now let us read together from my Bahrije."

My account of Piri-reis ben-Mohammed may lead some to suppose him an absent-minded old bookworm who was of little use to the Sultan. But in fact he was a man of acute intelligence in all concerning navigation and the sea, an eminent designer of ships, and a learned astronomer. His weakness was his book of Mediterranean charts, the Bahrije; like all authors he detested amendments and was vexed whenever the smallest addition became necessary. At heart he suffered from perilous ambitions and even dreamed of commanding a great fleet. But however eagerly he maneuvered his model squadrons about the sandbox, one could see at a glance that whatever else he might be he was no fighter.

I won his good will by listening to the more fanciful parts of his Bahrije, but he had no notion of my talents and preferred to treat me as a sympathetic listener rather than as a useful assistant. His conversation was no more than an exposition of his own views, yet I came away with an agreeable sense of having taken the first step along the path to success. In the blue twilight I strolled past the ruins of gigantic Byzantine palaces where poor Moslems still searched for treasure, past the high walls of the Seraglio, and so on down to the harbor and the house that Abu el-Kasim had rented.

Giulia had taken possession of the two inner rooms for our use and furnished them with things we had brought with us from Algiers. From behind the iron lattice and reed blind of her window she could survey the street unseen. She had already made the acquaintance of women in the neighboring houses and obtained their advice concerning the purchase of food and other domestic matters. The wretched deaf-mute was all at sea in these strange surroundings and dared not venture into the street; he sat in the courtyard strewing dust upon his head. My dog sat beside him equally bewildered, sniffing all the new smells and suspiciously eying the cats that in the evenings nimbly leaped upon the walls and mewed like wailing babies. Rael had an amiable nature but could not endure cats, and was ill at ease in a city that contained so many.

Lamps were burning in all the rooms when I returned, and Giulia, flushed with excitement, rushed to embrace me and tell me of her many purchases. She begged me to buy a eunuch to accompany her on her walks about the city, while Abu tore his sparse beard and pointed by turns to Giulia and his own head. In the glow of the new lamps our house looked like a palace from a fairytale. The expensive water cooler would no doubt have its uses in the heat of summer, but on that chilly autumn evening I longed rather for a hot drink, and was aghast to learn that Giulia had but a handful of aspers left out of my whole fortune. I exclaimed, "Giulia, Giulia! Everything is quite charming and I appreciate your motives, but you seem to have a false idea of my means. Why should we buy a lazy eunuch and feed him at our expense when he would bring us nothing but trouble? Eunuchs are the most expensive of all slaves, and even distinguished ladies are content with a slave girl to attend them."

Giulia was much dashed at my cool response and said, "I'm worn out with running about the city; my feet ache and I was laughed at when I haggled in the bazaar and with the greedy porter who carried the things home for me. And is this my thanks for trying to lay out your money to the best advantage? Of course eunuchs are expensive. But you could buy a Russian boy quite cheaply and make him into one."

"How can you suggest such a thing, Giulia! Never would I allow any man, whether Christian or Moslem, to be castrated just to gratify your vanity. Besides, the operation is dangerous; that's why the price of eunuchs is so high. We might lose our money. I must say I've never heard a sillier suggestion."

Giulia flared up. "Indeed! Even the Holy Father in Rome has a number of boys castrated every year for his choir, and many conscientious Italian parents send their boys to Rome of their own accord for that purpose, to secure for them a better future than their homes can offer. And it's not as dangerous as you say; you're only trying to annoy me and you don't love me at all."

She broke into bitter weeping and declared herself the unhappiest of women, since no one appreciated her good intentions. And because I saw that she was sincerely mourning our poverty and her broken dreams I sat down beside her with my arm about her neck, to console her by recounting my success with Piri-reis. Wiping away her tears she stared at me in utter amazement.

"Michael Carvajal! You, who have knelt before Allah's shadow on earth—can you have been so mad as to accept twelve aspers a day, and that for meekly serving a senile old creature like Piri-reis? Then you're no longer responsible for your actions. If there's a scrap of manhood in you, Michael, you'll go at once to the Grand Vizier and complain of such unfair treatment."

Deeply hurt, I replied, "Try to understand, Giulia, that my brains are my only fortune, and I shall be humbly thankful if by their help I can secure a comfortable income for us both without having to take risks. I never forced you to be my wife; you might have gone where you pleased. It's not yet too late. If you're as disillusioned as you'd have me believe, nothing need prevent us from going to the Cadi tomorrow. For a small sum he will dissolve our marriage, and you may use those different-colored eyes of yours to look about for a better man than I am."

It was unkind of me to remind her of the blemish which, though to me it was her chief charm, made every sensible man avoid her after the first glance; and she was greatly cast down. She sobbed and protested that she loved me, though she could not think why she had attached herself to a man so devoid of any trace of ambition. We wept and kissed until Abu el-Kasim felt it was time for him to withdraw, and soon we were planning together in all harmony how best to live on an income of twelve aspers a day. Giulia had to confess that the sum was at least twice as much as could be earned in Christian countries by a fully trained and experienced mercenary with a large family. At length she laid her white arms about my neck and said tenderly, "Ah, Michael! I love you more than I can say, but at least let me dream of the life we might have. By gazing into sand I can earn quantities of money as soon as my fame has spread in the city. Let me dream! I don't care about the eunuch. Perhaps I can train our deaf-mute to carry things for me. I won't ask you for anything more,

181

Michael, if only I may have one or two cats. The cats here have wonderfully bushy tails and a blue sheen to their coats; every fine lady has one, and the Prophet loved them. It's only fair that I should have a cat or two, since you have your dog."

She kissed me fervently and I was induced to consent. But a day or so later I was saddened to see how hurt my dog was, when two cats with bushy tails appeared and took possession of our two rooms. Rael thenceforward had to keep to the courtyard and hardly dared show himself in the kitchen, even for his meals. Giulia bought these prodigiously expensive creatures with the money that Piri-reis had given me, and even then remained in debt for part of the price.

One evening at dusk Andy arrived flushed with his potations, roaring German soldiers' songs and bringing a greeting from Master Eimer in whose tavern he had been celebrating his successes at the arsenal. The commander of the Sultan's artillery had been pleased to give Andy his hand to kiss, and to examine him as to Imperial armaments. He then appointed Andy foreman at the foundry with a wage of twelve aspers a day. Andy had met there a number of skilled Italians and Germans who worked either as free renegades or as slaves of the Sultan, and who all declared that they had learned much from the Turks and respected the artillery commander and his lieutenants. Andy was now to lodge at the arsenal and might not leave it without permission, because of the military secrets involved.

I was reassured to learn that Andy received the same pay as myself, for it showed that these rates were laid down by statute and that it would therefore be useless to complain of them. It was certainly mortifying to think that Andy, a single man and unable even to write his name, should receive as much as I did, but I was glad of his success and felt no resentment.

So began our life in Istanbul, and it continued thus throughout the winter—if winter it could be called. Snow fell very seldom and melted at once, though there was much wind and rain. Not long after our official reception, Torgut-reis received at the Grand Vizier's hands a gold-mounted horsehair switch, to be delivered to Khaireddin as the outward symbol of his new dignity as beylerbey. Torgut took back also a letter from the Sultan and three kaftans of honor.

During my life with Giulia I believe I developed more and acquired a greater knowledge of life than in all my former years of wandering. Compared with her, my first wife Barbara had been a straightforward, unpretentious woman, albeit a witch—or at least infected with witch-craft to some degree. Barbara had been content for us to live like two little mice in our hole and earn a bare crust, so long as we could be together. But Giulia was not afraid of life, nor did peace and quiet appeal to her. Idleness made her ill, and to satisfy her craving for action she committed the wildest follies, convinced that all she did was well considered and undertaken with the most praiseworthy motives. Moreover she was never satisfied. No sooner were the cats in the house than she disliked their color. When without my permission she bought a costly necklace, she found she had no gown suitable to wear with it, and wanted to renew her wardrobe, or at least buy some slippers sewn with the same kind of stones as were in the chain. She was amazed when I attempted to reason with her, and she explained patiently, as to a child, "You see, Michael, the necklace by itself is useless. And it would be waste to lock it up and never wear it. I'm only considering how to display it to the best advantage."

"Then why in the devil's name did you buy the thing?" I roared, infuriated. She looked at me indulgently and with a shake of her golden locks replied, "It was a unique opportunity and I was so fortunate as to have your month's salary in my purse. In Venice such a chain would cost three or four times as much; I should have been mad not to take it, especially as such things never lose their value and are an excellent investment."

"Allah help me!" I groaned. "I'm no miser, but neither am I a galley slave to live for days on end on pea soup and crusts, and all because of your extravagance."

Giulia raised her hands to heaven in a prayer for patience. Then she screamed, "Extravagance! When I think only of our future and place our money in valuables which neither moth nor rust doth corrupt! If you want better food, then in God's name earn a better wage."

"Allah! Allah!" said I. "I never spy upon you, Giulia, but I know you have many good things in your larder—expensive fruit juices, for instance, fruits preserved in honey, and sweet cakes from the pastry cook. That sort of food's no good to a man, but I can't endure your habit of inviting crowds of gossiping women to eat it and of prattling with them from morning till night, while your husband when he comes home after a hard day's work must put up with pea soup and stone-hard crusts."

Giulia flushed and cried tearfully, "I've never in my life known a more ungrateful man than you! Of course I must offer my neighbors as good cakes as I taste in their homes, if not better. It's the only way to sustain your reputation among them. You don't love me any more or you'd never treat me like this."

Our quarrels most often ended by my humbly begging Giulia's pardon and assuring her that she was the dearest and kindest and cleverest wife that ever a man had. I would also reproach myself for my bad behavior. But such phrases came ever more frequently from the lips only and not from the heart, and I stooped to utter them because my body craved for her and could not bear the abstinence that she would otherwise impose. An invisible rift widened between us and sometimes I would sicken of it all and join my dog in the courtyard under the cold winter sky, with his warmth as my only comfort. At such lonely moments I felt once more a stranger in the world, and wondered for what strange pattern the great Weaver could use so patchy and brittle a thread as myself.

Giulia's irritability arose partly from her ill success as a soothsayer, for although her neighbors politely clapped their hands and admired her powers she earned nothing. The capital abounded in so many fortunetellers, astrologers, and throwers of chicken bones, of all races and creeds, besides heiromancers who practiced divination by means of blood and entrails, that it was hard for a newcomer to compete with them. Though Abu el-Kasim diligently sang her praises in the bazaar, he was not a man to inspire confidence. We began to feel shut out again from this mysterious city, where success depended less on reasoned action than on chance.

I slipped imperceptibly into the Ottoman way of life and soon ceased to be regarded as a foreigner; with my gift for languages I combined the faculty of changing my skin, as it were, and assuming a new identity. Piri-reis's old sea janissaries were friendly, while his clerks and cartographers grew accustomed to seeing me among them every day. Now and again I would be given a task suited to my talents—some errand to the Seraglio library, perhaps, where learned Mussulmans and Greeks were busy with the translation and copying of ancient manuscripts. But among these scholars I found no one to be my friend.

I saw the Sultan once, at a distance, attended by a brilliant throng. A party of bowmen surrounded him as he rode, and as they might not turn their faces from him, those in front had to run backward. When on Fridays the Sultan rode to his father's mosque, anyone—even the poorest—might present a petition to him at the end of a long, cleft stick. Many of these petitions were actually read and were dispatched by the Divan to the appropriate officials, for the wrongs recorded therein to be redressed.

The more I thought about this vast empire, built up by the Ottomans from small beginnings and now comprising within its borders more races than I could name, the more deeply impressed was I by the remarkable statesmanship that held it together and made life there agreeable and safe. This realm was governed by milder, juster laws than those of Christendom, and the moderate taxes were not to be compared with the merciless extortions practiced by so many Christian princes. And further, the tolerance shown by Ottomans toward other religions was something unheard-of elsewhere; no one was persecuted for his faith save the Persian Shiites, the heretics of Islam. Christians and Jews had their own places of worship and might even observe their own laws if they so chose.

Christians indeed had one heavy tribute to pay, in that every third year they must hand over their sturdiest sons to be trained from their eleventh year upward as the Sultan's janissaries. But these boys did not complain; they were proud of the honor and became more vigorous champions of Allah than Moslems born and bred.

The High Porte was indeed the Refuge of all Peoples. Not only did the core of the Sultan's army consist of professional soldiers born of Christian parents, and adopted, brought up, and trained by Turks; the highest appointments in the Empire were held by men of every race who were slaves of the Sultan. To him alone they owed advancement, to him their heads were forfeit if they failed in prompt and meticulous execution of his commands. The Sultan bestowed great power on these men, but his incorruptible agents constantly toured every district of every province and listened to the people's complaints; thus the local governors were prevented from overstepping the limits of the authority vested in them by custom and the Sultan's laws.

My life was now bound up with the welfare and success of this empire, and so at first I strove to see everything in the most favorable light. There were signs that the Sultan was preparing for a great campaign, and without wishing ill to anyone I was keenly curious to know what would become of the King of Vienna. I had had experience of the Emperor's poverty and did not believe he could send much help to his brother; moreover an inherent feature of the Ottoman Empire was its tendency to expand. In this it followed the doctrines of Islam, which preached unceasing war against the unbeliever. Also the janissaries grew restless and discontented if the Sultan failed to lead them at least once a year into a war in which plunder and fresh honors were to be gained.

Whereas the Emperor Charles's campaigns cost enormous sums and far exceeded his economic resources, the Sultan's wars by an ingenious and farsighted arrangement paid for themselves. His regular cavalry, the spahis, drew their income from farms which they held from the Sultan and which were worked by slaves taken in battle. Thus these spahis served their sovereign for almost no wages. In districts bordering the Christian countries light cavalrymen, known as akindshas, lived on a war footing; their traditional banditry inclined them to enter the service of the Sultan. Similar tastes brought a vast number of idle men to the Sultan's colors as auxiliary troops, which were commonly thrown in as cannon fodder at the forefront of any attack. The Sultan therefore found himself in a far more advantageous position than the Christian leaders and could, even while sustaining losses, slowly but surely wear down enemy resistance. And so, when like Giulia I indulged in dreams of a splendid future, I saw nothing fantastic in the idea that one day I might find myself governor of some wealthy German city, in reward for my services.

But when I discussed Seraglio affairs with Giulia she warned me against relying too much on Ibrahim's favor, and asked in some derision what it had done for me so far. From our neighbors and at the baths she heard gossip enough, and knew that the Sultan's favorite slave, Khurrem the Russian, had already borne him three sons. This young and ever vivacious woman had so captured her lord's heart that he paid not the least attention to the rest of his harem, and had even shamefully dismissed the mother of his first-born son. It was now this underbred Russian woman on whom foreign envoys showered their presents; they called her Roxelana and sought by every means to gain her favor. Such was her influence over the Sultan that he would do anything to gratify her smallest wish, and envious voices in the harem had begun to hint at sorcery. Giulia said, "Grand viziers come and go, but woman's power over man is eternal and her influence stronger than that of even the closest friend. If in some way I could win Sultana Khurrem's favor I know I might do a great deal more for both of us than the Grand Vizier ever could."

I smiled at her simplicity, but warned her, "Speak low, woman, for in this city walls have ears. I came here to serve the Grand Vizier and through him Khaireddin, lord of the sea. And you're mistaken —nothing in the world is so fleeting as sensual passion. How can you suppose that the Sultan will be bound to one woman forever, when the choicest virgins of every race and country wait to obey his slightest sign? No, Giulia, women have no place in high politics; no future can be founded on a wayward houri of the harem."

Giulia retorted with some asperity, "I'm edified to learn from you that love and passion are such ephemeral things. I shall not forget. But perhaps some men are less fickle than you."

A few days later the Sultan held a Divan on horseback at which, according to ancient Ottoman custom, questions of peace and war were debated. He appointed Ibrahim commander in chief, or seraskier, of the whole Turkish army and once again confirmed Ibrahim's position as Grand Vizier, whose commands and ordinances were to be obeyed by high and low, rich and poor, as if they had been the Sultan's own. The proclamation was so comprehensive and detailed as to convince everyone that from now on Seraskier Ibrahim was, next the Sultan, the highest authority in the Empire.

In token of his favor the Sultan gave him, besides a great quantity of splendid presents, seven horsehair switches instead of the four with which he had previously been honored, and also seven banners —one white, one green, one yellow, two red, and two striped ones—to be borne before him always. The Sultan had further granted him a salary of ten thousand aspers a day: ten times that of the Aga of Janissaries, who held the highest rank of all the agas. In my lowly position I never caught so much as a glimpse of the Grand Vizier, but was delighted to find that my faith in him was justified. When I mentioned this to Giulia she answered, "Have it your own way, Michael. Pin your faith on the Grand Vizier, who has remembered you so often and to such purpose! But allow me to seek my fortune elsewhere."

Three days later the Sultan released King Ferdinand's envoys who had been imprisoned in the Fort of the Seven Towers, and bestowed upon each a well-filled purse in compensation for what they had endured. I was told that he addressed these words to them: "Salute

187

your master, and tell him he does not yet know all that our mutual friendship can achieve. But he will soon find out, and I mean to give him with my own hand all that he desires of me. Bid him make timely preparation for my coming."

To these playful words King Ferdinand's envoy replied, in a manner quite devoid of finesse, that his sovereign would be most happy to welcome the Sultan if he came as a friend, but that he would also know how to receive him as an enemy. Thus war was declared. But both official and secret agents of Christian states in Istanbul had already sent dispatches flying to their princes as soon as they heard that the Divan had met on horseback.

Spring advanced to the sound of drums and trumpets, and ceaseless rain turned the ground to mud. It was the custom, when the seraskier had set forth in advance to mobilize his troops, for the Sultan to march somewhat later at the head of his janissaries. But now every day small detachments started for the frontier in a prearranged order, and with the creaking, lumbering gun carriages went my brother Andy. For the second time in his life he found himself on the road to Hungary, though this time to fight for the Mussulmans instead of against them. He seemed dubious of the enterprise and wondered how the guns were to be conveyed along pulpy roads and across rivers swollen with the spring freshets. But, he thought, the Mussulmans had perhaps found some method of overcoming these obstacles, since they marched regardless of bad weather.

There was also great activity in Piri-reis's department, for the fleet was making ready for war. It was to patrol the coasts of the Black Sea and the Aegean, and some vessels were to make their way up the Danube in support of the advancing army. At this time I was sent on many errands to the arsenal and the forecourt of the Seraglio.

One exceptionally fine and sunny day after a long period of rain I was sitting and waiting in the Court of Peace, for my chief duty as messenger was to wait. I was by now familiar with the different dresses worn by the Seraglio servants—their materials, colors, badges, and headdresses—and no longer gaped about me like a stranger. Suddenly I saw a eunuch stumbling toward me. His fat face was swollen with weeping and he wrung his hands in despair as he asked me, "In Allah's name, are you not that slave of Khaireddin's, who brought the monkey? You may yet save me from the noose and the pit. Come with me quickly and I'll beg the Kislar-Aga to allow you into the

Court of Bliss, to coax the monkey down from the tree where it has been all night. A young eunuch has already broken his leg in trying to reach it."

"I cannot leave my important business to play with monkeys," I told him.

"Are you out of your mind? Nothing can be more important than this, for little Prince Jehangir is weeping and we shall all lose our heads if he continues."

"Perhaps Koko the monkey will remember me," I reflected, "for I tended her when she was seasick on the long voyage from Algeria. She will certainly remember my dog."

Rael lay curled up beside me, enjoying the warm sunshine, and when he heard Koko's name he pricked his shaggy ears. We hurried with the eunuch through the second and third courtyards where more eunuchs surrounded us and beat on little drums as a signal to the women to hide themselves. We reached the shining copper gates of the gardens where the Kislar-Aga awaited us—the highest official in the harem and commander of the white eunuchs. It was in vain that he sought to conceal his anxiety behind a dignified demeanor. I threw myself on the ground before him, and he gave orders for me to be admitted instantly to the gardens of the harem. To enter it without permission spelled death to any but eunuchs, and only with an escort of these and by the Sultan's command might merchants come in to display their wares. Not even a physician might pay a professional visit here without the Sultan's consent. But I was now hustled with such frantic speed into the most closely guarded gardens in the world that the eunuchs had no time to bathe me or give me clean clothes, as was the custom, and to my annoyance I had to appear as I was.

We raced along winding gravel paths, while my escort beat their little drums unceasingly and forbade me to look about me. At last we reached a huge plane tree in which four or five eunuchs with the courage of despair were clambering about in pursuit of the monkey. The monkey clung with hands, feet, and tail to the topmost branch. With cries and lamentations and kind words the eunuchs sought to coax it down to them, and exhorted one another shrilly not to let it fall and hurt itself. Just as I came up, one of these clumsy creatures slipped and tumbled shrieking from a considerable height. The top of the tree swayed as he crashed downward, head first, and lay senseless on the ground among the spring flowers.

Lamentable though this incident was, it was not without its comic side, and three well-dressed boys of whom the eldest was perhaps eleven years old burst into uproarious laughter at the spectacle. But the fourth wept softly. He was not more than five. He sat on the arm of a man in a flowered silk kaftan in whom to my amazement I recognized Sultan Suleiman himself. There was no mistaking his smoke-colored complexion, though in his plain dress and low turban he looked strangely short in stature. I at once threw myself down and kissed the ground before him and his sons.

All was confusion round the tree. Ropes lay about, ladders were propped against the trunk, and efforts had clearly been made to bring the monkey down by squirting water at it. Even at this distance I could see that it was sick, and it moaned as it clung helplessly to the bough. The Kislar-Aga bent low before the Sultan and suggested that I should be sent up the tree since I knew the monkey, and indeed had brought the bewitched animal to the Seraglio. If I failed he would have me beheaded, and so no harm would come of my admission to the forbidden gardens.

His harsh words so wounded me that I rose at once and said, "I never asked to come here; I was induced with tears and prayers to offer my help. Call down those blockheads. They scare the poor beast. And stop that drumming. Then give me a little fruit and I'll try to coax it down."

The Kislar-Aga said, "Is it thus you speak to me, miserable slave? And know that since early morning we have tried to fetch it down with fruit."

But Sultan Suleiman said curtly, "Call them down and send everyone away. You, too, have my leave to go."

When the chattering eunuchs had disappeared with their ropes, ladders, and syringes, complete stillness reigned. The little boy in the Sultan's arms had ceased sobbing, and only the moans of the monkey could be heard. Not venturing to address the Sultan I turned to his eldest son and said, "Noble Prince Mustafa, the monkey is sick. That's why it fled up the tree. I shall try to coax it down."

The dark, handsome boy nodded haughtily. I sat down upon the ground with Rael in my arms and called softly and coaxingly, "Koko! Koko!" The monkey peeped suspiciously through the branches and gave a few faint cries, but would not move. Then I said to Rael, hoping that the Sultan would hear, "Dear, faithful dog! Koko doesn't know me in my new clothes, and thinks I'm one of the eunuchs. *You* call her. Perhaps she'll remember playing with you on board ship. Try to call her down from the tree."

Rael looked up into the treetop, pricked his ears, and whined softly, then barked twice. The monkey climbed down a little way to get a clearer view, and Prince Jehangir still on his father's arm held up his little hands and called, "Koko! Koko!" The monkey hesitated, but as Rael went on whining she made up her mind and climbed swiftly down. She sped up to me, sprang into my arms, and hugged me with her white-whiskered cheek against mine, her whole spindly body shaking with fever.

Koko stretched out one arm and stroked Rael, then pulled his ears and tail, whereupon Rael gently caught her hand in his teeth and growled warningly. At the beginning of our voyage the monkey had tormented the life out of Rael, pinching him at every opportunity and then taking flight to the top of the mast, leaving the dog barking furiously below. But later they both enjoyed the game and became friends; sometimes they basked together on deck and Koko lay with her arms about Rael's neck, or with nimble fingers plucked fleas from his coat.

But now she broke off her play in a terrible fit of coughing, one tiny hand pressed to her chest. Tears flowed from the haggard eyes, and between paroxysms she uttered heartrending cries as if to tell me how wretched and lonely she felt. Rael too began to whine piteously, and licked Koko's limp hand as if he understood. The princes came to stroke the sick monkey and to my surprise the Sultan drew near too, and spreading out the skirts of his kaftan sat down beside me on the ground so that Prince Jehangir could touch the little creature. The Sultan said to me, "You must be a good man, since animals trust you. Is the monkey sick?"

I replied, "I have studied medicine both in Christian countries and among Moslems, and I know that this poor beast has fever. It will die, if Allah so wills. It could not survive this climate, and the night spent in the tree has worsened the chill. I think it fled up the tree to die there alone, for most of the creatures we try to tame prefer to die in solitude, away from humans."

Prince Mustafa said hotly, "The monkey has lived in warm rooms and worn warm clothes every day, for it's my brother Jehangir's pet. The slave who's to blame for its illness shall pay for it with his head."

I answered, "No one is to blame for this illness, for monkeys are most sensitive to changes of climate, and even in the palaces of sunny Italy they sicken and die. If this little monkey should perish too, it will be by the will of Allah and we cannot prevent it. Nevertheless I'll prepare a cough mixture to soothe the pain."

The Sultan said, "Will you indeed give this poor beast medicine? Most physicians consider it beneath their dignity to treat animals. Yet the Prophet loved them, especially camels and cats. Indeed animals, unlike men, are without guile and I hate to see them suffer. But I have many animal doctors in my service and shall need you no longer. Selim, give him the monkey's clothes. Mustafa, give him the chain. And you, Michael, dress the monkey and fasten the chain about its neck; then leave us."

The boys handed me a little wool-lined velvet kaftan and a thin silver chain, but Koko struggled when I tried to put them on her. At last I succeeded, and laying the end of the chain in Prince Jehangir's little hand I told the boys to give the monkey some warm milk. Then I rose, called my dog, and prepared to leave the gardens. But at this Koko flew into a passion, kicked and struggled and tried to bite the princes, then tore loose and ran after me. With the chain rattling behind her she scrambled up into my arms and clung there.

The Sultan was at a loss. He put down the little boy, who ran up to me crying, flung one arm around my leg and raised the other to stroke the monkey. It was then I noticed that the poor little fellow was club-footed, and that a hump was beginning to show beneath his silken coat. His sallow face was as ugly as the monkey's, and he was almost stifled with his sobs. Then Selim, the third prince, clutched his head and cried in a shrill voice that he was going to faint. The Sultan shouted, "Mustafa and Muhammed! Take Jehangir in at once and this man too, to look after the monkey. Send the Kislar-Aga to me and call the *tselebs.*"

As I bent to rub Prince Selim's temples the Sultan signed to me to go, no doubt meaning the boys to take me out of the harem gardens to their own quarters in the inner court. But the young princes misunderstood him and instead led me to Prince Jehangir's rooms where the monkey's cage was. I could feel the eyes of agitated eunuchs following me from behind the bushes, but did not then know enough to be afraid.

Carrying the monkey and leading Prince Jehangir by the hand I followed the boys to Sultana Khurrem's pavilion of many-colored tiles, thus committing all unawares the gravest possible offense. Mustafa, Muhammed, and Selim, all being over seven years old, lived with their *tselebs,* or tutors, in the third courtyard; but the sickly Jehangir, who was only five, remained in his mother's pavilion and was allowed to keep his monkey there. I was certainly somewhat startled to see the women attendants hastening toward us unveiled, in the belief that I was a eunuch, yet I still had no misgivings and entered Prince Jehangir's spacious room in which stood the monkey's gilded cage and its bed. I ordered the women to fetch some hot milk at once for the sick animal, while the boys sat down on cushions to watch all I did. Rael hurried round the room sniffing into every corner, and Prince Jehangir, like any other tear-stained and weary child, began crying for his mother.

All that had happened so far seemed purely the result of chance, and only later did I learn that Prince Selim was an epileptic. During his childhood the attacks could be controlled and suppressed by means of sedatives. They did not become serious until as a youth he began to drink too much wine. The Sultan naturally wished to keep this terrible disorder secret, and that was why he sent me so hastily out of the garden; he feared that the excitement might bring on an attack. Prince Mustafa was born of the Circassian slave whom Suleiman had dismissed in favor of Khurrem. He was thus only half-brother to Jehangir, and it had evidently been the Sultan's intention that Mustafa should take me to his own rooms; but Mustafa was generous hearted and of course thought it best for the monkey to be taken straight to its warm cage.

I did become exceedingly agitated, however, to hear a rippling laugh and see coming toward us an unveiled and richly dressed woman with a jeweled net over her hair. She put her arms about Prince Jehangir, and I at once flung myself to the ground, hiding my face in my hands. Yet I was as usual unable to master my curiosity, and stole a glance at her between my fingers, feeling that since in any case my punishment for entering the Sultana's pavilion must be death, it could make little difference if I had a glimpse of the woman of whom so many tales were told and whom Christian princes overwhelmed with presents.

My first impression was disappointing, for I had expected a ravishing beauty. This was the woman who, alone among countless lovely maidens from all corners of the world, had received the Sultan's handkerchief and for years after their wedding night had kept his favor. She was a fairly tall, plump woman, still young, but her face was unusually round and her nose anything but aristocratic. It was in her lively play of feature and continual laughter that her charm lay, though it seemed to me that her blue eyes had no part in that mirth. As she regarded the deeply bowing Mustafa over Jehangir's head I saw in them a singular coldness.

Prince Mustafa explained that he had been commanded to bring me with him to tend the sick monkey and prepare a draught for it. My dog now rose smartly on his hind legs and stretched forth his nose toward the Sultana, in whom he plainly saw the dispenser of titbits. Prince Jehangir giggled, and at once the Sultana sent her women after sweetmeats, which she then gave the dog herself, laughing her silvery laugh. Meanwhile a cup of warm milk had been brought and I was able to induce the monkey to drink a little of it; but it would not leave me and kept one arm tightly round my neck while with the other it tried to coax the dog to come to it.

Sultana Khurrem now turned to me and asked in Turkish, "Who are you, and how can a eunuch have a beard? Can you really treat sick monkeys?"

I pressed my forehead to the ground before her, while the monkey sat on the back of my neck and tried to snatch off my turban.

"Sovereign lady," I said, "I have not ventured so much as a glance at your radiant beauty. For the sake of my little dog and the sick monkey, protect me, for I'm no eunuch. Through no fault of mine I was brought to the gardens to coax the monkey down from the top of the plane tree, and I've not the least idea how I come to be in your presence, most lovely of all women in the world."

She answered, laughing, "Lift your head and look at me, you simple man, now that you're here. You've made my son Jehangir smile and he loves your dog. But the Kislar-Aga will no doubt receive the silken cord for his negligence, so you'll die in good company. Prince Mustafa deserves punishment for his stupidity."

In deep dejection I replied, "I welcome death, if it be Allah's will. But allow me first to give my dog to Prince Jehangir, if he is fond of him. After my death there will be no one else to care for the poor beast. I will also prepare a draught for the monkey and relieve its suffering. I'm not aware of having in any way offended against yourself or the Lord of all Nations, for it was not of my own will or with evil intent that I entered your presence. Nor can your beauty put me in a state of impurity, for how could one of my lowly estate raise his eyes to you?"

The poor monkey, still sitting on the back of my neck, was now overcome by another fit of coughing. I had to sit up again and take her into my arms. She coughed so violently that froth tinged with blood appeared at the corners of her mouth and she could offer no resistance when I laid her on the soft cushion in the cage, which was warmed by a charcoal brazier. Rael, replete with sweetmeats, jumped into the cage too, and curled up beside the monkey, which put an arm about his neck and tugged his ears. Prince Jehangir crept from his mother's arms, drew a cushion forward to the cage, and sat down cross legged to gaze with his big, sad eyes at his pet. I could see that he was a gentle boy, who would not ill treat my dog. I then rapidly recited the first sura and said, "Prince Jehangir, my dog is the cleverest dog in the world and has seen many countries. I bequeath him to you, since I am to meet the One who severs the bonds of friendship and silences the voice of happiness. Take care of Rael and be a good master to him, and Allah will surely reward you."

I was convinced that by the merciless laws of the Seraglio I must die. But the princes cared nothing for my melancholy fate; they clapped their hands and began to make much of their grieving brother Jehangir, in the hope that they too might play with my dog. Sultana Khurrem said, "Such an animal is no very becoming gift for the son of the Sultan; but he himself is not without blemish and perhaps the animal will be a comfort to him if the monkey dies—as I hope it will, for the smell of its cage pollutes the room. But I'm not hardhearted, and I will speak to the Sultan, if I should be so favored as to meet with him before the mutes have put the rope about your neck. But your entry into this pavilion without permission is so abominable a disgrace for the Kislar-Aga that he will hardly spare your life, and as the Sultan's slave I am bound to obey the Kislar-Aga in all things."

I knew enough of the laws of the Seraglio to realize that she was speaking the truth, and that without the Kislar-Aga's mediation she had not the least chance of approaching the Sultan. Suleiman himself had to submit to that official's complex ceremonial when wishing to visit the house where his slave women lived, and if one of these had dared to address him without leave it would have constituted an insult to the Sultan's majesty. For the same reason Suleiman could not visit his favorite without previously making known his intention. He could send for his children, to walk with them in the gardens, but at such times all the women had, on pain of disfavor and dismissal, to stay within doors and out of sight. Only by this strict rule could the Sultan be at peace, for without it his women would have been constantly slinking after him in an attempt to win his favor.

Having reflected as coolly as I could upon my unenviable plight, I said, "I was commanded by the Sultan himself to tend the monkey, so I must now fetch the necessary remedies. Should anyone slay me while I'm on this errand he will be acting against the Sultan's express command. I will go now; when—and if—I return, the Kislar-Aga may do with me as he pleases."

The Sultana broke again into a cooing laugh, and this continual mirth began to make me strangely uneasy. She said, "Don't think for a moment that you can escape. By looking into my face you have broken the strictest rule of the harem. For his own sake the Kislar-Aga will be forced to have you strangled as soon as he catches you, and even now, no doubt, is awaiting you eagerly at the Seraglio gates."

Prince Mustafa cried excitedly, "This should be good sport! Let's follow him and see what happens. My father the Sultan entrusted this man to my care, but if I can't save his life I should at least like to watch him die. Although I'm the Sultan's eldest son I have not seen many men die. Come, Muhammed!"

The smile faded from Sultana Khurrem's lips and her eyes turned ice blue, as if the shadow of death had glided through the room. Perhaps danger had quickened my wits, for I understood at once that Mustafa, on ascending the throne after his father's death, would have his brothers slain. It would be but in accordance with the law, for the gravest menace to the Ottoman Empire had ever been that of civil war between brothers. I had strayed into the gardens of death; what hope remained?

I believe only Prince Mustafa's arrogant manner saved me, for, since it stung Khurrem to hear him boast of his age compared with that of his half-brother, she made it a point of honor to protect me. She said, therefore, "Mustafa and Muhammed, go at once and find the Kislar-Aga. Tell him to come here instantly on pain of my most severe displeasure."

The princes were thus compelled to renounce the exciting game in which I was to be the bait. They tossed their heads and muttered, but at length obeyed. As soon as they had gone Khurrem turned to me and asked quickly, "Who are you and what is your profession? I hope I do not compromise myself by shielding an unworthy man."

Rapidly I told her of my travels and of how I took the turban, of how Khaireddin of Algiers had sent me to be the Sultan's slave because of my languages and my familiarity with conditions in Christendom. At this point the Kislar-Aga arrived in a state of unspeakable agitation, and pressing his forehead to the floor in repeated prostrations he said, "Sovereign lady! Most high Sultana! I cannot tell how the error occurred, but mutes await this impudent slave at the copper gates. The matter shall remain a secret and your fair fame unsullied. Not even the Lord of all Nations need hear what has occurred."

The flabby, ashen-faced eunuch stood there in his resplendent official dress and his eyes as he glared at me were dark with fury. But Sultana Khurrem said, "This slave was commanded by the Sultan himself to tend Prince Jehangir's monkey. See that he is given the drugs he requires and that he returns safely to my pavilion, unless you should receive contrary orders from the Sultan."

The Kislar-Aga was compelled to obey. He escorted me from the pavilion, and two strong eunuchs seized me and hustled me out of the gardens even more speedily than I had entered them. The Kislar-Aga, pouring forth an unbroken stream of abuse, never let me out of his sight for an instant until we reached the apothecary's shop in the forecourt. Here the Sultan's Jewish physician Solomon quickly mixed the medicine I asked for, though he seemed jealous because I was accompanied by the Kislar-Aga and asked spitefully at which learned university I had taken my medical degree. The Sultan's physicians were chosen from among the foremost specialists in the world and would suffer no outside competition. Humbly I explained that I was in attendance on a mere soulless beast which no man of distinction would deign to treat, and that I had studied medicine under eminent professors although I had never taken the diploma. The Kislar-Aga suddenly put both hands to his head and cried, "Blessed be Allah! Tell me again where you studied and graduated. If you're a physician you may of course practice in the harem itself, in the presence of eunuchs, if the Sultan so commands."

He offered me here the opportunity for a convenient lie, for I could have named any university and explained that I had lost my papers when taken into slavery by the Moslems. But had I sought such a

197

refuge I should have revealed myself as an untrustworthy character and so justified his earlier suspicions. After careful reflection I replied, "No, no. Allah be my witness that I'm an honest man and won't resort to falsehood even to save my life. When I have given the monkey its medicine you may take off my head, noble Kislar-Aga. I can claim no degree."

The Kislar-Aga stared and seemed not to believe his ears. Turning to the Jewish physician he said, "Truly this man is mad and afflicted of Allah! He refuses to profit by the most innocent lie to get himself and me out of trouble, although he would best serve the Sultan by so doing."

I repeated obstinately, "No, no. I cannot lie."

The physician stroked his beard and said smiling, "This man may not be a doctor yet, but he may become one at any time. All that is required is a diploma sealed with the seal of the madrasseh and signed by three learned *tselebs.*"

The proposal flattered my vanity, for the physician evidently believed me fully trained in medicine. But I knew that I could never satisfy the learned examiners.

"My knowledge is inadequate," I confessed, "and besides, I studied my texts in Latin, not in Arabic."

The Jewish physician answered slyly, "You know the suras and prayers; you're a pious Moslem, as your turban shows. Were so important a man as the Kislar-Aga to vouch for you at the madrasseh I don't doubt they would make an exception in your case and allow you to answer the more difficult questions through an interpreter. And were I that interpreter I could certainly express what you have to say in the most telling manner, and testify to your exceptional learning."

The suggestion greatly tempted me, for though it smacked of dishonesty, yet for this the Jew and not I would be responsible. I knew enough, I thought, not to harm my patients more than any other doctor, and was glad to think that the nickname "el-Hakim," given me in jest by Abu, was now to be ratified by a document signed and sealed. Such a diploma was worth much fine gold, and I should have been mad not to accept so excellent an offer.

With becoming reluctance I said, "I would agree to your proposal to oblige the noble Kislar-Aga, but I'm a poor man and cannot pay for the seal."

Solomon the physician rubbed his yellow hands together and said quickly, "Don't trouble yourself about that. I will pay for the seal and so forth if you, like an honorable colleague, will give me half of any fee you may receive for tending the monkey. I shall lose by it, of course, but in the name of the Compassionate I shall also acquire merit."

The Kislar-Aga exclaimed, "May Allah bless you! You walk in the true path, Jew though you be. If you will make a qualified physician of this man, discreetly and without undue chatter, you may be assured of my favor."

He lent his signet ring to Solomon and gave him a young eunuch to attend him. The physician then mounted a mule and rode away to speak with the learned *tselebs* in the medical department of the madrasseh. The Kislar-Aga committed me to the care of three armed eunuchs, ordering them to accompany me back to Sultana Khurrem's pavilion and not let me out of their sight for an instant. If I attempted to run away, or to address the Sultana, they were to strike off my head immediately.

Prince Jehangir was still sitting on his cushion with his head propped in his hand, watching the fevered monkey. My dog lay beside her, licking her dry nose from time to time. Koko had torn off her velvet kaftan and had not tasted the luscious fruits that had been set before her. In the dim corners of the room sat a few silent slave girls, deeply moved by the little Prince's grief.

I forgot my own fears and knew not whom to pity more—the dying beast or the deformed Prince, who with tears rolling down his cheeks sat motionless on his cushion, himself looking like nothing so much as a richly dressed monkey. I administered the soothing draught and applied a compress to the monkey's chest, and then sat with her in my arms. Prince Jehangir sat beside me and stroked the sick animal's coat from time to time.

I was fighting a hard battle with myself. Although I had promised to give my dog to Prince Jehangir only in the event of my death, I could not take Rael back, were my life to be spared, without deeply grieving the boy. It was clear that I must part with Rael in any event, and indeed the dog could have no better master than this solemn child. Here he would lack for nothing, while in my heart I knew it was only a matter of time before Giulia lost all patience with him. She would begin to ill treat him, and perhaps even do away with him altogether. I too was now very sorrowful; tears rose to my eyes as I recalled the adventures of my past life and I knew that never should I find a better or more faithful friend than my dog Rael.

The soothing medicine allowed the monkey to fall into a deep sleep; I laid her in the gilt cage and covered her warmly over. I then ordered my dog to keep watch beside her, and promised the Prince that I would come again next morning. The eunuchs led me away. Red and gold clouds hung over the Sea of Marmara and the air was crystal clear, as it so often is after a long spell of rain. The heavy scent of hyacinths lay over the gardens. As my guards led me toward the copper gates, I was filled with inexpressible sadness; everything seemed strangely unreal, as if I were walking by my own side and watching my journey through an incomprehensible world. At that moment I had no fear of death. The will of Allah was guiding me from cradle to grave; my life was an insignificant thread in his infinite web, whose pattern I could not see.

When we reached the Sultan's court the unarmed white eunuchs took charge of me and led me to their bathhouse where I was given a steam bath, massaged severely, and rubbed with sweet-smelling ointments. In the dressing room I was arrayed in fine new linen garments and a respectable kaftan. Hardly was I dressed when the hour of evening prayer had come, and I could perform my devotions after complete ablution and in the best possible frame of mind. I was then taken without delay to the Kislar-Aga's reception room where I found Solomon the physician and three long-bearded and short-sighted *tselebs*. Solomon had seated himself at a respectful distance from these ancient scholars. In a corner of the room sat the *tselebs'* scribe, with writing materials on his knee. A number of lamps suspended from the ceiling shed a clear light over the room.

Having saluted the *tselebs* with veneration, I was invited to sit on a low leather cushion before them, and Solomon made a long speech in my honor. Despite my youth, he told them, I had studied medicine at the foremost universities of Christendom; then, having found the true path, I had taken the turban and so been enabled to acquire valuable knowledge from ancient Arabian writings. He declared that I admired above all that school founded by Moses ben-Maimon and his pupils; but because of my imperfect knowledge of the language I needed help in displaying my talents, though I was well able to read Arabic texts. On the recommendation of the noble Kislar-Aga, an

200

exception had been made in my favor and I was to be allowed to answer the examiners through an interpreter.

It was of course most gratifying to hear the high opinion the learned doctor had formed of my attainments after so short a conversation. The *tselebs* listened attentively, nodded, and regarded me with benevolence. Each in turn put questions to me, to which I replied by a jumble of Latin. Solomon appeared to pay careful attention to what I was saying, after which he repeated appropriate passages by heart from the works of Avicenna and Moses ben-Maimon.

Several times in the course of the examination the *tselebs* disputed animatedly among themselves and plunged into far-reaching dissertations to display their own learning and profundity of thought. And having thus passed an agreeable hour they declared with one voice that I had given satisfactory proof of my competence in medicine. The scribe had already engrossed my diploma in a fair hand, and all three *tselebs* now signed this and pressed their inked thumbs upon the parchment. Solomon gratefully kissed their hands and gave each of them a leather purse in reward for their trouble, while the Kislar-Aga sent them a delicious meal from his own kitchen. I was not allowed to leave the Seraglio, however, and slept that night behind bolts and bars.

Immediately after the morning prayer the eunuchs led me back to Sultana Khurrem's pavilion, and the gleaming copper gates seemed as familiar to me as if I had been a daily visitor to the forbidden gardens. Prince Jehangir lay in a deep sleep on his bed beside the monkey's cage, and his plain little face bore traces of tears. The dog lay with his head across the boy's legs and wagged his tail in greeting as I approached.

But Koko had had a hemorrhage during the night, and her little heart was so worn out with fever that she had barely strength to hold my finger. A faint moan came, then a convulsion, and she was dead. What should I have done now, I reflected, if little Jehangir had been my own son? First I dressed the dead monkey in its fine clothes, drew the bedcover over it and carried it, bed and all, out into the garden. The eunuchs kept close beside me. I ordered an old gardener who was working there to dig a grave at the foot of the big plane tree. He obeyed, and having laid my burden in it I filled the hole, raised a little mound above it and told the gardener to plant a flowering shrub there before Prince Jehangir awoke. I then returned to the Prince's room and sat cross legged on the floor beside his bed. Only once did the Sultana appear in the doorway, signing to the eunuchs to let Prince Jehangir have his sleep out. I sat immersed in thought until my legs grew numb and time began to drag interminably. But Prince Jehangir, having been awake until very late the night before, was exhausted with grief and slept long and soundly, to the delight of his servants.

He awoke about noon, and as he rubbed his eyes with his thin hands the dog with wagging tail crept up to lick his fingers. A faint smile overspread the boy's face. Then he started and looked toward the cage, to find it empty. His face twisted, and fearing another outbreak of weeping I said hastily, "Noble Prince Jehangir, you're the Sultan's son. Face like a man that One who severs the bonds of friendship forever, for gentle death has freed your friend the monkey from pain and fever. Think of Koko as setting forth now upon a journey to a far country. Just as we have a Paradise, so I think have little monkeys and faithful dogs—a Paradise with rippling water brooks."

Prince Jehangir in his sorrow listened to my words as to a beautiful story, and pressed Rael to his breast. I went on, "My dog was a good playfellow for your monkey, and though today you've lost one friend you have gained another. I think Rael will serve you well, though just at first, like the faithful beast he is, he may miss me."

While I was speaking Prince Jehangir allowed himself to be washed and dressed, after which the servants brought in many delicate dishes and set them before him. He refused to eat, and the slave girls were beginning to weep for fear when I said to him, "You must feed your new friend and eat with him, that he may know you for his master."

The pampered Prince looked at me suspiciously, but I began at once to hand him such morsels as I knew my dog would like. The boy obediently bit a piece from each and gave the rest to Rael, and Rael understood that from now on he would be fed by Prince Jehangir instead of me. He looked at me in wonder, but ate avidly of the good food; and if the truth must be told I tasted a few of the dishes myself, for they were indeed excellent and I was hungry. So Prince Jehangir, Rael, and I shared that meal, while the slave women laughed and clapped their hands, blessing me in the name of Allah because the Prince wept no longer and ate like a man.

When we had finished he put his hand trustfully into mine and I took him into the garden to show him the monkey's grave at the foot of the plane tree. The gardener had planted an early-flowering cherry on the mound, and though Prince Jehangir understood little of graves and death he beheld the tree with delight. Then to divert his thoughts I showed him how to throw a stick for Rael to fetch and lay at his feet, how to make Rael walk on his hind legs, or guard anything that the Prince had dropped. In his wonder at Rael's intelligence Prince Jehangir forgot his grief and even laughed now and again, though timidly.

His ill-shapen body soon wearied, and when I had taken him back to the pavilion I felt it best to go. I kissed his hand when I took my leave of him, and bade my dog farewell, charging him to protect his new master as faithfully as he had protected and guarded me in years gone by. With head and tail drooping Rael stood obediently beside Prince Jehangir, gazing after me with longing. When I had come out into the garden I could no longer restrain my tears, though I told myself that I could not have found a better master for my dog. His life under Giulia's iron rule had become unendurable.

The eunuchs led me to the Kislar-Aga's door, where I had to wait some hours before he was pleased to receive me. He sat fat and flabby on his cushion, having kicked off his slippers, and with his chin on his hand he scrutinized me closely for a long time without uttering a word. Then he addressed me quite cordially, saying, "You're a riddle to me. You're either sincere in your simplicity, or else a very dangerous and guileful man whose intrigues I cannot fathom, accustomed though I am to every sort of roguery. They tell me you've won Prince Jehangir's friendship by giving him your dog, that you've asked nothing in return and stayed no longer in the Sultana's pavilion than was necessary, though by delaying you might have claimed princely gifts. I also hear that the Sultana was much pleased at the way in which you took her hint and poisoned that dirty monkey. But in speaking a good word on your behalf to the Sultan I might harm myself by commending a man whose aims are mischievous. Then again, if I speak ill of you, as I should like to do, I might offend the Sultan, because he pities Prince Jehangir for his deformity and thinks only of his welfare. But some reward I can obtain for you, for it would be most unbecoming for a slave to serve the Sultan unrecompensed."

He gazed abstractedly at the ceiling, rubbing his soft, hairless chin, and went on, "You will of course realize that the value of your reward depends entirely on my favor, since the Sultan has faith in my discretion. I've made inquiries about you, and know that since arriving in Istanbul you've lived a regular life, performed all your religious duties, and not sought to form secret connections with Christians. Yet all this may have been cunning on your part. You have been watched at your work at the Cartographer's Office, and no one has caught you copying secret documents. But if I tell the Sultan that you earn twelve aspers a day your reward will be proportionate, and cannot exceed two hundred aspers. If I speak in your favor and praise your talents, and in every way emphasize that through some mistake you've been given far too low an appointment, you may receive a fistful of gold and the opportunity to display your capabilities in some other field. You're therefore entirely dependent on my favor, and without me are worth no more than dung in the yard."

"I well understand this, of course," I replied, "but I've already promised Dr. Solomon half of whatever I receive. I hope that you'll be good enough to accept a quarter, so that something may be left for me. It would be a little hard if my trouble proved my only reward."

The Kislar-Aga stroked his chin and looked at me with his head on one side.

"The Seraglio is a strange garden," he said, "where a seed sown in secret may put forth unexpected flowers. There's no one so lowly but that chance, under Allah, may raise him to a lofty position. For the same reason death reaps a bounteous harvest in the Seraglio, and should a man be compelled to chastize another he would be wise to do it with noose or block, lest one day he find his victim placed in authority over him. If I allow you to live I must make a friend of you, so that your advancement may profit me. And to speak truly I am so amazed at your candor that with equal honesty I will do what I can for you."

I perceived from this that I had indeed won the favor of Prince Jehangir and his mother, so that for the time being my life was safe. Nevertheless, the good will of the exalted Kislar-Aga would also be of the greatest value to me. I said, "Let me be your friend, then, and first of all point out certain things which may be useful to you. If you've made inquiries about me, you must know that my wife has eyes of different colors and can therefore gaze into the future. Only allow her to display her talents before you, and as a shrewd man you will at once perceive the advantage to be gained from them. She is a gifted woman, more astute than I, and would certainly never foretell anything hostile to your interest. But first you must initiate her into Seraglio affairs and make known to her the circumstances that seem to call for judicious prediction."

The Kislar-Aga scratched the soles of his feet vigorously and replied, "Allah be my refuge! So your simplicity was but a mask. Yet I risk nothing by receiving your wife, and what you say of her has made me very curious."

We took leave of one another cordially, in no way underrating one another's intelligence. In token of his favor he allowed me to kiss his hand, but made me swear by the Prophet, the Koran, and my downy beard that I would not breathe a word of what I had seen and done in the Seraglio.

That evening a eunuch came to our house, attended by armed troopers, and handed me a silken purse containing two hundred gold pieces —a present from the Sultan. This was equal to twelve thousand aspers, or a thousand days' pay, and was considerably more than I had dared expect. But as I contemplated this great sum I realized how hasty I had been in promising Dr. Solomon half of whatever I received, when he would certainly have been content with less.

When the eunuch had again mounted his mule, whose saddle was ornamented with silver plates and yellow stones, Giulia sighed, "Ah, Michael, did you see how contemptuously that splendid man looked at our cramped courtyard and ruinous house, though he was well bred enough to conceal his wonder? Such a place may suit Abu el-Kasim, who knows no better; but now that you're in favor with the Sultan you should at once find a house in a better quarter. It need have no more than five or ten rooms, if only it be tasteful and furnished in a manner befitting your dignity, so that I needn't blush for shame when receiving visits from distinguished guests. Our best plan would be to choose some beautiful site on the shores of the Bosphorus or the Marmara, and there build a modest house according to our needs and tastes. It should not be too far from the Seraglio, although of course we should have our own boat or gondola, and an oarsman or two. They could look after the garden as well, and we might build a dwelling for them adjoining the boathouse. If one were married, his wife could help my women in the house, and we could put the sons into fine clothes and send them on errands into the city, so that all who saw them would form a proper idea of your rank and dignity."

I clutched my head at Giulia's wild talk, and could not utter a word for some time. At length I drew a deep breath and said, "Giulia, Giulia! You're planning my downfall. If we're wise we'll save every asper we can scrape together, lest evil times follow. A new house would

205

swallow up my present and future income; it would be like pouring money into a bottomless well, and I should never know another day's peace." Giulia's face hardened, and her eyes were stony with anger as she snapped, "Why must you always destroy my loveliest dreams? Do you grudge me a home—a place we could call ours? Think what we should save by gathering fruit from our own trees and growing our own vegetables instead of being robbed by rogues in the market. And suppose we had children! Ah, Michael! You couldn't be so hard-hearted as to give them a dirty street for their playground, and let them grow up like the children of donkey drivers?"

Tears were now streaming down her cheeks and her words so moved me that I too began to picture to myself a little dwelling on the Bosphorus, with a garden from among whose fruit trees I could watch the stars come out and listen to the lapping of the water along the shore. But reason told me that I could not be certain of keeping the Sultan's favor, and that houses were not built nor gardens laid out on twelve aspers a day.

Our conversation was cut short by a shrill squealing, and when we ran out into the evening sunlight of the courtyard we beheld Giulia's furry blue cat writhing on the grass plot. Giulia tried to take the cat in her arms, but it scratched her and at last hid beneath the house and refused to come out, coax as we would. The wailing grew ever more agonized and at last ceased altogether. Deathly pale and with hands clenched, Giulia walked to the corner of the court where the dog's bowl was kept. After putting Rael's food into it she had covered it with a lid which one of the cats in its greed had pushed off; the food was gone and I had only to glance at Giulia to see that during my absence she had mixed poison with it, to kill my dog and punish me for staying away all night.

Seeing that I understood she quailed and said faintly, "Forgive me, Michael! I meant no harm, but I was blinded by anger after wandering about sleepless all night thinking evil thoughts of you. Your wicked dog has tried my patience long enough, and tormented my cats when you weren't looking. He left fleas on my cushions, muddied my floors, and overturned my jars. And now to crown everything he has poisoned my pet cat and I shall never, never forgive either of you."

She worked herself up into a frenzy against me and my dog, but at least this melancholy interlude diverted her thoughts from her building schemes. We never had time to return to the subject, for hardly had we begun to tear up the floorboards to get out the cat's body when we heard the rhythmic tramp of marching feet. Someone thundered at the outer gate with a sword hilt, and when I opened it there entered an onbash of janissaries fully equipped for battle, with a white felt cap on his head. He greeted me and handed me an order from his aga to the effect that I must set forth at once to join the army in the town of Philippopolis, on the river Maritsa, and there report as interpreter to the Seraskier's intelligence corps.

As I read this appalling communication I became so greatly agitated that I could only stammer the suggestion that there had been a grave mistake, and that for his own sake the onbash would be wise to accompany me at once to the aga and have the matter cleared up. But the onbash was a stolid, unimaginative veteran who said he had his orders. These were to see that before the last hour of prayer I was beyond the city walls and on my way to the theater of war. I had better make haste, he said, if I wished to put up some provisions for the journey, and pack suitable clothes.

It all happened so quickly that I was really conscious of nothing until I found myself sitting uncomfortably in a basket on the back of a camel, swaying rapidly along toward the city gate on the Adrianople road. I lifted my hands to heaven weeping and bewailing my hard fate, but at this the ten janissaries who were goading forward my camel began to sing at the tops of their voices, praising Allah and proclaiming that they were bound for Vienna to overthrow the King.

Their eagerness for battle, the unclouded evening sky—transparently clear after so many rainy days—and last but not least the passage in the Aga's written order entitling me to thirty aspers a day from the Defterdar's treasury, cheered me by degrees and inspired me with fresh courage. I tried also to console myself by thinking that nothing occurred contrary to the will of Allah. If for some reason I was to be removed from the Seraglio, it could only be because the Sultan wished to test my efficiency on a campaign, and so discover in which high appointment he could best employ me.

We swung through the low arch in the city wall just as the sun was setting. The rolling slopes beyond glowed red and yellow with tulips, and the white columns of Moslem tombs caught the last dying rays. Dusk fell, the sky darkened to purple, and in strange accompaniment to the tramp of the soldiers and the grunting of the camel I heard the hoarse, distant voices of the muezzins calling the faithful to prayer.

All at once I felt as if someone had lifted a heavy, stifling blanket from me; I breathed freely once more, and enjoyed deep draughts of the fresh spring air.

Although I was now to take part in a campaign that threatened all Christendom, I was escorted by a squad of experienced janissaries who must answer for my safety with their heads. I had thirty aspers a day and if fortune favored me I had much to gain and little to lose. My dog was in good hands. Giulia could maintain herself very well until my return on the money that the Sultan had given me, and perhaps I might soon meet my dear brother Andy again among the gunners; his loyalty and strength could be of great help to me in time of need.

And so there was no reason for dejection. True, the camel smelled very evil, my legs were numb, and the constant swaying afflicted me with nausea; yet without effort I swung forward through the fragrant spring night. Sultan Suleiman's expedition against the Emperor's brother in Vienna was now to begin, and out of respect for the Sultan I will bring this book to an end and start another.

BOOK 5.

The Siege of Vienna

I SHALL say little of the hardships I underwent on that journey. Bad weather set in again, and every night I lay drenched and shivering in the janissaries' tent. Columns of infantry, troops of cavalry, and strings of camels struggled along all the roads toward Philippopolis; at night every farm was packed to overflowing so that neither by hook nor by crook were sleeping quarters to be had. I never understood how I was able to endure these discomforts without falling sick, accustomed as I now was to a life of relative comfort.

In justice to the onbash I must mention that he ordered his men to take the very greatest care of me. They cooked my food and dried my clothes, and I soon came to admire the excellent discipline prevailing in our little troop. Each of the ten men seemed to have his own task to perform whenever we camped for the night. One collected firewood, another cooked, a third cleaned the weapons and accouterments. While a fourth fed the camels, others would be pitching the tents, and so smoothly and speedily were all things done that very soon a cheerful fire would be crackling beneath the pot, while a tent offered a comparatively dry sleeping place. These toil-toughened men cared little for the ceaseless downpour, and indeed made it a point of honor to endure uncomplainingly every sort of hardship, even performing regularly the five daily acts of devotion, though it meant kneeling and prostrating themselves in the mud.

What most surprised me, however, was their consideration for the peasants. They neither struck them nor stole their cattle nor tore down their dwellings for firewood. They never set fire to their ricks or molested their women, as was the custom among Christian soldiery. In the civilized states of Europe the right to do these things was considered the lawful perquisite of every mercenary, and bitterly though the victims complained, they accepted it as they accepted floods, earthquakes, or any other scourge of nature. But my onbash paid for all food and forage in pure silver at rates laid down by the Seraskier, and told me that any janissary who stole so much as a chicken or trampled the smallest patch of corn within the Ottoman borders would be hanged. So lovingly did the Sultan care for his subjects.

The reader must not wonder at my asking what satisfaction a poor soldier could find in an expedition where these innocent and well-deserved enjoyments were forbidden. But the onbash reassured me, explaining that all would change as soon as we set foot in the countries of the unbeliever. There a man could rob and pillage to his heart's content and commit what deeds of violence he chose, for such was pleasing to Allah. The onbash hoped that he and his men would richly compensate themselves for the privations of the march through the Sultan's domains.

The swollen rivers were very difficult to ford, and peasants told me that no man living remembered a rainier spring. Floods submerged their fields, prevented spring sowing, and threatened the whole land with famine. Their words depressed me, but the onbash smiled sourly and said he had never known a peasant to appear satisfied with the weather. It was too hot, too cold, it rained too much or too little, and not even Allah could gratify his every wish, though by this the onbash would not be thought to cast doubts upon Allah's omnipotence.

When at last we drew near Philippopolis and I saw the plain by the brimming river covered with a huge encampment, I cried out in amazement and said, "I've beheld many wonders in this world, but never so vast a camp as this. I could wager there are at least a hundred thousand men gathered here, and as many animals."

The onbash replied that there might well be a hundred and fifty thousand armed men on the plain. To these would be added about twenty thousand janissaries under the Sultan's own command, besides the Tartar auxiliaries and the akindshas who would join us at the frontier. I was greatly consoled, and with real pleasure alighted from my spiteful and untrustworthy camel at the gates of Philippopolis. Once or twice the treacherous beast had flung me basket and all into the mud. Camels were meant for the scorching desert and are distressed by cold air and constant rain. Marshy ground gives them no proper foothold, and my mount stumbled so often and so badly that her gangling legs straddled in all directions and it was a marvel that she was not torn in two. I resolved at any cost to find myself a horse in Philippopolis.

This huddle of narrow streets may once have been a pleasant riverside town, but when I arrived there it was packed with troops. The damp houses and miry streets emitted a terrible stench and the place seethed with angry men. After a great deal of trouble I was shown at last to the house of a Greek merchant where I found a mob of clerks, map makers, officers, messengers, idlers, peddlers, Jews, gypsies, and even a runaway monk who had wandered barefoot through Hungary that winter to serve the Sultan's cause.

When I reported to the Aga of the Scouts, this much-tried man cursed and declared he could not find a crib for every donkey that the Sultan was pleased to send him. Nevertheless he bade me study the maps of Hungary and make a list of the wells and grazing grounds marked upon them, so that if need arose I could gather more detailed information by interrogating prisoners. I might billet myself where I could find room, for—as he added drily—he could always reach me through the paymaster, whom I would be sure to visit.

This unfriendly reception sobered me, but after my all too rosy expectations it was wholesome, and inclined me to humility and patience. I put a good face on it, therefore, and returned to my janissaries who had pitched their tents on the riverbank. I could not even be rid of my camel, since no one was so foolish as to give me a horse in exchange.

We were now in the month of May, and one night as I lay shivering in my wet clothes the river burst its banks. The wildest confusion arose in the rainy darkness, and I had only the alertness of my janissaries to thank for being still alive at dawn when I found myself high up in a tree, lashed to a sturdy bough. Below us the yellow waters eddied and swirled, carrying with them drowned men and beasts and all manner of stores. I was still dazed with sleep, my teeth chattered, and my stomach cried out for food. At first I felt no gratitude for my rescue, but mourned the loss of my tent, my clothes and weapons, and even my unserviceable camel, which had perished. But at dawn the onbash and the six janissaries whom his presence of mind had saved praised Allah and performed their devotions as best they might in so comfortless a situation. The onbash assured us that our wetting in the floods equaled a complete ablution and that Allah, taking our plight into account, would pardon our imperfect prostrations. The prayers of these men, so singularly performed in the tree top, gave true expression to their thankfulness, yet I, weighed down by my losses, could not feel reverence at so fantastic a sight. As the light grew, however, and revealed the desolation of that flooded plain where lately so huge a camp had stood, I realized the wonder of my preservation and the good reason I had to send up a sigh of thanksgiving.

Here and there clumps of trees rose out of the waters, with survivors hanging in them like clusters of grapes. Other men, shrieking in terror, clung to drifting roofs, to troughs, and even to the carcasses of drowned animals, and besought us in Allah's name to throw them a rope's end. But our tree could carry no more, and we needed all the ropes to keep us from falling in ourselves. Three days and nights we stayed there and would no doubt have succumbed had we not been able to cut pieces of flesh from the carcass of a donkey that lodged among the lower boughs.

I had begun to lose all hope of rescue when a flat-bottomed river boat came in sight, punted along by several men and constantly running aground on its voyage from tree to tree to pick up survivors. As it drew near we shouted and waved until the man in command brought it alongside and ordered us to jump down. My fingers were too stiff to loosen the knots in my rope and so I cut it, and tumbled headfirst into the boat; no doubt I should have broken my neck had not the man in charge caught me in his arms. His broad face and indeed the whole of him was plastered with yellow mud, and as he looked at me he cried in astonishment, "Is it you, brother Michael? What can you be doing here? Has Piri-reis sent you to chart these new Turkish waters?"

"Dear heaven, it's Andy!" I exclaimed. "But where are your guns?"

"Safe under these swirling waters; and as the powder has become somewhat damp they'd be of little use to me just now. From this we see how equitably fate orders our affairs. But you're in luck, for I've orders to bring you straight to the Sultan who will pay you compensation for your wetting. Others wiser and more prudent than you, who ran uphill in good time out of reach of the floods, win no prizes.

I wonder what can be the object of rewarding stupidity and punishing good sense?"

When we had taken so many men aboard that our gunwale was almost level with the water, he began to punt his way back, and was by now so familiar with the channels that he was able to avoid shipwreck on the ruins of houses, and other reefs. Soon we reached the foot of a slope where helpful hands dragged us ashore, rubbed our numbed limbs, and poured warm milk down our throats. We were then led to the top of the hill where stood Sultan Suleiman and Seraskier Ibrahim, gorgeously arrayed and surrounded by bowmen. At their command the Defterdar paid immediate compensation to every man saved. Janissaries received nine aspers each, onbashes eighteen, and I, having produced my written orders from the Aga of Janissaries, was given no less than ninety aspers. I hardly knew if I was awake or dreaming, for how had we deserved thanks by being caught in the floods? But the onbash loudly praised the Sultan and explained, "Janissaries have a traditional right to compensation for a wetting. If while marching with the Sultan we wade through water to the knees we're given an extra day's pay. If it reaches the waist, double. And if we're lucky enough to go in up to the neck in his service we get three days' pay. Therefore the Sultan does his best to avoid pools and streams, but he could hardly be expected to allow for the flooding of the Maritsa. I hope not too many were rescued, however, or funds will give out before we reach even Buda."

The sun shone. After the three days' fast the milk felt warm in my stomach and the good silver coins were agreeably heavy. Neither the Sultan nor the Grand Vizier appeared discouraged at the losses sustained by the army; on the contrary they laughed aloud and gaily welcomed the groups of survivors that were still coming ashore. Yet their seeming cheerfulness was but a custom, to encourage the troops after any reverse; and a good custom it was, for no sooner had I taken my money than I too began to make little of the sufferings I had undergone. Three pillars had been set up on the hillside, on each of which a head had been placed. Some of the rescued men amused themselves by pulling the beards of these; for they were the heads of three pashas whom the Seraskier held responsible for choosing the camping place and whom he beheaded, to propitiate the Sultan and to keep his favor.

My guide brushed the mud from his kaftan and told me to fetch the new clothes that the Sultan had promised me, and then go to the road builders' tent to await further orders from the Grand Vizier. But Andy turned his steps resolutely toward the field kitchens and I was compelled to go with him, for he had me by the arm. The cooks were easily identified by their white aprons and caps, and Andy addressed them respectfully, saying that he felt a little hungry; but they bade him join his father in the nethermost pit. Resenting this, Andy first assured himself that the broth in one of the cauldrons was not yet scalding, then seized the nearest cook by the ears and plunged his head into it. Next, lifting him out and holding him high in the air he said mildly, "Perhaps another time you'll treat a grown man like a man and not like a naughty boy."

The cooks raised a great outcry and brandished their carving knifes, but as Andy still stood firm and massive as a block of granite, pointing first to his mouth and then to his belly, they came like wise men to the conclusion that they would most easily be rid of him by giving him the food he asked for.

We sat down to eat, and Andy so gorged himself that afterward he could hardly move. He made a few feeble attempts and then stretched himself on his back; I, exhausted by three days and nights of exposure, laid my head on his stomach and fell into the deepest sleep of my whole life.

I fancy I must have slept the clock round, for when aroused at last by a great need to make water, I had no idea where I was and thought I had been carried on board a rolling vessel. But on raising my head I found myself comfortably reclining in a litter borne by four horses. Beside me on a down cushion sat a youngish, thoughtful-looking man who, seeing me awake, laid aside the book he was studying and greeted me kindly, saying, "Guardian angels have watched over you and shielded you from evil. Have no fear, for you're in good hands. I am Sinan the Builder, one of those in charge of the Sultan's road makers. You're appointed to be my interpreter in the Christian lands, which, if Allah so wills, we are to conquer."

I noted that I had been dressed in new clothes, but having hurriedly assured myself that I still had my purse I could think of nothing but my immediate need, and said, "Let us leave all phrase making, O Sinan the Builder, and order your men to rein in the horses, lest I wet your valuable cushions."

Sinan the Builder, who had been brought up in the Seraglio, was not at all offended. Raising the cover of a round hole in the floor he said, "In such matters slave and monarch are equal. May it remind us that on the Last Day the Compassionate will make no distinction between high and low."

In other circumstances I might better have appreciated this tactful speech, but now I could not spare the time to listen. Having eased myself, however, I turned to him again to find him regarding me with a frown, and I begged him to forgive my unseemly conduct. He said, "I don't complain of your conduct, but because of your great haste I had no time to turn away my head and so observed to my horror that you're uncircumcised. Can you be a Christian spy?"

Dismayed at the result of my negligence I greeted him hurriedly in the name of the Compassionate, professed my faith in Allah the one God and in Mohammed his Prophet, and recited the first sura to prove myself a true believer. I added, "I have submitted to the will of Allah and taken the turban, but a strange destiny has tossed me hither and thither and allowed me neither time nor opportunity to undergo that unpleasant operation. I will gladly tell you my story and so convince you of my sincerity, but must beg you not to betray the omission to others, for it may be the will of Allah that I should serve the Sultan and the Grand Vizier as I am."

He answered smiling, "We have a long journey before us, and I enjoy instructive stories, but your words are too glib to be true. However, if the Grand Vizier knows your secret I have no reason to mistrust you."

Slightly more composed I replied, "The Grand Vizier knows me and all about me, though he must have more important things to think of than the circumcision of a slave."

"I'm no bigot," he rejoined, "and won't conceal from you that I too have a secret sin; then neither of us need feel superior to the other."

He brought out a beautifully painted little keg and filled two mugs, handing one to me. I gladly swallowed the wine, believing that the burden of my sin would not be gravely increased thereby. I had often broken this rule before, and many interpreters of the law were of the opinion that repetition of a sin was no aggravation—that on the Last Day a hardened toper would receive no worse punishment than he who drank for the first time, knowing it to be sinful. We preserved polite silence in that swaying litter, and in the shade of its awning enjoyed the glow that coursed through our veins and to our eyes enhanced the colors of the landscape. At length I said, "I feel no concern for the morrow. Sufficient unto the day is the evil thereof and everything that comes to pass is in accordance with the will of Allah. It's from mere human curiosity that I now ask you whither we're bound?"

Sinan the Builder answered readily, "We're to cross the rivers of Serbia, my native land, and must hasten, for tomorrow the janissaries will march and after them the spahis, and for every day's delay on the timetable my chief, the road makers' pasha, must lose an inch of his beard. When his beard has gone, his head must follow. Therefore he is liberal with punishments among his subordinates. Pray that the sun may shine and the wind may dry the roads, for a single shower might shorten many men by a head."

I now had nothing to complain of. We traveled in swift comfort by night and day, and at fixed stages along our route fresh horses were in readiness, and food, and relays of akindshas to guide us. When any hitch occurred, Sinan the Builder had the culprits flogged without mercy. I pitied these poor men and chided Sinan for his sternness, but he replied, "I myself am an unassuming man, but an important task has been assigned to me and it would be foolish to tire myself needlessly or go hungry. I must conserve all my strength for work which I alone among all these men can do. Our greatest obstacle will be the river Drava, which now lies straight ahead of us. Hitherto, whenever spring floods have swept away the bridges there, not the devil himself has been able to build new ones until late in the summer. Yet I must build one now."

We did not make straight for our goal, however, but in obedience to orders brought by express messengers made one detour after another. Sinan the Builder marked the altered routes on his maps and sent his men ahead to mark the fords and throw booms across them as a measure of safety for those who lost their footing in the current. His courage was beyond question, for he never relied entirely on the scouts' reports, but waded out into the icy water himself, staff in hand, to test the bottom and direct the placing of stones where it was soft. Several times the current swept him off his feet and he had to be hauled ashore by a lifeline.

On reaching the Sava River he sent his men in their thousands to the woods to fell trees, or to the riverside to saw planks; wherever he appeared order and discipline took the place of chaos. But once again the heavens opened and floodwaters scoured away his works as if they had been spiders' webs. Rain fell in torrents from leaden skies, and when Sinan the Builder saw the river grow to a thundering cataract he calmed himself, sent his men to shelter, and ordered the slaughter of many sheep and heifers, saying, "Eat, drink, and rest until the rain stops, for nothing happens contrary to the will of Allah and the Sultan can hardly be in a greater hurry than the Merciful and Compassionate. Though the delay should cost me my head, I rejoice, for that head aches with figures and plans, and I cannot sleep at night for thinking of the bridge I must throw across the river Drava when we reach it."

Sinan the resolute, who had spared neither himself nor his men, now burst into tears of exhaustion. I put him to bed in the ferryman's hut and gave him hot wine to drink, so that he slept at last. In his sleep he babbled of a great mosque that he would build, whose like the world had never seen.

For five days the rain came down in sheets, and with my friend Sinan I suffered all the agonies of delay, pacing back and forth over the floor of the little hut. At any moment the army might march up to the riverbank, when the Grand Vizier would have our heads cut off and thrown into the river. Yet my fears were groundless, for not even Khosref, the road makers' pasha, appeared. At last a soaked and mud-bespattered messenger reached us through the downpour to report that the whole army was fast in a bog and that the Sultan had called a halt until the rain stopped. The messenger was so exhausted that he had thrown away his ax. His bell was choked with mud and he lacked strength even to sprinkle perfume from his flask, but sank to the ground proclaiming that Allah was one and indivisible and Mohammed was his Prophet. Blood then poured from his mouth, for he had run for many days and nights through drenching rain and along slippery bypaths, and his strength was at an end, although under normal conditions these runners could cover the distance between Istanbul and Adrianople in a single day.

Suleiman and Ibrahim submitted to the will of Allah and no one was punished for the delay caused by the rain. As the army marched slowly onward, many perished in the swollen rivers despite all precautions. Numberless pack camels, having had enough of the miry roads, closed their eyes and nostrils and sank down beneath their load, never to rise again.

The summer was already far advanced, bright poppies flowered on the plains of Hungary, and I had had more than my fill of the willow thickets and bogs of our route, when at last at the head of the army we reached the banks of the still flooded Drava, by the town of Esseki. The Turkish garrison had long since given up hope of crossing it and had paid for their feeble efforts at bridge building with scores of drowned men, for the current tore away the mightiest timbers as if they were straws.

In the town of Esseki we met at last our great chief, Khosref-pasha. He stroked his beard and surveyed the swirling Drava thoughtfully. At length he said in submissive tones, "Allah is great. Allah is the one God and Mohammed is his Prophet, peace be with him. The Sultan can scarcely demand the impossible of me, since I married his cousin and am thus related to him by blood. But Ibrahim, Grand Vizier and Seraskier, is a ruthless man. I must therefore bid farewell to my gray beard. You, my dear children and sturdy builders, would be wise to make your peace with Allah."

His men had formerly accompanied Selim the implacable on his many campaigns; they had built bridges over numberless rivers from Hungary to Egypt and by means of skillful sapping had reduced many fortified cities, including Belgrade and Rhodes. But even these veterans began weeping and tearing their beards as they cursed the Drava, the treacherous land of Hungary, King Ferdinand, and especially his brother, the Emperor of the unbelievers. But Sinan, having silently waited until the eldest among them had said their say, stepped forward and began, "Why, think you, did I cause thousands of camels and oxen to drag huge balks of timber from the hillsides of five countries to the banks of the Drava? Why have I sent the best smiths and carpenters to this miserable hole Esseki, on forced marches along unspeakable roads? As long ago as last winter detailed information was sent me at the Seraglio about the breadth of the Drava, the nature of its banks, and the strength of its current. Night and day I've wrestled with figures, that I might build a mighty bridge across this river. Shall all this have been in vain? No! I will not throw away my rule, compasses, and tables without at least attempting the great task."

The master builders, who had a lifetime's experience behind them, looked pityingly at the younger man and said, "Who is this Sinan, who gained his knowledge sitting on silken cushions in the Seraglio? The profoundest wisdom consists in submission to the will of Allah, and surely in this matter Allah has made his meaning plain."

Sinan glanced at the broad river, at the timbers stacked on the bank, and at the rafts already built. Then falling on his knees he kissed the ground before Khosref-pasha and said, "I'm young, but I've listened to the wisdom of the foremost bridge builders of our time. I have read the works of the Greek strategists and studied the description of the bridge that Iskender the Great threw across the river Indus. Give me your hammer, noble Khosref-pasha, and in the sight of all raise me to the rank of your son. Then, despite all obstacles, I will bridge the Drava. Ride meanwhile to the Sultan and beg him for three days' grace. He will need those three days himself to rest his troops. But I must ask for the help of all the thirty thousand janissaries."

Khosref-pasha shook his head and for a long time he demurred. Yet there was something so persuasive in Sinan the Builder's assurance that at length he gave in.

"Well, I will be a father to you," he assented, "and share your disgrace if you fail. But I mean to share the honor also, if by the help of Allah and his angels you achieve the impossible. Take my hammer— and let all of you, my sons, obey young Sinan!"

He handed his jeweled and gold-hafted hammer to Sinan, laid a hand upon his shoulder and declared in the presence of many witnesses, "You are flesh of my flesh, my son Sinan the Builder."

He then rapidly recited the first sura in confirmation, sent for his horse, and set forth with his suite to meet the Sultan.

I hardly know how to account for Sinan's bold behavior unless it was that having been born in this region he knew the ways of Serbian rivers, or perhaps had reason to believe that the rainy spell was now at an end. Be that as it may, by next day the level of the water had fallen and Sinan sent thousands of men into the river to sink caissons and fill them with rocks, and to drive massive piles into the river bed at points carefully calculated and marked in his plans.

Each end of the bridge was strengthened by sturdy abutments to withstand any further floods, and work did not cease even at nightfall. Swarms of naked men waded through the dark waters by the light of torches and flares. Above the rushing of the torrent, the din of hammering and sawing could be heard in Esseki itself. Sinan the Builder took further advantage of his new authority by promising unheard-of sums to every man who hastened the work, and ordered the Marabouts to proclaim that all who drowned or were crushed by falling timbers or in any other way lost their lives should win direct to Paradise exactly as if they had fallen in battle against idolatrous unbelievers. Even the janissaries caught something of his dauntless energy, for unlike the experienced engineers they could form no clear idea of the magnitude of the task.

Sinan could not indeed complete the bridge by the third day, when the Sultan and Grand Vizier arrived with the main army, but he explained ingeniously that the three days he asked for were to be reckoned from the time the Sultan reached the banks of the Drava. And when the Sultan saw that despite seemingly insuperable difficulties the work was really going forward, he did not question this new interpretation. He and the Grand Vizier, plainly dressed and with pointed helmets on their heads, made their way to the scene of operations attended by a few green-clad *tsaushes*. In this way they could judge for themselves which men worked hardest and behaved most creditably in moments of danger. And although Khosref-pasha, who now began to suspect that Sinan might succeed, hastened to sit in the younger man's tent, study his plans, and issue orders right and left as if he were the true leader of the enterprise, the Sultan was not deceived. It was Sinan alone whom he watched, with an expressionless face, though never once during the work did he speak to him.

At the last moment the camels came up and also a number of trained elephants, which so far as I could see were of great service. Between their great ears sat the Indian mahouts looking like little monkeys, and the clever, ponderous beasts obeyed their every sign, walking in single file into the river, groping for foothold, and catching one another by the tail to form a living breakwater for the laborers. On their gilded tusks they lifted timbers that not ten men could move, and carried them easily to the place where they were needed. But Sinan the Builder said, "Those animals are more trouble than they're worth; they splash about and get in everybody's way. However, they amuse the Sultan and the janissaries and keep my workmen in a good humor. But your brawny brother Andy is worth ten elephants to me."

I noticed that Andy had risen high in rank among the builders and was wearing the turban of a bimbash. But unable to sustain his new dignity he toiled away ax in hand, ever ready to raise and bear on his shoulders a log that the efforts of many men had not availed to shift. His feats inspired awe and fear, yet he seemed to me to lack the qualities needful for a bimbash, or captain of a thousand. He found it difficult to direct the work of others and preferred to tackle all awkward tasks himself, to demonstrate how he thought they should be done. Having watched his foolish behavior for some time I could no longer keep silence, and for the sake of our long-standing friendship I went up to him and said, "It's unseemly for a bimbash to behave like a peasant in front of his subordinates, and you shame others of your rank by appearing with a sooty face and tarry hands. You've broken your fine plume, and no bimbash ought to roll up his sleeves until he draws his sword in battle."

But Andy answered, "This work is only temporary, and it really hurt me to watch how these fumbling Moslems handle an ax. And then Sinan begged me on his knees to help, and he's a good fellow, whose only fault is to let you loiter about and make silly remarks."

On the sixth day the bridge was finished, and for four days and nights the army crossed it in an unbroken stream, while the cautious Sinan watched to see that no excessive strain was placed upon it. Sultan Suleiman called Khosref-pasha and Sinan to his tent on the first evening of that march, together with their immediate assistants. Andy had therefore to wash his hands and don a red kaftan that Khosref-pasha had given him. But at this moment of triumph Sinan lost all his self-assurance, and was disconcerted when the janissaries ran at his heels loudly singing his praises and clashing their ladles against their cooking pots. When we reached the gorgeous awning that shaded the entrance to the Sultan's tent, Sinan turned in his agony to Khosref-pasha and asked him point blank, "Dear father! An adoptive son has the same right of inheritance as other sons, has he not? And you acknowledged me as your son before all the builders, confirming it with the first sura?"

Khosref-pasha, beside himself with delight, tenderly embraced Sinan and assured him that a foster son inherited from the foster father and vice versa. We then entered the tent and Khosref-pasha kept his arm fondly about Sinan's shoulders, to show that he was ready to share the honors of the undertaking with his dear son. At Suleiman's right hand, in garments sparkling with precious stones, stood the Grand Vizier. He praised our achievement with eloquence, and the Sultan himself addressed a few words to Khosref-pasha and Sinan the Builder, assuring them of his special favor. But outside the tent the janissaries beat ever more enthusiastically upon their cooking pots, and at last Sinan could contain himself no longer. Drawing a paper from his bosom he unfolded it with trembling hands and began to read aloud the rewards that he had promised the janissaries and builders. When he had finished he looked the Sultan straight in the eye and said, "Lord, as you hear, the bridge will cost two million, two hundred thousand aspers in gifts alone, but in this I do not include the cost of materials, transport, and manufacture, nor that of forging, stone cutting, and other minor expenses. But my dear father Khosref has pledged his fortune that my word may be kept, and for my part I gladly sacrifice the inheritance he has promised me, for lack of other property. If I may judge from the noise outside I fancy the janissaries are impatiently awaiting their reward, and I beseech you to pay them at once the two million, two hundred thousand aspers. My father and I will then make out a joint receipt for the sum. I shall do my utmost to redeem my share of this, provided you will entrust me with profitable building works in the future."

Khosref-pasha, crimson in the face, thrust Sinan the Builder violently from him and shrieked, "It is true that I recited the first sura when I adopted him as my son, but he wormed himself into my confidence with false pretenses and I cannot answer with my whole fortune for a madman's promise. On the contrary I shall have him beheaded immediately."

He raised his hand to smite his son Sinan, in the very presence of the Sultan, but fortunately he could not accomplish this disgraceful act, for at that moment a blood vessel burst in his brain and he sank powerless to the ground.

This lamentable incident was certainly our salvation, for it gave the Sultan time to recover from his amazement; the smoke-colored face regained its customary composure. Ibrahim had been anxiously watching his expression, but Suleiman lived up to his reputation for nobility and said only, "My small change seems likely to be exhausted before we reach even Buda. But we must give thanks to Allah that Sinan did not promise the janissaries the moon from heaven."

Grand Vizier Ibrahim laughed quickly, and we all joined in as heartily as we might until even the Sultan smiled. Only Sinan the Builder was grave. The Sultan then ordered the Defterdar to distribute the rewards according to Sinan's memorandum. He bestowed upon Sinan a splendid purse containing a thousand pieces of gold, while lesser sums were given to his assistants. I contrived to stand in so prominent a position as to receive ten gold pieces for my services as bridge builder, while Andy was given a new plume set in a jeweled clasp to replace his broken one, also a hundred gold pieces.

The highest reward went however to Khosref-pasha, for his discrimination—as the Sultan rightly said—in choosing the best man for the work. And Sinan was content that it should be so. But for a long time afterward, Khosref spoke thickly and gave orders by nods and signs, which Sinan interpreted as best suited him.

Once over the bridge the army divided and marched away by different routes toward the great plains of Mohacs, where Janos Zapolya, the ruler-elect of the Hungarian people, was to bring his forces to swell the Sultan's army. Sinan and I traveled in our horse litter along the Danube, above whose rapids nearly eight hundred vessels had been assembled to carry guns, ammunition, forage, and provisions up the river; we moved level with these transports.

After many days' journeying through thicket and swamp we came at last to that melancholy battlefield where three years ago the fate of Hungary had been sealed. But in fact it had been determined long before, when the King of France begged the Sultan's help against the Emperor. The Most Christian King's alliance with the Moslem ruler was a more decisive factor than any battle. Poppies were already waving above the burial mounds: a reminder—to me, at least—of the vain sacrifices resulting from Christian disunity.

As Sinan and I were borne over these ghostly plains we were overwhelmed by a sense of the pettiness of human life and the vanity of statecraft. Beneath our feet lay bones washed bare by torrential rains. Nothing distinguished Hungarian skulls from Turkish. Both gazed with blank eye sockets at a blank universe. The warriors lay among cannon balls and battered shields, their broken swords still in their skeleton hands, their only visible memorial the alien, Oriental flowers that blossomed about them. The seeds of these had fallen from Turkish wagons or mingled with the blood-soaked soil in the droppings of horses and camels, and at the sight of the thorny, broad-leaved plants with their blue flowers I was overcome with melancholy and cried, "Hail, field of Mohacs! Europe's grave, memorial to Western statesmanship! Your bleached skulls bear witness of a continent that tore itself to tatters, as a maniac rends his own body. Bitterly do they tell of the princes of the West, who wrought one another's destruction by treachery while night fell over Europe, and the crescent of Islam shone in menace from the East. Mohacs! Dark

225

token of the decline of the West; bright promise also of a future when men shall not be required to give their lives for other men's blind lust for power, and when East and West shall be ruled by the same just ruler, in the name of the Compassionate! His law will bind rich and poor alike and none shall persecute, strangle, burn, or torture another for his faith. People will live in concord within the pale of wise government and be free to practice their religion without making war. This is what we must achieve, and quickly, or there is no meaning in the world and no reason for living."

In this highflown manner did I apostrophize the whitened bones of Mohacs. But then an unspeakable anguish seized me as I remembered the glorious cathedrals and smiling cities of Christendom, from whose steeples the hoarse voice of the muezzins might soon be calling the faithful to prayer. My blood, the faith in which I had been bred, and the memory of my forefathers bound me to the nations of the West which by their divisions had dug their own grave. Yet I was severed from the fallen Mohacs by my desire to live, even in changed conditions; I felt no urge to die for a faith that had doomed itself.

At that moment we heard the thunder of many hoofs, and the wind bore to us the clashing music of the janissaries' drums and cymbals; life itself seemed on the march toward this field of death. Sultan Suleiman was proceeding to the scene of his greatest victory, and though in general his troops marched as silently as shadows, on this day the Sultan allowed the bands to play and the banners to fly before he called a halt for the night. With this martial music ringing in our ears we perceived the futility of our reflections, and hurried to our tent on the banks of the river.

Like magic the mighty camp sprang up on the desolate plain. Each man knew what he had to do, and soon the janissaries were seated in their groups of ten about the cooking pots and crackling fires. The Sultan's pavilion with its awning stood on the highest knoll whose slopes were covered, as with a living carpet, by the bodyguard. The duty of these men was to sleep on the bare ground about Suleiman's tent, with their bows beside them. While herdsmen watered the camels and oxen at the river and mowers cut hay for the spahis' horses, Grand Vizier Ibrahim, attended by a brilliant retinue, rode forward to meet King Zapolya.

Next morning when we had washed ourselves and said the morning prayer, I met Master Gritti, who was evidently suffering from the effects of a carouse. He hastened to embrace me and said, "For the love of God, Master Carvajal, tell me where in this accursed camp a keg of refreshing wine may be had! Later today I have to accompany King Janos to the Sultan, lest he forget the Hungarian bishopric he promised me."

I was far from pleased to see this licentious and scheming man, but common humanity required me to help him. Just then Andy, who had spent the night inspecting his cannon aboard the newly arrived rafts, came up to us and I asked his advice. After some deliberation he went to borrow a couple of horses for Master Gritti and myself to ride, and walked beside us to the camp of the Christian akindshas half a mile away. Unlike the Moslems they were filthy in their habits, and had befouled a lovely grove of beeches with their garbage and ordure. Janissary patrols, far from inspecting this camp, kept as far away as possible. In return for Master Gritti's gold the ruffianly akindshas dug up a cask of excellent Tokay that they had buried and eagerly invited him to quench his thirst.

Like the experienced toper he was, Master Gritti drank only enough to bring the blood back to his head and put him in a good humor, for important tasks awaited him. Then we left the camp and he hastened to his tent to change his clothes and prepare to join King Zapolya's suite. In order to receive the King in a worthy manner, the Sultan paraded his great army on either side of the reception tent, so that when after the noon prayer the lawful King of Hungary approached with his following he seemed like a drop that at any moment might be swallowed up by the ocean. I was not admitted to this ceremony, but afterward Master Gritti gave me a detailed account of what had passed. It seemed that the Sultan was pleased to walk three steps to meet Zapolya and to extend his hand to be kissed, and that he then invited him to take his seat beside him on the throne. I fancied that in thus honoring Zapolya the Sultan but honored himself, but Master Gritti had a better explanation to give.

"The cause goes deeper, for although Janos Zapolya is a man of no consequence and brings only six thousand horsemen, yet he has in his possession a magic talisman of far greater importance than an army, and it was this object that the Sultan by his flattering reception was able to secure. Zapolya is better as a scout than as a soldier and his partisans have by cunning caught and held the keeper of St. Stephen's crown. I was compelled to confide this secret to my brother Ibrahim, or the Sultan would scarcely have troubled to receive the fellow."

I answered politely that I failed to grasp his meaning, since a mere crown made no man king. To win a kingdom a powerful army was needed. But Master Gritti said, "Holy Stephen's crown is unlike any other. The Hungarians are still a barbarous and superstitious people and recognize no one as king of Hungary until he has been crowned with this crown. Therefore it is their greatest treasure and the Voivod Zapolya removed at least half the obstacles in his path when he discovered its secret hiding place. And now this credulous man has sold it to the Sultan, for a matter of four horses and three kaftans, and five hundred trustworthy spahis are on their way to fetch it before King Zapolya repents of his bargain."

It seemed that Master Gritti was right, for during our continued march to Buda I observed that no one took much notice of King Zapolya. He and his followers brought up the rear of the column, and the janissaries referred to him disrespectfully as Janushka. Three days after leaving Mohacs, we pitched camp in the vineyards about Buda. The walls of the city appeared exceedingly massive and the German garrison kept up so lively a fire that I hastened to visit the warm springs of the region, while Sinan the Builder set his men to sapping and mining in preparation for the siege.

The Sultan and the Grand Vizier, wearing plain kaftans and helmets and attended by a few of the bodyguard, made a tour of inspection to hearten their men before the assault. I had the good fortune to meet them as I was bringing food to Sinan, who was so engrossed in his work that he often forgot to eat. When the Sultan, no doubt to display his excellent memory, addressed me kindly by name, some unexplained impulse made me mention a dream I had had.

"I've been told that your wife also has dreams," the Sultan remarked, "and that she can see coming events in a bowl of sand. Tell me then what you saw in your dream."

I was taken aback, and stammered, and glanced at the handsome Ibrahim, who seemed not altogether pleased at the Sultan's words. It was a mystery to me how Suleiman could know anything of Giulia, but now I had begun there was nothing for it but to continue.

"Yesterday I bathed in the marvelous springs of this region, and was afterward so weary that I fell asleep. I dreamed, and saw the fortress of Buda and a vulture flying heavily over it, bearing in his

228

beak a strange crown. The gates of the citadel opened and the defenders prostrated themselves before the vulture. Then the Son of the Compassionate stepped forward and the vulture set the crown upon his head. This I saw, but a wiser man than I must interpret the vision."

I had indeed had this dream, which was no doubt suggested by Master Gritti's account of St. Stephen's crown, though in fact I had seen the crown fall from the vulture's talons, crushing all Buda beneath its weight. My vision of the opened gates was no doubt born of a lively desire to see the city fall as rapidly as possible into the Sultan's hands, that I might escape the perils of an assault.

So, as is usual, I improved the dream a little, yet not too transparently, I thought, since neither the Sultan nor the Grand Vizier could know what Master Gritti had blabbed to me of St. Stephen's crown. Nor did they seem to suspect any deceit; they looked at one another in the greatest astonishment, and the Sultan exclaimed, "Allah's will be done!" Even Ibrahim's handsome face brightened. Later I received from the Sultan a new coat and a well-filled purse in reward for my dream.

It is hard to assess the value of dreams as omens, yet this one was fulfilled, in as much as Buda fell after six days' siege, before even a breach had been shot in the walls. No one was more astonished than myself, for I had been far from expecting so speedy a conclusion.

When the two captains of the garrison saw the mighty forces of the Sultan and the large numbers of cannon that had been brought ashore from the rafts, they opened negotiations and consented to leave the city provided they might retain their arms and personal possessions. The Sultan gladly agreed to these moderate terms, for summer was far advanced and the main object of the expedition still lay a great way off.

To the beat of drums and clash of cymbals the janissaries paraded smartly on either side of the city gates to allow the German garrison to march out, and to show with words and gestures what they thought of them. At first the Germans walked humbly, exhorting one another to remember the suffering and scorn to which our Lord Jesus Christ had submitted; but when the janissaries vied with one another in treading the Cross underfoot and in subjecting the vanquished to every sort of mockery they could contain themselves no longer. Their faces darkened as they cursed their officers and reminded one another that they were German *landsknechts,* before whom the whole world

229

trembled. Some paused to reply to those janissaries who spoke in German; the adversaries stood screeching nose to nose with outstretched necks, like fighting cocks. This gave me an opportunity to see and even handle the new light muskets, fitted with wheel locks, which many of the Germans treasured as their most precious possession. The janissaries who had come off worst in the battle of words could no longer master their thievish desires, and now tried to wrench these weapons by force from the Germans' hands. Struggles ensued; the conflict spread with ever increasing savagery, and it was not long before most of the Germans were slain and their weapons and stores were in Turkish hands.

I believe no more than five or six of the garrison escaped the massacre and hid in the willow thickets. All the ground between the city gates and the riverbank was strewn with heads, arms, legs, and other portions of dead *landsknechts*. The janissaries returned to their camp well pleased, to try their new weapons, or fight one another for them. The episode did great harm to the Sultan's reputation in the world. Both the Emperor Charles and his brother of Vienna made haste to proclaim the Sultan's treachery, though the noble Suleiman was so deeply stricken by the conduct of his janissaries that he retired into his tent and would not show himself for three days.

Shortly after this I was summoned to Ibrahim's tent by Master Gritti, who escorted me thither. The Grand Vizier was sitting cross legged on a cushion studying a map. He invited us cordially to sit down beside him, then with a smile of mockery in his dark, sparkling eyes he said, "I am obliged to you for your dream, Michael el-Hakim, but I forbid you to have any more—or at least to tell the Sultan about them without my permission."

Somewhat hurt I replied, "I can't help my dreams, and my intentions were of the best. Moreover my dream came true, for Buda fell without a blow struck."

Ibrahim gave me a searching glance and said, "In this instance your dream did indeed come true, and that is why I've sent for you. How could you guess what would happen? What was your object? Who put the words into your mouth? Was it to make the Sultan suspect me, his slave, of coveting the crown of Hungary?"

I froze at these words, but he went on relentlessly, "How can I trust you? Do you think I don't know how you've curried favor at the Seraglio and entered the service of Sultana Khurrem? As a sign

230

of your loyalty you even gave your dog to her son, though she is a false woman and hopes to injure me. Confess that it was she who paid you to follow me on the campaign and dream these noxious dreams!"

I was too stunned to take in a word of what he was saying. Master Gritti looked at me through narrowed eyes and shook his head. Suddenly the Grand Vizier took out a great silken purse from under his cushion and flung it into my lap. A second and a third followed until my knees sagged beneath their weight. Then he cried, almost in fear, "Weigh that gold in your hands and think carefully—which of us is the richer, I or the Sultan, and which of us can reward you most liberally? I must admit that hitherto you've had no great profit from me. But that gold is yours if you will only confess that Khurrem the Russian has won you over and set you against me, for it's hard to lay hold of an adversary in the dark and I must know what her intentions are."

Notwithstanding my agitation I could estimate that each of the three money bags contained at least five hundred gold pieces—a vast fortune for a man in my position. With this money I could buy a beautiful house and garden on the Bosphorus as well as slaves and boats and all that my heart could desire. I saw before me the plump face of Sultana Khurrem, the cold blue eyes, the irregular features, the perpetually smiling mouth and dimpled cheeks. I owed her nothing and was in no way bound to her, yet I hesitated to reply—not for her sake but because I found it difficult to lie to the Grand Vizier. Ibrahim watched my face closely and said, "Fear nothing, but speak openly. You need never regret it, for I alone require certainty on this point. This is my secret and the Sultan shall never learn of it."

At last I said, "You have led me into cruel temptation, but I cannot lie to you—not even for all this gold."

Tears of indignation rose to my eyes as I thrust the bags aside, and I told him how I had entered the harem and how I came to give my dog to Prince Jehangir. I ended bitterly, "I'm a fool to tell you this when a lie would make me a rich man. But I've never been able to work solely for my own advantage—a fault that my wife continually complains of."

The senseless loss of the money caused me to burst into tears and curse my own weakness. Master Gritti and Seraskier Ibrahim looked at each other in wonder. Then Ibrahim stroked my shoulder soothingly and asked, "How then can the Kislar-Aga have made your wife known to the Sultana, so that she now pays almost daily visits to the harem to gaze into sand and to sell all kinds of lotions and ointments for the complexion?"

I struck my hands together in astonishment and replied, "Of this I had not the least idea, though it's true that I spoke a word to the Kislar-Aga on my wife's behalf and extolled her talent."

Giulia's great good fortune encouraged me to prattle on about her until the last shadow of the Seraskier's suspicions melted away and he said with a smile, "I believe you. I cannot doubt your sincerity, though I've not yet made up my mind as to whether you're a simpleton or a man of excessive cunning."

To my sorrow he took back the money bags and hid them again under the cushions. But then he clapped his hands and dismissed the mute who had been standing hidden behind a curtain with a skein of colored silken cords over his shoulder. The sight of this man sent cold shivers down my spine and the Grand Vizier said, "If you had confessed to plotting against me you would have been given the gold, but little time to enjoy it, for I could not have allowed you to live. But your honesty deserves recognition, so ask of me what you will, within reason."

Quaking with both fear and gratitude I threw myself to the ground before him and cried, "I will ever be your faithful servant, as hitherto— but tell me what you mean by 'reason,' for I would not insult your munificence by requesting too petty a token of your favor."

At this the Grand Vizier laughed aloud, but gave me no help. I was indeed in a dilemma, for though I was loath to ask too little I feared to anger him by too bold a request. I rubbed my moist palms together in an agony of indecision, until at last I summoned up my courage and said, "I am a man of small pretensions, but my wife has long desired a dwelling that we might regard as our own home. A little house, however modest, with its own garden somewhere on the shores of the Bosphorus, not too far from the Seraglio, would be the most wonderful gift you could make me. I would bless you all my life long. You own large properties on the outskirts of the city—countless gardens, palaces, and summer villas—and would never notice the lack of one little corner on the shore."

No request could have been more acceptable to the Grand Vizier. A smile overspread his handsome face as he stretched forth his hand to be kissed and said, "Your request is the best proof of your sincerity, for if you had meditated treachery you would certainly not have asked for a house near the capital, but rather such reward as could be carried abroad. And there is no lovelier city than Istanbul. Allah himself designed it to be the capital of the world, and if he wills it I mean to beautify it further with fine buildings and mosques. I will make over to you a spacious plot of ground next to my own summer palace on the Bosphorus, and Sinan shall build for you and your family a roomy wooden house to harmonize with the landscape and gladden the heart and the eyes. He may draw the necessary funds from my treasury and employ *azamoghlans* to help in the building. In confirmation of which I now repeat the first sura."

Master Gritti shook his head at my stupidity, but my own joy knew no bounds and I saw that fate after all had been kind in sending me to this war.

But we wasted many valuable days at Buda, and when at last the army moved off the heavens opened once more, so that even the toughest of the janissaries began to fear that Hungary was infested with raging jinn, while the shivering dervishes foretold another deluge. Yet the Sultan's army was too big for anyone to doubt its ultimate success. Not even the Hungarians doubted it, for when on our way up the Danube valley we came to the strong fortress of Gran, Bishop Varday surrendered at once and so far sacrificed himself as to join the Sultan's suite, in order to save what could be saved of the property of the Hungarian church.

We pursued our way under great difficulties, and it was pitiful to see the camels in that icy rain, slipping and stumbling along the swampy roads and tearing the pads of their feet, until they lay down to die. By the time we reached Vienna we had hardly twenty thousand camels left, though we had started with over ninety thousand, and it will be understood how hard it became to carry supplies for so vast an army.

September was drawing to an end when at last our forces took up their positions before Vienna, and in his gorgeous pavilion the Sultan sat shivering before a charcoal brazier. The gold-embroidered lining of the tent gave little protection against the cold and was not even rainproof.

But from the hills of Semmering, the rich and populous city, with its cathedral spire soaring into the sky, seemed almost within reach. The walls looked as slender as threads while the hastily thrown up

233

breastworks and palisades held no menace. Truly, I cannot think how we failed to capture Vienna with its slender fortifications and relatively small garrison, though this indeed was stiffened with a few veterans whom King Ferdinand had been able to install there before prudently taking flight into Bohemia.

But in all fairness I must mention that the defenders lived up to their reputation and did all they could to increase the homesickness of the besieger. They were supported by a firm and well-justified belief that time and the forces of nature were on their side, and I fancy also that they regarded themselves as the guardians of the last Christian stronghold. If this fell, nothing could hold back the tide of a victorious Islam from flooding in over Germany and all Europe. I felt this strongly as I looked out over Vienna from the Semmering heights, and renegade though I was I could not be sure for which side I desired victory. And when I saw the incredible valor of the besieged I felt very painfully my apostasy, though the understanding reader will appreciate my sincerity and singleness of heart in matters of faith.

I had little time for profitless brooding, for Sinan the Builder soon set me to work in earnest. As his interpreter I had to interrogate every prisoner we had taken at the capitulation of Buda; he even sent me to the prison camp to question fugitives whom the akindshas had captured, and learn from them details of streets, houses, walls, towers, and new fortifications in Vienna. He gave me no rest. Panting, I dashed from one informant to another and noted on my map which houses were stone built and which were of timber, which had lost their roofs and which had been torn down to make room for artillery, where trenches had been dug, which streets were closed to horse traffic and who had command of the various gates, towers, and bastions. I became really exasperated at last and cried, "Allah preserve me, what trouble you give yourself! Make a breach in the walls, no matter where, and the janissaries will do the rest—if only for the sake of warming themselves at last in front of a good fire."

But Sinan the Builder replied, "No, no. First I must note the slope of the ground and discover any subterranean springs, establish the water table, and note the depth of soil, lest my saps become flooded or brought up short by a wall of rock. I must know all there is to know about Vienna."

I was already so familiar with the plan of the city that I could almost have found my way about it blindfold. Thousands of its inhabitants who were unfit to bear arms had been driven forth most mercilessly, and fell an easy prey to the savage akindshas. Their numbers so increased that there was scarcely room for them in the slave pens; nor was it possible to maintain an effective guard. Thus it was that many of them succeeded in escaping and carrying back useful information to the defenders.

If these defenders had been mindful of their small numbers and had followed the rules of war by waiting quietly behind their walls for our attack, life in our camp might have been bearable, despite the weather and the shortage of provisions. But these reckless Germans and Bohemians hindered us in every possible way. When after much reflection and calculation Sinan began at last to dig toward the Carinthian Gate, the German gunners in the city descended into the underground galleries beneath the walls. There they sat with ears pricked and eyes fixed upon the surface of water in a bucket and upon a handful of peas scattered on a drum. When the peas began to dance and the water to quiver with the vibration of our works, these godless men at once embarked on countermeasures. So, when at last we had tunneled right under the wall and there stacked our powder until such time as we could explode all the mines at once, these impudent and thievish Germans dug through to our saps from inside, stole all our powder, and carried it back into the city, having first blown up and destroyed all that we had achieved in the course of weeks of hard and dangerous labor.

One evening the Seraskier, impatient at the slowness of the sappers, brought his light fieldpieces into position before the Carinthian Gate and bombarded its towers throughout a night of torrential rain. There could have been no better demonstration of the incomparable skill of the Turkish artillery, for they kept up an unbroken fire, loading and discharging their pieces almost as rapidly as in dry weather and by daylight. The constant thunder of these guns greatly stiffened my courage, but Andy thought it useless to expose the gunners to the drenching rain and so worsen their chills. The coughing of a hundred thousand Moslems was more alarming than a cannonade, he said, and alone would shatter the walls of Vienna.

I felt no desire to leave my comparatively dry quarters, for which Sinan the Builder had procured a brazier. I spent a cheerful evening with him there over a flask or two of wine, and as a result we fell into a deep sleep. Suddenly we were roused by a terrific explosion.

Certain picked troops of the garrison—Germans, Spaniards, and Hungarians—had made a surprise sortie through the Salt Gate and hurled themselves upon our unsuspecting men. They set fire to all the brushwood we had so painfully collected, to Sinan's store sheds, the slave pens, and all the tents they could reach. It would have gone ill with the whole camp had not everything been too wet to burn properly.

The worst panic was caused by the grenades that the assailants flung into the tents and whose smoking, hissing fuses glowed in the darkness like the tails of comets. Their shells of earthenware or glass were filled with stones, nails, and other rubbish which at the moment of explosion flew in all directions, inflicting many wounds.

Sinan and I were in a daze of sleep when the storm broke and would certainly have come to a melancholy end if we had not managed to creep into an attack trench and so along to a tunnel whose mouth was concealed by a bush. The roar of the battle overhead was so terrifying that I lay there quaking, but Sinan the Builder wrapped his cloak about his head and fell at once into profound slumber.

When at dawn the janissaries began marching down the hillsides in close order for the counterattack, the enemy, as might have been expected, were panic stricken and at least five hundred of them were cut down. The janissaries, furious at losing their night's sleep, pursued so closely on the heels of the rest that they would have followed the fugitives into the city had not the Germans hurriedly closed the gates, thereby leaving a number of their officers outside.

Heads by the hundred were borne on poles to the Sultan's tent, while the janissaries played their music and the agas boasted of their great victory. But the destruction in the camp was many times greater than the German losses, and the agas allowed no one to count the Turkish dead, whose bodies were hastily thrown into the Danube. Preparations for our assault were delayed and the powder—stacked in readiness beneath the walls—became damp. Time was on the side of the defenders. The everlasting coughing of the Turks resounded through the camp night and day, disturbing the Sultan's sleep and exasperating him, for he read it as a sign of rebellion. Who knows but that he had some grounds for his suspicion?

We were now nearing the middle of October, and supplies were running very short when at last we succeeded in exploding two mines and bringing down part of the wall near the Carinthian Gate. Almost before the flying debris had reached the ground the agas with swords and whips drove their men to the assault. For three days these attacks were repeated, but the men no longer believed in victory; the fighting spirit was out of them and many confessed that they would rather be killed by the scimitars of their own leaders than by the frightful two-handed swords of the Germans which at one stroke could cleave a man in half.

Even Sinan the Builder was threatened by the Seraskier's displeasure, for too many mines had exploded ineffectually. However, further frantic efforts resulted in the widening of the breach, and the final decisive assault began. Company after company was flogged and goaded into the thick of the struggle until the ground before the Carinthian Gate was strewn with fallen Turks. Fog lay over the ground and through it the tips of the Turkish tents stood up like the white columns of tombs. All noise was curiously muffled in this spectral sea, and it was as if legions of spirits were in conflict before the walls. No wonder that the janissaries had no heart for the enterprise. When at dusk their last attack failed, they streamed back in full retreat and began to strike their tents, that they might depart without delay from the neighborhood of this uncanny city.

When the Germans became aware of this they rang all the church bells and fired salvos in celebration of their joyful and unlooked-for victory. But when darkness fell, bonfires of a different sort blazed up in our camp. The infuriated janissaries were burning all that came to hand—enclosures, store sheds, grain sacks, and a great part of the plunder that the roving akindshas had brought in from sixty miles around and which, because of the lack of pack animals, could not be carried away. They slew the prisoners, impaled them or threw them into the flames, and although scores escaped in the confusion and were hauled up into the city by ropes, yet hundreds of Christians were burned alive in revenge, that their shrieks might reach the city and subdue the unseemly jubilation of the defenders.

Thus ended our triumphal march into the German states. The hideous menace that had brooded over Christendom melted away, and instead I was fated to witness Sultan Suleiman's first and sharpest defeat. It was not the will of God, it seemed, that Christendom should fall.

Hitherto, experience had seemed to show that God concerned Himself but little with warlike operations, but recent events made me alter my opinion. On leaving Rome I had thought of Christendom as a plague-ridden and already doomed carcass, but now I understood that some good must have remained in it since God in His patience granted it a short period of grace, as He would have been willing to do for Sodom and Gomorrah had ten righteous men been found in them.

I shared these solemn thoughts with Andy as we wandered quietly among the heaped-up bodies of the dead, emptying purses and collecting the jeweled daggers of officers. The superstitious Moslems dared not seek out the bodies of even their own dead after dark, but Andy and I had no such scruples, and even though our business might appear to some people a little unbecoming, it would have been worse to behave like Turks and burn Christian prisoners alive. We also tended the wounded as well as we could, and ended our work of mercy by helping a moaning *subashi* into camp.

Having thus come safely past the guards we returned to Sinan the Builder's quarters—and only just in time, for he was already preparing to leave, and one of the Sultan's bodyguard had come thither to bring Andy and me before the Seraskier. So startled was I at this unexpected summons that the burden I bore beneath my kaftan fell to the ground with a crash. With or without reason my conscience pricked me; I feared that the Grand Vizier might have heard of our little excursion to the battlefield and would have us hanged for looting the dead.

A moment's reflection showed me that this was not possible, however, and having stowed away my booty in a chest I entrusted this to Sinan, who alone had porters at his disposal. Yet I might have saved myself the trouble, for before we reached even Buda on our homeward way all our baggage was lost in a bog. We had no time to remove our bloodstained garments, for the hour was late and the Grand Vizier was pacing impatiently up and down his tent. Seeing us he halted in surprise and cried bitterly, "By Allah, are there still men who do not fear to bloody their clothes in their sovereign's service? Are renegades to restore my faith in Islam?"

It was clear that he put a wrong construction on our appearance, yet I would not venture to correct so exalted a lord. With almost unseemly haste he dismissed his servants from the tent, made us sit beside him and began speaking in a whisper. As he spoke he glanced about him continually, as if afraid of eavesdroppers.

"Michael el-Hakim and Antar! Sultan Suleiman has come to the conclusion that Allah will not yet permit us to capture Vienna. Tomorrow therefore he will strike camp and start for Buda with the main army, leaving me with the five thousand spahis to follow as rear guard."

"Allah is Allah and so forth," I said, with unfeigned relief. "May his angels Gabriel and Michael protect our flight. The decision is indeed wise and I cannot sufficiently praise the Sultan's prudence."

But the Grand Vizier ground his teeth and said, "How dare you talk of flight! Not even in error must you pronounce so loathsome a word, and any man who dares distort the truth about our great victory over the unbeliever shall receive a hundred strokes of the rod on the soles of his feet. But the game is not yet over, Michael el-Hakim; if Allah permits I will yet lay Vienna at the feet of the Sultan."

"And how in God's name is this to be done?"

"I shall send you and your brother Antar into the city!" His brilliant gaze transfixed me as he went on threateningly, "If life is dear to you you'll not return with your mission unfulfilled. I am giving you a unique opportunity to serve the cause of Islam."

Believing that adversity had bereft him of his wits I answered soothingly, "Noble Seraskier, I know what faith you have in my talents and Antar's valor, but how are we two to capture a city that two hundred thousand men and a hundred thousand camels have failed to take?"

Andy too looked doubtful, and said, "It's true that I've been compared to Samson—though far be it from me to vie with any holy man of Scripture—and Samson, they say, brought down the walls of Jericho by blowing a horn. But I have no such horn and humbly beg you to find some worthier man for the task."

But Grand Vizier Ibrahim said, "You shall not be alone in Vienna, for I've chosen and bribed a dozen men from among the German prisoners, and I shall send them two at a time into the city on the same errand as yourselves. You too must dress like German *landsknechts* and mingle with the others. On the third night from now you must set fire to the city as a signal to me that you've succeeded in your task, and then open the Carinthian Gate so that in the confusion of the fire my spahis may ride in. If I should see no fire I must submit to the will of Allah and ride after the Sultan, hoping one day to meet you and your bold brother Antar in Paradise."

He paused for breath, but presently continued, "I've little confidence in the Germans I have bribed, but you I trust and I shall ask a certain loyal Jew named Aaron to help you. You will find him in a quarter

239

called by Christians the City of Affliction, where the Jewish inhabitants of Vienna are penned up behind boards and barricades. Embittered by Christian persecution Aaron pins his faith on the Sultan whom he regards as his deliverer. Therefore he will certainly help you if you show him this ring."

The Seraskier raised his shapely hand and spread out his fingers to choose one of the splendid rings upon them. From his little finger he drew a diamond no larger than the tip of a child's finger, but so pure and brilliant as to emit blue fires as he turned and twisted it in the light.

"Aaron knows this stone. He can give you no active help for fear of injuring his fellows, for Christians commonly visit the fault of a single Jew on all others in the city and sometimes on those of other cities as well. But he will advise you and if need be hide you. Tell him I will gladly redeem the ring for two thousand ducats. You shall wear German clothes and be escorted with blows to the prisoners' enclosure. Go in peace, then, and be assured of my favor if you succeed and I find you alive among the charred ruins of Vienna."

But now both Andy and I spoke with firmness, and I told Ibrahim that if he were so anxious to be rid of a faithful servant he would do better to strike off my head at once. Ibrahim saw he would gain nothing by that, and after vain attempts at persuasion he said, "Very well, let it be as you wish. But why do you think I spared you circumcision if not to send you on just such an errand as this? Since you refuse, I can no longer delay the fulfillment of my religious obligations and must have the matter attended to at once."

So saying he clapped his hands for the guard and sent him to fetch a surgeon. He then expressed satisfaction that Sinan the Builder had drawn his attention to a circumstance which his many duties and cares had caused him to forget. Andy and I had barely time to exchange a despairing glance before the surgeon appeared with a tube and a knife, which he began to sharpen, assuring us meanwhile that all would be over in a moment and that we should find it no more painful than the extraction of a tooth. Yet I felt the most intense repugnance to the operation and to the loss of my last link with Christendom, where I might yet seek refuge were disaster to overtake me in the Sultan's domains. Andy also fidgeted and at last said, "I think I prefer to serve Islam by going into Vienna, so long as there may be no further talk of mutilation if I survive. Good Moslem though I am, I cannot believe that on the Last Day Allah will have nothing better to look at than—"

I said quickly that as ever I would share my foster brother's fate for good or ill, and as for circumcision, I would defer it until I felt it a matter of conscience, and then submit to it of my own free will.

The Grand Vizier dismissed the disappointed surgeon and said smiling that he relied upon us and was persuaded that we should do our best like honest men. He then handed each of us one hundred German and Hungarian gold ducats, in the worn leather purses common among mercenaries. In his presence we changed into clothes taken from fallen Germans, and as soon as Andy had drawn on the familiar striped breeches the old German oaths rose unbidden to his lips and he was aware once more of the unassuageable thirst of the mercenary. The wine that the Grand Vizier then offered us sustained us under the blows and buffets with which we were driven into the pen of captives, though our escort seemed to me overconscientious in obeying Ibrahim's order to treat us like the rest and thus allay suspicion.

So it was that I had a black eye and a swollen lip when in the raw morning mist we broke out and stumbled over the familiar battlefield to the Carinthian Gate, and there cried piteously in the name of God to be admitted. Many of our fellow prisoners had been almost too weak to stand, far less escape, but at least a dozen women pressed through the gap that Andy had made in the fence and followed us, screaming. Hearing the noise of these poor women, who seemed to imagine that the louder they shrieked the faster they could run, the sentinels on the walls made ready for us and lowered ropes and ladders, at the same time discharging a swarm of arrows at our pursuers, whom the mist concealed.

Trembling and dizzy we crawled up the walls, and friendly hands helped us over the top. We were thumped on the back and offered bread and wine, and as we ate we helped to haul up the women who with screams and flapping petticoats emerged like distracted hens from the sea of mist.

These women were fairly young and handsome, for the akindshas on their raids chose always the best for the slave market and slew the rest. Both Germans and Bohemians yelled with delight at the sight of them and welcomed them as a gift from heaven. Having helped them from the wall they at once threw them down on the bare ground, all breathless as they were from their flight, and raped them so quickly that they hardly understood what was happening.

This lively scene was interrupted by a red-haired ensign who came dashing from the guardhouse to beat his men on their hinder parts with the flat of his sword and revile them shrilly for being worse whoremongers than the Turks. He then ordered them back to their posts lest the enemy should gain possession of the gate by a surprise attack.

The seasoned veterans, with their bloodstained bandages, singed beards, and blackened cheeks, laughed in the stripling's face and invited him to kiss this and that. But they let the women go and hauling up their breeches returned to the watch tower. The ensign now addressed us in harsh tones and threatened to hang us with his own hands if we proved to be Turkish spies. He pointed to a number of German-clad bodies dangling from gallows at the top of the wall, and declared we should suffer the same fate unless we at once made full confession.

But Andy knew how to handle such young cockerels as this. He stepped up to him, belched wine fumes in his face and said he would teach him how to treat the Emperor's loyal servants, who escaped in peril of their lives and rescued a flock of Christian women from the fate awaiting them in Turkish harems. So convincing was his eloquence that the young man blenched, addressed him as sir, and assured us that for his own part he had no suspicions, but that his duty required him to be strict. He begged us therefore to comply with regulations by making water before him and giving our names, and the names of our regiment and commanding officer. When he had entered these particulars in his guard book we could obtain passes from the town hall.

We could not refuse so moderate a request, and when we had given him the visible proof he asked for that we were not Moslems, Andy explained that we belonged to the advance guard of the *landsknechts* who had been sent to Vienna's relief from Italy and that our leader was the Emperor's famous general Bock von Teufelsburg. It seemed best not to mention any well-known man for fear of detection, but I hastened to emphasize that the name spoke for itself, having won honor and glory in seventeen years' campaigning, and it was not our leader's fault if our troop had been surprised by the akindshas and dragged away for questioning. We two, I said, were the only survivors.

The ensign listened open mouthed and protested eagerly that the name of Bock von Teufelsburg was familiar to him. He repeated his instructions to report at once to the town hall for further interrogation. Then he seemed to hesitate; he bit his lip in some embarrassment and said, "The prosecutor and provost marshal are somewhat severe, as is natural, in view of Turkish cunning. They would rather hang ten innocent men than allow one suspect to escape. Nor are deserters kindly received, and as a good Christian I warn you that you'll be imprisoned in any case until you can find someone to vouch for you. Failing this you will be hanged."

Then in a burst of candor he went on, "You and your comrade would be wise to shun the town hall and the provost marshal's men like the plague until the Turks have withdrawn. You'll have no difficulty, for there are many other deserters hiding in taverns and in the lodgings of softhearted women. Go in peace and fortune go with you. Drink a cup now and then to my health and success."

With that the good-natured boy threw us a silver schilling and left us. Andy and I slipped away into the October mist.

I was for seeking out Aaron at once, but Andy, holding my arm negligently between finger and thumb, trudged along the filthy streets under the blank gaze of charred, roofless houses, and as he went he sniffed the air. Just as a compass needle quivers to the north, so Andy amid the desolation of this city made unerringly for a tavern, whither a mob of drunken, quarrelsome, boastful, dicing Germans, Spaniards, and Bohemians had preceded us. When we had settled ourselves on two empty barrels with a stoup of wine before us Andy said contentedly, "I feel a better Christian every moment, and can hardly believe that only yesterday I wore a turban and washed my head and neck five times a day."

"I've nothing against a morning draught," I said with some reserve, "but the task we've been set weighs on my mind. No doubt we should be wise to buy up straw, wood, and pitch in good time, so as to make a fine blaze of this sour and squalid city."

But Andy with a rattle of his purse called for more wine and said, "The hairs of our head are numbered and not a sparrow falls to the ground unless shot, so it's needless to take thought for the morrow today."

He was soon chatting with a couple of scoundrels who peered greedily into his purse, embraced him, and swore he was their best friend. Andy flung down three Hungarian gulden and ordered the innkeeper to serve drink to both these brave defenders of Vienna. But a pock-marked, villainous fellow with a bloodstained Turkish kaftan thrown over his shoulders resented Andy's openhandedness and in his turn poured a heap of gold onto the slimy, bespewed table, coughed hoarsely, and cried, "In the name of Christ, the Virgin, and all the saints! *I* will pay, for I've escaped from Turkish imprisonment, killed one of their pashas, and performed such feats as no one would believe were I to relate them. Let these Turkish coins speak for me; I take it as unfriendly that anyone should seek to forestall me."

Andy quietly swept his coins back into his purse, declaring that he had no wish to insult so great a hero.

In time all were thoroughly fuddled, and the ruffian with the gold ordered the tavern keeper to bar the door. He then delivered the following speech.

"Are we not all brave men? Have we not all done deeds that for a thousand years will be praised by Christians everywhere? But who thanks us? We've had neither pay nor the smallest chance of plunder— yet is not the town ours, since we preserved it from destruction? It is but fair that the inhabitants should pay us what we're owed, and as soon as the cavalry have set off in pursuit of the Turks we shall have our chance."

The topers roared that this was the most sensible talk they had heard since the siege began. But, said they, we're few and the provost marshal is a ruthless man. Rope and stake await everyone who seeks justice.

The pock-marked man lowered his voice and his eyes glowed as he said, "Let us bring the good news to all trustworthy comrades, and tomorrow evening after vespers set fire to the city! The marshal's men will be too busy quenching the flames to hinder us in our good work."

The soberest of the company fell silent and began looking about them for a way of escape. But others reflected, and admitted that the plan was a good one. The speaker went on, "We're not alone in this. We're many! I have comrades who will speak of this elsewhere, and certain bold warriors are at work even now recruiting for the cause." He drew forth another purse and emptied it upon the table. "I'll pay five gulden at once to anyone who will promise to set fire to some house he knows of."

At this point the tavern keeper abandoned the wine cask to its fate and slunk out, followed by one or two of the less inebriated. But Andy, to my great dismay, turned crimson in the face and roared, "This man is a spy and a traitor and offers Turkish gold to brave men! Strike him on the mouth and hand him over to the provost marshal!"

In vain I tugged at Andy's sleeve and sought to silence him. When the pock-marked man dashed at him with drawn sword, Andy overturned the table, hurled an empty barrel at his head, snatched his weapon, and began roaring for the marshal. In the ensuing confusion the drunken soldiers rapidly grabbed at the spilled coins that were rolling all over the floor, and then with savage imprecations hurled themselves upon the agitator to seize and bind him. Outside could be heard the drum of the marshal's men and soon we were following the unhappy traitor, with oaths and clenched fists, to testify against him at the town hall.

It was not only in our tavern that such incidents took place, and the provost marshal's men, reinforced by a few armed troopers, marched through all the streets of Vienna, raiding every alehouse and arresting all who scattered money in too ostentatious a manner. When we reached the town hall we found a crowd there already, bawling death and destruction to all traitors. We yelled as loudly as the rest. Andy said, "It was a pity to break up the party so soon, but the fellow was too talkative and would have been caught anyway. There are enough witnesses without us, but let us stay here in the background, for no one would dream of seeking us in this place."

I said bitterly, "You should have let him talk on, for then we might have waited with folded arms till all was ready. Now there's no time to be lost and we must quickly buy our fuel, or incur the Grand Vizier's displeasure."

Andy stared at me goggle eyed and said, "Are you out of your wits, Michael? This man has disclosed the whole plot and we've no chance of taking the authorities by surprise. All that's left to do is to save our own skins. The Grand Vizier should have remembered that too many cooks spoil the broth."

Meanwhile the questioning went on, and to the people's great delight two deserters found skulking in a tavern were hanged at once. Five suspects who had been too free with their money were put to the torture. Their howling penetrated the massive stone walls and could be heard out in the market place. It was not long before proclamation was made from the doors of the town hall that these five had confessed to having been bribed by the Aga of Janissaries to return and fire the city, and in the confusion open the gates to the Turks.

To pacify the people the five men were dragged into the market place—for they could no longer walk—to be broken on the wheel and then quartered; their dismembered bodies were then impaled on stakes in the sight of all. When these stakes were set up I felt very cold and spewed up my wine, and in a faint voice I pleaded with Andy to take me away.

But the crowd was now in an ugly mood. Men looked askance at one another and soldiers began shouting that the Jews must be in league with the Sultan since they had crucified our Lord. They set upon a terrified Jew who had strayed by chance into the market place, stoning him and hurling him to the ground to kick his yellow face, before streaming away toward the ghetto.

Heedless of my pitiable state Andy gripped my arm and soon we found ourselves before the barred gate of the City of Affliction, which from what we could see well deserved its name. Sunlight could never penetrate the stinking alleyways, all doors and windows were shut, and not a living soul was to be seen. As soon as the soldiers began breaking into the houses the rabbis and elders who had fled to the cellars sent a swift messenger by secret ways to the Christian duke, to offer him the customary protection money.

When the officers had allowed their men to wreck the houses, throw out and smash the furniture, and violate two luckless Jewesses, they sent mounted men to put an end to the tumult and drive the excited mob back into the city. The horsemen took their time over this and addressed the pillagers in a friendly tone, explaining that while they would not seem to defend the butchers of Christ, yet it was wise to let them survive because they were useful, and a Christian could always squeeze a few coins from them at need. Meanwhile Andy and I hid ourselves under some straw in a stable, and having emptied the last drops from a little Hungarian keg he had brought with him from camp, we sank into the deep sleep of exhaustion.

It was night when we woke, but the Jews were still singing songs of lamentation and strewing ashes in their hair as they examined their ravaged dwellings. So mournful and eerie was the sound in the darkness of night that cold shudders ran down my spine, but Andy said, "That's an old song. I've heard it in every Christian city where Imperial troops have been quartered. Let us seek out Aaron, for hunger rumbles in my belly."

246

I went with him to the house whence came the terrible lamentation, but the singing died away when we appeared among the crouching figures and asked for Aaron. I believe they were accustomed to the sudden arrival of strangers in their midst at night, for they were not at all alarmed. Having assured themselves that we were to be trusted they opened a secret trap door and took us down into a cellar, from which through evil-smelling underground passages we came to Aaron's house.

Aaron was an emaciated man with an expression of suffering. He seemed unsurprised at the sight of Ibrahim's ring, but kissed it reverently. Bowing deeply before us, he said, "We hoped for a miracle from Jehovah and believed that the new Solomon would ride into the city on a white horse; we would have welcomed him with green boughs, as a conqueror. But Jehovah would not have it so."

He rubbed the diamond against the sleeve of his black kaftan and admired its brilliance in the light of a smoking oil lamp. Then he sighed, "Keep the ring, if you think it safer with you than with me. I should only send it back to the Grand Vizier, for I can do nothing in this matter."

We spent the night in Aaron's house and the following day also, for we did not know what else to do. But with the approach of night —the night which the Grand Vizier had appointed for the fire—Andy said, "I should like to do at least something to deserve the ring that Aaron refuses to take, and am weary of being cooped up in this miserable house. Let us go back into the city, brother Michael, and inspect the King's powder magazine and grain store. Perhaps we could manage at least a small fire, though the Grand Vizier can have little use for it now."

To avoid the soldiers posted at the gates of the ghetto, we crept out of the place through the sewers, according to Aaron's directions. I should mention that this honest Jew refused to take a penny for his help and protection, and merely begged us to speak a good word for him to the Grand Vizier. We found that the powder magazine and the duke's stables were guarded by numerous sentries; we had no chance, therefore, of starting even the most innocent little fire and so fulfilling in part our promise to the Seraskier.

In the market place a great crowd of women had assembled about the cooking pots from which compassionate monks were distributing food to the fugitives, who would otherwise have perished from hunger. But on the doorstep of a deserted house I saw a young girl; she

247

had thrown her petticoat over her head and was rocking silently to and fro. Her mute distress so moved me that I spoke to her and offered alms; but she looked up and retorted sharply that she was no trollop to be bought with money. I was startled to see how beautiful she was and to learn that she was one of those who thanks to Andy had escaped from the Turkish camp. She recognized us too, and with a cry of surprise asked how we had come off with our lives, when all other escaped prisoners had been hanged for deserters.

I begged her to be silent for the love of God, and not attract the attention of the guards, for our lives were now in her hands. She was very lovely, though her hair was soaked with rain and her clothes tattered and muddy. We learned that she and her parents had fled from Hungary—where her father owned an estate near the Transilvanian border—to join King Ferdinand, but during their flight to Vienna the akindshas slew all the household save herself, whom they led away into slavery.

When she told her name and sought protection with the military authorities in Vienna, she was received with scorn and her dead father reviled as a rebellious Hungarian. Every Hungarian herd maid, they told her, who escaped from the Turks became a nobleman's daughter as soon as she entered Vienna. However, for her beauty's sake one of the court gentlemen promised to take pity on her and sleep with her regularly, provided she would enroll herself among the prostitutes and earn her bread honestly like other fugitives. Twice, because of her hunger, she had spoken to soldiers in the street and begged them for the love of God to give her food and shelter. But these men, having eagerly promised their help, merely led her into some side alley to debauch her, and then left her lying in the mire. She said, "I would give anything to return to my home and seek the protection of the Turks and King Zapolya. Perhaps he would let me keep my father's estate since I am the only survivor, and then marry me to one of his followers. Not even Turks could treat me as badly as Christians do."

Just then heavy raindrops began falling. Andy looked up at the murky clouds and said, "We're in for a sharp storm, so let's seek shelter. There we can discuss the matter further, my fair young lady, for your youth and your distress have cut me to the heart."

But the poor girl crossed herself and vowed that never again would she go with strange men into alleyways, but would rather perish of cold and hunger where she sat. But we reassured her so earnestly and the rain came down so hard that after anguished hesitation she agreed to go with us. With lowered eyes she told us in a faint voice that her name was Eva, and gave her family name also, but it was one of those heathen Hungarian words that no one can pronounce. We knocked at the doors of many houses but no one would let us in. Fortunately we met one of the hucksters who supplied the *landsknechts,* pushing his handcart along the street and looking about for shelter. He sold us bread, meat, and cheese and told us of a respectable brothel—the only place where we could be safe from the provost marshal's men, as the mistress of it paid the marshal a substantial sum to be allowed to carry on her business in peace.

The brothel keeper received us cordially as soon as she saw that we were well supplied with money, nor did she try to foist her own girls upon us. Judging by the noise, they were busy enough already. She gave us a clean attic room with the assurance that no one would disturb us before the morning; she even lit the fire so that we might dry our clothes. In return, and to ensure that she would not inform against us, we bought a pitcher of wine from her at an exorbitant price. Brothel keepers are as trustworthy in business matters as Jews, and for the same reason—their lives depend upon it. Not that fools cannot lose their money there as easily as anywhere else, and even be thrown into the street in their underclothes with a chamber pot over them for good measure. Such things must happen when one fails to observe the customs of the house.

We ate, drank, and warmed ourselves, and when Andy and I had removed our clothes to dry them at the stove, our companion ventured to do the same, retaining only one of her petticoats. Although her clothes were torn I saw that they were of durable and costly stuff, which went far to strengthen my belief in her story. I lent her my comb, and now that wine had brought color to her cheeks I saw that she was an unusually charming, bright-eyed, and clear-skinned beauty. Andy, too, when he had eaten, gazed long at her while the rain drummed on the roof above our heads. At length he said, "Your other petticoats will be dry by now, and you'd better put them on. The Scriptures tell us not to lead one another into temptation, and I should be loath for my thoughts to go astray because of your bare shoulders."

Yet he gazed with ever increasing rapture at the lovely girl, who had evidently been well brought up, for she kept her long-lashed eyes modestly lowered and ate very delicately. As he gazed his eyes grew

249

rounder and he began to fidget and breathe heavily. I had never seen Andy so discomposed in the presence of a woman. He drummed on his knees, clawed at his neck, or scratched his back; for a time he strove to keep his hands demurely folded and when all else failed he thrust them resolutely beneath him and sat upon them with all his weight. Feeling that he had eaten and rested enough I said, "I fancy I hear the vesper bell, so now is our last chance to carry out our plans."

At that moment a violent thunderclap resounded above our heads; heaven's sluice gates were opened and hailstones the size of pigeons' eggs clattered upon the dripping roofs and flooded streets. After listening to this din for a while Andy said with a sigh of relief, "It was not Allah's will. This deluge would quench the fiercest fire in a moment and had we foreseen it we need never have come to this devil-ridden city."

The storm showed no sign of abating, and indeed grew more violent. For some reason I was beginning to feel much irked by Andy's presence, and I said, "Perhaps it would be well if you stood guard outside the door, for this shy and charming girl would no doubt like to discuss with me in private how best we may help in her great need."

I believe my intentions were of the best, but the girl misunderstood me, and catching Andy by the arm with both hands she cried in a fright, "Dear Master Andrew, I beg you not to leave me alone with your brother, for he glares at me like a wolf and I trust no one any more."

Andy reddened, shook his fist at me, and then lifting the girl gently on to his knee he put his forefinger under her chin and said, "Have no fear, noble Mistress Eva. Trust me, and if Allah wills it I will take you safely back to your homeland. I should tell you that my brother and I are in the Turkish service and we too are trying to get away from this vile city."

The girl did not struggle in his embrace, but looked straight into his round gray eyes and said, "Though you were kalmucks, devils, or sorcerers I would go with you rather than stay here. The Turks have treated me more mercifully than the Christians, and in these few days I've conceived such a loathing of Christendom that I can well understand how a brave man might rather serve the Sultan than King Ferdinand. I've admired you since I first saw you among the prisoners, for your strength and chivalry and kind heart. You're no doubt of noble German birth, since you speak that hateful language so well."

250

Drops of sweat stood on Andy's brow as he replied, "I learned the language on my campaigns, and only your kindness could call my camp talk good German. I was born in the wilds, in a land of fir trees and wolves and bears, and no prince ever had the wit to bestow on me the spurs of knighthood. Yet in the Sultan's army I wear the heron's feather plume of the master gunner, which surely more than equals a pair of gilded spurs."

Mistress Eva, gladdened by these words, leaned her dark head trustfully on Andy's shoulder. Presently he lifted her from his knee and laid her gently on the edge of the bed, where he stood for a time bending over her and sighing.

"Ah, how warm you were in my arms, Mistress Eva! Your rosy cheeks are smooth and downy as peaches and to me you're fairer than the moon."

Mistress Eva lowered her eyes and said in deprecation, "No, I'm not beautiful. I'm but a helpless orphan, and not even at King Zapolya's court have I any protector to win back for me my father's estates."

Andy pressed both hands to his chest and quivered like a tree about to fall.

"Allah be gracious to me!" he whispered. "This must have been written in the book of fate long before my birth. Tell me, how big are your estates? How many horses and cattle have you? Are the buildings in good repair? And what is the soil?"

Horrified at the turn things were taking I prepared to leave them, beseeching Andy in our own language to have his way with her at once rather than commit himself with such rash talk. But he implored me to remain, saying that he had known nothing like this before and was at a loss what to say to her, and that I must be his spokesman. Mistress Eva looked at us in bewilderment, but meekly replied to Andy's questions. "My father told me little of his affairs, but our estates were big enough for modest landed gentry like ourselves to live upon. We had wet and dry soil, clay and sand. We had forests, and game in plenty. It took a day and a night to travel from end to end of our land, though my father was constantly going to law with his neighbors whom he accused of shifting the boundary stones and allowing their flocks to graze on his pastures. I suppose we had some hundred thousand sheep, a thousand horses, and a few cattle. At any rate my father's Jewish intendant gave him money whenever he asked for it."

Andy sighed, cleared his throat, and said pleadingly, "Michael, I may be possessed of the devil, but I really am deeply in love with this girl and want to marry her, so that I may watch over her interests and restore to her her father's property. Speak for me, Michael, for you can choose your words better than I. If you won't, I must—but then if I fail and she refuses me I'll break every bone in your body!"

Deeply though I deplored his conduct I had no choice but to address the girl in well-chosen words and say, "I think my brother may be out of his mind, but he wants to marry you. As a wedding gift he offers to speak to King Zapolya and regain your estates. He has a chance of succeeding, being in favor with the Grand Vizier, whose best friend is King Zapolya's adviser, Master Gritti. My brother is of undistinguished birth, though with a good conscience he may call himself a von Wolfenland zu Fichtenbaum, or a de Wolf of Spruce, and he swears his heart has been on fire from the moment he first saw you."

Mistress Eva's cherry lips parted in mute astonishment and her face was suffused with a blush. It was now her turn to tremble and wring her hands. Then she abandoned all womanly hesitation, and throwing herself on the floor at Andy's feet she clasped his knees and sobbed, "With all my heart I will be your wife, noble Master Andrew, and could dream of nothing better. For I'm a poor orphan, robbed of goods and virtue. If you'll have me for your wedded wife I will share both good and ill fortune with you, and submit to you in all things. All I ask is that you will let me keep my Christian faith and pay some good priest to unite us in the sacrament of marriage."

With the sweat pouring down his face, Andy turned to me and said, "Do me one last service, Michael, and find me a priest. If you haven't brought one within the hour I shall take this girl under my arm and fly with her from Vienna, leaving you to shift for yourself."

He spoke so desperately that I feared he might do as he threatened. I set my teeth grimly, therefore, and went in search of our hostess. This vigilant woman was still up, selling wine to her customers and emptying the purses of those who slept. She told me of a trustworthy priest who was ready at any hour of the day or night to perform his sacred office without indiscreet questions, so long as he was liberally paid. It was not the first time he had been summoned to the house, and twice that week he had administered the Viaticum and Extreme Unction to customers who had come to blows over questions of religion. I gave her a gold piece and she sent a pot boy for the priest, in the belief that somehow or other I had got the better of Andy in a struggle for the girl and that he now lay at the point of death. When I returned to our room Andy snatched his hand from Eva's neck with a scowl at me. But he quickly regained his good humor and said, "Forgive me for speaking to you so sharply just now, my dear Michael. This is the happiest moment of my life, and I could never have dared to hope that such a lovely and well-born girl could grow fond of me."

Just then we heard the ringing of the priest's bell outside. What was my amazement when I opened the door to admit him to find that I knew that bluish, puffy face with its crimson beak of a nose. There in a cassock, tonsured and with a stubble of beard, stood the man who during my student years in Paris had given me my first dearly bought lesson in the falsehood and treachery of the world.

"In the name of the Compassionate!" I cried. "May all the saints protect us, Reverend Father, but are you not Master Julien d'Avril, the blackguard from Paris? Where did you steal that cassock and how comes it that you were never hanged? Surely there is *some* justice in the world?"

It was indeed Julien d'Avril, though greatly aged and more drink sodden than ever. At first he turned ashy pale. Then, like the fox he was, he quickly recovered himself, enfolded me in his malodorous embrace and with tears of emotion exclaimed, "Ah, my dear boy, my dear Michael de Finlandia! What happiness to see again your open, honest face. Blessed be the hour that unites us once more. How is it with you, and why do you need the services of Holy Church so urgently as to drag an old man out of bed?"

With this unlooked-for meeting I may fitly end the story of the siege of Vienna, and having conscientiously told all and hidden nothing of my share in this unhappy campaign, I will begin a new book about my subsequent adventures.

BOOK 6.

The Light of Islam Returns

ANDY too was much shaken when he recognized Julien d'Avril, but he soon recovered and showed him the reverence due to his cloth.

"The past is forgotten," he said, "and I bear you no grudge, Master Julien, although at one time I would gladly have flayed you alive and hung your hide to dry on the branch of a tree. But no one is free from guilt and who am I to cast the first stone? Tell me one thing— are you a properly ordained priest, empowered to administer the Sacraments?"

Julien looked at him reproachfully and replied, "Can you doubt it? Forget my former sin-polluted name and call me Father Julianus, for so I am known to all Vienna as a pious army chaplain. I have brought with me the Host and the holy oil, and wait to serve you, though I can see no one here at the point of death."

Andy said, "Reverend Father Julianus, produce your sacrament of marriage and read the necessary words over me and this Hungarian orphan girl; she must tell you her own name, as my stiff tongue can't get round it."

Father Julianus showed no surprise, and his eyes wandered abstractedly over the bare shoulders of the bride as he remarked, "Your purpose is praiseworthy, but what has the mistress of the house to say to it? Have you paid her for the girl? She incurs much trouble and expense in her profession and I should be loath to do her an injury, for we're good customers to one another."

Andy stared at him uncomprehendingly, but Father Julianus raised his hand and went on, "Don't think I doubt your sincerity or mean to slight your bride in any way. Many a marriage embarked upon in the heat of the moment or in a fit of drunkenness turns out well, and a prostitute often makes the best wife for a professional soldier. She gathers firewood for him, carries his cooking pot, and washes his clothes. Nevertheless allow me as an experienced curer of souls to suggest that you would be wise to sleep on the idea."

When at last Andy grasped the chaplain's meaning he flew into a passion, drew his sword, and would certainly have stabbed Father Julianus to death had I not sprung between them. I reproached our guest very volubly for his suspicions, and explained that Andy's sweetheart was of noble birth and the heiress to a great Hungarian estate. The wedding must necessarily be a quiet one, I said, because of the unhappy conditions prevailing in her own country. Father Julianus should have three ducats for uniting them and an extra ducat for the poor box.

But Father Julianus only half believed me; peering at all three of us suspiciously, he said, "There's something fishy about this affair. You wouldn't have summoned me at this time of night and to a brothel if you had nothing to hide. I won't risk my neck by being a party to it—at any rate not for four ducats."

Andy in his madness made no attempt to bargain, but offered the blackguard twenty Hungarian ducats, which only made him the more suspicious. Nevertheless he opened his book, read the necessary benedictions, and joined the pair in matrimony without further remark. Even in his impious mouth the ancient Latin words had a solemn sound.

Finally he asked Andy for the ring, that he might set it upon the bride's finger and declare them man and wife. In his extremity Andy asked me for Grand Vizier Ibrahim's valuable diamond ring—a request so outrageous as to do more than anything to convince me that his mind was unhinged. Storm and swear as I would, he snatched it from my purse by force and handed it to Father Julianus, who slipped it on the girl's finger. So it left our possession for ever.

At the sight of this magnificent stone Father Julianus looked much disconcerted and seemed to wonder what sort of men we really were. He brought the ceremony speedily to a close, pronounced the benediction with all the power and authority of Holy Church, swept the coins rapidly into his greasy purse, and prepared to leave. He said, "I have talked myself dry and will gladly drink to your welfare and success if you wish it. No doubt you will stay here for the rest of the night to fulfill the first obligations of matrimony, and I will visit you again to bestow the blessing of the Lord upon you both."

I suspected that we had walked into a trap, but Andy caught Father Julianus by the ear, poured wine down his throat, and said hospitably, "Drink, dear Father. For once at least swallow enough to know that you have drunk. Tonight I care not what it costs. Michael can fetch us another couple of flagons of this nectar."

Father Julianus struggled violently, spluttered and protested, but Andy forced his swollen nose into the stoup and bade me fetch more wine. When he released him for a moment the pious Father at once began accusing us of treachery and cursing us for renegades, and swore that the first time he saw us in Paris he could smell the sulphurous fumes of heresy about us. Andy soothed him, saying, "This is for your own good, dear Father Julianus, but if you'd rather have your throat cut I've nothing against it. Don't tempt me too far, for I can't forget your dastardly desertion of us at the inn outside Paris, when you left us a curt letter as sole memento of all our cares and troubles."

He drew his knife, spat into his palm, and began to whet the blade. Father Julianus at once fell silent and his face turned gray. The villain had known every twist and turn of fortune, and saw that he would be wise to submit to the inevitable. In a faint voice he asked for more wine, and I went at once to fetch it.

It was not long before he began assuring us that he had always regarded Mohammed as a most eminent prophet, and that the Church had taken up a very narrow-minded attitude to polygamy, notwithstanding the good example set by the patriarchs. He went on to lament the harshness of the provost marshal to a poor army chaplain in begrudging him his modest earnings. But when he began to stammer and hiccup and prop himself against the edge of the table Andy told me to go, and to take Father Julianus with me. After many vain protests I staggered with the chaplain down the steep stairs and our kind hostess helped me to carry him into another room. She then offered me the services of her establishment, but I was in too dejected a mood to avail myself of them and crept into bed beside the snoring Father Julianus, where for greater safety I tied his left leg to my right. I then fell asleep, with a clear conscience as my only pillow.

I slept very heavily and was only awoken by Father Julianus tugging violently at my leg. He was sitting up beside me and having said a prayer he whispered, "Don't move, for we've fallen into the hands of robbers. They have bound me so that I can't get out of bed, and one of my legs is so numb that I haven't a vestige of feeling in it, though I've done all I can to rub it back to life."

He pummeled my own leg in despair until in pity I untied it from his and showed him where his right leg lay safe under the blanket. Having regained his composure he remembered what had happened. His face darkened, and I had just time to catch him by the shirt before he sneaked through the door. I warned him that I was quicker on my feet than he, and could easily take his life if he tried to betray us. He heaved a sigh of resignation and proposed that we should taste a drop of mulled wine together.

I had nothing against this proposal and in all harmony we crept downstairs, picked our way among sleeping soldiers and all the sordid confusion of the night's orgies, and heated wine for ourselves over the glowing embers of the hearth. Remembering Andy and his bride I saved wine and bread for them, and being wishful to shake the dust of the city from my feet as quickly as might be I went at once to their room in company with the chaplain.

Andy lay snoring on his back, while his young wife lay in a deep sleep with her face pressed to his hairy chest and her arms about his neck. I quickly covered their nakedness with a blanket, to spare Father Julianus's feelings, but the sound of the hot iron hissing in the wine woke Andy as by magic. His eyes flew open, and hastily thrusting the naked girl away from him he drew the blanket up to his chin and cried, "What in the name of Allah has happened? Who is this shameless woman? Take her away!"

I spoke soothingly to him as with hair on end and an expression of utter amazement on his face he swallowed a stoup of wine. Little by little memory returned to him and he sat muttering to himself, uncertain whether to be glad or sorry at his sudden marriage. So absurd did he look that I too hardly knew whether to laugh or cry.

But a cup of scalding wine is the best remedy for perplexity. We forgot our worries and broke spontaneously into a French song, as an aubade to the young bride.

But for all our din the girl never moved; indeed she scarcely seemed to breathe. She lay motionless, her lips parted and her clear skin looking even paler for the dark hair that lay in disorder over the pillow, and for the long lashes that shaded the rings beneath her eyes. Andy gazed at her fearfully and poked her with his forefinger, but she only stirred a little and went on sleeping. Tears rose to Andy's eyes as he told us to be quiet, and with a shake of his head he said, "Let the poor child sleep. She's a tender little foal and must be very tired, though I held her as gently as I could. I know already that this is one of the very few marriages that angels in heaven have arranged; but for all that I shall demand my legal rights and fight tooth and nail for my wife's interests. We had better hasten at once to Hungary, to be there in time for the counting of the livestock."

The eyes of Father Julianus glistened as he said quickly, "What will you give me besides my freedom if I help you to pass through the city gates unscathed?"

"No, no, dear Father Julianus," said Andy with a wave of his hand. "Why should we part now that we have found one another again? If you'll escort us out we can consider what return to make you afterward, at our leisure."

The wine had inspired me with a most excellent idea, and I put in quickly, "Be reasonable, good Father Julianus, and you shall not regret it. It's possible that you may return to Christendom to devote yourself to very different tasks. Only trust me. But good counsel is now precious, and we won't haggle if you can really get us out of this carefully guarded city."

After much argument we agreed, while cursing his rapacity, to pay him a hundred ducats for safe conduct, twenty-five to be handed over at once.

"I don't mean to go on foot," he said. "You must get good horses for all of us and dress as richly as you can."

He refused to explain why this was necessary, and as we were forced to trust him we had no choice but to send the pot boy with a message to Aaron. Thanks to this honest Jew, four fairly good horses, ready saddled, stood at the door by noon, and Andy and I were able to don cuirasses inlaid with silver, though somewhat bloodstained. For the young woman Aaron provided a gown of silk and velvet and a veil of the kind women use to conceal their faces while traveling.

But with these things came a reckoning that made me gasp for breath. The charge for each item was shown separately, and the total came to no less than nineteen hundred and ninety-eight ducats. But, wrote Aaron, if we had not this sum with us he was willing to take the Grand Vizier's ring as security, and had given the bearer two ducats in coin, thus bringing the loan to two thousand ducats, or the value of the ring.

Aaron's shrewdness in taking advantage of our desperate situation cut me to the quick, and when I saw Andy glancing sideways at the ring on his sleeping wife's finger I declared that though he might be ready to steal her wedding ring I could never find it in my heart to commit so mean an action. I therefore took the two ducats from the messenger and made out a bill for two thousand ducats in the Grand Vizier's name, to be honored by the Sultan's treasurer. I perceived certainly that this paper might cause us some trouble if it were ever presented, but I fancied that Aaron would never have the opportunity to arrange this if only we could get away quickly.

But here I was entirely mistaken, being ignorant of the amazingly swift business communications existing among Jews. Incredible as it may seem, the bill was presented at the Sultan's treasury in Buda long before we reached that town ourselves. The Grand Vizier accepted it, although it had passed through so many hands and been increased by so many costs and charges that by the time he saw it the sum amounted to two thousand, three hundred and forty-two ducats. All too late I perceived that to Jews such a document was almost safer than coin during wartime and when great distances were involved; Aaron therefore gained rather than lost by the transaction.

The rustle of the silken gown roused the young lady; she rubbed the sleep from her long-lashed eyes and sat up to wish her husband a tender good morning. Andy sharply bade us turn our backs, and urged his wife to put on the new dress with all haste. Nevertheless our journey was further delayed by her refusal to wear the gown until it had been altered to cling more closely to her figure. There ensued a desperate running to and fro with scissors, needles, and thread, and many tears were shed before we were able to mount our horses and leave that pleasant house, having richly rewarded its proprietress for all the trouble and vexation we had caused her.

To my surprise Father Julianus made straight for the Salt Gate, which stood wide open. Crowds of people on foot or in ox carts were streaming through it out of the city. Noting our silver cuirasses the guard thrust the mob aside to make way for us and greeted Father Julianus with jovial quips, to which he replied with benedictions seasoned with salty oaths, as befitted an accomplished army chaplain. The guard commander thrust his lance suspiciously into a wagon load of

262

hay on its way into the town, but paid no heed to those who were leaving it, and it was more from curiosity than professional zeal that he asked Father Julianus whither he was bound. The old fox replied that he was escorting the noble lady von Wolfenland zu Fichtenbaum back to her estates, and with that we rode through the archway and left the city of Vienna behind us.

My heart, which hitherto had been in my mouth, returned to its proper place and I felt so profound a relief that I gladly paid Father Julianus his second twenty-five ducats, asking how in the name of God he had known that we could leave the city so easily. He answered, "Even yesterday crowds of vagrants were going and no one stopped them, since they were only a burden to the citizens. For safety's sake I asked you to wear good clothes, so that if necessary you could behave like noblemen and whip off any inquisitive people. Surely you don't imagine that I would have consented to come with you if I had believed there was any danger?"

We rode forward along the squelching roads past the ruins of Moslem camps that formed a great arc about the city and extended to the distant hills. We were soon overtaken by a troop of horsemen bound in pursuit of the Turks. They hailed us with friendly shouts and warned us against Turkish patrols that might yet be lingering in the region. Toward evening the sky appeared through rifts in the clouds. It grew colder, and we knew that snow might soon be expected.

It fell that night, but Andy and I welcomed it as a reminder of our distant homeland, and it was in any case to be preferred to the mire of autumn. But the snow soon melted, leaving the roads worse than before. We were never in doubt as to our course, for pillars of smoke by day and the glow of fires, which at night lit up the horizon, showed us the route of the retreating Turkish army. An even surer indication were the headless, plundered corpses that we found impaled on stakes in the burned-out villages. All houses and barns within the radius of a day's march from the route were burned and the inhabitants slain, and not even the soulless beasts had been spared.

The ghastly scenes filled me with revulsion; I longed to leave all such wanton devastation behind me and seek the blessings of peace. In a day or two the traces of the retreating army were fresher. Smoke still rose from the heaps of ashes as we passed; blood still flowed from the wounds of the slain. At last we came up with a few bowmen who were busily engaged in throwing corpses into a well to poison the water. We approached them and by way of credentials showed them the Grand Vizier's ring on Mistress Eva's finger.

They wanted to kill Father Julianus at once because of his cassock, and had already dragged him from his horse when Andy exerted his great strength and held them off. They withdrew a few paces and raised their bows; I can think of no bleaker sound than the twang of a bowstring on a chilly morning.

But I summoned up my Turkish vocabulary and threatened the spahis with the Grand Vizier's fury if they carried out their threats, and at the same time offered them princely rewards if they would bring us to him immediately. Yet I fancy it was the sight of Mistress Eva that made them relent. No doubt they expected to get a good price for her, and perhaps hoped to sell Andy and me as well. The janissaries would certainly buy Father Julianus, for they loved to stimulate their religious fervor by roasting Christian priests alive over their campfires. These men were therefore content to deprive us of our horses, and did not even trouble to throw a noose round our necks, but merely prodded us forward with their lance butts.

We first saw the Seraskier when we reached Buda, and perhaps it was as well that we could not burden him with our own troubles until the army had halted here to rest before the remainder of the homeward march. The Sultan now proclaimed Hungary to be a friendly country and forbade his troops to plunder the villages or carry away their inhabitants into slavery. To what extent the maddened janissaries obeyed his decree I prefer not to say.

For all the hubbub of victory instigated by the Sultan I soon noticed that the mood of the army left much to be desired. On his arrival in Buda the Grand Vizier had caused the holy crown of St. Stephen to be brought forth and placed in his tent for public display. Andy and I, standing like beggars by the tent door, watched the high pashas come out shrugging their shoulders and exchanging scornful smiles. We realized that our welcome would be none the warmer for delay and sent in our names to Ibrahim, who as usual received us in the middle of the night. He was fingering the crown as we entered, and beside him sat that bird of ill omen, Master Gritti. We prostrated ourselves and kissed the ground before the Seraskier, but his reception of us was less cordial than it might have been.

"You dogs, you devil's spawn!" he cried. His handsome face was violently flushed with wine. "I never sent you to Vienna to lie wallow-

264

ing in a brothel! Where are your turbans? Where is my valuable ring? Did I ask you to get into debt with your whores? I had to argue for hours with the Defterdar before he would honor your draft."

Andy answered mildly, "Don't condemn us unheard. Your ring's not lost; I gave it to my wife. I'll pay for it when I can."

The Seraskier turned to Master Gritti with a look of despair.

"What are we to do with these mad dogs? They even boast of their misdeeds." To us he went on, "You should at least have set fire to Vienna, like brave men; but it seems you settled down in a house of ill fame and misconducted yourselves to the value of two thousand ducats, before crawling back to offend me with your dissipated faces."

Andy reddened and said warmly, "Allah be good to you! How you distort the truth. I tell you I've entered into Christian matrimony, so there's no question of misconduct; and as for Michael, he's too badly scared of the French pox to think of it. As a great general you should know that it would take a platoon of men to spend two thousand ducats in a brothel. Thanks to our boldness and enterprise we escaped a hideous death and so saved you two irreplaceable servants. Think shame of your base accusations, and beg our pardons before I lose my temper."

He looked so solemn that Seraskier Ibrahim burst out laughing and wiping tears of mirth from his eyes he said soothingly, "I was but testing you, for I know you have done your best. But not even the bravest man can turn bad fortune to good, and Aaron has put in a word for you through his colleagues. I do regret my ring, however, for the stone was of rare purity. May I see your bride and satisfy myself that she is worthy of it, or do you prefer as a good Moslem to conceal her face from me?"

Andy replied delightedly that being a Christian his wife observed no undue modesty where her face was concerned; she was therefore summoned, and with her Father Julianus slunk into the tent. At the sight of him the prejudiced Seraskier instinctively made horns with his fingers and said, "How can you allow a Christian priest to pollute my tent? I see by his cassock and his beardless chin that he belongs to the most pernicious order of idolater."

I explained hurriedly, "I rescued Father Julianus from Vienna and at peril to my own life brought him here, thereby doing you a greater service than you know, for I have a plan which I would prefer to set before you in private."

Meanwhile Mistress Eva drew aside her veil, revealing her shyly smiling face and dark eyes. The Grand Vizier gazed at her with pleasure and said politely, "She is indeed fair. Her brow is whiter than jasmine, her eyebrows are musk, and her mouth like the pomegranate. I regret my ring no longer and rejoice with you, Antar, in the capture of so lovely a prize. And I will admit that both you and your brother have proved your loyalty to me, though Allah preserve me from any more such costly demonstrations."

I was delighted to find that like a true nobleman he freely submitted to the will of Allah and meant to retain us in his service. Andy profited by the auspicious moment and said promptly, "Naturally I ask no reward for my fruitless labors, yet I should be overjoyed if you would show your favor by speaking a word to King Zapolya on behalf of my wife, so that her estates on the Transilvanian border may be restored to her. Eva, my dear wife, tell the noble Seraskier your family name."

Master Gritti was already tearing his hair and when Mistress Eva modestly pronounced her name he broke out in lamentation, "Do not listen to this Antar, dear Grand Vizier! Every renegade in the army has hastened to marry some nobleman's daughter in order to claim her inheritance, and Hungary would be lost if all these unlawful claims were granted. King Zapolya has therefore followed my advice and is amalgamating these properties so as to place them in the hands of a few trusted persons. Instead of the tens of thousands of small estates that now exist, there will remain only a thousand or so large ones. You will realize how greatly this must simplify the work of the taxgatherers and strengthen the present government, since the new landowners will be fully aware that they stand or fall with King Zapolya."

The Grand Vizier said wearily, "I don't want to interfere in Hungary's internal affairs, but I must protect the Sultan's subjects and the interests of my own servants. Antar shall therefore take possession of his wife's estates, but in order not to impede King Zapolya's excellent land reform I will gladly allow him to add other properties to his own and so make it as large as the rest. See that my wishes are respected, Aloisio Gritti, if you would remain my friend."

I nudged Andy to make him fall on his knees and kiss the Grand Vizier's hand, and the delighted bride followed her husband's example. The Seraskier then dismissed them. But I remained, meaning to strike while the iron was hot, and held Father Julianus by the arm. When Master Gritti had left a great weariness came over Ibrahim's handsome face; I noticed that he had grown thinner during the campaign and that lines had appeared on his smooth white brow. He said with a yawn, "It's late, Michael el-Hakim. Why do you burden me with your presence any longer?"

I answered, "The moon shines while the sun reposes. Night is the moon's time. Let me speak and so serve you, mean slave though I am."

He said, "Be seated, my slave, and let the Christian priest sit also, since he is so much older than we."

He brought out a flagon and three goblets from under his cushions and allowed us to drink to his prosperity. Sipping a little himself, he said, "Speak your mind, Michael el-Hakim."

I replied in carefully chosen words. "There is but one war—that between the Sultan and the Emperor, Islam and Europe, the Crescent and the Cross. The Emperor himself has often said that his main object is to unite all Christian lands in a common crusade to crush Ottoman power. Any Christian who opposes the Emperor is therefore —whether he knows it or not—the Sultan's ally. The heretic Luther and his followers are the best of these and you would do well to give him secret support, further his aims, and above all champion the cause of religious freedom."

The Grand Vizier gazed at me searchingly and asked, "During your wanderings in Germany did you ever hear of a certain Margrave Philip, the ruler of a principality called Hesse? He has taken Luther under his protection. Is he a powerful man? How large is his domain? Can he be trusted?"

I felt a pang at my heart as he spoke that name. I saw in my mind's eye a fair-haired, blue-eyed man in armor surveying the gashed body of a priest who lay in a pool of blood; I saw him sitting in the sunshine with his hands about his knees, before a church door in Frankenhausen. Since those violent days an eternity had passed and I had lived many lives; but now I realized to my surprise that only five years lay between me and that chance encounter. I answered eagerly, "I know him. He told me in jest that he thought of appointing Luther to be his house chaplain. His province is a modest one and he is burdened by debt, unless he has since enriched himself by the theft of church lands. But he is a warlike man and a fine horseman. I can't answer for his integrity, for he struck me as a singularly cold-blooded creature to whom religion was an instrument of temporal profit rather than a path to salvation."

The Grand Vizier flung his golden goblet at my head and cried, "Why have you never told me all this before, you dog? I could have made good use of it last spring when King Zapolya was negotiating with Duke Philip's secret envoy."

I rubbed the growing bump on my forehead and retorted in injured tones, "Why did you never ask me? Now perhaps you understand what you lose by denying me your confidence and ignoring my knowledge of Christian politics. You have treated me like the meanest of slaves and shut me up with that senile old fellow Piri-reis, to play with toy boats in a sandbox. But now tell me honestly what agreement you have made with Duke Philip and the Protestants. Pay no heed to Father Julianus, for he understands nothing of our language and will keep quiet so long as he has a wine jar within reach. I am curious to hear these things and will gladly give you my advice."

The Grand Vizier looked a little ashamed of his hastiness, and said, "It's true that I've underrated your capabilities, Michael el-Hakim, and I should have placed more faith in your stars, as Khaireddin did, and my friend Mustafa ben-Nakir. Last spring, having made his protest before parliament, this Philip of Hesse sought to unite the other Protestant German princes in an alliance, to defend their faith against the Emperor and his power. For the same reason he sent secret envoys to the court of France and to King Zapolya, to beg for help. He was shrewd enough to foresee the inevitable clash between the Emperor and the Protestants, and as soon as he heard that the Sultan was preparing to march on Europe he declared himself willing to raise the standard of revolt in the German states. But the other princes feared attack by the rest of Germany if they joined us; and I suspected his own good faith, knowing that these heretics quarrel among themselves and hold conflicting beliefs. I therefore urged this fiery duke, through King Zapolya, to seek first religious unity within his party. No doubt the foremost prophets—the prophet of the Swiss Confederation, for example, and those of Germany—are now met together in some German city to arrive at a common religious formula. In such circumstances the German Catholics will find themselves squeezed between the Protestant princes in the north and the Confederation in the south, as a glance at the map will show."

I answered candidly, "Luther is an obstinate man, as I know. He likes to be cock of the walk and will tolerate no other prophet beside him. Sectarianism is in the very nature of heresy, for once men begin to interpret the Scriptures for themselves each does it as best suits him until all is confusion and every prophet vows that God speaks directly through his mouth. Nevertheless they are all Christians, and a united Protestant Germany would turn with equal repugnance from both Islam and the Pope."

"No, no, you're wrong, Michael el-Hakim. No bitterer hatred exists than that between sects of the same religion. Do you not remember that when Mohammed the Conqueror brought Constantinople under Ottoman rule the Greek church chose Sultan rather than Pope, and it was this schism rather than the weapons of the Osmanlis that brought about the downfall of the Greek Emperor? In this case also I believe that the Protestants will choose the Sultan rather than submit to the Emperor's will and the teaching of the Pope."

He sank into profound thought, and waved us away. Father Julianus walked through the camp with me and back to the city, so unsteadily that I had to hold his arm. He had not understood a word of what was said, but declared thickly that Grand Vizier Ibrahim was a most remarkable statesman, since not the Emperor himself had better wine in his cellar than he.

Next morning the Grand Vizier sent me a princely kaftan of honor and a horse whose saddle and bridle were adorned with silver and turquoises. My salary was raised to two hundred aspers a day, so that I was now a man of some consequence and could look the future boldly in the face. I was of course compelled to feed and clothe Father Julianus and give him great quantities of wine. I presented him with the dress of a learned *tseleb*, to shield him from the hostility of the janissaries who bore intense hatred to Christian priests.

Andy obtained leave from the Grand Vizier to set off to Transilvania to inspect his property, but was expressly forbidden to remain in King Zapolya's service. He was to return to Istanbul at latest in the following spring, and leave a trustworthy tenant in charge. This arrangement had no charms for Andy, who had hoped to live henceforth a life of lordly idleness on his own estates. It was now necessary for him to procure suitable gifts for the Grand Vizier, Master Gritti, and his new lord, King Zapolya. But since the mementos we had gathered outside Vienna had all been lost in a bog together with the Grand Vizier's baggage, poor Andy had not an asper more than I.

We turned in our need to Sinan the Builder, but he had already spent what the Sultan had given him on quantities of books and manuscripts. At last to his great shame Andy was forced to beg his wife for the Grand Vizier's ring, to pawn it. But Mistress Eva for all her youth was a woman of sense. She asked in surprise, "Why don't you go to a Jew? It was my father's custom. The Jew can claim repayment from your steward and you'll be spared these unbecoming worries."

Andy approved of this advice and we went at once to a Jew who had been recommended by one of the Defterdar's clerks. He received us in a murky cellar dwelling, bewailing the evil times that prevented all profitable business. Andy realized that he could not demand too much from this man who was evidently burdened by many cares. He had thought of asking for a hundred ducats as journey money, but now his heart failed him.

"Allah preserve me from adding to your trials," he said. "Perhaps we could manage with ten—"

Before he could pronounce the word "ducats," the Jew cried aloud to Abraham and explained volubly that for so large a sum he must have better security than a promise and a note of hand, and although I had always had my doubts of Mistress Eva's estates I began to suspect the Defterdar's clerk of talking nonsense about this man's great fortune, since he made such a song about ten ducats. I said to Andy, "Come away! I can lend you that much if need be. I only hope you can pay me when sheep-shearing time comes round."

I was wearing the kaftan that the Grand Vizier had given me, and the Jew no doubt mistook my rank and position, for he now bowed to me very eagerly and said in an altered tone, "You shall not leave me empty handed, most worthy gentlemen, for it would bring me bad luck. Let us talk the matter over. I know of the favor shown you by King Zapolya, but allow me to tell you that sheep shearing in Hungary is not the profitable business you seem to think. How can we tell who will shear them next spring? The Tartars, Moldavians, and Poles are even now taking advantage of the general confusion to steal sheep and other livestock, and no doubt this is happening on your estates also, my dear sir. Indeed it was a desperate gamble on your part to take possession of these domains, and I fear that without responsible backing you will as time goes on merely increase your debt."

He spoke so honestly and benevolently that Andy believed him and even I began to wonder whether he was justified in advancing ten gold ducats on Andy's problematical flocks. Andy said, "If things in Buda are as bad as you'd have us believe I had better return papers and seals to Janushka and tell him to look for a bigger simpleton than I am to take over these estates."

The Jew rubbed his hands together and bowed till his corkscrew curls swept the floor, and having begged to see King Zapolya's deed of conveyance he said, "Noble Sir Andreas von Wolfenland, I understand that in the Sultan's dominions you have been used to living in a style superior to that customary in our poor land. Should the lambing fail or war ravage your domains, a promissory note might cause you embarrassment. Furthermore, I shall incur expense if I have to collect my money from Istanbul. Yet risks must be taken if any profit is to be made. Let us talk no more of promises and notes of hand. I will advance the sum you ask in return for the shearing rights of your flocks for the next two years. I may suffer great loss by this, but all is in the hand of God."

Andy glanced at me in doubt and I whispered quickly that he should close with this offer, since ten ducats in the hand were worth a hundred sheep in some godforsaken corner of the Hungarian steppes. But Andy weakened on seeing the Jew wipe tears from his eyes, and he said, "No, no. I'm an honest man and you have a wife and children to feed. I cannot agree to your risking your modest fortune for my sake. Let us make out a binding promissory note, and for your trouble and expenses I am ready to pay ten or even fifteen per cent."

The Jew dried his tears and his face darkened as he said, "You're greedier than noblemen in general are wont to be; you grudge me a fair profit. Nevertheless, to confirm the good understanding between us, you shall have the money in return for only one year's shearing rights. In that case I shall expect the trade monopoly in all your villages, including the salt traffic. My agents shall inquire into the breed of sheep in the region and all other matters concerning the estate. You can rely on me for the best terms, for I'm an honest man and would be a father to you."

Andy thanked him politely, and replied, "Why should I resist when you're so bent on risking your money? All I ask is that you won't reproach me if things go wrong. You must feed my flocks and keep my sheepdogs and horses in good condition, however, or I shall make no further bargains with you next time I visit my estate."

The Jew's face lit up as he answered eagerly, "From the first moment of our meeting I was charmed by your honest character, for you did not treat me with contempt as most Hungarian noblemen do. I respect you because you know how to hold your own; therefore I agree to your proposal on condition I may pay you the sum in silver and change it into gold for you myself. In this way I can profit by the exchange rate, that is to say six aspers per gold ducat, which will enable me to feed my wife and children, even should I lose by the deal."

This seemed to me a very moderate request, though it was easy to reckon out that he would gain one ducat on the ten. He now begged us to excuse him while he worked out his gains according to the day's rate of exchange, and to fetch out the money, which in wartime he had to keep hidden. We were taken to an adjoining room which to my amazement was richly furnished with costly rugs, gilt chairs, velvet curtains, and Venetian mirrors. A servant brought us a gigantic silver dish heaped with grapes, pears, and other good Hungarian fruits. After inquiring whether we were strict Mussulmans the Jew also ordered wine to be served. It was clear that he wished to keep on good terms with Andy, though his lavish hospitality seemed out of all proportion to our business.

We ate the fruit and drank the wine, and when the Jew returned nothing was left upon the dish but a few cores and the skeleton of the grape bunch. Yet he was not at all distressed at this, and smiled radiantly as he led us back to the mean counting house. And here we stared; for on the table a mass of gold coin lay neatly stacked beside a number of sealed leather bags. The Jew evidently misunderstood our astonishment, for rubbing his hands together in some embarrassment he said, "Ten was the sum mentioned, was it not? Ten thousand ducats in silver are equal by statute to six hundred thousand aspers. But at today's exchange rate only five hundred and forty thousand when changing gold to silver, and five hundred and seventy thousand, silver to gold. I take as a rule one asper per ducat for costs and charges. So I give you five hundred and forty aspers in silver. By changing this to gold at the current rate you receive nine thousand, four hundred and seventy-three ducats, and thirty-nine aspers in silver. One asper per ducat for charges comes to one hundred and seventy-five ducats and twenty-three aspers. Your net total is therefore nine thousand, two hundred and ninety-eight ducats and sixteen aspers, and I have laid this sum on the table. Pray be so good as to count it yourselves, and note that each of the sealed bags contains five hundred ducats. As a matter of form, sir, I would ask you to sign this lease. I trust your word entirely, but I'm an old man and may die at any time, and your life too is one of hazard."

Andy said sulkily, "You wouldn't make a fool of me, good father?"

The Jew tore his beard and said in some heat, "Sir, such cheese paring is unworthy of you! I am entitled to reckon my charges at the rate of fifty-four aspers to the ducat, though you pay fifty-seven. The difference amounts to only five hundred and twenty-five aspers, and a distinguished gentleman like yourself should think shame to accuse me of dishonesty for such a trifle."

Andy said, "No, no. But I have little head for figures, so you must round off the sum to nine thousand three hundred ducats, and I will gladly acknowledge the receipt of ten thousand ducats for a year's lease of my sheep."

With a sigh the Jew took sixteen aspers from the table and replaced them with two worn gold ducats which I perceived at once to be underweight. The coins on the table were all newly-minted and whole, however, and so I willingly forgave him this slight deception.

Andy asked me to read the contract aloud to him, and we found it to be fully in accordance with what had been agreed, and though nothing was mentioned as to the care of the livestock, the Jew pointed out that it would be to his own interest to take good care of the farms, for he hoped that next year the contract might be renewed on slightly better terms for another five or ten years. Our eyes were by this time fully open to the excellent stroke of business Andy had unwittingly done in dragging that poor little wench from the gutters of Vienna and making her his wife.

But our dealings with the Jew were not yet over, for though I guessed that King Zapolya and Master Gritti would prefer ready money, the Grand Vizier at least must be offered something more personal, and for this no one could have given us better advice than the sagacious Jew. Such things as precious stones, ornaments, saddles, and damascened gold harnesses the Grand Vizier already had in abundance, so something entirely special must be found. At last Andy bought from the Jew a most marvelous clock of Nürnberg make, which struck both hours and quarters. It showed also the day, the month, and the year, and would thus be of great advantage to an absent-minded person, though unfortunately it was based on the Christian measurement of time. However, we guessed that because of his wars and other dealings with European countries the Grand Vizier might be glad to keep count of the Christian reckoning.

This clock was so complicated and so ingeniously built that I could not understand how a human brain could have devised it. The case was of beautiful workmanship, and the Jew contrived to set it going long enough for us to see how at each hour a little secret door flew open and a smith, followed by a priest and a knight in full armor, stepped forth to strike the hour on a little silver bell, and then disappeared through another door on the opposite side of the clock.

Its only fault was that it did not go, and the watchmaker to whom it had been sent for repair had been sold into slavery by the Turks. Nevertheless the Jew hoped he might yet be found, and we could then give him to the Grand Vizier with the clock, to regulate it and keep it going. Because the mechanism was for the present out of order the Jew sold us this treasure for only twelve hundred ducats, which Andy gladly paid, and we then took a cordial leave of this wealthy man.

When after a great deal of difficulty we were able to trace the clockmaker, Andy paid no less than sixty ducats for him, without bargaining, though there was little left of him but skin and beard. In his free-handedness he even gave the old fellow new clothes, and after a bellyful of food the man wept copious tears, tried to kiss Andy's hands, and blessed him as his benefactor. He at once set to work on the clock, declaring that he knew its caprices, and even without the necessary instruments and parts was able to make it work well enough to convince the Grand Vizier of its surpassing excellence. He swore by the saints that once in Istanbul he would make this timepiece the marvel of the Seraglio and would devote the rest of his life to tending it. Thus it was that the clock secured him a carefree existence as the Grand Vizier's slave.

We now ordered four strong slaves to carry it carefully to Ibrahim's tent, where the clockmaker set it going; the Grand Vizier marveled greatly at it and thanked Andy for the princely gift. I fancy Andy rose notably in the Grand Vizier's esteem, for as a further mark of favor Ibrahim sent him and his wife two magnificently caparisoned saddle horses and provided an escort of a hundred spahis to attend them to their estate.

Andy, having now done everything possible to secure his position, made ready to leave for the Transilvanian border. When I saw that

274

in his black ingratitude he was forgetting me, his unmerited successes smarted within me and I said, "The frog puffed himself up until he burst. The money is yours; you can throw it down the jakes if you wish. But your coldness to me is very wounding, and I think you owe a morsel of consideration to one who is all but your own brother, and whom alone you have to thank for your prosperity."

My words and my unfeigned tears brought Andy to a better frame of mind, and as icy winds chased the snow clouds over the towers of Buda, we seemed transported to our own land. We wept on one another's breast; we swore that nothing in the world should sever our friendship and that we should be godfathers to one another's children. When at last we parted Andy pressed upon me a thousand ducats, saying that even this sum was but slight acknowledgment of my long and faithful friendship.

We had by now reached the end of October. The Sultan ordered the camp to be struck and the janissaries with many forebodings began the long march home. Before we left Buda, the Grand Vizier summoned me and Father Julianus once more to a nocturnal discussion and said, "It may be that you're right, Michael el-Hakim, and are more familiar with German religious questions than I am. King Zapolya's secret representative at the court of Margrave Philip reports that the heretic prophets have met in Marburg, the capital of Hesse, but that after a couple of days' debate they separated in open hostility without having reached a single agreement. It seems that Luther and Zwingli did nothing but accuse one another of error and arrogance. I therefore agree to your plan, Michael el-Hakim, and will send you to the German states to sow even more bitter dissension among the Protestants and so draw them nearer Islam."

I was aghast at his words, and made haste to reply, "You have quite mistaken my meaning, noble Grand Vizier, for I'm no orator. No, no, it is Father Julianus who should be sent to Germany, for he is an experienced preacher who can smell out heresy afar off. He will choose the right man in every town for the work; he will sow the seeds of Islam in people's minds so that in their enthusiasm for the new ideas they will forget all that Christendom holds in common and rally round separate articles of faith. One will preach the one God, another the sinfulness of idolatry, a third predestination, and a fourth polygamy as justified by Scripture. I believe that Father Julianus knows

275

his Bible so well that within a few days he could find texts to support all these arguments."

Father Julianus stared at me as if the ground had opened at his feet and the devil in all his hideousness had appeared.

"Get thee behind me, Satan!" he cried. "Would you make a heretic of me? Never will I consent to it; I will choose rather the glorious death of the martyrs."

"But can you not see, Father Julianus," I said, "that in sowing dissension among the heretics you do Holy Church the greatest possible service? I am persuaded that the Grand Vizier will furnish you with money enough to keep you well provided with wine and beer in the German lands—well enough even to invite others to share it with you. Should you be suspected of disseminating false doctrines, you have only to deny all you've said and blame your imperfect knowledge of the language for any errors there may have been. But if all goes well— you should need no more than a couple of years to complete the task —and if you send me details of all those, young or old, learned or simple, poor or rich who are in any way inclined to embrace and proclaim the new teaching, I am sure the Grand Vizier will so reward you as to enable you to spend the remainder of your days in peace and comfort before a never failing wine jar."

Conflicting thoughts were mirrored on Father Julianus's puffy face, and I could read there lingering fears for his immortal soul. Persuasively I went on, "Who knows but that the Grand Vizier might approach the Curia through a Venetian banking house, and buy you a bishopric in some retired corner of France or Italy? There you might enjoy a well-earned rest without molestation by inquisitive people."

A warm gleam came into Father Julianus's eye; he gazed dreamily into the distance, and at length exclaimed with a sob, "How devoutly I would serve in that exalted office, wretch and sinner that I am! Truly, Michael, from now on I will reform and do all I can to be worthy of the blessed task entrusted to me."

Falling on his knees he kissed the Grand Vizier's hand and watered it with his tears. I feared that Ibrahim would recoil from the expense of my plan, and I said quickly in Turkish, "Take no thought of the outlay, noble Grand Vizier, for Father Julianus will hardly get out of Germany alive to claim his bishopric. These new prophets are at least as fanatical in the defense of the purity of their faith as the Holy Office. Yet if by any miracle he should survive, it would be no bad

276

thing for you if a Christian bishop were to owe his position to Islam."

Ibrahim nodded and said, "As you will, Michael el-Hakim. I trust you, and leave you a free hand with the details. If it fails, *tsaushes* will bring you the black kaftan and the silken noose, and will stay to see that you do not misinterpret the significance of the gift."

Perhaps this reminder of my mortality was wholesome. At any rate I began to see that I was meddling very rashly with matters that in no way concerned me. Nevertheless the plan was adopted and the details arranged by which Father Julianus could transmit his reports secretly to Istanbul.

By degrees Buda was emptied of Turkish troops and Father Julianus set forth in good heart upon his return to Vienna, where he meant to preach about his miraculous rescue from the hands of the Turks. After that he would make for the German states. Having seen him safely off, I bought some war mementos and other presents for Giulia and then embarked on one of the transport vessels. This carried me down the Danube until I was able to join Sinan the Builder once more, in whose litter I completed the journey to Istanbul in comfort.

Of the obstacles and hardships encountered by the army on its homeward march I will say only that the losses sustained were greater than those of the siege itself, and that at least ten thousand Hungarian and German slaves perished on the way. For my part I could think only of Giulia and of our future home on the shores of the Bosphorus. Sinan the Builder, thin, worn, and unable to sleep after his unremitting toil and anxieties, was weary of my chatter long before we reached Istanbul and at length seized his hammer and threatened to crack my skull if I would not be quiet.

The nearer we came to Istanbul the more impatiently did I long to hold Giulia in my arms again, as I had done in the moments of our greatest happiness. I longed to tell her how well I had prospered, for with my two hundred aspers a day she could no longer look upon me as an inept and unenterprising man. By a singular irony of fate, the weather improved as we came nearer home. The rain ceased, wintry chill gave place to springlike warmth, and our eyes, weary of bleak mountains and heavy cloud, were now dazzled by the fresh green of countless gardens, although plane trees and acacias had long since shed their leaves.

The air was like well-cooled wine, the sun shone from a cloudless sky, and the smell of the sea came to us on the wind as the Sultan

277

rode into his city at the head of his janissaries amid deafening acclamation. Drums and cymbals clashed and the captive slaves dragged themselves along, glancing sullenly to right and left as they beheld the vast extent of the Ottoman capital. Bonfires blazed everywhere that night. Even in Pera, the Venetian quarter, they glowed like strings of pearls.

On fire myself with longing I rode straight to Abu el-Kasim's house, mounted on the horse given me by the Sultan. On my head I wore a broad turban adorned with a tuft of feathers in a jeweled clasp. From my belt under the kaftan of honor jingled a heavy purse and, besides my copper pen case, I wore a saber in a silver scabbard. I had hoped to find the gate flung wide and Giulia, warned by the sound of music, trembling in the doorway and blessing the day that brought me safely home from all the perils of war. Such was my fancied homecoming. But having waited so long outside the closed gate that inquisitive neighbors began to gather about me, I drew my sword, leaned forward in the saddle, and hammered on the gate with the hilt.

My horse was whinnying and dancing about and I had great difficulty in keeping my seat when at last I heard the clash of bolts and Abu el-Kasim's deaf-mute stood before me in the gateway. When he recognized me he quite lost his head and flung the gate open with a crash, uttering many incomprehensible sounds meanwhile. The horse reared, shied, and bolted into the courtyard, whence Giulia's furry blue cat dashed away in a fright with bushy tail erect. At this my mount kicked and leaped sideways, throwing me headfirst to the ground. It was a marvel that my neck was not broken, though as it was my drawn sword made a deep gash in one calf—my first and only wound of the campaign.

The deaf-mute flung himself to the ground in remorse, beating his brow and breast with clenched fist so that I had not the heart to chastise him. At this moment a dark-skinned Italian appeared in the doorway with coat unbuttoned and striped breeches open at the waist. Smoothing his gleaming black hair he demanded angrily who dared to disturb his noble mistress's siesta. He was young and well built, though his dark complexion hinted at low birth; his features were as faultless as those of a Greek statue, and as expressionless. His brilliant eyes seemed light in comparison with his skin, and his thin lips showed determination, though at the moment they were distorted by a sneer.

I have described him thus fully to show that outwardly he was in

278

no way repellent; yet from the first I felt a deep distrust of him. For this his arrogant behavior was not to blame, for when he realized who I was he displayed a flattering awe, and having restored some order to his own dress began respectfully shaking the sand from my kaftan. He then addressed me in well-chosen words. "I beg you not to be offended at so miserable a welcome, noble sir. We could not guess that you would return so soon. Regard for your lady should have impelled you to send word of your coming, that she might have prepared the house for celebration and received you in a fitting manner. Just now she is taking her midday rest, but I will rouse her instantly."

This I sternly forbade him to do, saying that I preferred to wake her myself and so afford her a pleasant surprise. I then demanded in some irritation who he was and how he dared give himself the airs of the master of the house and try to prevent me seeing my own wife. He changed his tone at once and said on a note of humility, "Ah, Master Michael, I'm but Alberto the slave, from the city of Verona where my father still works as an honest tailor. I ought to have chosen his trade, but I was lured away by my craving for adventure and later captured by Turkish pirates. For a while I toiled as a galley slave and was then offered for sale in the bazaar here in Istanbul. Mistress Giulia took pity on my wretchedness, bought me, and installed me here as major-domo. Yet I have no servants under me save this feeble-minded deaf-mute, who is not worth the salt in his broth."

I asked how Abu el-Kasim could have approved of this purchase, since both house and slave were his. Alberto looked surprised and answered, "I have never seen this Abu el-Kasim, though the neighbors mentioned some shady drug dealer of that name. I believe he left here in the summer for Bagdad. Who knows if he will ever return?"

I perceived that many changes had taken place since my departure, and snapping at the Italian to keep his eyes lowered when addressing me as befitted a slave, I stepped into the house. He kept close at my heels and strove to push past me when I paused to look about. I hardly recognized the rooms, so cluttered were they with trash from the bazaar, and I constantly stumbled over stools, cushions, censers, and bird cages. When at last I reached the curtains concealing the entrance to Giulia's room Alberto thrust himself in front of me, and falling on his knees he cried out, "Do not wake her too abruptly, noble sir! Let me give her a little warning by banging on a tray!"

Touched by his consideration for the lady of the house, I was nevertheless resolved to give myself the joy of surprising her. I pushed aside the agitated Italian, drew the curtains and tiptoed into the room. And there, once my eyes had grown accustomed to the half-darkness, the sight of Giulia abundantly rewarded my starved senses.

She must have been tossing restlessly in her sleep, for she lay quite naked amid the tumbled bedclothes. Her face looked thin and there were dark rings beneath her eyes, but her golden hair lay in abundance over the pillow, her breasts were like rosebuds, and her limbs like musk and amber. Never in my most amorous dreams had I seen her so alluringly fair.

I gasped and praised Allah for according his champion so glorious a homecoming. Then I bent over her, caressed her gently with my finger tips, and whispered her name. Without opening her eyes she stretched herself voluptuously, wound her white arms about my neck and sighed in her sleep, "No more, no more, you cruel man!"

Nevertheless she made room for me beside her, groped for me with her hands, and whispered, "But you may take off your clothes and lie beside me!"

I was startled at her readiness until I realized that she was enjoying some delightful dream and talking in her sleep. With a smile I did as she asked, flung off my clothes, and crept onto the bed beside her. Throwing her arms about my waist she pressed me to her and begged me sleepily to caress her. The depth of her slumber surprised me, but I could see that she did not want to cut short her dream and was putting off the moment of waking.

I did as she asked until in my excitement I made too abrupt a movement and woke her. Her wonderful eyes flew open. If I had had the smallest doubt of the soundness of her sleep I could have asked no better proof of it than her behavior now, for when she discovered what was happening she was quite beside herself with fright; she tore herself away and hid her nakedness beneath the covers. Then she burst out sobbing with her face in her hands, thrusting me away when I sought to comfort her. Filled with compunction for the trick I had played, I humbly begged her forgiveness. When at last she could speak she asked in a quavering voice, "Is it really you, Michael? When did you come, and where is Alberto?"

Hearing this, Alberto, who was standing behind the curtain, called out reassuringly and told her not to be alarmed by the blood on my trousers; the wound was slight, he said, and had occurred when I fell off my horse in the courtyard. His prattle so enraged me that I swore at him and told him not to stand there spying upon us. But Giulia said, "In fear and trembling I have counted the weeks and months of your absence—and are oaths the first words I must hear from you when at last you return? Don't insult that faithful servant who has so well protected me since Abu el-Kasim left me in the lurch. Have you no more regard for me than to force your way in and place me in so degrading a situation before my own servant?"

This was the Giulia I knew, but she had evidently been badly startled and it relieved her to scold me. Even such words as these rang pleasantly in my ears after so long an absence and I tried to embrace her, but once again she broke loose from me and snapped, "Don't touch me, Michael. By the rules of your religion I ought first to wash myself, and you too are dusty from your journey. You never were considerate to me, but at least remember your duties as a Moslem and leave me alone until I have bathed and made myself beautiful."

But I protested that she had never been lovelier than in her present disordered state, and so begged and pleaded with her that at last she gave in and surrendered herself to me, muttering the whole time about my thoughtless and insulting conduct and so depriving me of half my pleasure. Afterward she rose quickly, turned her back upon me, and began to dress without a word. Receiving no answer to any of my humble questions I too became angry and exclaimed, "So this is the homecoming I have so long awaited! But why should I have expected anything else? You've not even asked how I am—and as for that scoundrel Alberto, I mean to send him straight back to the galleys where he belongs."

Giulia spun round and spat like a savage cat. With blazing eyes she cried, "I see no change in you, either! You only talk like that about Alberto to hurt me. He's as good a man as you—perhaps better, for at least he comes of honest parents and has no need to make a secret of his birth. And what may you have been up to in Hungary? I could never have guessed the sort of thing that goes on at these campaigns if I hadn't heard about it at the harem."

Hurt though I was by her unworthy suspicions, I understood that her jealousy had been aroused by the malicious gossip she had heard. For the women of the harem were in the habit of bribing the Defterdar's eunuchs to spy upon the Sultan and the Grand Vizier, so that these exalted gentlemen had to pay dearly for any little adventure they might engage in.

I said, "The Sultan and the Grand Vizier are men of virtue and it's unseemly to speak ill of them. But your groundless jealousy shows perhaps that you still love me and care what becomes of me. Therefore I will swear on the Koran—and on the Cross, too, if that will satisfy you—that I never went near a woman, much as I desired to at times. There is no one like you, Giulia. And if at any time I did forget you, a wholesome dread of the French pox restrained me from thoughtless conduct."

Hearing my grave words Giulia regained a measure of composure, though she still sobbed and laughed by turns as if someone had been tickling her. Then she said, "Still the same old Michael! Tell me then what you have done and what presents you have brought for me, and then you shall hear how to the best of my woman's ability I have sought to build up a stable future for us both."

I could contain myself no longer and told her of all my successes—of the two hundred aspers a day and of the Grand Vizier's promise of a piece of land and a house. I talked on ever more eagerly and boastfully, until at length I noticed that Giulia's brow was black as thunder and her mouth twisted as if she had bitten into a sour apple. I broke off in a fright and asked suspiciously, "Do you grudge me my prosperity, my dear Giulia? Why aren't you glad? We have left all our anxieties behind us and I cannot imagine what is on your mind." Giulia shook her head dejectedly and said, "No, no, dear Michael. Of course I am glad of all your success, but I'm afraid for you. With your usual credulity you've given yourself entirely into the power of that ambitious Ibrahim. He's more dangerous than you suspect and I would rather see you halt in time than be swept to perilous heights by clinging to the skirts of his kaftan."

I retorted hotly that the Grand Vizier was the noblest man and finest statesman I had ever met. It was a pleasure to serve him, not only for his munificence but also for his princely conduct and his brilliant eyes. Giulia's face darkened still further and she vowed he had bewitched me as he had bewitched the Sultan—for in no other way could she explain the strong and sinister friendship that bound Suleiman to his slave.

Greatly discomposed I told her that she with her eyes of different colors would do well not to talk of witchcraft, whereupon she burst into bitter weeping, saying that never had I so deeply, so unforgivably wounded her. I was surprised at her susceptibility on this point, for it was long since she had deplored her eyes; she had come rather to regard them as an asset, which indeed they were.

"You know I love those eyes above everything," I assured her. "The left one is a brilliant sapphire and the right a shining topaz. Why are you so irritable today?"

Stamping with rage she cried, "Fool! I know best what my eyes are worth. But I can't forgive you for going behind my back and getting house and land from the Grand Vizier. The idea was mine from the beginning and you opposed it. I've already found a site and the needed building materials. I wanted to surprise you and show you what an exceptional wife you have. Now you've spoiled everything. Nothing you could have done could hurt me so deeply."

In my tender mood I could well appreciate the bitterness of her disappointment. To the best of her feminine ability she had secured a home for us, though of course it could not be so fine and tasteful as the one I meant to build. I fell on my knees before her, begged forgiveness for my ill-considered behavior, thanked her for the sacrifices she had made, kissed her slender fingers, and assured her that I had thought only of our common good and had never meant to steal a march upon her.

"But," I asked, "what is this place that you have chosen? Above all, how could you find the money for it, for I know that nothing costs so much as building."

"It's an excellent site," said Giulia, "and need not be paid for until some convenient moment. For the materials I was able to borrow money on remarkably good terms. The wives of certain wealthy Greeks and Jews desire my friendship because of my connection with the Seraglio, and their husbands have been generous with their advice and with the loan of money, with your salary as security. I hoped that the house might be ready by your return, when you could have accepted it as a present from me with nothing to do but pay for it."

I was aghast, but she looked at me with such artless pleasure that I had not the heart to reproach her. She pressed her face against me and said with a sob, "I'm glad you're home, though you startled me so badly. Now you can help me in all my perplexities and see to these everlasting accounts. The house would have been finished by now but for the labor of clearing the ground, for the site is on the Marmara shore near the Fort of the Seven Towers, among the ruins of the ancient Greek monastery. That was how the Greeks were able to sell it without asking leave of the Sultan. No one has ever built there before because of the cost of clearing the site, and that was how I was able to buy it so cheaply."

I dimly remembered having seen that dreary field of ruins, haunted since the fall of Constantinople by stray dogs alone. Her senseless action set me trembling in every limb as I strove in vain to master my feelings. Giulia stared at me wide eyed. Her face took on a greenish pallor and suddenly she rose and vomited, while tears ran down her cheeks. Forgetting all else in my concern I took her gently by the shoulders and said anxiously, "My dearest! My own wife! My most precious treasure! What is it—what ails you? Is it fever, or have you eaten too rashly of salad or raw fruit?"

Giulia moaned, "Don't look at me now, Michael, when I'm so ugly. Nothing ails me—perhaps the worry of the house has been too much—and then you looked so stern. Pay no heed. Tell me I'm an extravagant wife sent to you by God for your sins."

I could only beg her forgiveness from the bottom of my heart. I bathed her forehead with cold wet cloths and gave her vinegar to inhale until the color returned to her cheeks. The best tonic, however, was my saddle bag, from which I now produced all the presents I had bought for her in Buda—necklaces, earrings, and a most beautiful Venetian mirror whose handle was formed by the consummate art of the silversmith into a likeness of Leda and the Swan. I was not so strict a Moslem as to shun representations of animals and men; and in any case Giulia was a Christian.

So at last we achieved perfect harmony, and Alberto hastily prepared for us a savory Italian meal. He served me attentively and showed me every mark of respect, but although in my present mood I desired to be in charity with all the world, some little thorn seemed to have lodged in my heart and I could not be reconciled to this man who hovered about us continually and with his queer, pale eyes noted every expression of my face. What vexed me most was Giulia's invitation to him to sit with us on the floor and share our meal. Fortunately he had the grace to retire to a corner and content himself with what we left. When at last he took the plates away for the cats and the deaf-mute to lick clean I could remain silent no longer and announced with some heat that I did not care to dine with my slave, and in any case could not endure the way this repulsive man padded and slunk about me.

Giulia, deeply offended, said, "But Michael, he's a Christian like myself. Would you deprive me of the pleasure of conversing now and then in my own language with a fellow countryman? You have your brother Andrew; you talk together in your mother tongue so that I can't understand a word you say. Why grudge me this little consolation in my loneliness?"

I was moved by Giulia's innocence of heart in this matter, when as a rule she was so shrewd and experienced. I said gently, "Dear Giulia, don't misunderstand what I am going to say. Not in my wildest dreams could I ever suspect you of unfaithfulness. Yet as a husband I find it irksome in the extreme to share my house with a young man, and one whom simple-minded people might consider good looking. I know that I can trust you, but it's my duty to safeguard your good name. I could endure him better if he were a eunuch —and indeed," I went on, fired by the idea, "it's not too late to make him one; he's still fairly young. Though at one time I thought the risk of financial loss too great, because of the frequent fatality of the operation, I saw many in Buda—some of them older than Alberto— who were none the worse for it. Let us see to this immediately. Then neither I nor anyone else can have the least objection to his living in the house."

Giulia gazed at me very searchingly as if wondering whether I were in earnest. Then a queer smile overspread her face and without a word she clapped her hands to summon Alberto. When he came she said to him, "Alberto, your master suspects that your presence here is harmful to my reputation and wishes to make a eunuch of you. He declares that the operation will not injure your health. What have you to say to this?"

Alberto's dark face paled a little, perhaps, and he glanced at me as if judging the size of my neck. Then he turned to Giulia with an expressionless smile and answered meekly, "Madam, if I must choose between gelding and the galleys, you know what my answer will be. I don't pretend to look forward to so disagreeable an ordeal, but my consolation is my utter indifference to women. My one desire is to devote my life to your service, and if I can please my master by submitting to this operation I will seek out a competent surgeon without delay."

The noble candor of this speech made me ashamed of my meditated brutality. At the same time a great weight was lifted from my heart, for if he was indeed as indifferent to women as he averred I had nothing to fear on Giulia's account. Giulia, narrowly watching my face, said, "Well, Michael, I hope you're properly ashamed? Is a slave to teach you nobility of conduct? You see now that there are still unselfish and loyal people in the world, and that everyone is not as ill natured as yourself. Make a eunuch of him if you like, but if you do I will never set eyes upon you again, so despicable would you then appear to me."

By this time I was feeling like some unnatural monster, but seeing my indecision Alberto fell on his knees before me in tears and cried, "No, no, my dear master! Don't listen to her, but have me castrated at once, for I cannot bear your distrust. I swear I shall lose nothing by it; to me women are no more than sticks and stones. The good God has given me the heart of a eunuch, for all my beard."

They worked on me together until to my own surprise I found myself begging Giulia not to treat this selfless man so harshly. She wept and agreed to let all be as before, provided I never mentioned the matter again or insulted her faithful servant with my base suspicions. She further reminded me that if the Sultan could eat with his slave, so could I, and that Alberto was no scullion but a major-domo, such as was found in the most distinguished Venetian families.

Though still reluctant, I was ready to agree to anything that might mollify Giulia. We went early to bed that night and she showed herself fully reconciled to me.

Of her doings in the Seraglio she would not speak. All in good time, she told me; for the moment I need know no more than that the Kisler-Aga was singularly well disposed toward her, and that she had received countless presents from the women of the harem and from her Greek and Jewish friends. I did not press her, or sadden her by remarking that most of the presents seemed to me worthless trash.

Early next morning a richly dressed eunuch arrived to take me to the Seraglio, where he bade me present myself to the Kislar-Aga. This fat, ruthless man, whose Negro blood gave his cheeks a gray tinge, received me most cordially and allowed me to help him to his feet, that he might accompany me to the Court of Bliss.

This unwonted civility greatly astonished me, but the whole Seraglio was in a sunny mood because of the Sultan's return. Nowhere was a surly face to be seen. From the meanest slave to the highest official all were smiling—all dispensed blessings to right and left. I was showered with benedictions; my footsteps and my very toenails were blessed, and I was told that I was fairer than the moon, despite the scar left on my cheek by de Varga's teeth, which had somewhat disfigured one corner of my mouth. The torrent carried me with it and I exerted myself to make ever more graceful replies, calling down blessings on the very shadows of those I met.

The Kislar-Aga told me that Sultana Khurrem had presented the Sultan with a daughter during his absence, in whose ear the name Mirmah had been whispered. She was fairer than the moon and the Kislar-Aga could not sufficiently praise the Sultana for bearing her lord a child each time he went to war, and being consequently ever merrier and more beautiful on his return than she had been at his departure. The Kislar-Aga was evidently satisfied that Sultana Khurrem still enjoyed the Sultan's favor.

Engrossed in this animated conversation I had not time to look about me until the Kislar-Aga suddenly kicked the back of my knee as a hint to prostrate myself. We had come through the Court of Bliss into the Princes' playroom, and to my amazement I found myself in the presence of Suleiman himself. With the Grand Vizier beside him as usual he was showing his sons how to work some toys of Nürnberg make, which he had brought home for them. There was a horse that moved its legs and drew a cart, a drummer that beat his drum, and many other marvelous things such as had been found in profusion in the nurseries of Buda Palace.

The boys knelt about him on the floor. Mustafa the eldest looked on in dignified silence; he was as dazzlingly beautiful as his mother—now fallen from favor—was said to be. The lively Muhammed shrieked with delight. Selim stretched out his hands for every toy, while nearest his father stood little Prince Jehangir. He rested his chin trustfully on Suleiman's silken sleeve so that the hump, alas, showed all too plainly beneath the little kaftan. His dark eyes gazed at the gaily painted toys as if penetrating their vanity, as if in his heart, child though he was, he meditated upon the baffling mysteries of life and death.

When the Sultan saw me he dropped the toys, smiled for once without constraint, and said merrily, "Blessings on you, Michael el-Hakim, from the crown of your head to the soles of your feet! May every hair of your head and beard be blessed and may your wife bear you only sons. But in the name of Allah do not bless me in return, for I've weathered such a storm of benisons already that now as soon as anyone opens his mouth I begin to laugh. Pay no attention to me, for it is Prince Jehangir who wishes to receive you in a worthy manner."

I rose to my knees to kiss Prince Jehangir's thin hand. His sallow face flushed with joy and he stumbled excitedly over his words as he patted my cheeks and cried, "O Michael el-Hakim, Michael el-Hakim! I have a surprise for you—a bigger surprise than you can ever guess!"

This was enough to show me that at least no evil had befallen my dog, and I was now to learn that Rael had earned high regard and had founded a family. Prince Jehangir hurried me off to see three adorable black-and-white puppies lying with their mother in a kiosk that had been fitted out as a splendid kennel.

"Allah is Allah!" I cried, and the tears ran down my cheeks at Rael's ecstatic welcome. "How has this come about?"

Prince Mustafa said to me in his grown-up fashion, "We didn't know that breed of dog, and the kennel master despised Rael. But when I saw how faithfully he served my little brother I thought I would find out more about him. The Venetian envoy knew the breed and said that in spite of harsh treatment in the past, Rael had all the points of the best variety of Italian house dog. We bought a mate for him from the Duke of Mantua, and the result you may see in that basket. Tell me how Rael came into your possession and what his pedigree is, so that we can record it in our kennel book, with the names of the puppies."

I was at a loss for what to say, for I had picked Rael up as a stray in the courtyard of Memmingen town hall. All I knew was that he was a good, pious dog that had resolutely endured the torture of the Holy Inquisition and been acquitted. I explained this to Prince Mustafa and told him how faithfully Rael had served me and how he had saved my life when I lay dying of the plague among the corpses in the streets of Rome.

The Sultan and his sons listened sympathetically to my story, and the Grand Vizier said thoughtfully, "Feel no concern about the dog's pedigree, Prince Mustafa. He will begin one for himself. Perhaps there is greater honor in founding a noble line than in basing one's position on old and tainted blood."

288

At the time I paid no heed to Ibrahim's words, but later I had reason to remember them, for they had acquired a terrible significance. And indeed no sooner were they spoken than he started, and passing his hand over his brow he smiled and said hastily, "Ah, Prince Jehangir, the audience is not ended. Remember that the son of the Sultan has the privilege of requiting gifts with even richer rewards."

Prince Jehangir clapped his hands and a red-clad eunuch entered the room bearing a sealed leather purse which he handed to me, and which I judged to contain at least a hundred ducats. I offered Prince Jehangir my best thanks and we returned to the playroom. But my good fortune was not yet complete, for there the Sultan said to me, "My friend the Grand Vizier has spoken of you and I know you have exposed yourself to great danger in my service. For that very reason you were absent when I was dispensing rewards to my warriors outside Vienna, and so you missed your share. I must not insult my son Jehangir by giving you more than he did, so you shall claim an equal sum from the Defterdar. But with the Grand Vizier I can and should compete in generosity; tell me therefore what he has promised you!"

The day was indeed ruled by my lucky star. I glanced at the Grand Vizier and at his encouraging wink I prostrated myself and babbled eagerly some quite incomprehensible words. My behavior must have been most ridiculous, for the Sultan laughed till he cried. The Princes laughed too, and tried to mimic my stammering. Then Suleiman said, "I gather that the Grand Vizier has promised you many remarkable things, but try to speak a little more coherently."

"A plot of land!" I gasped at length. "The Grand Vizier has promised me a little plot of land from his gardens on the Bosphorus, and a small house, for my dearest wish has ever been to serve you, O Commander of the Faithful, and after all my checkered years of wandering I long to find a home. The Grand Vizier has even promised to pay the costs of this from his own coffers."

The Sultan laughed again and said, "And to vie with him I authorize you to take from the Seraglio storehouses such carpets, cushions, mattresses, cooking pots, dishes, and other furniture as you may need to put your house in a habitable condition. From the arsenal you may take a light rowing boat roofed at the stern, that you may be sheltered from sun and rain on your journeys to and from the Seraglio."

But this day of marvels was not even yet at an end, for when I visited Defterdar Iskender to claim the extra purse, this noble gray-bearded *tseleb* bent a hostile look upon me and said sternly, "For some reason that passes my understanding you are climbing into high favor, Michael el-Hakim, and I feel it my duty to remind you of your position. As Defterdar I cannot permit any slave of the Sultan to get into debt, far less seek the aid of Greek and Jewish usurers. Why should I waste money thus, instead of allowing it to circulate freely within the Seraglio and at length return to the treasury? You should pay for your building works through me, Michael el-Hakim, for I would give you good terms. You treat me most unfairly by employing idolatrous riffraff for work which might otherwise bring into the treasury a portion at least of all that has been lavished upon you in gifts."

Much disturbed, I stammered, "Noble Defterdar-*tseleb,* you are quite mistaken, for the work is to be carried out by Sinan the Builder and I have no intention of depriving the treasury of its dues. But my wife I regret to say is a Christian, and in my absence she was so foolish as to incur debts in my name. I fear she has fallen into the hands of rascally Greeks. To behead these men at once would be the simplest way of releasing me from the burden of debts, whose total I have not dared to ascertain."

The Defterdar glanced at the roll in his hand, gritted his teeth, and hissed, "Your debts have reached the dizzy figure of eight hundred and fifty-three ducats, thirty aspers, and I cannot think how those shrewd Greeks dared give your wife so extensive a credit."

I snatched the turban from my head and wept, saying, "Noble Defterdar, forgive me, and take these two purses in part payment. Be assured that I will live on bread and water and wear garments of sackcloth until I have discharged this terrible debt. You have my salary as guarantee."

My sincere consternation moved the hardhearted Defterdar, and he said, "Let this be a warning to you. A slave cannot contract debts, for in the last resort the treasury must pay them and may have no other way of reimbursing itself than by making use of the silken noose. Nevertheless your lucky star has prevailed, for by order of Sultana Khurrem I have already discharged to the last asper the debts your wife so frivolously contracted. Be thankful, therefore, for your unmerited good fortune and in future keep your wife under better control."

He gave me a list of the receipts, and as he did so he looked at me searchingly as if pondering what manner of man I was. He knew that thanks to the Grand Vizier my salary had been increased, and he must have wondered how at the same time my wife could be in favor with Ibrahim's rival, the Sultana. It was evident that he himself belonged to the Sultana's adherents, and of course I had every reason to be grateful for her generosity to my deluded wife. Yet I would not be so foolish as to modify my loyalty to the Grand Vizier on that account.

Hardly had I come home and begun to tell Giulia of these events than her face darkened and she asked sharply what I had to complain of, since the Sultana had been so bountiful as to discharge our debts. Any other man, she said, would have thanked and praised his wife for such skillful management, but from now on I might handle my own affairs and she would not lift a finger to help me. I said, "I ask no better. But now let us inspect your plot of land and consider the best way of getting rid of it."

We hired a boat and glided first along the shore of the Bosphorus, past Galata and the dervish monastery. When we had gazed for some time at Grand Vizier Ibrahim's beautiful gardens Giulia relapsed into a very thoughtful silence. We returned across the Golden Horn with its myriad shipping and on beyond the Seraglio until we could see the Palace of the Seven Towers before us. We went ashore below the ruins, and a steep goat track led us up through their desolation to a little herb garden and a quantity of water-logged timber. At the bottom of the hole that the workmen had dug for the foundations of Giulia's house could be seen the broken arches of ancient brick vaults. The place was bleak, barren, and in every way uninviting for a human dwelling, though the view over the Marmara was very beautiful. As I stood silently pondering what was to be done, a most excellent idea came into my head and I said, "Now that Andy is married, Giulia, he is sure to need a house in Istanbul. Why should we not let him have this valuable land for a modest sum? He loves to work with stones and here he can do that to his heart's content. I could make him comfortably drunk before I show him the property."

For some reason I had not troubled to mention Andy's wealth or to confess that it was to him I owed my well-filled purse and the presents

I had bought her; she therefore observed scornfully that he could never afford it. My brilliant idea so carried me away that I told her of his good fortune and of his wife's estates. Giulia stiffened and an ugly expression came over her face as she exclaimed, "O Michael, you blockhead! Why in God's name did you not marry the girl yourself? As a Moslem you're allowed as many as four wives. But it was like you to let the chance of a lifetime slip through your fingers for the sake of that oaf of a foster brother."

In her fury she turned pale again with another attack of nausea, but when she had recovered I said soothingly, "Giulia, my dear one, how can you suppose I should ever think of any other wife but you?"

Giulia answered with a sob, "I could have brought up a callow girl like that in the best possible manner and treated her like a sister. Later when she had borne you a child, who knows but what she might have swallowed some unwholesome mushroom sauce, or fallen sick of the fever that's so common in Istanbul? Stranger things have happened. We could then have inherited her property. I think only of your welfare, Michael, and would never stand in the way of your good fortune."

I repented now more than ever of having so imperfectly appreciated the merits of the young Hungarian girl, but consoled myself with the thought of selling that useless land to Andy. On our way home Giulia stared at me repeatedly and shook her head as if baffled by my irrational behavior.

When we were at home again and seated at our meal, Alberto's hovering presence irritated me so much that I said angrily, "Last time I was in the Seraglio I hit upon an excellent plan to dispel all suspicions about Alberto and safeguard your reputation, Giulia. Tomorrow I shall buy him a eunuch's dress which in future he must always wear. No one will ask awkward questions so long as he acts the part on his walks abroad."

My sensible proposal appealed to neither of them; they exchanged glances that revealed their loathsome complicity and Giulia so far forgot herself as to say, "Why, eunuchs are beardless! Alberto's beautiful curly beard makes such a disguise impossible."

She stretched forth her hand with the freedom of ownership to feel his short beard, but I snatched back her hand and said, "He must shave it off—he must shave twice a day if need be—and he must eat rich food until his cheeks are plump and oily. Things cannot go on as they are."

Despite vehement opposition I had my way in this matter and the weeping Alberto was compelled to shave off his beard and array himself in the yellow garments of a eunuch. For Giulia soon perceived the advantage of this arrangement—eunuchs fetched a far higher price than ordinary slaves, and she felt both wealthy and distinguished when she walked about the city with the seeming eunuch in attendance. I now did all I could to fatten him and at times made him eat a whole dish of greasy food, regardless of his cries for mercy. Soon I had the satisfaction of seeing his cheeks grow round and glossy and his empty Italian beauty fade into plumpness. The fatter he grew the better I liked him.

So our life came gradually to run in more peaceful channels, and not many weeks had passed before Giulia came to me, pressed her cheek to mine and murmured that I was soon to be a father. I marveled that she should have discovered this so soon, but she declared she was experienced in these matters; also she had had a dream in which she held my child in her arms. I both doubted and hoped, but soon my physician's eye detected the outward signs of her condition.

Ineffable joy filled my heart; I no longer thought only of myself, for the expected increase in my family laid new responsibilities upon me and I dreamed ambitious dreams for my unborn son. Giulia showed me great fondness and I did all I could to avoid distressing her. So throughout that lovely spring we lived like a pair of turtle doves, building our nest.

I shall begin a new book to tell of my house and of my advancement in the Seraglio, of Grand Vizier Ibrahim's statesmanship, and of Abu el-Kasim and Mustafa ben-Nakir, who had been so long absent from my sight.

BOOK 7.

The House on the Bosphorus

THAT spring, radiant with fair hopes, did not pass in idleness; my new duties in the Grand Vizier's service kept me fully occupied. The times seemed not to favor the Ottoman Empire, for the Emperor Charles, having succeeded in making peace with the King of France and the Pope, now strove to consolidate his power in the European countries and to unite them for a decisive assault on Islam. After the successful defense of Vienna he induced the Pope to crown him emperor in Bologna, and in the course of the spring he called a German Diet in Augsburg to prepare a final attack on the Protestants.

Khaireddin alone, from his base in Algeria, waged war upon him and won a great victory over Admiral Portundo, who was convoying the coronation guests on their return from Italy to Spain. For these noblemen and courtiers alone, Khaireddin extorted ransoms amounting to tens of thousands of ducats, though for Admiral Portundo himself he demanded only Captain Torgut in exchange. This officer had been taken prisoner by Christians and chained to a rower's bench, where he had time to meditate upon the melancholy consequences of rash and foolhardy behavior.

I had my own share in this naval triumph, which gave striking proof of how formidable an opponent Khaireddin had become even for the united navies of the Emperor. Having carefully studied the situation and observed the scornful resentment felt by the sea pashas for this hero, whom they continued to regard as a barbarous and untrustworthy pirate, I sent word to Khaireddin in Algeria advising him to cease his futile raids on the coasts of Italy and Spain and instead attempt a real victory over the Emperor's fleet. I also suggested that he should cease dyeing his beard. The Sultan's sea pashas were all aged men, and in the Seraglio a long gray beard was regarded as the most convincing sign of experience and ability. As soon as news of the great victory reached the Seraglio I hired a young poet named Baki and a couple of street singers to compose and perform suitable verses in Khaireddin's honor until his name was on everyone's lips. In bazaar and bathhouse he was hailed as a light of Islam. His beard was reputed to reach to his waist, and the Prophet himself, they said, had appeared to him in a dream.

To restore the balance after his naval defeat the Emperor bestowed the island of Malta and the fortress of Tripoli upon the Knights of St. John. This was the severest blow that could have been dealt Khaireddin, and indeed the Sultan's whole sea power, for having drifted hither and thither without firm foothold since the fall of Rhodes, these ruthless crusaders whom Mussulmans called bloodhounds of the seas became once more a menace to merchantmen and pilgrims. Their war galleys, also, continually patrolling the sea routes and convoying Christian vessels, would soon greatly hinder Khaireddin's lawful traffic.

One day on returning home I was met at the gate by Alberto who ran up to me in his yellow eunuch's dress and in a state of great agitation announced that Giulia's labor pains had begun. These terrible tidings made me cry out in fear, for it was not more than seven months since I had returned from the war and so premature an infant could hardly be expected to survive.

Despite my medical experience I was no midwife, having practiced chiefly as an army surgeon, and reflecting now upon the delicate organism of a woman I felt ill equipped indeed. I was therefore greatly relieved to learn that the skillful Solomon had been sent for and was even now at Giulia's side. As he had attended Sultana Khurrem at her confinements, I knew I could wish for no more competent man. He came out to the courtyard, his arms bloody to the elbows, and assured me cheerfully that all was going as well as could be expected. At his frightful appearance my knees turned to water; I exhorted him to do his best and promised him lavish presents if only my son might survive. But the honest Jew explained that he had been sent by Sultana Khurrem and that for certain reasons he could accept nothing from me. He wearied of me at last, saying that my woeful presence did more harm than good, and urged me to go for a brisk walk to restore the color to my cheeks.

In vain I told myself that millions and millions of boys had been born into the world before this one, many of them prematurely. I found no comfort. The sun was sinking behind the hills when like a thief I slunk back to Abu el-Kasim's house, hoping to see some strange woman run joyfully toward me crying, "What will you give me for bringing you glad tidings?"

But I heard no joyous voices and the women squatted like crows in that silent house, avoiding my eyes. I feared the worst when Solomon came to me with a child in his arms and said in a tone of compassion, "It was not Allah's will, Michael el-Hakim. It's only a girl. But mother and child are well."

I bent forward fearfully to look at the infant, and to my unspeakable joy perceived that she was no defective embryo, but fully developed and healthy, with a little dark down on her head. She opened her deep blue eyes and gazed at me from her paradise of innocence with a look that made me clap my hands and praise Allah for this miracle.

When Alberto saw how great was my relief he too smiled happily and wished me joy. Until then, no doubt, he had feared that being a Moslem I should find no delight in a daughter. When I again expressed my wonder at Giulia's short pregnancy he assured me that he had heard of many similar cases, and cases also where the opposite had occurred. There had been for example a distinguished lady in Verona whose child was born eighteen months after the death of her husband. Therefore, said Alberto, not the most eminent physician could predict these events with certainty; so much depended on the physical structure of the woman and other circumstances, and perhaps even on the husband. Lowering his eyes respectfully he went on, "Voyages, campaigns, and pilgrimages, which impose long abstinence on a man, seem to increase his virility so that children engendered after such journeys come sooner into the world than most. Such at least is the opinion commonly held in Italy."

In my great happiness I lost all my antipathy for Alberto, and indeed secretly pitied him because I had forced him to shave and assume the yellow robe of a eunuch. I therefore spoke kindly to him and let him admire the child in my arms. He pointed out how strongly she resembled me, until I soon saw that she had not only my chin but also my ears and nose, though what most delighted me was the perfection of her eyes. Both, like Giulia's left one, were sapphire blue.

I care to say no more of this little daughter of mine, the touch of whose tiny fingers melted my heart as if it had been wax. For her sake I spoiled and pampered Giulia as she lay scolding me for all the things I forgot or left undone.

Because of some lingering weakness and to preserve the youthfulness of her breasts she insisted on my finding a wet nurse for the child, and from a Tartar in the bazaar I bought a Russian woman who was still suckling her year-old son. My mind misgave me that she would neglect my daughter and save most of her milk for her own boy, but when the Tartar offered to knock the child's brains out without extra charge I could not agree to so godless an action, and consoled myself with the thought that I could keep the infant and train him up as a houseboy.

The purchase of the nurse was not the only great expense incurred at that time, for when the house that Sinan had designed, with all Giulia's alterations and additions, began at last to rise on the sloping shore of the Bosphorus, I was appalled at its size. All unknown to me it had grown and grown until now it was almost as large as the palaces of the agas. Giulia's vanity further demanded that the whole property should be enclosed by a high stone wall—the principal mark of distinction in a house. I went in deadly fear as Sinan presented even longer and longer reckonings, though he employed young *azamoghlans* from the janissary school for the work and I was permitted to buy the building materials through the Defterdar's treasury at the Sultan's price.

Long before we moved into our mansion I had to buy two Negroes as boatman and gardener's boy, and of course a Greek head gardener. Giulia dressed the Negroes in red and green with silver belts, and as the gardener swore by all the Greek saints that he had never encountered two such lazy and impudent blacks as these I had also to buy a meek Italian boy to help him. So large a household required a cook, the cook required a slave girl, and the slave girl needed a woodcutter and a water carrier to help her, until at last I felt as if I were being sucked down into a whirlpool.

When after two and a half years' absence Abu el-Kasim returned from Bagdad his house was so full of yelling, squabbling servants that he did not recognize it, and had to go out into the street again to make sure he had come to the right place. And truth to tell I had long forgotten that I was a mere guest in his house and was making use of what belonged to him. But the deaf-mute, half starved, ragged, verminous, and long since banished to the obscurest corner of the yard where he dragged out a miserable existence beneath a roof of woven withies, at once recognized his lord. He squealed and scampered about and fawned upon him, like a faithful dog welcoming his returning master.

At first I hardly knew Abu. He wore a large turban and a kaftan with jeweled buttons, and on his feet were slippers of red leather. With a gesture of command he bade his three donkey drivers unload the bales of merchandise from the backs of their beasts. The donkeys were gray, sturdy creatures; silver bells jingled on their harnesses and from the great bundles they carried floated a fragrance of musk and spice. Abu el-Kasim himself smelled of musk and rose water and had even pomaded his sparse beard. It was clear that he had prospered on his travels.

Before I hurried out to greet him I glanced about me and to my shame observed the hideous confusion prevailing in his house. His cooking pots were dented, his pitchers chipped, and his costly rugs worn threadbare. Baby clothes hung out to dry in the yard, the two Negroes lay snoring on the porch, and in the midst of all sat the Russian woman with knees apart and eyes half shut, suckling my daughter and her son. The scales fell from my eyes at last and I perceived how neglectful Giulia had been of Abu el-Kasim's house. She was not even at home now, but had gone to the Seraglio or the bathhouse, "to attend to her work," as she would say whenever I questioned her.

My fingers were ink stained. I had slept badly and was worn out with trouble and anxiety, but despite my weariness and shame a wave of warmth swept through my heart as I embraced Abu el-Kasim and with tears of joy welcomed him home after the hardships of his perilous journey, from which I had feared he would never return. Abu looked about him with his monkey eyes and was on the point of tearing his beard, but recollected himself in time and said bitterly, "I can see for myself that my return was unexpected. But I'll endeavor to control my tongue if you will at once fetch me a little water that I may perform the lesser ablution and repeat the prayer of homecoming."

While he was engaged in his devotions I contrived by savage imprecations and blows to restore a measure of order. The slaves cleared part of the house by throwing out our own belongings and helping the donkey drivers to carry in the bales. Having ordered the cook to prepare a meal instantly, I accompanied Abu el-Kasim ceremoniously into the house and led him toward the place of honor. But Abu paused before the Russian woman, who had never learned to veil her face in the presence of men, and gazing enchanted at her and the two children at her breast he said, "I see that you have taken another wife, Michael el-Hakim, and evidently not a moment too soon, since Allah has already blessed your household. Never have I beheld a finer boy. He is fairer than the moon and the image of his father."

He took the child in his arms and wept with delight when the boy clutched his beard with his little fingers. The Russian was delighted at this condescension; she modestly covered her bosom and even drew a veil over her round face as she gazed moist eyed at Abu el-Kasim. I snapped, "She's no wife but a bought slave. It is my daughter who is fairer than the moon and out of regard for the Sultan I have whispered the name Mirmah in her ear, after the Moslem manner, since the Sultan's own daughter has been given that name. But I forgive you, Abu el-Kasim, for no doubt you have not yet rubbed the dust of travel from your eyes."

He handed the boy back reluctantly to the mother, stroked my daughter's cheek out of politeness, and seated himself in the place of honor. A scullion, trembling with fear, brought sherbet in a silver goblet and spilled some of the sticky liquid over Abu's knees. Abu fished a dead fly from the cup, tasted the drink, and said with a grimace, "What delicious sherbet! Its only defect is that it's too warm —but then it's so much the sourer. However, for the sake of your child I forgive you everything, Michael el-Hakim, though I confess my first impulse was to send for the cadi and two competent witnesses to assess the damage you have done to my beautiful house. But for thirty years no little hand has tugged at my beard. I will not be petty. I can afford to look the other way, and indeed have always been magnanimous."

To cheer him I explained that my new house would soon be ready, and even promised to have certain repairs carried out in his own. When we had eaten a good meal together and opened a jar of wine all awkwardness between us melted away; our conversation grew ever more animated and Abu el-Kasim told me of the marvels of Bagdad

302

that not even Genghis or Tamerlane had been able to destroy. He spoke too of the Persian rose gardens, of Tabriz and of Ispahan, and praised in glowing terms that long-hallowed land of poets. As to his own affairs, however, Abu was reticent, and he was unwilling to open his bundles, though it was not long before the whole house was fragrant with them. The smell of musk wafted out into the street, bringing the neighbors to our gate to shower blessings on Abu el-Kasim at his most happy homecoming. Moved to tears he distributed the remainder of our meal among them—more indeed than I had intended to give away—and sobbed with the nostalgia born of wine, "Ah, Michael! My name is Abu el-Kasim, but you have never even asked me why I so call myself and what became of my son Kasim. Today I felt a child's hand playing with my beard for the first time in many years; time rolled backward, the fount of tears was unsealed, and I looked for a moment into the well of my own life. Woe, woe is me! So dearly did I love my only son that at his birth I tempted Allah by changing my name to Kasim's Father, Abu el-Kasim."

He plunged again into sorrowful memory. Presently he looked up and said in an altered tone, "That reminds me that on my journey I met our friend Mustafa ben-Nakir. At the moment he is studying poetry under the guidance of the most eminent poets of Persia. He's also associating with dissatisfied dignitaries who resent the tyranny of young Shah Tahmasp and want to abandon the Shiite heresy while there is yet time, to return to Sunna, the true path."

Only now did I understand in my innocence that Abu el-Kasim and Mustafa ben-Nakir had gone to Bagdad and Persia to gain knowledge that would be of use in the event of war in the East. Much disturbed I exclaimed, "Allah! You cannot mean that the Grand Vizier is secretly spreading dissension in the Persian dominions? The Sultan has given firm assurance of his desire for peace, and he needs all his forces to defend Islam against the Emperor's planned attack."

Abu el-Kasim replied, "Unfortunately Mustafa ben-Nakir has obtained incontrovertible proof that Shah Tahmasp, to Islam's shame, has begun negotiations with the Emperor and asked his help in a war against the Sultan. The time is indeed ripe for all Mussulmans to lift up their voices and cry across the world, 'To our aid, all true believers!'"

At his words I seemed to hear the roar of an avalanche and I choked over my wine. For if the Sultan were forced to wage a double war and defend himself against both Emperor and Shah, then indeed evil days were dawning for us all. Abu el-Kasim blinked at me and went on, "In their blindness these infernal Shiites would rather fight on the side of the unbelievers than submit to Sunna and the rule of uncultured Turks. Much indignation has also been aroused by the rumor that the Grand Mufti has issued a *fatwa* by which in any future war the Shiites may be deprived of their property and sold into slavery, though they themselves are Moslems."

"That's no rumor," I said innocently. "It's true, for what army would make the arduous march to Persia merely to protect the life and property of the inhabitants? But such talk is absurd. The Sultan has no intention of attacking Persia. He is secretly equipping a new army to march again on Vienna and the German states."

But the wine had gone to Abu el-Kasim's head and made him quarrelsome. "You're a renegade and grew up in the West, Michael. You're Europe-mad. But what good would those impoverished and divided countries be to us? They have not even the same religion. No, the Eastern lands are the lands for the Sultan. Islam has grown from a tiny seed into a tree, under whose shade the whole world may rest. First Suleiman must unite Islam and extend his domains to wealthy India; then if he chooses he can turn his eyes to cold, barren Europe. You should have seen Bagdad with its thousand minarets, the countless ships in Basrah harbor, the mosques of Tabriz, and the treasures in the bazaars of Ispahan! Then you would turn your back on the penniless Emperor of the unbelievers and set your face toward the East."

Clearly he on his part was Orient-mad, and I did not care to bandy words with him in matters that I understood better than he did, honored as I was by the Grand Vizier's confidence. I called the nurse and laid her son in Abu's arms, then picked up my daughter Mirmah and touched her hair with my lips, marveling again at the freak of nature that had given her black hair, when Giulia's was golden yellow and my own fair rather than dark.

Either the wine or Abu el-Kasim's talk sharpened my wits, and I perceived that my position as Ibrahim's confidant was less simple than I had supposed. I was paid a good salary as an adviser on German affairs, but if such fanatics as Abu el-Kasim and Mustafa ben-Nakir were to induce the Sultan to maintain peace in the West, then the Grand Vizier's interest in Germany would diminish and I should

304

lose my pay. In my own interest therefore I must firmly oppose Abu's and Mustafa's plans. But, I reasoned, should we meet with such another reverse as that of Vienna, all supporters of attack in the West would fall into disfavor and must give place to those who advocated war on Persia.

At this point in my reflections it occurred to me that all the Sultan's advisers—including perhaps the Grand Vizier—were in the same position as myself. Their political attitude must be governed by private interest, irrespective of what was best for the state. These thoughts so bewildered me that I could no longer tell right from wrong.

At dusk Giulia returned, attended by Alberto. She was infuriated by the disorder in the house, swore at Abu for returning unannounced like a thief in the night, and snatched my daughter from my arms lest in my drunkenness I should let her fall. I blushed for her uncontrolled behavior, but Abu el-Kasim unpacked a flask of genuine Persian rose water for her, and begged her to commend him to the ladies of the harem, that they might receive him from behind a concealing curtain and inspect his marvelous wares. Giulia was pleased by the gift and flattered that he should have appealed to her for help, and very soon they were conferring together in perfect harmony as to how much must be given to the Kislar-Aga, how much to the doorkeepers, and how much she was to have for herself.

I did not interfere in Giulia's affairs, having troubles enough of my own. I was now forced to acknowledge Alberto's merits, for during the difficult days of moving he kept the good of the household continually before his eyes. He accompanied Giulia everywhere and so spared me all uneasiness on her account. But what most moved me was his affection for my daughter Mirmah. At every opportunity he took her in his arms and could silence her weeping far more quickly than I could. His whole behavior showed how well he had adapted himself to his role of major-domo, and more than once I was ashamed of my groundless dislike of this most willing man.

Once we were settled in our new house on the Bosphorus his value became even more apparent, for the slaves obeyed him, and soon he achieved so perfect an order in the household that I had nothing to think of but how to earn enough to meet our ever increasing expenses. The number of these was incredible; sometimes I was left too poor to buy paper and ink for the translation of the Koran that I had secretly begun. I had more than ten people to feed and clothe and an expensive

305

carrying chair to buy as well as harness and saddlery; I must be lavish in almsgiving, and whereas I had fondly believed that our garden at least would be productive, the reverse proved to be the case. Indeed it swallowed more than all the other expenses put together, for I was compelled to grow the same sorts of flowers as were to be seen in the gardens of the Seraglio. I soon ceased to wonder that so apparently humble a post as that of Seraglio gardener was regarded as one of the most desirable and lucrative of any in the realm. The Indian and Chinese ornamental fish alone cost a small fortune, and as many of these died for lack of care Giulia was able to persuade me that in the end it would be cheaper to buy a skilled man to tend them. I prefer not to recall the price of this dried-up, shivering Indian.

There were thus limits to my happiness, as I sat on my billowing down cushions, wandered among the brilliant flowers in my garden, or lingered by the pool to feed the colored fish. Constant money worries chafed me like an ill-fitting shoe. I had hoped that Giulia and I might enjoy our new-found abundance in peaceful seclusion, but she soon made it clear that we could derive neither profit nor enjoyment from our house unless we invited important guests to view it for themselves.

Though it entailed a day's exile from my domain I was undeniably flattered when Sultana Khurrem herself, accompanied by some of her ladies, arrived in her lord's pleasure barge to admire our house and wander through the gardens. The honor this visit conferred upon us far outweighed the expense of a new marble landing stage, thought Giulia. Armed eunuchs stood guard about our house all day, so that even the dullest must observe in what high regard my wife and I were held. Soon the Grand Vizier with his suite came to visit us and see what had become of all his money; Sinan the Builder and I had to undergo a thorough cross-examination before he was smilingly pleased to understand that it was solely out of regard for his own dignity that we had been compelled to build so fine and handsomely appointed a house.

Proud of his work, Sinan the Builder often brought distinguished pashas and sandshaks to inspect it, in the hope of further commissions. I had thus the opportunity of making useful acquaintances, though some of the more eminent among them treated me haughtily because I was a renegade. These guests put me to great expense, as each of them had to be entertained in a manner befitting our respective dignities.

I grew thin and pale from this life of luxury, and pangs would shoot through the pit of my stomach at the thought of the future. But one day Giulia came to me and putting her arms about my neck for once she said tenderly, "Dearest Michael, we can go on like this no longer. You must see that for yourself."

Much moved I replied, "Ah, dear Giulia, you're quite right. A roof and a dry crust are enough for me so long as I have you beside me. We have forged golden fetters for ourselves, and already I feel a silken noose about my neck. Let us humbly confess our error, sell this place, and return to that simple life which is surely better suited to us both."

But her face darkened and she said, "You misunderstand me. A crust of bread and a cup of water in your company would of course satisfy me, but we have our daughter Mirmah's future to think of. I've put up with your lack of ambition too long. I must take the reins into my own hands, since you seem unable to handle them."

She paused to choose her words before continuing, "It's not for a simple woman to meddle with statecraft, but a certain exalted lady feels alarm at the perils threatening the Ottoman Empire and is not convinced that the Grand Vizier's precautions are the best. His overweening pride and conceit are no secret from her." Noting the expression on my face she went on hurriedly, "But why enlarge on that? All I meant to say was that many of the most influential men in the realm are dubious of those dangerous schemes of conquest in the West. If the janissaries must be sent into battle they would do better in Persia, which is a weak, divided country."

To this I replied, "All in good time. The great menace of the Emperor must first be removed. That is the sum of the Grand Vizier's policy."

"You speak like a fool, Michael," said Giulia impatiently. "How can the Sultan defeat the Emperor, who has himself conquered and imprisoned the King of France and the Pope? It may be that Charles bears no ill will to the Sultan and would have nothing against his expansion in the East, so long as he maintained peace with him and his brother. Let the Emperor rule the West and the Sultan the East; there's room in the world for them both."

She spoke with such assurance that I began to feel misgivings, for she could never have worked these things out for herself. She gripped me with both hands and shook me, whispering, "Great sums are at stake, Michael! Though the Grand Vizier may boast of his incorruptibility there are other more receptive purses. I've good reason to think that the Sultan is secretly inclined to a lasting peace with the Emperor, for he realizes the terrible consequences of defeat. And I know from reliable sources that the Emperor desires nothing better than a secret treaty with the Sultan for the partition of the world. But these of course are very secret matters and for appearances' sake the Sultan must feign hostility to any such plans."

"But," I objected, "how can the Sultan trust the Emperor? Even now the Persian envoy is at Charles's Court. How can we be sure that Charles will not attack these dominions as soon as the Sultan's back is turned?"

"Whether he likes it or not, the Sultan is forced to wage war on Persia to crush Shah Tahmasp, who otherwise with the Emperor's support will attack him. But this would prove costly for Charles, who is disinclined to meddle with Oriental affairs in which he is not directly concerned. Look at it how you will, Michael, you must see that peace with the Emperor can only be to the Sultan's advantage. You can lose nothing by working for so good a cause."

This conspiratorial talk did not appeal to me at all, for to my mind reason and not secret gifts of money determined the rights and wrongs of a case. But when I hinted as much to Giulia she shook her head at my simplicity and said, "God pity you, Michael! Nothing you can say will tip the scale either for or against peace, but our style of living has persuaded certain credulous persons that you enjoy the Grand Vizier's confidence. By this you see the importance of outward show. A hundred thousand ducats have been staked on peace, though I dare not hint even to you whence this money comes. But gold speaks for itself, and here are a thousand ducats to prove that those of whom I speak are in earnest. When the Sultan has made peace with Ferdinand there'll be another five thousand for you."

Taking out a little leather bag Giulia broke the seal and let the coins roll jingling across the floor. I freely admit that the ring of money spoke more eloquently in the cause of peace than ever Giulia could. Yet she went on persuasively, "Blessed are the peacemakers. The distinguished lady I spoke of wishes to save the Sultan all unnecessary opposition, and Grand Vizier Ibrahim can easily be sent to Persia as seraskier. The lady sincerely hopes to gain the Grand Vizier's trust and friendship, for she believes that they both have the Sultan's interests at heart. For this reason she is deeply hurt at the malicious rumors put about by him concerning Sultana Khurrem and her sons. It is slander to say that Prince Selim is epileptic. Prince Jehangir's deformity is no more than a trial sent by Allah, such as any woman might have to bear, and the other two Princes are certainly more gifted than the haughty Mustafa, who in no circumstances should be favored at his half-brothers' expense."

I fancy Giulia was somewhat carried away by her enthusiasm and said more than she intended. I was so greatly agitated by her proposal that I lay awake until nearly morning. Conflicting ideas whirled round in my head and when at last I fell asleep I was tormented by nightmares in which I seemed to be wandering over a quagmire and vainly seeking firm foothold. I stumbled and fell; the purse dragged me down and down until my mouth was filled with marsh water and I was all but suffocated. I awoke with a shriek, bathed in cold sweat.

It seemed to me that this dream was an omen, and early in the morning I ordered the boatman to row me to the city. Having performed my devotions in the great mosque I turned my steps to Ibrahim's palace, where I sought out a clerk of the secret intelligence and told him I had a matter of the greatest importance to communicate to the Grand Vizier in person.

I had to wait all day and far into the night until Ibrahim returned from the Seraglio, and when at last he received me it was with coolness and the request that I would not add to the great burden of his cares.

I told him all that Giulia had said and in confirmation would gladly have handed him the thousand ducats, had not Giulia already taken charge of it and dropped it into Alberto's bottomless purse. The Grand Vizier flushed with anger and ground his teeth as he said, "Enough is enough! If that false, fanatical, scheming woman dares to meddle in statecraft I shall give her something to remember it by. God knows what devil beguiled the Sultan into laying his cloth upon that feline shoulder. She has brought him nothing but her sickly, epileptic blood. Better had her puny brats been strangled in the cradle—though not the Sultan's best friend could have suggested such a measure."

When he had stormed for some time I ventured to ask what I should do with the money.

"Keep it," he said. "It's of no significance. I am the one who decides questions of peace and war, for no one is powerful enough to oppose me. The Sultan follows my advice for he knows I'm the only one who cannot be bought—the only one with whom his interests come first. By the most sacred oaths of Islam he has sworn never to remove me from my appointment as Grand Vizier or do anything to harm me, for in all the world I am his only true friend. This was the condition upon which I took my place at his right hand."

Resting his great brilliant eyes upon me he smiled and continued, "Perhaps I have neglected my friend the Sultan of late. I must procure him some fresh diversion and prevent that witch from vexing him every night with her mischievous whisperings. Master Gritti is in Buda, as you know, but you have a beautiful house, Michael el-Hakim, at a suitable distance and surrounded by a wall, so don't be surprised if you should be visited one evening by a pair of wandering brothers. You'd do well to take a few poor poets under your patronage and treat them to a cup of wine and a kaftan. Beautiful poems, good wine, and ravishing stringed instruments can count for much in the destiny of nations. Your position will be much strengthened if you're known to entertain eminent guests in secret. But for safety's sake send away your wife and let her spend the night soothsaying in the harem."

He broke off and smiled, and for the first time I saw a cruel line about his mouth as he added, "Suppose I were to make Sultana Khurrem the present of a prediction! Your wife sees in the sand what best suits her. Persuade her if you can to foretell the succession of one of Sultana Khurrem's sons to the throne. Every prophecy if it is to carry conviction must contain something of the quaint and unexpected. Let her say that Selim the epileptic will succeed, and we shall see what follows!"

He smiled broadly, but I could not share his amusement.

"Why the sickly Selim?" I asked. "My wife's predictions have a disconcerting way of coming true, and I dislike trifling with these matters."

Ibrahim bent forward and his eyes burned with anger as he said, "The Sultana is as blind as any other mother. She would see nothing strange in such a prophecy. But let her once hint a word of it to the Sultan and the scales would fall from his eyes. He has that fine boy Mustafa. How could he contemplate for a moment the accession of a feeble-minded epileptic to the throne of the Osmanlis?"

He added after a pause, "I can no longer rely on Master Gritti, who

310

thinks only of his own advantage. I need a new meeting place where I can converse privately with foreign agents. Why shouldn't you profit by this as Master Gritti did, since I have invested such vast sums in your house? Spread the rumor that in return for substantial gifts you can arrange secret interviews with me, and I will undertake to prove the rumor well founded, provided you don't call upon me needlessly or for trifling matters. But that I may trust you absolutely you must keep careful account of all the presents you receive, and draw equivalent sums from my treasury. Only thus can I be sure that you won't betray me out of sheer avarice."

Thunderstruck at his munificence I stammered blessings, but with a laugh he bade me be silent, picked up his violin, and began to play a merry air that Venetian vessels had brought to Istanbul. Now it was that I glimpsed the full import of his proposal, for if the mightiest man in the Ottoman Empire made me his confidant I need set no bounds to my ambitious dreams. Bowing to kiss the ground before him I murmured, "Why, my lord Ibrahim? Why choose me?"

He touched my head carelessly with his henna-dyed fingers.

"Perhaps life is no more than a feverish dream. Then why not take a sleepwalker for guide? I may be fond of you, Michael el-Hakim, weak and pliable though you are. If I were a little fonder of you than I am I would strip you of wealth and send you out as a mendicant brother to seek Allah in the desert and among the mountaintops. Don't expect too much of my confidence, for even if you knew my deepest secrets, me you would never know. But you once said something that went straight to my heart—that a man must be true to at least one human being. Perhaps that is the task confronting me, for in fact a man can never be true to anyone but himself. My star, my destiny, a curse, or perhaps some inner power has raised me up above all other men. The essential condition for my existence is therefore unflinching loyalty to my lord the Sultan. His welfare is my welfare, his defeat my defeat, and his victory is for me too a victory."

I returned through the darkness to my lamplit house whose every stair was fragrant with rose water. Giulia was still awake and came to meet me with glowing cheeks and sparkling eyes. But a strange sense of unreality held me in its grip and I stared at Giulia as at a wraith—a wraith I did not know.

"Who are you, Giulia, and what do you want of me?"

Startled she drew back, saying, "What ails you, Michael? You're quite pale. Your turban's on one side and you're staring like a madman. If you've heard some foolish tale about me, don't believe it. I would rather you came straight to me than lent your ear to unfounded slander."

"No, no, Giulia. What could anyone say against you? It's just that I cannot understand myself or discover what it is I want. Who am I, Giulia, and who are you?"

She wrung her hands and burst into tears.

"Ah, Michael! Have I not warned you a thousand times not to drink so much? Your head won't stand it. How can you have the heart to frighten me so! Tell me at once what has happened and what the Grand Vizier had to say."

At her urgent whisper I awoke from the strange trance. The walls of the room returned, the table was solid beneath my hand; Giulia too was a creature of flesh and blood and I could see that she was very angry. But I looked upon her as upon a stranger and in a clearer light than formerly. I saw deep lines about her eyes and a look of malign cunning hardening at her mouth. Heavy ornaments clinked at her wrist and throat and the necklaces had made red marks on the lifeless white of her bosom. I felt no longing to gaze into her eyes and there seek peace and oblivion, as I had been wont to do.

With a sensation of pain I looked away and said, "Nothing ails me, Giulia. I'm only tired after a somewhat exacting conversation with the Grand Vizier. But he trusts me and I think will give me much of Master Gritti's former work. He expressed no opinion about the war, but he has not forbidden me to counsel peace. The cup of success is full to the brim, but why—ah, why is it so bitter?"

Hardly had I said this than I began shivering in every limb and realized that I was gravely ill. Giulia at first fancied that I had been poisoned in the Grand Vizier's palace, but having recovered from the first shock she put me to bed and administered sudorifics. I had succumbed to the fever so prevalent in Istanbul; indeed it was a wonder I had escaped it so long. It was not dangerous, but was characterized by a very severe headache.

When Grand Vizier Ibrahim learned of my disorder he showed me the greatest kindness, sending me his own physician and causing an astrological table of diet and medicines to be drawn up for my use. He also visited me in person, thereby giving rise to much whispering in the palace. The result was that during the course of my sickness I received a number of presents of the kind that pass constantly from hand to hand in the Seraglio.

Giulia was overjoyed and talked unceasingly of these gifts and their givers, and of the presents that it was my duty to offer in return. The most sensible plan would have been to pass the same things on, since this was in no way contrary to accepted custom. But Giulia was incapable of letting anything out of her hands once she had firm hold of it, however ugly or useless it might be. Thus my illness proved very costly because of all the presents I must buy, while in the Seraglio speculation grew as to what could have become of all the great bronze urns, Nubians in armor, and other strange objects that had drifted about the Seraglio for years.

When at last I began to recover, Giulia showed herself kinder and more considerate than she had been for a long time, and taking my hand one day she said, "Michael, how is it that you talk to me less openly than you used to? Has your heart been turned against me by some malicious rumor? You know what a nest of gossip the Seraglio is, and my close friendship with Sultana Khurrem has aroused such jealousy that it wouldn't surprise me in the least if the most terrible things were told of me. Believe none of it, my dear Michael. You know me better than anyone—you know how openhearted I am."

Her needless suspicions saddened me and I answered kindly, "There's no reason for my gloomy mood. It's all part of my sickness and will soon pass. Forgive me, and try to be patient with me as always."

In this I was not quite frank, having seen that to be loyal to Ibrahim I must behave with reserve toward Giulia. I was sure that she would pass on to Sultana Khurrem all that I told her, and thenceforth I was very circumspect. Hitherto my candor had been excessive, a fact that was to be of great advantage now, since Giulia had come to believe me incapable of concealment.

Mindful of the Grand Vizier's advice I now began inviting poets and eloquent dervishes to my house—ragged fellows who cared little how they earned their bread so long as they might live untrammeled among like-minded companions. Though Mussulmans, they were much addicted to wine drinking, and were glad enough to accept my invitation. I fancy they even conceived a certain liking for me, for I was content as a rule to listen silently to their talk and their poems.

As I came to know them better I was astonished at their daring, for

313

they did not hesitate to compose biting epigrams on the Grand Vizier's vanity, the haughty silence of the Sultan, and the various errors of which other noted men were guilty. They even wrote ambiguous verses about the laws of the Koran. The Persian art of versifying they held to be supreme and many of them were diligent in translating Persian poems into the Turkish language. They trimmed and polished their works as a jeweler polishes stones, and when they hit on some new or startling piece of imagery they rejoiced as if they had found a treasure. Yet I could not take their skilled game as seriously as they did. To them the composition of a poem seemed as admirable and important as the conquest of a kingdom or a voyage into the unknown world; they even claimed that in the golden pages of history the names of bards would outlive those of eminent generals and learned interpreters of the Koran.

Their chief merit was never to be wearisome. Caring little for this world's goods they could sprinkle their ragged cloaks with the gold dust of fantasy, and though ever willing to compose eulogies to order for the rich and powerful, yet the pleasure of the work was of greater value to them than rich reward, and if they hit upon some happy witticism at their patron's expense they would rather forfeit his fee than omit the jest.

The friendship of these curiously free men came to me at a fortunate moment, for I was still unduly complacent over my position, my house, my riches, and my worldly success. It was good for me to hear their acid comments on jeweled girdles, plumed turbans, and silver-mounted saddles. A bright flower or a scarlet fish swimming through crystal water was for them as breath taking a sight as any diamond. When I attempted to explain that diamonds had other merits besides beauty, the poet Baki, who neglected both ablution and prayer, drew the corner of his mantle over his dusty feet and said, "Man possesses nothing. In the end it is rather things that possess man. The only true value of a diamond is the beauty hidden within it, and beautiful things can enslave as easily as ugly ones. Wiser therefore to love a tulip-cheeked girl from a distance, for to possess her may be to become her slave and lose one's freedom, and loss of freedom is a slow death."

Giulia could not understand what pleasure I could take in the company of these disreputable men, from among whom I very carefully chose a few whom I could count on as my friends. She spent many of her days and nights at the Seraglio and I was not inquisitive. Un-

314

known to her I was preparing for the hour when the Sultan and the Grand Vizier would visit my house in disguise to pass the evening in the company of poets and wits, as they had been wont to do in Master Gritti's house.

Sometime after this the Sultan was assailed by one of his heavy fits of melancholy, and the Grand Vizier sent me an agreed signal. Late the same evening there came a sound of knocking at my gate and two slightly inebriated men, their faces hidden under a fold of their kaftans, stepped inside declaiming verses to the porter. They were of course attended by a number of guards, but these together with two deaf-mutes remained outside the house. No greater proof of Ibrahim's confidence could have been given me. I led my visitors into the house, where they sat down somewhat apart to sip wine and listen to a learned dervish who was just then reading aloud his translation of a Persian poem.

But the others were too shrewd to be taken in by the newcomers and soon perceived that these were no ordinary guests. It would have been insulting if they had not, for Ibrahim rightly considered himself the finest-looking man in the Ottoman Empire, while Sultan Suleiman was equally assured that his own demeanor betrayed him for the nobleman he was, despite the mask he held before his face. But my guests had sense enough to feign ignorance. At his request they addressed the Sultan as Muhub the poet, and pressed him eagerly to read aloud his verses. He demurred for some time, but at length drew out a roll of paper covered with beautiful script and read from it in a musical voice. His hands shook as he did so, for he believed himself unrecognized and knew that he was in the presence of the foremost experts in the city. It was evident that he feared their candid criticism. So far as I could judge his work had no other fault than a slight verbosity, a slight monotony, and a slight touch of the commonplace, at least in comparison with Baki's allusive, whimsical style.

His hearers expressed courteous appreciation, but no more, their self-respect as poets not permitting them to fawn even on the Sultan where their art was concerned. They raised their goblets to Muhub and praised him until a frank smile of delight overspread the Sultan's pallid face. But Baki, the young and unabashed, added, "With a liberal hand Muhub the poet has cast pearls and gold before us, and to listen now to anything inferior would be most unbecoming. But if anyone of us can play an instrument we might in that manner venture to compete further with the incomparable Muhub."

I fancy that all he meant by this flowery speech was that he could bear no more of the Sultan's stilted poems and hoped that Ibrahim would pick up his famous violin. It was not to be expected, however, that Suleiman should catch the fine irony of Baki's remark. He eagerly assented and begged Ibrahim to play. None of us had reason to regret it, for when Ibrahim, having first drunk a little wine, filled the room with his marvelous music, all the passion, joy, and longing of our fleeting lives sang to us in every cadence, until I trembled and could not restrain my tears. Even Baki wept aloud.

I need speak no more of that night. It passed away in a sedate and seemly manner, and when the guests became unduly drunk the Grand Vizier took his violin again to quieten them with his playing. No one fell asleep but Murad-*tseleb,* who indeed understood little of music. The rest of us were in the gayest possible mood, and when the stars began to pale we carried Murad-*tseleb* out and dropped him into the fishpond to sober him, Baki holding his head above water by the beard. The keeper of the fish, roused by the shouts and splashings, dashed from his hut in only his loincloth, to throw stones and curse us with the wild curses of his homeland, until we took to our heels and lost our slippers in the flower beds. Muhub the poet even lost his turban, and laughed until the tears ran down his cheeks.

But now in the gray light of dawn the mutes grew uneasy at their lord's long absence and knocked upon the door. At the sight of these two dark-skinned giants we turned suddenly very sober, as if under a cold shower. Still breathless from the chase and soiled with earth from the flower beds, Muhub the poet scrambled into his carrying chair, and with great difficulty dragged the Grand Vizier in beside him.

Sultan Suleiman visited my home about a dozen times, and met there not only poets and wise dervishes but also French and Spanish sea captains and well-informed adventurers, most of whom had not the slightest idea who he was. In the presence of foreigners and unbelievers he remained silently in the shadows and was content to listen carefully to what they had to say, putting in a question from time to time about life and conditions in European countries.

Thus it was that I came to know Sultan Suleiman, called by Christians the Magnificent, though his own people named him merely the Lawgiver. No one is a prophet in his own country. And the better I

316

knew him, the less he charmed me; the melancholy that held him prisoner made him wearisome company. With all his faults Ibrahim remained a man among men, whereas the Sultan withdrew himself into his secret solitude, seemingly as remote from his fellow creatures as heaven is from earth.

Perhaps it was this that caused him suffering and overwhelmed him at times with that restless, gnawing fear. Because of the suspicions of his father he had lived for much of his youth in the shadow of a lurking death, when every night he lay tensely awaiting the coming of the mutes. It seemed to me that this unnaturally passionate friendship for the Grand Vizier had something in it of compulsion, as if by showering favors upon Ibrahim and investing him with limitless power he sought to convince himself that there was at least one man in the world whom he could trust.

The longer I think about Sultan Suleiman the more clearly do I perceive how little I know of his inner nature and thoughts. As lawgiver he made life easier and pleasanter for his subjects than it had formerly been—certainly better than it was in Christendom. His own slaves were the exception, for although they were free to essay the steep ladder to power they never knew whether a horsehair switch or a silken noose awaited them at the top.

My own position as the Grand Vizier's confidant was singular. As a rule I would visit him after dark, entering the palace by a side door or through the servants' entrance. Yet it was common knowledge in the Seraglio that petitions and reports could be most rapidly conveyed to the Grand Vizier through me. It was a mystery to everyone therefore how my wife Giulia could come and go in the harem as freely as if she lived there, how she could enjoy the Sultana's favor, foretell the future for her and her ladies, make purchases for them in the bazaar, and—no doubt for a handsome consideration—obtain audiences with the Sultana for certain wealthy Greek and Jewish women.

Little wonder that the strangest stories about me began circulating in the Seraglio and the foreign quarter. Sometimes my influence was exaggerated, sometimes I was said to be harmless because I frequented poets and learned dervishes. When I began to receive Christian adventurers in my house my fame spread to the West and even as far as the Imperial Court. The Christians who visited me came either on secret missions, or to investigate the chances of entering the Sultan's service, or again to establish profitable business connections in Istanbul. More

317

than once I was able to do these men substantial services, and it was told of me that although I accepted presents the information I gave was strictly accurate.

It was of course natural for me to accept presents from both friends and enemies, as did every influential man in the Seraglio, for without offering them no suppliant could ever dream of gaining an audience. It was by no means an official's salary that determined his position or the regard in which he was held, and the presents that his appointment brought him constituted by far the greater part of his regular income. The Grand Vizier himself accepted gifts, even from King Ferdinand's envoys, these presentations being openly made and regarded merely as a courteous acknowledgment of his high station.

Because of my special duties I received many presents in secret, though for my own sake I rendered an accurate account of these to the Grand Vizier. This the givers had no notion of, and because I was apparently so easy to bribe I earned a bad reputation among Christians, who fancied that their gifts were the price of the favors done them. But thanks to Ibrahim's liberality my conscience remained clear and I never succumbed to the temptation of deceiving him.

I may mention that the Christians threw their money about very foolishly in seeking to steer Ottoman politics in a direction favorable to themselves, and in return were often kept dangling with empty words and fair promises. Not until they were on their way home would it dawn on them to what extent the wool had been pulled over their eyes. Official ambassadors were as a rule royally received. Throughout their stay in Istanbul they were attended by a brilliant suite and a special guard of janissaries; houses and servants were assigned to them and as much as twenty ducats daily allowed them for subsistence, and they were frequently received in audience by the Grand Vizier, who was a master of procrastination.

At long last the envoys would be ushered into the golden-colonnaded chamber of the Divan, though not until they had first been dazzled by a display in the janissaries' courtyard. Here elephants with gilded tusks were to be seen, and the magnificent procession of the viziers and their retinue. Dazed and bewildered by these splendors they found themselves bowing before the Sultan—a sultan seated upon a pearl-incrusted throne. With every breath the thousand jewels of his golden robe winked and flashed, and the ambassadors soon perceived how highly they were honored in being permitted to kiss that jeweled hand

and listen to the meaningless compliments with which Suleiman was pleased to greet them. Throughout their stay in Istanbul they had felt entangled in the meshes of an invisible net; at best all they received was a signed letter from the Sultan to take home with them, and they had soon to confess that the document was worth no more than the embroidered purse in which it lay.

Such was the treatment meted out to official negotiators, and matters were no better when the Grand Vizier consented to come to my house and there, over a cup of wine, interview some Spanish nobleman or Italian adventurer who at the Emperor's behest sought a private audience. Through such agents Charles V sought to feel the Grand Vizier's pulse on the question of the partition of the world. By boasting of his influence with the Sultan, Ibrahim would lead his opponent on to reveal his true motives and aims. Yet however warmly he appeared to approve the proposals he was careful never to commit himself. The Sultan himself made no pronouncements, and where this subject was concerned would have nothing whatever to do with foreign spokesmen. Nevertheless he was always intensely interested to discover through the Grand Vizier how far the Emperor was willing to compromise.

I believe that both Sultan and Grand Vizier sincerely wished for peace at this time, yet all the fumbling conferences came to nothing because neither side would trust the other. It was in principle impossible for the Sultan, as Ruler of the Faithful, to consider a lasting peace with unbelievers, since the Koran expressly forbade such a policy. And for his part the Emperor, like the cynical statesman he was, would naturally take the first opportunity of uniting the Christian countries against the Sultan regardless of fair promises and secret treaties, because he rightly saw in the Ottoman Empire a constant menace to imperial power and to Christendom itself.

Sorrowfully I now learned the futility of all politics and saw that however lofty his motives, man cannot control the march of events. The Grand Vizier required my presence at these meetings so that if necessary I could testify that he had ever acted in his lord's best interests. And as I listened I acquired a widening knowledge of political problems. I learned that one could talk long and eloquently and yet say nothing, and all too plainly I beheld the pettiness, selfishness, vanity, and weakness of mankind. The company of poets and dervishes had trained me in discerning the emptiness of worldly honors. I tried

319

not to set too much store by my position, provided I might keep my fortune, for thanks to this, Giulia could live the life she craved and I was spared her eternal nagging. She measured success in money and valuables, and in her more amiable moments she would even admit that I had not proved so unenterprising as she had feared. She would have liked to see me stand with folded arms and modestly lowered eyes in the colonnaded chamber of the Divan when the kaftans of honor were conferred, but happily she found enough food for her vanity among the ladies of the harem. Even the Sultan's mother received her in the Old Seraglio, though she suffered a severe heart attack because of Giulia's prophecies. For I had cautiously guided Giulia's thoughts in the right direction, and she was so rash as to predict that Sultana Khurrem's son Selim would succeed to the Ottoman throne. Strangest of all, Giulia herself implicitly believed her own prophecy and began to behave toward Prince Selim with the utmost respect and veneration.

From time to time she would bring me news or warnings plainly originating with Sultana Khurrem and intended by that guileful woman to reach the Grand Vizier through me. But for his part, Ibrahim could not reconcile it with his dignity to enter into any communication with the Sultana with Giulia as intermediary. In this he made a great mistake and underrated the Sultana's terrifying strength of will and vigilant ambition. But who at that time would have done otherwise?

In the courts of the West the Sultana was known as Roxelana, the Russian woman. Presents, even from Christian princes, streamed to her through the golden portals of the harem; incredible stories were told of her luxurious way of life and her gorgeous clothes. One of her gowns was reputed to have cost a hundred thousand ducats. There were also tales of her cruel jealousy that made life in the harem a hell. If any woman there sought to attract the attention of the Sultan, or if he by chance glanced at one of them, Sultana Khurrem laughed gaily and saw to it that she disappeared.

I cannot say with certainty what gifts were sent her by the Emperor's secret envoys or the King of Vienna, but during those uneasy months she did her utmost, Giulia told me, to induce the Sultan to make a treaty with the Emperor. Politically, of course, this was madness, for the Emperor had just been crowned by the Pope and had concluded peace with France, and thus stood at the height of his power. In the Diet of Augsburg he even succeeded in frightening the Protestant princes into obedience, and confident of victory was now preparing to make war on the Sultan. Indeed, in his quality of Most Catholic Majesty he implicitly obeyed the exhortation of Scripture not to let his right hand know what his left hand did. While secretly offering his left hand to the Sultan in token of peace, he slipped his right into a steel gantlet to deliver a crushing blow. Never before or since can the Ottoman Empire have been in such peril, and the Sultan's desire for peace was easy to understand.

Fortunately, the only result of Charles V's ultimatum to Germany was the founding by Philip of Hesse of a league of princes, in support of Luther's teaching. King Zapolya and the King of France certainly had a finger in the pie, but the secret and I believe decisive reason for the princes' defiance was Ibrahim's promise of support in the event of war between them and the Emperor.

Which of these princes had their religious zeal stimulated by Turkish gold I cannot say, but Philip of Hesse at least found means to pay and equip his troops in a manner unaccountable to the Christians. I had my own reasons for frequently recalling the thin face and cold blue eyes of this man. Compared with the league he had formed, Father Julianus's harmless preachings through Germany were of small significance. Luther and his pastors were now beginning to watch over the purity of their doctrine as jealously as ever did Holy Church, and to my sincere grief I must record that Father Julianus never returned to claim his bishopric. He was stoned to death in a small provincial town.

Thanks to the Schmalkald League, we were relieved of the heaviest of our anxieties, and the Sultan had no further need to listen to the advocates of peace. Grand Vizier Ibrahim on the contrary revived his ambitious plans for the conquest of the German states, with the Protestant princes' support.

I disliked war, yet since for the well-being of the army a fresh campaign was necessary, it seemed to me that we had much to gain and nothing to lose by marching once more on Hungary. Among the mountains and barren wildernesses of Persia even a large army could vanish like a needle in a haystack. But in Germany the Schmalkald League bound the Emperor's hands, and so favorable an opportunity might never return.

For Andy's sake above all I looked upon war as something absolutely necessary, and I blamed myself for having neglected and forgotten my loyal friend for so long. One spring morning, when the tulips in my garden had unfolded their bright red and yellow cups, and fresh sea winds swept in from the sparkling Bosphorus, Andy knocked at my gate. Hearing the shouts of the porter I hurried up and at first failed to recognize my old friend. He came in barefoot with a sack on his back, wearing dirty leather breeches and a ragged turban, and I took him for one of the beggars that squatted in such numbers about my door. When I saw who it was I cried out in amazement, for Andy's sturdy legs trembled with weariness, and his pale, staring face was twitching. He dropped the sack, pulled off his turban, and having gazed dully at me for some moments he said, "In the blessed name of the Prophet, Michael, get me something to drink—something strong—or I shall lose the remainder of my poor wits."

I took him to the boathouse, drove out the Negroes who slept there, and with my own hands fetched him a keg of rare malmsey from the cellar. Andy knocked out the head of the keg, which he carried to his mouth, and in great gulps he drank half of what it contained. Soon the trembling in his limbs ceased and he sagged to the floor with a thud that shook the boards and sent dust flying from the joints of the walls. Then, hiding his face in his hands, he drew a deep breath and uttered so rending, so despairing a sob that I in my turn began to quake for dread.

"Michael," he said, "I don't know why I should burden you with my sorrows, but a man must turn to some friend at such a time. I don't want to grieve you, but things are bad with me—as bad as they can be. Better if I had never been born into the misery of this world."

"What in the name of Allah has happened?" I cried, in the deepest agitation. "You look as if you'd murdered someone."

His bloodshot eyes were upon me as he answered, "I've been dismissed from the arsenal. They tore the plumes from my turban and kicked me out—they shook their fists and threw my belongings after me. I'm wretched, wretched."

Relieved that it was no worse I admonished him, saying, "Is that all? You should have known what comes of drinking. But even if you have lost your pay, you've your wife's fortune to turn to."

With his head still in his hands he retorted, "I care nothing for the arsenal. We had an argument about the cannon and I told them their war galleys were only good for firewood. I wanted them to build

322

bigger vessels to carry heavy ordnance, like the Venetians and Spaniards. So I went. He laughs best who laughs last. But I'm a sorrowful man and don't expect to laugh ever again in this world."

He seized the keg and poured more wine down his throat before continuing, "Your good colleague Master Gritti is behaving like a maniac in Hungary, and all the Transilvanian lords are at each other's throats. But whether Hungarians or Moldavians, Wallachians or Tartars, all are agreed that no Mussulman shall own land in Hungary. My deed of conveyance from King Zapolya they put to what they considered its fit use before my very eyes, and have long since divided my flocks among themselves, slaughtered my cattle, and razed all the buildings to the ground. That poor Jew will suffer great loss, and I can't get back a penny on all my lands, though they're so wide that it takes a day and a night to ride from end to end of them. Sweet songs are brief songs, they say, and I own little but the breeches I have on."

"But—but—" I stammered, realizing that I should have to take care of poor Andy once more, despite the friction this would cause with Giulia. Then, summoning courage, I clapped him on the shoulders and said, "We'll find some way out, my dear Andy. But what has your wife to say to all this?"

"My wife," said Andy absently. He raised the keg and emptied it at a draught. "I must have forgotten to tell you. The poor little girl is dead. And it was not an easy death. She suffered for three days before she went."

"Jesus, Mary!" I cried, striking my hands together. "That is, Allah is Allah—Why did you not tell me this at first? I feel for you most deeply in your great sorrow. How did she die?"

"In childbirth, in childbirth!" said Andy in a tone of wonder. "And that was not the worst, for the child died, too."

And so at last I learned all that had befallen Andy. He hid his face in his hands again and broke into such terrible weeping that the walls of the boathouse shook. I could find no words to comfort him in his boundless grief.

"It was a boy," he managed to say at last. Then, enraged at his own weakness, he swore for the first time in many a long month in his own rough mother tongue, *"Perkele!"*

Without a word I returned to the cellar and fetched another barrel of wine. He wiped his eyes with the back of his hand.

323

"My little foal! Her cheeks were like peaches and her eyes like bilberries. I don't understand. But even in the early days the Jewish physician advised her to take the baths at Bursa, and I'm glad to remember that she made the journey like a princess, though at the time I grumbled foolishly at the expense. The physician told me in his learned jargon that her organs had grown askew from too much riding as a young girl. And her loins were hard as ash, for young Hungarian ladies are in the wicked habit of riding astride like men."

"Dear Andy, my brother and my friend! All these things were written in the stars before your birth. Sweet songs are brief songs, as you say, and you lived in your happiness so long as it pleased Allah. Who knows? She might have lived to weary of you and make eyes at some other man."

Andy shook his heavy head. "Stop chattering, Michael, and tell me—were their deaths sent to punish me for deserting the Christian faith? I believe I'm as good a Moslem as any, though I can't recite all the prayers. In my heart I've never denied our Lord or His mother—Mussulmans venerate them, too—and I've been sneered at for never treading the Cross underfoot. But as I was roaming about the city in my anguish I chanced to enter the Christian church, and when I heard the intoning of the priest and the ringing of the bell I seemed to hear also the devil himself laughing at me in mockery, because I'd forsaken God of my free will and at your bidding. For God's sake, help me, Michael, and give me peace again. My son was not baptized and my wife neglected both confession and communion after our marriage, though in other ways she was a good Christian. It is frightful to think that because of my falling away they must burn in eternal fire."

I could not but reflect seriously upon what he said. With trembling hands I raised the wine to my lips and sought in it the courage that I lacked. I thought it unfair of Andy to blame me for his defection, and said with some heat, "Pray remember that we took the turban independently of one another; I never asked you to do it. Though if we must go to hell for our sins I admit we shall most likely go side by side—indeed, for once I may be a step ahead of you, being a scholar and therefore more answerable for my actions than you."

Andy replied impatiently, "I'll account to the Lord for my own actions without troubling you. But why did He strike down my wife and son? What sin can my little boy have committed? I learned as a child how vain it is for a poor man to hope for justice in this world, but all the more confidently did I hope for it in the next."

I know not whether the wine had given me courage or merely clouded my judgment, but for the first time in my life I confessed to myself that I was the worst of all heretics.

"Andy," I said gravely, "I'm weary of quibbles and of juggling with words. Only in a man's own heart is God to be found, and no man can save another by expounding texts, be they in Latin, Arabic, or Hebrew. If indeed there is an eternal, omnipotent, and omniscient God, would He trouble to aim His wrath at a poor worm like you?"

Andy's head shook and tears rolled into his great hands as he said, "Perhaps you're right, Michael. Who am I that God's great cannon should be trained on me? Give me a truss of straw to lie upon for a few days, Michael, and a little bread; I will get over this as best I may and consider how to start life afresh. It's only in stories that men win a princess and half a kingdom. In the days of my great happiness I used to fancy that I must be dreaming, and soon I think I shall be able to believe it. First I will take the edge off sorrow by getting properly drunk; then in the drabness and headache of waking I shall remember the past in all humility as a dream too fair for an oaf like me."

His resignation so deeply moved me that I too wept, and together we mourned the sorrows and vanities of life. Andy being already very drunk I fetched a sleeping draught from my medicine chest, and mixed enough of it with his wine to stun an ox. Soon he sank back unconscious on the floor, to all appearances dead save for a faint whistling in his nose.

He slept for two days and nights, and when he woke he took a little to eat. I did not vex him with needless chatter, but left him alone to dangle his legs from the jetty and stare at the restless waters of the Bosphorus.

Some days later he came to me and said, "I know I'm a burden to you here, and especially to your wife, so I shall keep out of the way and live with your Negroes in the boathouse, if you'll let me. But give me work to do—the heavier the better. Idleness irks me, and I would like to do something in return for my food and sleeping place."

I was abashed at his words, for Giulia had indeed pointed out somewhat sharply that Andy ate at least three aspers' worth of food a day and used a mattress and blanket that properly belonged to the Negroes;

325

she also suggested that he should bestir himself a little to earn his keep. And although I should have preferred to see Andy treated as an old friend of the family, I summoned Alberto and asked him to find suitable work—a request that he seemed to have been expecting. He took Andy at once to the northwest corner of the garden, which had not yet been cleared, and told him to break stones and build a terrace there. It was an improvement long planned, and postponed because of the expense. Andy also chopped wood and carried water to the kitchen, and all with such good will that even the slaves began leaving him their work to do. He tried to avoid us, but Giulia often purposely stood in his path to gloat over his degradation. Nevertheless it seemed to me at times that Andy, as he bowed and shambled off to do her bidding, was silently laughing at her; this I took as a sign of his recovery.

War was again imminent, and this time camel trains set forth months in advance, carrying bridge-building materials to the banks of the Danube tributaries. Charles V proclaimed the Turkish peril in all the German states, and by thus spreading alarm among the people he succeeded also in inflaming them against the Protestant princes. I could not but admire his astute use of a situation on which the Grand Vizier had based his own hopes for a successful campaign. I observed these things with the impartial eye of an onlooker, and one with personal experience of German lands of which Ibrahim, as a Moslem, could have only a dim idea.

To my great joy Ibrahim thought it best for me to remain in Istanbul in charge of his secret business, though I could not tell from his expression whether this order was a mark of special favor or a sign of lessening confidence. Mustafa ben-Nakir had lately arrived in the Sultan's capital, having journeyed first from Persia to India in company with old Suleiman the eunuch, Viceroy of Egypt, and then after countless adventures returned to Basra aboard an Arabian smuggler. He had grown thinner and his eyes seemed bigger than before, but he was otherwise unchanged. The scent of the costly oils with which he anointed his hair spread agreeably through the room, the silver bells jingled at girdle and knee, and the book of Persian poems was worn with diligent use. I greeted him as a long-lost friend, and Giulia, too, was glad to see him. He sought out Andy and sat for a long time cross legged in the grass watching him break stones for the terrace. But although Mustafa ben-Nakir's sole purpose in coming seemed to be to describe in glowing colors the wonders and the wars of India, he had in fact secret business with me and took me to meet the renowned eunuch Suleiman.

Suleiman the eunuch was at this time a man of some seventy years, and so fat that his little eyes had almost disappeared. Four strong slaves were needed to raise him to his feet when once he had sat down. He had attained the viceroyalty of Egypt by his unswerving fidelity. In the past, otherwise competent viceroys of wealthy, decadent Egypt had fallen a prey to all manner of ambitious dreams until it seemed as if a curse lay over that ancient land.

But because of his enormous bulk and his age, Suleiman was too lazy and also too astute to contemplate rebellion against the Sultan, and had of course no sons to whom he might be tempted to bequeath a crown, nor any ambitious wife to egg him on. And although he looked with delight upon beautiful slave girls and kept two of them about him to scratch the soles of his feet, this was, so far as I know, his only indulgence. He did not even care to rob the Sultan to any great extent, and punctually remitted his yearly tribute without arousing among his subjects the customary lamentations. He was thus a most unusual man and because of his independent position was almost equal in rank to the Grand Vizier. It was a great honor for me to be received and addressed by him.

"Deeply though I deplore the needless trouble he puts himself to," he began, "and his restless wandering from place to place, yet because of the beauty of Mustafa ben-Nakir's eyes and his bewitching manner of reading poetry aloud I find myself compelled to listen to him. But now, no doubt because of his unpleasant experiences of Portuguese pirates in India, he has taken it into his head that the honor of Islam requires the liberation of the princes of Diu and Calicut from the Portuguese yoke. In the course of his long journeys he has formed useful friendships to this end, and has heard from reliable sources that these two unhappy princes would gladly welcome the Sultan's sea janissaries as liberators."

Mustafa ben-Nakir regarded me with his clear, innocent eyes and said, "Those brigands have stopped the Mussulman spice trade and carried away the cargos in their own ships round Africa to Europe. They oppress the inhabitants of Diu and rob the Arabian merchants— indeed, they rob even their own king by sending inferior spices to Lisbon and keeping the pepper to sell to Moslem smugglers at usurers'

327

prices. The Portuguese have instituted a reign of terror in India that is a disgrace to all Islam—to say nothing of the loss of trade, both to the Sultan's dominions and to our true friends the Venetians. The unhappy Indians yearn for the coming of the Deliverer."

"Allah is Allah!" I said. "Let me hear no more of deliverers, Mustafa ben-Nakir; I am older and wiser than I was in Algeria, and the word leaves a taste of blood behind it. Speak out and tell me what you want and what I am to gain by it, and for the sake of our friendship I will give you what help I may."

Suleiman the eunuch sighed heavily and glanced at Mustafa ben-Nakir, saying, "What times we live in! You youngsters have no notion of the pleasure to be found in leisurely bargaining, and you stifle the art of conversation for which so admirable an opportunity has now arisen. What fever has overtaken the world? Whither are you hurrying? To the grave? But you may give my purse to your greedy friend, Mustafa ben-Nakir, if you can come at it beneath my cushions."

Mustafa ben-Nakir felt beneath the heavily flattened cushions and brought out a handsome purse whose weight at once convinced me of Suleiman's sincerity. With hands folded over his vast belly he sat sighing with contentment, while a lovely girl scratched the sole of his right foot. He closed his eyes, curled his toes voluptuously, and said, "Though all is vanity and a chasing after shadows, yet despite my age I have been entranced by the flowery lyrics of Mustafa ben-Nakir's speech and inspired to accomplish heroic deeds. Being an old sailor I'm also assailed by a senile jealousy of the much-praised Khaireddin, who is and ever will be a pirate. For a man of my girth a large ship is the safest and most comfortable means of transport, and I know nothing more agreeable than sitting beneath an awning on the poop deck, gently rocked by the sea breezes. My digestion functions incomparably better at sea than on land, and that for a man of my age and proportions is of supreme importance. During storms or when roundshot sing over the vessel my bowels display an incredible activity. Regularity is the foundation of health, young men, and for that reason alone I should like to build a Red Sea fleet and so spend as much time as I may on the water. I should have no objection if Ottoman historians were to record that Suleiman-pasha the eunuch conquered India for his stomach's sake. There is nothing to laugh at, Michael el-Hakim. Disorders of the stomach have influenced world history before now

328

and will do so again. Nothing is too petty or too insignificant for Allah to make use of in weaving his great carpet."

I could not forbear smiling at the singular pretext he had chosen, but Mustafa ben-Nakir looked at me with the utmost gravity and said, "You're a man of perception, Michael el-Hakim, yet even reasoned conclusions may lead one astray. My friend Suleiman, unlike most men, is under no necessity of lying. Were it gold he coveted, he would find more than enough of it in Egypt. As for military glory, he rates it about as highly as the bodily function of which he has so eloquently spoken. But I read in your eyes that you don't believe him, from which we must regretfully infer that no one in the Seraglio will believe him either—perhaps not the Grand Vizier himself."

Suleiman the eunuch wheezily interposed, "That is why we need your advice, Michael el-Hakim. And besides this, the sea pashas approve no fleets but their own. The money, vessels, and materials secretly offered me by the Signoria only increase the delicacy of the matter. In short, I cannot submit my plans to any but the Grand Vizier himself. You must convince him that there is nothing wrong in what I ask. Let him then persuade the Sultan to remit, say, a third of the annual tribute from Egypt for the next three years. With that sum I can build the Red Sea fleet. Warships are the most expensive toys ever invented, and I should be loath to impose extra taxes on Egypt. At the same time it would be beneath the Sultan's dignity to allow his fleet to be paid for entirely by foreign powers."

Twist and turn the matter as I would, I could only conclude that Suleiman was sincere and that apart from his digestion, solicitude for the Sultan alone induced him to put forward these proposals, so as to bring the vast profits of the spice trade once more under the Sultan's control. Mustafa ben-Nakir watched my expression narrowly and said, "You must see that Suleiman-pasha cannot propose this of himself. After seeming opposition to the plan he will give in and build the fleet, and take it to India if the Sultan so commands. Michael, here is the opportunity of your life. If you succeed and have a share in this enterprise from the beginning, the princes of the West will one day envy you your riches."

Suleiman stretched his fat legs and curled his toes luxuriously, saying, "I have few passions, but I love to collect human beings. I love to see the varied forms in which Allah molds his dust, to inspire it with the breath of his nostrils. I have taken a fancy to your anxious

329

eyes, Michael el-Hakim, and marvel at the deep line so prematurely drawn between your brows. You will ever be welcome to Cairo as my guest, and the time may come when you'll be glad of a refuge and a protector beyond the range of the Sultan's artillery. Victory and defeat are in the hands of Allah, and who knows what the morrow may bring?"

Indian affairs so captured my imagination that I did all I could to secure Ibrahim's support for Suleiman's plan. And although because of the impending war the Seraskier had many other things on his mind, he did not fail to mention the matter to the Sultan, who secretly commanded Suleiman the eunuch to build his fleet, ostensibly to defend the Red Sea against the ever more daring raids of Portuguese pirates. But for this the Sultan would accept no help from Venice.

Once again I begin a new book, and this time in the name of Allah, the Merciful and Compassionate. For my eighth book will show how the worm of decay was already nibbling at the fairest of blossoms, and perhaps also poisoning my own poor renegade's heart.

BOOK 8.

Roxelana

THERE is but little to tell of the Sultan's next campaign. It lasted from spring to autumn of the Christian year 1532, and came to nothing. Yet the march was eased by wise planning and perfect weather; strict discipline was maintained among the troops, and the three hundred pieces of artillery followed the marching columns without mishap. No general could have hoped for better conditions. But those who followed the progress on their maps noted with surprise that it slackened more and more as summer advanced. From midsummer onward, it became clear to the least experienced observer that indecision was delaying the march, until at last the whole of that gigantic army slowed to a halt and camped during August and September before the insignificant fortress of Guns.

Advocates of peace in the West made the most of this period of delay and doubt. Envoys from the Persian governor of Bagdad and from the Prince of Basra brought conciliatory messages to the Sultan, and their arrival seemed timed to show that at the most favorable moment for energetic action in the East the Seraskier had sent the army away to make needless and unprofitable war on the Emperor. Little wonder then that the Sultan paused so hesitantly before Guns, embittered by its stubborn resistance, yet for appearances' sake he was compelled to persevere. Instead of proceeding to Vienna, however, he marched from Guns toward imperial Carinthia, and his vanguard had reached the gates of Graz before he felt justified by the lateness of the season in beginning his homeward march. And though the grisly trail of slaughter left by his forces struck terror to the hearts of Christians everywhere, yet this great enterprise turned out to be nothing but a disorderly, planless raid, bringing Suleiman no honor and causing trouble in his empire that was out of all proportion to the result.

The only people to profit by this campaign were the Protestant princes of Germany, whom it enabled to make a pact with the Emperor at Augsburg. This for the time being ensured their religious freedom. Thanks to the pact Charles was even able to induce Luther to preach in favor of a united crusade against the Turks. Thus Grand Vizier Ibrahim's hopes fell to the ground, and it became clear that yet again the Christians had made shameless use of their secret commerce with the Porte to secure concessions from the Emperor for their own ends.

But I have not yet mentioned the hidden but decisive reason for the Sultan's strange hesitation before the walls of Guns. At the opening of the spring offensive, a fleet of seventy sail had put to sea to defend the coasts of Greece. Early in August, on almost the very day that Ibrahim pitched his pavilion before Guns, this fleet was sighted by the combined navies of the Emperor, the Pope, and the Knights of St. John, as they lay at anchor in Preveza Bay. At the same moment a Venetian fleet of forty war galleys was seen rapidly approaching; these neutral vessels anchored at a convenient distance to await developments. It is my belief that the hot, windless days of August, 1532, decided the fate of the world for centuries to come. The Emperor's navy was commanded by Andrea Doria, undoubtedly the greatest admiral of all time, whom Charles had made Prince of Malfi. The commander of the Venetian fleet was Vincenzo Capello, who was strictly bound by the secret instructions of the Signoria. But the names of the Turkish sea pashas I shall not mention. I was informed of their shameful conduct by Mustafa ben-Nakir, who was eyewitness to these events.

Like his sovereign, Doria was a cautious man who would never give battle unless he were certain of winning. Perhaps he considered the Turkish war galleys too dangerous, although he numbered among his vessels the terrible carrack, that marvel of the seas—a floating fortress so lofty that her serried cannon could fire over the war galleys that commonly preceded her. Doria, then, did not attack, but secretly boarded the Venetian flagship to beg the commander to unite his force with the rest. No Mussulman fleet in the world could withstand them then, he said; they could proceed unhindered over the Aegean to the

334

Dardanelles and destroy the fortresses there in the twinkling of an eye. Then Istanbul itself, its ancient walls denuded of defenders by the Hungarian campaign, would fall an easy prey to the Christian navies.

But it was by no means to the Signoria's advantage that the Emperor should by this single stroke attain to world dominion, nor was it desirable to put a spoke in the Sultan's wheel. As the only well-matched opponent to the Emperor, he kept the nations of the world in healthy equipoise. Capello, therefore, as an obedient son of the illustrious Republic, politely declined on the grounds of the secret instructions he had received, though no one knows what these were. Then, mindful of the bonds of friendship uniting Venice with the Porte, Capello informed the two Turkish sea pashas of Doria's intentions. As a result these valiant men quite lost their heads, weighed anchor that night, and rowed back with might and main to the shelter of the Dardanelles, leaving the Greek coasts to their fate.

The return of the Moslem fleet in the utmost disarray, with its rowers half dead from exhaustion, threw Istanbul into a state of panic. The united navies of Christendom were expected to appear before the city at any moment. Wealthy Jews and Greeks began hurriedly packing their possessions for dispatch into Anatolia, and many of the highest officials discovered that their health required an immediate visit to the baths at Bursa. The garrisons of the Dardanelles fortresses were reinforced, and all available weapons supplied to them, while repairs were begun on the ruinous walls of Istanbul. The valiant caimacam was said to have sworn to die sword in hand at the gates of the Seraglio rather than capitulate, and this report, though intended as encouragement, gave the final impetus to the mad rush from the city.

So witless and cowardly had been the action of the Turkish fleet that not one of the Sultan's warships dared show herself at sea for a long time afterward. It was left to a young Dalmatian pirate, a beardless boy who later won renown under the nickname of the Young Moor, to bring to Istanbul the comforting tidings that Doria had abandoned his plan because his forces, unaided by the Venetian fleet, were insufficient to ensure victory. Instead he was laying siege to the fortress of Coron in Morea. The Young Moor had come to Istanbul to sell Christian prisoners from one of Doria's supply ships, captured by him off Coron. He had at his disposal one little felucca and a dozen

335

boys of the same mettle as himself, his only effective armament being a rusty iron cannon. Yet he seemed not to understand that he had done anything heroic in attacking Doria's whole fleet with one little vessel, though the Sultan's sea pashas had fled without even engaging it.

The news he brought restored calm; the caimacam sent an express to the Sultan at Guns to report that all was well and that the campaign might continue, while the inhabitants of Istanbul hailed the Young Moor as a hero and pointed the finger of scorn at the sea pashas.

Mustafa ben-Nakir had returned to Istanbul with the demoralized fleet, and on entering my house found Giulia and Alberto packing up my most valuable possessions with the help of the terrified slaves, while I studied the maps for the best route to Egypt where I meant to beg the protection of the good eunuch Suleiman. He passed on to us the Young Moor's reassuring news.

"Roll up your maps, my dear Michael," he added. "Doria's too old and cautious for such a gamble. Venice has saved us."

Giulia's eyes sparkled with indignation.

"Khurrem-sultana will never forgive the Grand Vizier for enticing the Ruler of the Faithful away into this foolish war and leaving us exposed to these perils. And if you had the least notion of how troublesome it will be to unpack all these pots and pans and ornaments and jars and mirrors and to put back all the curtains and carpets, you'd not laugh like that. I believe the Sultana is frightened enough to summon Khaireddin. Indeed he would have been sent for long ago had not the Grand Vizier been so eloquent in his praise; the Sultana is inclined to mistrust anything proposed by that ambitious schemer. But it's to be hoped that after this ill-managed affair his days are numbered."

Mustafa ben-Nakir answered mildly, "Let's not kick a man when he has already fallen. If the army returns safe and sound from Hungary we can allow the Grand Vizier to continue trusting to his star of fortune, this time in Persia. Sooner or later he'll break his own neck. The Sultan and Ibrahim are together. They encounter the same dangers and the same obstacles and no doubt share the same tent. The Sultana would be most unwise to hurl accusations at the Grand Vizier as soon as he returns, for half would fall on the Sultan, and not even an ordinary man can endure reproaches after an enterprise which in his heart he knows has failed."

Giulia opened her mouth to retort; yet she had been listening attentively and allowed Mustafa ben-Nakir to proceed without interruption.

"Persia is a big country; its mountain passes are treacherous and Shah Tahmasp with his gilded cavalry is a terrible foe—especially if, as I've heard, he is receiving arms from Spain. Would it not be wisest to send the Grand Vizier to that savage country alone? The Sultan is not obliged to go with the army; for once he can remain in the Seraglio to govern his people and make good laws, and remain beyond the all-too-powerful influence of his friend. If only I might have the opportunity of speaking to the most radiant Sultana, even through a curtain, I could whisper much good advice into her no-doubt seductive ear. It would be no sin for the slaves of the harem to speak to one of my sacred brotherhood, so long as the Kislar-Aga gave his permission."

He glanced at Giulia and then contemplated his polished nails, to give her time to reflect upon his proposal. But her flushed cheeks and averted eyes made it clear that she was only too anxious to convey Mustafa ben-Nakir's request to the Sultana as quickly as might be. And when shortly afterward I beheld our graceful boat speeding over the water to Seraglio Point I spoke warningly to Mustafa ben-Nakir.

"You frighten me. Don't count on me to join you in going behind my lord Ibrahim's back. And remember, he is the grand master of your order."

Mustafa ben-Nakir's fine eyes flashed as he replied, "How shortsighted you are, Michael! We must play the Russian's game so long as circumstances favor her. And I long to see for myself whether or not she is a witch. The Grand Vizier will be defenseless on his return, which is why we must persuade Khurrem that she would weaken her own influence by seeking his overthrow. No one could replace him, for he is the greatest statesman ever seen in the Ottoman Empire. And he will be master of the future if all goes as we hope. Without him the Sultan would be a reed bending to every wind. You don't want that epileptic boy of his to succeed?"

"But Prince Mustafa, not Prince Selim, is the eldest!" I exclaimed in astonishment.

"If the Sultan were to die, none but Ibrahim would dare to send the mutes to Khurrem's sons. So long as one of them is alive, a bowstring is all that can be predicted with certainty for Prince Mustafa."

I remembered little Prince Jehangir with his sad, sad eyes, and I

337

thought also of my dog. Sultana Khurrem had not treated me badly; on the contrary, she had saved my life and shown great kindness to my wife Giulia. I was filled with repugnance at the thought of what my loyalty to the Grand Vizier might one day entail. Mustafa ben-Nakir went on, "Grand Vizier Ibrahim will certainly not be defeated in Persia. Bagdad and Basrah will be in our hands before the outbreak of war, and our object this time is for Ibrahim to lead the army alone and garner the undivided honors of victory. The army must learn to look upon Ibrahim as their highest commander, and in the eyes of the people the crushing of the Shiite heresy will cover him with glory. The strongest will and the wisest head will govern Islam—with or without the Sultan. Only thus can Islam rule the whole world and the Prophet's promise find fulfilment. Peace be with him."

I looked at him with growing suspicion, never having seen him so carried away by his own words, and I could not but feel that for all his seeming candor he did not mean to reveal more than suited his own schemes.

"But," I began doubtfully. "But—"

I found no more to say, and there we left it. In the meantime I had my safe house on the Bosphorus, and in revulsion from a troublous world I slipped into indifference, drifting passively with the tide in the knowledge that were I to muster all my strength and resolution I could not alter the preordained course of events.

The fright I had had reminded me that my fortune and possessions were but a loan of which a defeat or a whim of the Sultan might deprive me at any time. Fortune had come too easily for me to believe that it could last, and thus it was that I took to visiting the great mosque where, beneath the celestial dome and surrounded by the Emperor Justinian's porphyry pillars, I would spend hours of quiet meditation.

Returning home one day I witnessed a curious incident. Stillness reigned in the garden and no slaves were to be seen, but when I stepped softly indoors so as not to disturb Giulia's customary midday rest, I heard Alberto's hoarse shout on the floor above, and Giulia's voice quivering with rage. I hurried up the stairs and as I drew aside the curtain I heard a sharp slap and a scream of pain. I stepped in to see Giulia bending sideways in fear, with tears streaming down her face. She held both hands to her cheeks, which were red from the blow, while Alberto stood before her with feet apart and hand uplifted, like an angry master chastising his slave. I stood petrified and incredulous, never having seen Giulia so meek and helpless. But perceiving that Alberto had really dared to strike her, I was filled with blinding rage and looked about for a weapon with which to slay this insolent slave. At sight of me they both started, and Alberto's face from being black with fury now turned ashy pale. I lifted a costly Chinese vase, meaning to bring it down on his head, but Giulia sprang between us, crying, "No, no, Michael! Don't smash that vase—it was a present from Sultana Khurrem. And this is all my fault. Alberto is innocent and meant no harm. It was I who angered him."

As I stared at her she took the vase from my hands and set it down carefully upon the floor. At first I thought I must have had a touch of the sun, so preposterous did it seem that Giulia of all people should permit a slave to strike her in the face, and then defend his action. We stood all three staring at one another. Then Alberto's face relaxed and with a meaning look at Giulia he turned and hurried out, ignoring my call to him to return. Giulia threw herself at me, stopped my mouth with her hand, and with tears still running down her swollen cheek she panted, "Are you out of your mind or drunk, Michael, to behave so? Let me at least explain. I should never forgive you if you wronged Alberto through a misunderstanding, for he's the best servant I ever had, and quite innocent."

"But," I said, rather flustered, "he'll get away before I can catch him. I mean to give him a hundred good lashes on the soles of his feet and send him down to the bazaar to be sold. We cannot keep a raving madman in the house."

Giulia seemed ill at ease, and said, "You don't understand, Michael, and you'd better be quiet. It's I who owe Alberto an apology; I lost my temper and struck him for some trifle that I've already forgotten— and don't stand there staring like an idiot! You madden me. If my face is swollen it's from toothache and I was on my way to the Seraglio dentist when you came in and interfered—slinking in to spy on me, though God knows I've nothing to hide. But if you lay a finger on Alberto I shall go to the cadi and in the presence of witnesses declare myself divorced. Alberto has suffered enough from your bad temper, though he's a proud, sensitive man and not baseborn like you."

At this I flew into a passion and seizing her by the wrists I shook her and shouted, "Are you really a witch, then, Giulia—a devil in human shape? For my own sake I would not believe it, but even the strongest pitcher can go to the well too often. Never do I want to think ill of you, for I love you still. But to let a slave strike you and go unpunished is unnatural. I don't know you. Who are you, and what have you to do with that miserable wretch?"

Giulia burst into violent weeping; she flung her arms about my neck and stroked my cheek with her hair. Then with downcast eyes she said faintly, "Ah, Michael, I'm only a foolish woman and of course you know best. But let us go into our room to talk it over. It's not fit that our slaves should hear us quarreling."

She grasped my hand and I followed her unresisting to our bed-chamber where, having dried her tears, she began abstractedly to undress.

"You can talk while I change my clothes. I must go to the dentist and cannot show myself at the Seraglio in this old rag. But you may go on talking and reproach me to your heart's content for being so bad a wife to you."

As she spoke she removed everything but the thin shift that she wore next her skin, and took out one gown after another to decide which best became her. Truth to tell it was long since she had accorded me the joys of marriage, and was most often assailed by a violent headache when I approached her. Therefore when I beheld her naked in the clear light of day I was spellbound by her alluring white skin, the soft curves of her limbs, and the golden hair curling freely over her bosom.

She noticed that I was staring at her, and sighed plaintively, "Ah, Michael, you've only one thought in your head! Don't glare at me so."

She crossed her arms over her breast and looked sideways at me with those strange eyes that in my unreason I could not forbear loving. My ears sang, my body glowed, and in a tremulous voice I begged her to wear the green velvet gown embroidered with pearls. She took it up, then let it fall again and instead chose a white and yellow brocade with a jeweled girdle.

"This yellow dress is more slimming to the hips—"

Her face took on a soft expression as she stood there with the gown in her hands, and she said, "Michael, tell me truly. Are you weary of your wife? Since you've taken to entertaining those new friends of yours you seem less close to me than you once were. Be honest with me. You've only to go to the cadi to be divorced from me. How should I force upon you the love your indifference has so often wounded?" She sobbed, and after a pause went on, "The love of women is a capricious thing and must ever be wooed afresh. It's long since you brought me flowers or showed me any other attention. No, you push a purse into my hand and tell me to buy what I want, and this coldness has hurt me deeply. That's why I have been so irritable—and perhaps that's why I struck Alberto, who bears only good will to both of us. So you see it has all been your fault, Michael, and I cannot remember when last you took me in your arms and kissed me as a man kisses the woman he loves."

Her wild and groundless accusations took my breath away, but shyly she drew near me and pressed her warm white body against me, saying, "Kiss me, Michael! You know you're the only man I ever loved—the only man whose kisses really satisfy me. Perhaps in your eyes I seem old and worn out, and like all Moslems you desire a new and younger wife. But kiss me!"

I kissed her treacherous lips, and what ensued need not be told, for the wise man will guess and for the fool all explanations are vain. All I can say is that barely an hour later I went readily down to Alberto to beg his pardon on Giulia's behalf because she had so exasperated him as to make him strike her. I asked him to overlook the hard words I had flung at him, and ended by giving him two ducats. Alberto listened without betraying by the flicker of an eyelid what he was thinking, but he took the money and confessed freely that his behavior had been most unbecoming. Peace reigned in the house once more. Giulia hid her somewhat weary eyes behind a thin veil and was rowed to the Seraglio. May a wiser man rebuke my blindness; I cannot. A man in love is always blind, be he the Sultan himself or the meanest of slaves, and it is easy for a landsman to be wise about a shipwreck. Let the clever man cast a glance at his own marriage before sneering at mine.

I was not the only blind man. Sultana Khurrem received Mustafa ben-Nakir in the presence of the Kislar-Aga and spoke with him first from behind the curtain; later she revealed to him her laughing face. When the cool Mustafa returned from the Seraglio he was like another being. He sped to me on winged feet. His eyes shone and his pale face glowed. The first things he asked of me were wine and roses, and with an autumn rose in his hand he said, "Ah, Michael! Either I've lost my understanding of character or we have been entirely mistaken in this woman. Roxelana is like the glow of morning. Her complexion is snow and roses, her laughter is silver, and to look into her eyes is to see a smiling heaven. No evil thought could lurk behind that white forehead. I'm out of my senses, Michael, and know not what to think of her or of myself. For Allah's sake melt amber in wine, call musicians, sing to me, for devine poems are welling up in my heart and no one has lain under such a spell before."

"Allah be gracious to you, dear Mustafa ben-Nakir!" I stammered at last. "Surely you cannot have fallen in love with that diabolical Russian!"

"How should I dare to lift my eyes to the gates of heaven? But no one can forbid me to drink wine mixed with amber, to scatter my verses to the winds, or to play upon a reed pipe in praise of Khurrem the beautiful."

He wept tears of rapture while I surveyed him with distaste and said, "The Sultana is a shameless woman to flout custom and the law by unveiling her face and so leading you into temptation. How could the Kislar-Aga permit it? But tell me, did you speak to her of the Grand Vizier? And what did she say? That, after all, is the most important thing."

Mustafa ben-Nakir dried his tears, and forgetting for once to polish his rose-colored nails he looked at me in wonder and said, "I don't remember. I recall nothing of what we said, for I listened only to the music of her voice and her laughter until she unveiled her face. Then I was so bewitched that when she left me my head was like a blown egg. Compared with the miracle that has happened all else is indifferent to me."

Giddy with wine he sprang up and began to dance, stamping rhythmically and joyously ringing the silver bells at his girdle. And as he danced he crooned love songs until I began to suspect he had been eating hashish. Yet his delirium infected me and filled me with an irresistible desire to laugh. I blended drops of fragrant ambergris in the wine and soon I seemed to see how destiny sped like a gazelle from the swiftest hunter, and mocked the vain pursuit.

At the beginning of winter the Sultan and the Grand Vizier returned with the army from the campaign in Hungary, after striking terror to the hearts of all Christendom and revealing the formidable might of the Ottoman Empire. For five days there were celebrations in the city and the nights were bright with bonfires. From the arsenal, colored fiery serpents sprang into the air, and burning oil was poured upon the waters until waves of fire rolled over the dark surface of the Golden Horn.

In this joyous tumult discord was drowned. The price of slaves dropped, the spahis found cheap labor for their farms, and the Sultan distributed lavish presents among his janissaries, so that harmony and peace prevailed. The people are ever willing to forgive the errors of princes, but upstarts come off less lightly. Nevertheless, Ibrahim was too proud to show how deeply he was hurt by certain stifled murmurs.

He would not allow himself to be blinded by his own proclamations of victory, or by the fireworks that he had commanded. From the steps of his palace he surveyed with a wry smile the crowds that filled the Atmeidan, and said, "War was inevitable, Michael el-Hakim. The Western menace has been removed and the time has come to set our faces to the East. Spread the news as widely as you can, and above all tell your remarkable wife, that she may bring it to the knowledge of Khurrem-sultana."

Throughout the winter and spring Ibrahim had great need of my services. Besides an ambassador from King Ferdinand, there arrived also one from Venice to claim recompense for the service rendered us in Preveza Bay. The Venetian colony in Galata received their envoy with high honors. The Sultan, in token of his displeasure with the sea pashas, promoted the Young Moor to the command of four war galleys with which to blockade the port of Coron in Morea, recently captured by Doria. To show how lightly he valued Coron compared with Hungary, he sent thither battle-scarred old Jahja-pasha with five thousand janissaries and the curt command to decide for himself which he valued most: his own battered head or a horsehair switch at the top of Coron tower.

The Young Moor blockaded Coron from the sea, but in the summer Doria came cruising off the point with the united navies of the Pope and the Knights of St. John, meaning to break through to the fortress with provisions and powder. The sea pashas, enraged by the Sultan's disfavor, followed the Moor with some seventy sail to Coron, where the young hero, crying on the name of the Prophet, bore down upon Doria and threw his supply ships into confusion, heedless of the guns of the terrible carrack. For very shame the sea pashas were compelled to take a hand.

Doria now found himself forced into open battle, though his inten-

343

tion had been merely to run the blockade and then make off at once. The Young Moor sank several transports while others were driven onto the rocks. Then he attacked the first of the Knights' galleys, hove grapnels over her rail, and had already captured her by the time the sea pashas came to his support.

Amid the roar of cannon that echoed among the hills, amid the billowing, concealing smoke, the splintering of oars, and the yells of the combatants, the Young Moor showed the pashas how sea battles are fought. And these worthies in their fright forced their way in among Doria's vessels to form a ring about the galleys of the Young Moor, whom they dragged forcibly from the deck of his prize. He was wounded in the head, arm, and side, but still he wept and cursed and cried to the devil for aid. After rowing aimlessly hither and thither and colliding with one another, the valiant pashas at last extricated themselves from the enemy and removed the Young Moor's two remaining galleys to safety.

Doria, greatly startled by the unexpected belligerence of the sea pashas, did not attempt pursuit, but was content to land his supplies with all speed and stand away for home. The sea pashas Zey and Himeral at first could not believe in their glorious victory over the hitherto invincible Doria; then, in triumph, they hoisted all their flags and pennants and even unwound their turbans to stream them in the wind, amid the noise of trumpets, drums, and cymbals. The only flaw in their triumph was the unseemly behavior of the Young Moor, who with clenched fists and tears of indignation abused the pashas as cowards and traitors.

But who could long harbor resentment on so glad an evening? They freely forgave the stripling on the grounds that he was delirious from fever, and bound him to his cot lest he leap overboard.

Nevertheless the boy was cheered by Jahja-pasha who, having followed the course of the engagement from the shore, rowed over to the Moslem flagship that evening, bawling curses all the way until the most hardened sea janissaries turned pale. Once aboard, this doughty warrior, whose head was the stake in the game for Coron, seized Himeral-pasha by the beard and smote him in the face. The one object of the naval action, he screamed, had been at all costs to prevent the relief of Coron, and by failing in this simple task the pashas had prolonged the siege possibly for weeks, though Coron had been on the point of capitulation. The sea pashas saw that the fear of losing his head had made him mad, and with united strength they cuffed and buffeted him back into his boat.

Yet because of the foolhardy conduct of the Young Moor, not all the supply ships had reached the fortress, and a state of famine still prevailed there. The Greek inhabitants of the town lacked the endurance of the Spaniards, and during the night they crept beyond the walls in search of roots and bark. Some of these men fell into the hands of Jahja's janissaries and at his orders were gruesomely tortured next morning in full view of the garrison. This spectacle had its effect; the Spaniards surrendered and were permitted to embark and sail away with full military honors.

Thanks to the agents of the Knights of St. John, Doria kept abreast of Seraglio affairs and was well aware that Sultan Suleiman had offered Khaireddin the command of all his ships, ports, islands, and seas. It was said that Khaireddin welcomed this appointment with tears of joy, and having left the reins of government in the hands of his young son Hassan—under the guardianship of a trustworthy captain—he at once set sail for Sicilian waters in the hope of cutting off Doria's retreat from Coron and crushing him between the Algerian vessels and the Sultan's fleet, which he naturally supposed would give chase. Doria eluded him, however, and after a profitable engagement with a pirate, Khaireddin sailed away with his prizes to meet the sea pashas. These received him with the proper honors, though grudgingly, and Khaireddin reviled them for their cowardice and their failure to do their part in the capture of Doria. He then ordered them to release the Young Moor, whom he embraced and treated like his own son.

All this I learned from hearsay, but that autumn I saw for myself how Khaireddin's forty ships glided majestically up the Marmara and anchored in the Golden Horn. From Scutari on the Asiatic side to the hills of Pera, the shores were white with people, and the Sultan himself stepped onto his marble quay to watch the vessels pass. Their thunderous salute echoed over land and sea and was answered by the guns of other ships anchored in the harbor. The most eminent pashas and renegade captains made haste to greet Khaireddin as he stepped ashore.

Khaireddin stood beaming under a gold-fringed canopy to receive the manifold welcome. His once-red beard was now venerably gray, and reached, with some artificial aid, to his belt. He had painted wrinkles on his face and shadows about his prominent eyes, so as to

345

vie in age with the Sultan's sea pashas, though I believe he was then not a day over fifty.

The inhabitants of Istanbul had much to divert them during this time. On the third day after his arrival Khaireddin set off in ceremonial procession to a reception at the Seraglio. He was attended by janissaries in red and gold, and a hundred camels followed laden with gifts for the Sultan—bales of silk and brocade and such curiosities as an uncultured pirate would collect in the course of years. Worthless trash and priceless treasures lay higgledy-piggledy together. The greatest sensation was aroused by two hundred lovely young girls bearing gold and silver dishes in which lay purses filled with gold and silver coin. These slaves had been selected for the Sultan's harem from every known land, though the greater number were from Sicily, Italy, and Spain. When with faces unveiled they bore their treasure into the Sultan's presence even the staidest Moslems were dazzled by their beauty; they were obliged to hold their hands before their faces and only peep through their fingers, lest they be brought into a state of impurity before the hour of prayer.

In the hall of pillars with its starry roof, Sultan Suleiman received Khaireddin, first allowing him to kiss his foot, which rested on a cushion covered with diamonds, and then stretching forth his hand in token of special favor. It was certainly the proudest moment in the life of the erstwhile potter, the spahi's son from the island of Mytilene. When first he spoke he stammered and shed tears of joy, but the Sultan smilingly encouraged him, bidding him tell of Algeria and other African lands—of Sicily, Italy, and Spain, and above all of ships, seafaring, and the sea. Khaireddin needed no second bidding and spoke in bolder and bolder fashion, not forgetting to mention that he had brought with him the Prince of Tunis, Rashid ben-Hafs, who had fled from his bloodthirsty brother Muley-Hassan and come under Khaireddin's protection to seek comfort and help from the Refuge of all Nations.

To my way of thinking Khaireddin acted unwisely in so promptly revealing his own selfish aims. He would have done better to speak of Doria and his big guns, the carrack of the Knights of St. John, and such things as had won him the honor of an audience with the Sultan. I believe that his childish boasting did him more harm than the slander of his bitterest enemies; in the middle of the ceremony Iskender-*tseleb's* scornful laugh was plainly heard. Khaireddin, drunk with

346

good fortune, responded only by a broad smile, but the Sultan frowned.

Despite the princely gifts he brought with him, Khaireddin therefore made by no means so good an impression as he fancied. The Sultan allotted him a house to live in, as the custom was, but let him wait in vain for the three horsetail switches that had been promised him. Meanwhile Zey-pasha and Himeral-pasha vied with one another in spreading tales of his unseemly way of life, his conceit, untrustworthiness, cruelty, and greed. These stories were the more dangerous in that they contained a grain of truth. Yet Khaireddin's greatest error had been to stay too long at sea, for when at last he came to Istanbul, Grand Vizier Ibrahim had already started for Aleppo to open the Persian campaign, whereby Khaireddin lost his strongest support in the Divan.

But my account of Khaireddin has led me to anticipate. Between the dispatch of his invitation and his arrival, negotiations with Vienna were brought to a favorable conclusion, and having thus secured a lasting peace and permanent frontiers in the West, the Grand Vizier set his face toward the East. Many Persian noblemen who had sought the protection of the Porte accompanied him to Aleppo, the assembly point for the campaign.

I should mention that Khaireddin ignored me in a most ungrateful manner, and in his blindness seemed to think that he now needed neither my help nor the Grand Vizier's. Hurt though I was, however, I knew the Seraglio and bided my time. Only a few days later I observed—and not without a certain malicious pleasure—that his house stood unvisited and that silence had fallen upon his name, while the townspeople began uttering ever louder complaints of his seamen. For these renegades, Moors, and Negroes, who during the summer had fought and plundered afloat and in the winter roistered and brawled in Algiers, knew nothing of the well-mannered customs of the Sultan's capital and assumed that they could behave there as they did in their own harbors. They even went so far as to stab two Armenians who did not get out of their way quickly enough—an unheard-of occurrence in the Sultan's city where even to bear arms was an offense and where the janissaries who kept order carried nothing but light bamboo canes. At first Khaireddin would not hear of executing the culprits, explaining that Armenians were Christians, to slay whom was an act pleasing to Allah. Only when he found that his reputation suffered and that the Sultan remained inaccessible and silent within the Seraglio did he climb down and have three men hanged and ten flogged.

But it was too late. With growing dismay he noted how abrupt were the turns of fortune in this city, and he took to dictating childish letters to the Sultan in which he alternately groveled and threatened to leave his service for that of the Emperor. Fortunately Khaireddin's *tseleb* was intelligent enough to destroy these letters at once.

As a last resort, the puffed-up sea captain humbled himself and sent for me to discuss certain matters. To make clear to him my rank and standing I sent him word again that my door stood open if he wished to consult me, but that I could not spare the time to go running all round the harbor looking for him. After tugging his beard for three days he came, bringing with him my old friends Torgut and Sinan the Jew, who were as shocked as himself at the Sultan's behavior. He looked about him with wonder at the marble steps of my landing stage and at my splendid house that rose dreamlike from terraces ablaze with flowers, though the autumn was far advanced.

"What a city!" he exclaimed. "Slaves live in gilded mansions and wear kaftans of honor, while a poor old man whose whole life has been devoted to increasing the Sultan's honor on the high seas must creep in rags to the throne without winning so much as a kind word for all his labors."

To give outward expression to his injured feelings he had put on a plain camlet kaftan, with only a little diamond crescent in his turban in token of his dignity. I attended him with all due honor into the house and bade him be seated. Then I set the cooks to work and summoned Abu el-Kasim and Mustafa ben-Nakir, that we might all confer together as in the old days in Algiers. They came promptly. Khaireddin sent for the wares he had brought from his ship and lavished on us presents of ivory, ostrich feathers, flowered gold brocade, and silver vessels adorned with Italian coats of arms. Sighing heavily he followed these up with a purse of gold for each of us.

"Let all discord between us be forgotten," he said. "After bestowing these presents I'm a poor man and hardly know where my next meal is to come from. Forgive me for failing to recognize you when you came aboard my ship to greet me. I was already dazed by all the rejoicings—and then you've grown so much handsomer!"

When we had all eaten and drunk, Khaireddin at last came to the point and asked the meaning of the Sultan's silence. I therefore told him frankly all I had heard in the Seraglio and reminded him that he had needlessly aroused the resentment of the sea pashas and offended even the gentle Piri-reis by deriding his model ships and his sandbox. And he had come too late, I said: the Grand Vizier was in Aleppo and in his absence the pashas gave the Sultan no peace. They told him he stained his honor by taking into his service a ruffianly pirate, when in the arsenal and Seraglio there were many experienced pashas who had served him long and faithfully without thought of reward. Khaireddin ought not to be trusted with war galleys, for he would only make off with them as his brother had done and fight less for the glory of Islam than for his own temporal profit.

I enlarged upon this and did my best to mimic the whining tones of the pashas until Khaireddin flushed, tore his beard, and sprang up exclaiming, "What foolish and wicked accusations! I have never done anything but labor for the greater glory of Islam. These raises in their silken kaftans who sit on dry land and play at battles with their maps and compasses and sandboxes! It would do them good to smell powder and burning pitch now and then. But thanklessness is all our reward in this world."

At this point Giulia drew aside the curtain and stepped in, wearing her lovely golden-brown velvet dress and a pearl-sewn net over her hair. She feigned alarm, made as if to draw her diaphanous veil across her face, and exclaimed, "Oh, Michael, how you all startled me! Why did you not tell me we had guests—and such welcome guests, too! I couldn't help overhearing something of what you were saying, and I shall therefore give you a piece of advice. Why do you not appeal to a certain exalted and sympathetic lady who has the Sultan's ear? If you wish I can speak a word to her on your behalf, provided Khaireddin will beg forgiveness of her for his most wounding and inconsiderate behavior."

Khaireddin demanded wrathfully how he could have offended Khurrem. He had presented her with ten thousand ducats' worth of ornaments and fabrics—enough surely for the most pampered and exacting woman. But Giulia shook her head with a smile.

"How stupid you men are! One of Sultana Khurrem's gowns alone costs ten thousand ducats, and she receives ten times that amount yearly in pin money from the Sultan. Your present is neither here nor there, but she was greatly incensed at the two hundred girls you sent, as if there were not already enough of the useless creatures in the

349

harem, without your pock-marked, squinting scarecrows! The Sultana was obliged to distribute them among the governors of remote provinces. For many years past the Sultan has had no eyes for any woman but Khurrem, so you may fancy how you have hurt her. However, I have spoken on your behalf and assured her that being an uncultured seaman you've not yet learned how to behave in the Seraglio."

Khaireddin was scarlet in the face and his eyes goggled as he cried, "I put my faith in the one God! With the eye of an expert I chose each one of those girls myself; they were lovely as the virgins of Paradise and as pure—that is, generally speaking. Even the most devoted husband may weary of one wife and whet his blunted desires elsewhere, only to return to her with the greater ardor. Yet if Khurrem-sultana is really able to keep her husband's love to herself alone, then indeed I believe in her power and I'm sure that she can help me to the three horsehair switches that have been promised me."

"But it was Ibrahim who summoned you hither!" I exclaimed in dismay. "It would be altogether wrong for you to be indebted to Sultana Khurrem for your advancement, and I suspect in this a subtle intrigue to humiliate the Grand Vizier."

Giulia shook her head and there were tears in her eyes as she replied, "Ah, Michael, how little you trust me, though I've told you a thousand times—the Sultana bears no ill will to anyone! She has promised to speak to the Sultan on Khaireddin's behalf and is willing to receive Khaireddin from behind the curtain. Let us go at once to the Seraglio, that the Kislar-Aga may prepare a reception for Khaireddin and his senior captains—for it would be well for Khaireddin to arrive at the Seraglio with a brilliant retinue, that all may witness the favor he enjoys."

As Khaireddin's former slave I went with them to watch developments on the Grand Vizier's behalf. Our arrival at the Seraglio was unpromising, for the janissaries made scornful gestures and the eunuchs turned their backs, but by the time we took our departure the news had spread. Blessings now rained upon us and the janissaries sitting by their cooking pots sprang up and cheered. It was a plain indication of the influence that Sultana Khurrem now exerted in the Seraglio.

She spoke with Khaireddin from behind the curtain and laughed her rippling laughter. But having flattered him and told him that he was the only adversary worthy of Doria, she chattered on about trivial matters, to my great relief, and ordered her slave women to serve us with fruits preserved in honey. Nevertheless she promised to speak for Khaireddin to the Sultan.

"But," said she, "the sea pashas are irascible old men, and I would not hurt their feelings. All I can do is to tell my lord of the excellent impression I have of you, great Khaireddin. I will chide him gently for so long neglecting to give you the reward you deserve. He may reply, 'It was the Grand Vizier's suggestion, not mine, and the sea pashas in the Divan opposed it.' Then I shall say, 'Let the Grand Vizier decide! If having seen Khaireddin he is of the same mind, then bestow at once on the great man the three horsehair switches you promised him, and show him honor.' The Grand Vizier has full powers and not even a unanimous Divan can reverse his decision."

I could hardly believe my ears. She was renouncing in favor of the Grand Vizier all the advantages she would have gained had Khaireddin been indebted to her for his promotion. Charmed by her voice and her purling laughter I began to think that jealousy alone had inspired the Grand Vizier's opinion of this lovely woman.

Accordingly, Khaireddin left for Aleppo, and shortly afterward Abu el-Kasim came to me and rubbing his hands together in some embarrassment he said, "Your enchanting daughter Mirmah is getting her teeth and no doubt will soon cease to suck at that opulent breast. I have a great favor to ask of you, Michael el-Hakim. Will you sell me that round-cheeked nurse and her son? for I feel old age creeping upon me and would gladly have so soft and white a pillow for my head. The boy shall be my heir."

I was astonished, for from motives of thrift Abu el-Kasim avoided feminine society almost entirely. Nor was I sure whether I could grant his request. I said, "Giulia may not agree to this. And there is another point. I would be loath to hurt your feelings, Abu el-Kasim, but you are after all a dirty, skinny, stringy-bearded old man, while the nurse is in the flower of life. My conscience forbids me to sell her to you against her will."

Abu el-Kasim sighed and wrung his hands and enlarged upon his passion, and when I asked how he meant to pay for the woman and her son he suggested hopefully that we might effect an exchange.

"I will give you my deaf-mute whom you've always coveted. That scar on your head should remind you how conscientious a watchman he is, and you will never regret the bargain."

I burst into a fit of laughter at this idiotic proposal, until it occurred to me that he would never have made it unless he believed me the greatest simpleton Allah ever created. My laughter ceased and I replied with asperity, "Not even on the strength of our friendship should you suggest such a thing. I'm no pander and I refuse to hand over this woman to your senile lust for so paltry a return."

Abu el-Kasim hastened to explain further.

"But I was in earnest, for my deaf-mute is a treasure of whom I alone know the value. Have you not often seen him sitting among the yellow dogs of the Seraglio and observing all that goes on? When you lived in my house you must also have noticed how queer strangers came to visit him and converse with him. He is not the fool you take him for."

I did indeed recall a couple of powerful Negroes who sometimes sat with him in the courtyard making rapid signs to him with hands and fingers. Yet such visitors in no way enhanced the value of Abu el-Kasim's feeble-minded slave, and again I refused sharply even to consider the matter. But Abu el-Kasim, looking about him cautiously, bent forward and whispered, "My slave is a treasure, but only in the neighborhood of the Seraglio. To take him back with me to Tunis would be to bury a diamond in a dunghill. He is as faithful to me as a dog because I'm the only man in the world who has shown him kindness, but you too would gain his devotion by a friendly word or two and a pat on the shoulder. Now you must often have seen three deaf-mutes pacing through the courts of the Seraglio. Their clothes are blood red, and over their shoulders they wear silken nooses of different colors. No one looks them in the face, for their striking dress gives passers-by enough to think about. There are seven in all, and when on duty they walk about in threes. They bring a silent death and even the most exalted pashas tremble at their blood-red clothes and dragging footsteps. Being deaf-mutes they cannot utter a word about their work, but such men can converse among themselves in a language understood by deaf-mutes in all lands. My slave is on good terms with these fellows and they chatter together in sign language to an extent altogether unsuspected by the Sultan. I have taken pains to learn their signs and have acquired much terrible knowledge, though in my position I can make no use of it. But you have won to a high position and the day may soon come when knowledge of what the deaf-mutes say to one another may be of inestimable value."

I had noticed certain incidents that bore out what he said, yet I still did not fully appreciate his offer, for the deaf-mute inspired me only with repugnance. Nevertheless a quite unexpected impulse of generosity caused me to answer, to my own surprise, "You're my friend, Abu el-Kasim, and a man of my rank and standing should show liberality to his friends. Take the Russian, if she consents to go with you, and her son too; you shall have them as a present from me, in the name of the Compassionate. And I will take care of your slave. He shall sleep in the porter's hut or under the boathouse, but had better keep out of sight during the day. The less Giulia sees of him the better."

"Believe me," said the old rogue piously, "you won't regret the bargain. But never hint the reason for it to your wife. Learn the deaf-and-dumb language secretly; if Giulia seems inquisitive, blame me and say I persuaded you into this foolish bargain when you were in your cups. This she will readily believe."

In the course of the winter Khaireddin returned from Aleppo, much shaken by his long ride. Ibrahim had received him with all honor, confirmed his appointment as beylerbey in Algeria and other African countries, and decreed that he should take precedence before all governors of similar standing. This alone was a high honor and carried with it membership in the Divan, but the Grand Vizier also dispatched a letter to the Sultan, having first read it aloud to Khaireddin to leave him in no doubt as to where thanks were due for his promotion.

"In him," the letter ran, "we have at last found a true seaman worthy of the highest honors, whom you may appoint without misgivings as pasha, member of the Divan, and admiral of the fleet."

The Grand Vizier sent me a copy of this letter and added, "Khaireddin is at heart even more childish than I thought, however bold and cunning he may be at sea. Honors go to his head like incense, for he cannot forget his low birth. He is won by flattery—the grosser the better—and this makes him an easy prey to the intrigues of the Seraglio. Therefore I have thought it best to load him with as many honors as possible, that there may be nothing left for others to tempt him with. I believe also that because of his childish nature he is relatively honest; nevertheless keep a sharp eye on him and let me know at once if he should show the least sign of treachery to me or to the Sultan. Africa is Khaireddin's weak spot; we must support his enterprises in Tunisia lest the Emperor tempt him with it. Tunis can also serve as a good base for our conquest of Sicily."

Regardless of my warnings, Khaireddin puffed himself up like a frog and prepared a long speech to the Sultan, to be delivered before the Divan. On receiving Ibrahim's letter the Sultan hesitated no longer; indeed, I believe he was overjoyed that for once his beloved Khurrem and Ibrahim were agreed, and he lost no time in calling the Divan. At this assembly he presented Khaireddin with a sword whose hilt and scabbard sparkled with countless diamonds, and he conferred upon him the Vizier's standard of three horsehair switches and the title of Kapudan-pasha of the navy, with unlimited powers at sea. This represented something very different from the authority vested in senior Venetian officers, for example. The eyes of the Signoria were ever upon these men and their powers were limited by the sealed orders issued to them beforehand to cover different situations. But the Sultan nominated Khaireddin independent governor of all his ports and islands, with supreme command of all vessels and their captains. In naval matters he was subordinate to none but the Sultan, and at meetings of the Divan he took his place beside the Sultan's viziers. Thus the erstwhile potter was elevated at a stroke to rank with the four or five most eminent men in the Ottoman Empire.

In acknowledgment of these unprecedented honors, Khaireddin delivered a voluble and bombastic address in a voice with which he was used to make himself heard above the roar of the elements, until some of the eunuchs cast anxious glances upward, fearing the collapse of the starry roof. He brought the speech to an end with the following words: "In short, I mean to inflict as much damage as I may upon the unbelievers and carry the Crescent to honor and victory upon the seas. First I shall overwhelm, destroy, annihilate, and sink the idolater Doria, who is my personal enemy. Let me conquer Tunis as I have so often besought you, and thereby gain an important base for the fleet. For centuries the caravan routes from the Negro lands beyond the desert have converged upon this city, and I shall be able to send you and your harem an abundance of gold dust and ostrich feathers. But dominion of the seas is naturally my chief aim. And believe me, O Commander of the Faithful, he who rules the sea soon comes to rule the lands about that sea!"

I have quoted this much of his address to show how irresponsible, childish, and rash was Khaireddin's conduct in the Seraglio. Little did he know of the ways of the Divan when he thus trumpeted abroad his private schemes. A whisper in the Divan quickly arrived at every court in Europe, and no earthly power could prevent it even when, according to ancient Ottoman tradition, the Divan was held on horseback to discuss questions of peace and war. Yet strange as it may seem, once at sea Khaireddin outdid all his rivals in cunning, and because of his notorious guile the Imperial envoys would not believe that his main objective was indeed Tunis. They laughed at him up their sleeves for fancying he could delude them. The Knights of St. John were convinced that he intended the capture of Malta, while others believed that Rome itself or Cartagena was in his mind.

Yet however ludicrous Khaireddin's behavior in the Divan, it must be stressed that in seafaring matters he had no equal. No sooner had the horsetail switches been bestowed than he rolled up the sleeves of his kaftan of honor and started a great turnout of the arsenal. Many useless heads ended under the archway of the Gate of Peace, and to replace various Seraglio-trained striplings in silken kaftans Khaireddin appointed seasoned renegades. He laid down the keels of new war galleys and reorganized the distribution of sea pashas among the islands and along the coasts, so as to bring back capable men to arsenal and ships.

The spring cleaning of the arsenal stirred up the same conflicts that had cost Andy his plume, though this time the roles were reversed. Having now encountered the terrifying carrack of the Knights of St. John, the old sea pashas at last showed an inclination to move with the times and demanded larger craft to carry heavier armaments. But although Khaireddin fully appreciated the firing powers of these great Christian vessels, yet he considered them too slow in maneuvering and, as an experienced pirate, attached far more importance to speed and mobility than to size.

It was now Khaireddin's business, through my mediation, to be reconciled with Chief Pilot Piri-reis, whom he had so deeply wounded by his contemptuous behavior, for notwithstanding his sneers he had the greatest respect for the famous book of charts and valued the old man's advice more than he would admit. They debated long together as to the respective merits of large and small vessels, but whereas Piri-reis spoke in favor of the former, Khaireddin remained unconvinced and preferred to act upon his own experience.

355

After the spring rains the Grand Vizier began the march from Aleppo to Persia at the head of his magnificent army, and at once the Sultan was seized with a great restlessness. Fresh winds were blowing, and the stuffy air of the Seraglio so irked him that despite all tenderly whispered dissuasion he was minded to set out in time to lead the forthcoming campaign.

Meanwhile Khaireddin hoisted sail and the greatest and best-appointed fleet ever seen off Istanbul stood out to sea. Andy sailed with him in the flagship as master gunner, Abu el-Kasim embarked also, while I remained behind to spread helpful rumors as to Khaireddin's real intentions. I succeeded best with the story that he was bound for Genoa, to recapture that city on behalf of the French King, for everyone knew what a triumph it would be for him to swoop on Doria's very aerie. This attempt of mine to keep Doria within the shelter of his city succeeded beyond all hope, and I was thus of far greater service to Khaireddin than if I had gone to sea with him as his adviser.

The Sultan had much to attend to before setting forth to war, including the imprisonment of Rashid ben-Hafs, Prince of Tunis, which was so secretly effected that Khaireddin's own officers believed the Prince had sailed with them and was merely staying below decks because of the rolling seas. But undoubtedly the most important step taken by Suleiman was the appointment of Prince Mustafa as Governor of Anatolia. The Prince was now fifteen years old and had ruled as sanjak over a district; this new appointment finally confirmed the Sultan's choice of Mustafa as his lawful heir, though many had been led by Sultana Khurrem's ever increasing influence to doubt this. Pious Moslems, dazzled by the incomparable splendor of their military and naval forces, were persuaded that the great age of Islam had dawned. Only Sultana Khurrem was silent.

One day toward the end of summer, I was crossing the janissaries' deserted courtyard, with my perfumed handkerchief to my nose because of the stench of severed heads from the vaults of the Gateway of Peace, when a limping onbash came up to me, struck me roughly on the shoulder with his cane, and having made sure of my name announced that he had orders to arrest me—to throw me in chains and confine me in the Fort of the Seven Towers.

356

I shouted aloud for help and insisted that there must be some terrible mistake, since I had nothing to hide and all my actions could bear the light of day. But the onbash silenced me with a blow across the mouth, and before I was fully aware of what was happening he had taken me to the smith, who riveted shackles about my ankles and held out a sooty hand—I must reward him for neither burning me nor breaking my bones. A sack was drawn over my head lest any in the street should recognize me. I was lifted onto a donkey and led the long way from the Seraglio to the Fort of the Seven Towers.

The constable, a thin-lipped eunuch, received me in person, for my rank and position were well known. He made me undress, searched and removed my clothes, giving me a worn camlet kaftan, and asked me politely whether I would have a cook of my own or be content with prison fare, which would cost me only two aspers a day. This sudden stunning blow of fate had so clouded my understanding that in a faint voice I declared myself satisfied to eat the same food as other prisoners. I was resolved to mortify my flesh and pass my time in pious meditation after my life of luxury in the Sultan's service.

I bade the eunuch take from my purse a sum befitting his rank and dignity, and hoped that in return he would inform my unfortunate wife as to where I was and what had happened. But he shook his head and told me that this was out of the question, since all state prisoners must be kept as completely cut off from the outer world as if they dwelt in the moon.

This eunuch showed me the greatest consideration and respect, and even exerted himself to climb with me up the steep stairs to show me the view from the marble pinnacles of the Golden Gate. At the same time I had the opportunity of observing the measures taken to defend the fort against assailants, and I believe that the walls alone that linked one tower with the next were enough to sever us from the outer world.

In the square marble tower of the Golden Gate he showed me bricked-up, windowless vaults into which food was passed through an opening the width of a hand. These were designed for the highest princes of Osman's line and for viziers and members of the Divan, whose rank did not permit them to be shackled. With pardonable pride he pointed to one wall and told me that not even the oldest warder knew who lived behind it, and the prisoner himself could not tell him, as his tongue had been cut out on his arrest many, many years ago. He then showed me the deep hole through which corpses were thrown into the moat and thence carried away into the Marmara. For my further entertainment he pointed out the bloodstained block where executions by the sword took place. Above a long-since bricked-up gateway a faded gold inscription in Greek letters could still be seen, surmounted by the two-headed eagle of the Byzantine emperors. Of this only the heads had been hewn away, to spare the feelings of pious Moslems.

At length, with many apologies, he showed me my own accommodation—a roomy stone cell with windows looking out over the courtyard. I might wander freely about this court and eat if I chose beside the wooden cookhouse.

He left me to my misery, and for three days and nights I lay on the hard wooden bench in my cell, without appetite or desire for company. Desperately I puzzled over the reason for my arrest, and indeed wondered that anyone had dared to order it, since to judge from Ibrahim's letters I still enjoyed his favor. I passed all my actions in review, and even my secret thoughts, but without finding anything to justify my plight. Yet the more earnestly a man broods over possible guilt, the guiltier he feels. After three days and nights of self-examination I was so keenly aware that at least in my heart I had broken many laws, both of the Prophet and of man, that I was left like a guttering candle, and felt of all outcasts the most wretched.

On the third day the duty onbash came to me with a bundle of clothes, my old copper pen case, and a letter from Giulia. She hinted obscurely that I had only myself and my ingratitude to thank for my hard fate. "Never should I have thought that you would deceive me so," she wrote. "If you had revealed your base scheme to me I could at least have warned you. And now, but for my tears and prayers, your head would have been cut off and your body thrown into the pit. I can do no more for you; you have made your bed and must lie on it, thankless Michael. I can never forgive your conduct, for soon I shall be forced to pawn my jewels to meet household expenses."

Her incomprehensible letter put me altogether beside myself. I rushed to the eunuch, burst into passionate reproaches, and ended, "I can bear this uncertainty no longer—I am going out of my mind. What am I accused of, that I may at least defend myself? When the Grand Vizier returns he will inflict terrible punishment on everyone

358

who has dared to lay a hand on me. Have my irons struck off, my good man, and release me at once from this prison, or even you may lose your head."

The eunuch was annoyed at being disturbed in his exacting work of casting accounts. Yet as became a man trained in the Seraglio he kept his temper and answered pleasantly, "Ah, Michael el-Hakim, in five or ten years when you are a little more composed we will discuss the question again. Very few state prisoners know what they're accused of, for the essence of the punishment decreed by the Sultan in his wisdom lies in that very torment of uncertainty. Not one of our distinguished guests knows whether he will remain here a week, a year, or his whole life. At any hour of the day or night the deaf-mutes may come and lead you to the brink of the pit; at any hour the gates of the prison may open before you and release you once more into the world of men, to attain perhaps to even higher distinctions than before. You would be wise to devote this favorable time to mystic contemplation, until like the dervishes you come to understand that in the eyes of Allah all is illusion, whether it be imprisonment or freedom, wealth or poverty, power or serfdom. Therefore I shall be happy to lend you the Koran."

But it was easier to discuss these things in the sweatroom of the bathhouse than behind the iron bars of a prison. I lost all control of myself and began to stamp and shriek until he was compelled to have me seized by janissaries and caned on the soles of my feet. My fury soon dissolved into tears of pain, and the janissaries held me under the arms and half-carried me back to my cell, where they touched brow and floor with their finger tips to convey their continued good will and respect. The swelling and agony of my feet distracted my thoughts, as the wise eunuch had intended, and so in time I composed myself and began to live each day as it came. My one hope was that when the Grand Vizier returned from Persia he would miss me and, Seraglio intrigues notwithstanding, discover my whereabouts.

The five daily prayers and ablutions helped to pass the time, and having nothing else to do I diligently studied the Koran. I also took the friendly eunuch's advice and performed the breathing exercises of the dervishes, and fasted now and then. But I soon found my faith too weak for me to attain the state of supreme rapture extolled by Marabouts and holy dervishes.

359

At last, therefore, I abandoned these exercises and was content to maintain my body in good health and to eat with appetite. All day long I strolled about the courtyard while flocks of migrating birds swept with a rush of wings overhead against the turquoise sky of autumn. In this way I came to know my fellow captives, among whom were many eminent Mussulmans and also Christians who were of value to the Sultan for the exchange of prisoners. They idled the days away lying on the grass about the cookhouse, though some of the more industrious busied themselves with carving tallies of the days of their imprisonment, and proverbs, on the smooth stones at the base of the towers. Twice I met Rashid, the Prince of Tunis, and heard him revile Khaireddin and Sultan Suleiman for their dastardly betrayal.

Weeks passed, the acacias in the courtyard shed their leaves, the days grew chilly, and I wearied of the company of my fellows. I was consumed with yearning for my beautiful house on the shores of the Bosphorus, and could imagine nothing more desirable than to recline on a soft cushion on the terrace as dusk fell over the waters and one by one the stars came out. I longed to see again my red and gold fish, to hold my little daughter Mirmah by the hand and guide her steps as she struggled toward the faithful Alberto's embrace. I wasted away with longing and believed myself abandoned by everyone.

One clear autumn day as I stood on top of the marble tower I looked across the misty blue sea and beheld sails, pennants, and silver crescents, and like an echo from another world I heard the boom of cannon from Seraglio Point. The turrets of the Gateway of Peace shimmered dreamlike in the distance, while at my feet the billowing landscape, sprinkled with white tombstones, glowed golden in the clear autumn air. A dusty, chalk-white road wound its way among the hills and vanished in the distance.

The freedom, the beauty of the scene cut me to the heart, and I was sorely tempted to hurl myself down from the giddy height of the tower and find release from this world's vanity, suffering, and hope.

Well that I did not, for that day brought an unexpected turn in my fortunes. At dusk three deaf-mutes came to the prison. With dragging steps they crossed the courtyard to the marble tower on the side nearest the sea, where the death pit was. Here in silence they strangled Prince Rashid and cast his lecherous body into the hole, from which incident I concluded that Khaireddin had captured Tunis and so had no further use for Rashid ben-Hafs.

Like all the other prisoners I was aghast at the arrival of these deaf-mutes. Of the three I recognized at once the ashen-faced, cruel Negro who used to visit Abu el-Kasim's slave. As he crossed the courtyard he gave me an expressionless look, but with his fingers he made a reassuring sign to show that I was not altogether forgotten.

This greeting was the first message I had had from the outer world since Giulia's letter, and I was seized by so feverish an agitation that I could not sleep that night. On the third day after the deaf-mutes' appearance I was summoned by the eunuch, who ordered my fetters to be struck off, gave me back my clothes and money, and accompanied me to the gate as a mark of his unchanging regard. Thus I was released as suddenly and mysteriously as I had been imprisoned so many months ago.

Outside, to my amazement, I found Abu el-Kasim awaiting me in a splendid palanquin, and no one will blame me for bursting into tears at the sight of him. I wept like a fountain, leaning against his scrawny shoulder and breathing in the bitter, spicy smell of his kaftan as if he had been my father.

Abu drew me in beside him and under cover of the curtains gave me a little wine. Recovering slightly from my agitation I asked him eagerly whether I was indeed free, what I had been accused of and what had been happening in the world since I had been snatched from it. Abu el-Kasim said, "Ask no foolish questions. The matter is of no importance and will become clear to you in due course. All you need do now is come home, recite the first sura, and give me the Russian woman and her son according to your promise. It was only to fetch them that I returned, and for the rest of my days I shall live peacefully in Tunis. Thanks to Khaireddin that town has been liberated from the Hafsid tyranny and now celebrates its freedom under the vigilant protection of the janissaries."

Not until he had assured himself that I meant to keep my word and give him the Russian did he heave a sigh of relief and tell me the reason for my imprisonment.

It seemed that when Khaireddin set sail in the spring he made first for Coron and supplied the fortress with new cannon. Then for the first time in history the Mussulman fleet sailed openly through the

361

Strait of Messina to display its strength, after which it cruised slowly northward and systematically raided the coast of the Kingdom of Naples. Doria dared not come out to meet Khaireddin, since because of seemingly well-founded rumors he believed the fleet to be bound for Genoa. Most unluckily a Christian slave, in return for his freedom, promised to show Khaireddin's land forces the way to the castle of Fondi, where there was reputed to be immense treasure.

"It appeared, however," said Abu el-Kasim, "that the slave had greatly exaggerated the value of this, and in their fury the janissaries broke into the chapel, plundered the coffins of the dead lords of the castle, and scattered their bones. The lady of the castle, a widow of ripe years named Giulia Gonzaga, fled in her nightgown. Khaireddin had never heard of her, but after her escape she spread the most colorful stories of her flight. Since her widowhood she had been wont to entertain poets and other riffraff, in the frivolous Italian manner, and in return for her hospitality these poets hailed her in their verses as the most beautiful woman in Italy. You know what poets are—there was no harm in any of it. But in her crazy vanity this woman spread the report that Khaireddin had stormed her castle solely on her account, because he meant to send her to the harem of his lord, Sultan Suleiman. She told the tale so often that she began to believe it herself."

"Allah be good to us!" I exclaimed, deeply shaken. "Now I understand. Small wonder that Sultana Khurrem was angry when she heard of this, for she must have believed that Khaireddin had betrayed her confidence at my instigation. I can only marvel that my head remains on my shoulders. A woman scorned is more savage in her jealousy than an Indian tiger."

"The Venetian Signoria took care that this entertaining story should reach the ears of the Sultana, and she was the more eager to believe it for a certain disharmony that had arisen between her and the Sultan over Prince Mustafa, just before Suleiman went to war. The best proof of its falsehood is that the groom who risked his life to save Giulia Gonzaga was slain afterward at her order, because he laughed at her story and said that the Sultan would certainly prefer a sack of flour to the lady's somewhat flabby charms."

"Then," I remarked, "the misunderstanding must now have been cleared up and Sultana Khurrem will know that I am innocent. But if not, I must flee to Persia and seek refuge with the Grand Vizier, loath though I am to encounter Shiite swords."

Abu el-Kasim said, "She believes in your innocence, and Khaireddin's princely gifts have entirely dispelled her groundless suspicions. But now Grand Vizier Ibrahim is reported to have marched with great pomp into Tabriz, the Shah's capital, and so reached the peak of his glory. The Sultan has joined him there and lovely Khurrem can only sit and bite her nails. For many days Istanbul has been rejoicing at the conquest of Persia, and now new fires are being lit to celebrate the capture of Tunis."

We embarked in my boat, and as the stars came out and sparkled like silver sand against the blue of the night sky I saw far away my beautiful house and garden, and the high walls rising in terraces above the shore. So unreal did all things seem to me that life itself appeared but as a dream, a flower, a song. I drove my nails into the palms of my hands in an effort to control myself, impatient for the moment when I could once more hold my wife Giulia in my arms. The slaves had hardly raised their oars to let the boat glide noiselessly to the marble landing stage before I leaped out, and on winged feet sped up the steps to my house. Seizing the first lamp I saw I hastened to the upper floor, calling out Giulia's name in the hope that she might yet be awake. Hearing the noise, the faithful Alberto came rushing to meet me with his hair on end, breathless from astonishment. He hastened to fasten his yellow coat and threw himself at my feet weeping for joy at my return, and embracing my legs with his powerful arms. Not until he heard Giulia calling to me in a faint voice did he come to his senses and release me.

Giulia was lying limply on her bed, her hair curling over the pillow. "Oh, Michael, is that you? I thought by the noise that thieves had broken in. I can't think how it is you're here so soon, for Sultana Khurrem and I agreed that it should be tomorrow. Someone has been negligent or taken a bribe, and deserves severe punishment for the fright you've given me. My heart is still thumping and I can scarcely draw breath."

She sounded indeed so breathless and frightened that I raised the lamp to look at her, and although she quickly drew up the coverlet and hid her face in her hands I could not but see that her left eye was bruised and that there were red weals across her shoulders as though from a cane. Aghast, I snatched off the coverlet and beheld her shivering, naked body covered with red blotches.

"What is this?" I cried. "Are you ill, or has someone beaten you?"

Giulia began to sob, and wailed, "I slipped and fell on those treacherous stairs, striking my eye and rolling right to the bottom. By a miracle I broke no bones. Can you wonder that I'm bruised and shivering? Alberto helped me to bed and when he had gone I drew off my shift to look at my bruises and rub them with salves. I hoped to be quite well again to welcome you tomorrow—and then you come storming in like a wild beast with no consideration for me whatever."

She was talking so excitedly that I could not get a word in, and as I had often slipped on those stairs myself, especially after drinking wine, I had no reason to doubt her word and was aware only of a deep thankfulness that she had suffered no worse injury. Yet somewhere in the depths of my heart that evening—though I would not admit it even to myself—the vile, scorching truth was revealed.

Having humbly begged Giulia's pardon for my thoughtless behavior, I called Abu el-Kasim to enter, since owing to her injuries Giulia could not leave her bed. But Abu was out of humor because Giulia had allowed the Russian nurse to go out with the other servants to celebrate the Sultan's victories. He fidgeted about the room for some time, scratching himself, and at length set forth in search of the woman to protect her virtue from the mob.

I was not sorry to see him go, for now at last Giulia and I could be alone. Inflamed by wine and my own suspicions I could not master myself, but embraced her to deaden my thoughts, though she begged me to spare her bruised body. My passion only burned the hotter as the agonizing truth forced its way deeper and deeper into my heart. Giulia submitted ever more willingly and at last began to respond faintly to my caress. Artlessly she asked me whether I still loved her, and I could only grit my teeth and declare that of all women on earth I loved only her—that no other could satisfy my desire. This was the hideous truth and I hated myself for submitting to her spell.

At length I sank to rest beside her, and she began to chide me gently. "What an unnatural father you are, Michael! You've not even asked after your daughter. Would you not like to peep at her while she's asleep? You could never guess how she has grown and what a beautiful girl she promises to be."

At this I could control my thoughts no longer and said, "No, no, I won't see her. I won't even think about her. She has Alberto. All I ask is to bury my thoughts, my will, my hopes, my future, and my bitter, bitter disillusionment in your arms. I love you only and can do no other."

At my violent and despairing words she raised herself quickly on her elbow. Her face was strangely flushed and there was a cruel look about her lips as she stared at me in the yellow lamplight. But dissimulation came easily to me now, and presently she shrugged her white shoulders and lay down calmly at my side, saying, "You talk very foolishly, Michael. You should not neglect your own child for my sake. Mirmah has often asked after you, and tomorrow you shall walk with her in the garden, to show both her and me that you're a tender and thoughtful father, though I know you care little for children. So much at least you can do for me, when I ask you so prettily."

Next morning she brought Mirmah to me and I took the child into the garden to look at my red and yellow Indian fish. For a while she held my hand obediently, as no doubt Giulia had bidden her, but soon she forgot me and began throwing sand into the water with both hands to scare the fish. I cared little for the fish, but narrowly scrutinized the child that Giulia called mine. She was in her fifth year— a capricious, violent child who went into convulsions if her smallest wish was opposed. She was beautiful; her features were regular and faultless as those of a Greek statue, and her complexion was so smooth and dark as to make her eyes seem strangely pale. While we strolled in the garden Alberto followed us like a shadow, as if fearing that I might throw the little girl into the pool. But how could I have harmed her who had no share in the sin or in the death of my heart? When she had tired of teasing the fish Alberto took her quickly away and I sat down on a stone bench that was warmed by the sun. My head was empty and I did not want to think.

I was not many years over thirty, but the gnawing uncertainty of my imprisonment had led me to doubt the purpose of my life, and on my return the corroding truth took up its dwelling in my heart. I was overcome by a desperate longing to flee from the city of the Sultan and find somewhere—as far away as possible—a peaceful corner where I might live out my life like other men and in quietness increase my knowledge.

Yet how could I give up Giulia and my beautiful house, my comfortable bed, the good food served in porcelain and silver, my friends the poets and dervishes and above all the Grand Vizier who trusted and needed me? I could not desert him—least of all now, when despite his brilliant successes the shadows were clustering thick about him. I strove to make a bold decision, but I could not tell what was best for me. Time slipped by like a swift stream, the worm gnawed at my heart, and vainly I sought comfort in my cups and oblivion in cheerful company.

To all appearances, the Ottoman Empire had never known so golden an age. The conquest of Tunis had brought with it control of Africa's ancient caravan routes over the desert from the Negro lands; along these routes poured gold dust, black slaves, ivory, and ostrich feathers. Tunis was also a base for the conquest of Sicily, and already the Knights of St. John—the greatest menace afloat—were thinking of withdrawing from Malta to the security of the Italian mainland.

From Tabriz the united armies of the Sultan and the Grand Vizier embarked upon an arduous march to Bagdad, and news of the blood-less capture of the holy city of the caliphs came as a climax to many victorious tidings. Yet these successes could not provoke Shah Tahmasp to a decisive encounter, and the march on Bagdad claimed more than its share of victims. I received a letter from the Grand Vizier of which the very handwriting betrayed a disturbed state of mind, commanding me to join him in Bagdad.

The war was by no means ended. The army was to winter in Bagdad and in the spring renew its attack on Persia. But treachery lurked among the troops, he wrote, and did more damage than the weapons of the Persians. Iskender-*tseleb* the Defterdar was the cause of all the trouble, and since Aleppo he had brought about utter confusion in the finances. He had deliberately sent ten thousand men to certain death in an inaccessible mountain pass, and it was becoming more and more evident that the whole campaign had been planned to discredit Ibrahim as Seraskier. Ibrahim must be constantly on his guard against assassins—who were not sent by Shah Tahmasp. But, he wrote, he would turn the conspiracies of his foes against themselves; he would root out the treachery that had sprung up in the army and show who was Seraskier-sultan of the Ottoman Empire. From me he required a report of all that had happened in the Seraglio during his absence, and meant to entrust to me a further task, which could not be mentioned even in a secret dispatch.

366

I was filled with forebodings and fears that the noble Seraskier, distracted by the hardships and reverses of the war, had taken to suspecting treachery in the most innocent places. Yet since he commanded me, I must go to him. I will therefore begin my last book and relate how Grand Vizier Ibrahim's star burned dim just as he attained to the highest position ever held by a slave in the Ottoman Empire.

BOOK 9.

Grand Vizier Ibrahim's Star
of Fortune

BY FAIR words Abu el-Kasim persuaded my daughter's Russian nurse to renounce her Greek religion and embrace Islam, that he might marry her lawfully in the presence of the cadi and two qualified witnesses. The woman so warmly admired Abu's broad turban, his kaftan with the jeweled buttons, and his glittering monkey's eyes, that she clapped her hands for joy when she understood his honorable intentions. I knew not whether to laugh or cry when I saw how tender Abu was of his wife's reputation and how he even overcame his avarice for the time, that the wedding celebrations might be as splendid as possible. All the poor of the quarter were feasted for many days in succession, pipes and drums resounded, and women sang in shrill voices their ancient nuptial hymns.

To my delight Giulia made no opposition, though she failed to understand how I could hand over a woman still in her prime to such a man as Abu, still less incite her to renounce her Christian faith, schismatic though it was. Abu el-Kasim swore that he would make her son his sole heir if he should have no children by her, and at the boy's circumcision he gave him the name of Kasim, so that in Tunis it might be thought that he was Abu's son.

By the time I received the Grand Vizier's anxious letter from Bagdad I had already accompanied Abu el-Kasim and his family to their vessel and seen them off with many blessings. A singular, almost morbid conviction had grown upon me of late that a curse lay over my house, and I rejoiced at the Grand Vizier's summons, plainly though it showed that the stress of war had deranged his mind. Dread of my own house

371

inclined me to this long journey, and as feverishly as during my imprisonment I had longed for Giulia, I now yearned to be parted from her for a time, that I might meditate in peace and quiet upon her and upon our relationship.

Giulia made no objection to my journey, envied me my sight of Bagdad, and gave me a long list of things to buy for her in the bazaars. As the day of departure drew near she displayed increasing affection, but shortly before I left she spoke a few grave words. "According to news received by a certain distinguished lady, Grand Vizier Ibrahim has secretly summoned to Bagdad a number of eminent statesmen, and it's certain that he is up to no good. But the Sultan, blinded and bewitched by his friendship, cannot see the danger, though the ambitious Ibrahim has assumed a new title and in the Persian manner signs himself Seraskier-sultan. Fortunately Khurrem was able to persuade the Sultan to send thither the loyal Defterdar, Iskender-*tseleb*, to advise the Seraskier and at the same time to hold him in check. Yet Ibrahim has tried in every way to hinder Iskender-*tseleb* in his work and to undermine his authority."

"I know all this," I replied curtly. Her words distressed me, for the attempt, foiled by the vigilance of the Grand Vizier, to steal part of the Sultan's war funds had aroused much excitement throughout Istanbul and fantastic rumors were current in the Seraglio. But nothing would deter Giulia from pouring poison into my ear.

"Believe me, Michael—be wise and don't walk blindfold into disaster. Take careful note of all the Grand Vizier says. Calm him; prevent any hasty or ill-considered action. For although Sultana Khurrem wishes him no ill, he will be setting the noose about his own neck if he continues to persecute her friends and faithful servants. Iskender-*tseleb* in particular enjoys the Sultana's favor, and it was only to cast suspicion upon him that Ibrahim bribed men to steal the camels laden with part of the war funds."

"I take a very different view of that incident," said I. "Why should the Seraskier steal his own money? And besides, he has the written confession of the accused—a confession which throws a strange light upon the Defterdar, as should be evident to all right-thinking persons."

Giulia's face darkened.

"And it was extorted under merciless torture! Perhaps you can explain why the Grand Vizier was in so great a hurry to take the lives of those unhappy men as soon as they had confessed, if not to silence inconvenient witnesses."

"Allah be gracious to me!" I cried in exasperation. "Only a woman could reason thus. How in wartime could he have pardoned the men so dangerous an offense? As Seraskier, he was compelled to make an example of them, to prevent the spread of sedition."

A queer gleam came into Giulia's eyes, but with a great effort she controlled herself and answered, "You refuse to see the truth, Michael, and you will have a terrible awakening. Don't blame me if when the time comes I can do nothing to save you. I wish you a good journey to your dear Grand Vizier, and hope that on the way you will find time to think the matter over. Be sure that rich rewards await you if you come to your senses in time."

According to Ibrahim's commands, I traveled the long road to Bagdad with the greatest possible speed. I was blind and deaf with exhaustion, my cramped limbs ached, and I was in agony from saddle sores when at length I slipped from my mount with my companions to press an aching brow to the ground and stammer prayers of thanksgiving. The countless mosques, minarets, and towers of this fabled city were like a mirage amid the flowering gardens crisscrossed with irrigation canals, and the holy tombs of Islam lay more thickly here than anywhere else in the world. Bagdad was no longer the city of the caliphs, for after the days of the great Imam the Mongols had looted and burned it more than once. Yet in my eyes it seemed rich and splendid, and with all the tales of Arabia in my thoughts I rode in through the city gates preceded by runners who hastened to inform the Grand Vizier of our coming.

As we slowly crossed the empty, arcaded market place I saw in the middle a gallows guarded by janissaries, from which hung the body of a bearded man. The unexpected sight aroused my curiosity; I rode nearer and to my amazement recognized that face, now blue in death, and the well-known shabby kaftan with its ink-stained sleeves.

"Allah is Allah!" I exclaimed. "Is this not the body of Defterdar Iskender-*tseleb?* How comes it that this man—the richest, noblest, and most learned in the Ottoman Empire—hangs on this gallows like the meanest malefactor? Could he not at least have been given the green silken noose, so that in the name of the Compassionate he might have taken his own life in the privacy of his room?"

Some of the high court officials who had journeyed with me in obedience to Ibrahim's summons hid their faces, turned their horses, and rode back to the gates, determined to leave the city without delay. The janissaries guarding the gibbet said fiercely, "It is all the fault of the accursed Grand Vizier. The Sultan is innocent, and we never begged this honor. Who can doubt now that Ibrahim is plotting against the Ottoman Empire? The mufti proclaimed a *fatwa* entitling us to plunder these heretics of their possessions and to sell them into slavery. But Seraskier Ibrahim, that winebibber and blasphemer, denies us our right to pillage. We should like to know how much the merchants have paid him for that. Wages cannot compensate for this injustice and serve only to show that Grand Vizier Ibrahim is suffering from a tender conscience."

One could sympathize with the janissaries if their tale was true. Iskender-*tseleb's* wealth, piety, and pure Turkish origins had won him great regard throughout the Ottoman Empire, so that indeed it can have been no pleasure to stand sentinel over his dangling corpse. I rode on, oppressed by dark forebodings. At the palace chosen by the Grand Vizier for his headquarters I was received with the greatest suspicion; my clothes were repeatedly searched by the guards, who even ripped up the seams of my kaftan in search of poison and hidden weapons. From this I realized the state of terror prevailing in Bagdad. When at length I was led by the elbow into the presence of the Grand Vizier, I found him too greatly agitated to keep still. He was pacing up and down the marble room, his handsome features were puffy and his eyes bloodshot with strain and lack of sleep. His usually well-kept nails were bitten, and he paused often to take a draught of spiced wine. At the sight of me he forgot all his dignity and hurried forward to embrace me. He dismissed the guards and cried, "At last I behold one known and trusted face among the traitors! Blessed be your coming, Michael el-Hakim, for never did I stand in such need of a clear-sighted, impartial friend."

As coolly and dispassionately as he could he gave me a brief account of the progress of the campaign since the departure from Aleppo, and as I thought the matter over I saw that Ibrahim was in possession of so many proofs of Iskender-*tseleb's* treachery as to leave no room for doubt. Against the Seraskier's will, Iskender had been appointed kehaya, or steward, of the army and, blinded by his hatred of the Grand Vizier, he had acted throughout the campaign against the best

374

interests of the troops. Not until the outset of the terrible winter march from Tabriz to Bagdad was Ibrahim able to persuade the Sultan to dismiss the Defterdar from his post as kehaya, and then it was too late, for when snow set in and floods came and roads were transformed into bottomless swamps, the wretched state of the supplies and equipment was revealed, as also the confusion and disorder brought about by secret agents. The Grand Vizier did not hesitate to cast the blame on Iskender-*tseleb* both for the ruinous condition of the baggage wagons and for the lack of forage, as a result of which the draft animals dropped from exhaustion. The Kehaya's reconnaissance and route planning had been most imperfect; indeed, he seemed to have chosen the worst roads in order to undermine the morale of the troops and to incite them to revolt against the Seraskier.

"Vanity led me to follow his deceitful counsels and march on Tabriz without waiting for the Sultan to join me, for it would have been a triumph if I could have defeated the Shah unaided," said Ibrahim candidly. "All too late I realized that Iskender's encouragement was born of his secret wish to destroy me and discredit me in the eyes of my lord and sovereign. I now have proof that the Defterdar was in secret communication with the Persians throughout the whole march and gave them all needful information as to our routes and objectives, so that they were able to withdraw in time and avoid a pitched battle. If that is not treachery, tell me what is! In the end it was either his head or mine. Yet since his execution I've been oppressed by a feeling of impotence. I feel caught in a net. My head is at stake, and there is no one whom I can trust."

As we sat drinking wine together, agitated servants in gilded helmets hurried in to tell us that the Sultan had woken from his midday rest and seemed out of his mind. He was screaming and tearing at his breast and no one could quiet him. Together Ibrahim and I raced to the Sultan's bedchamber, where we found him standing in the middle of the floor staring into space. His face was wet with sweat, and he trembled all over. The sight of the Grand Vizier seemed to bring him to himself; he wiped his face and dismissed all anxious questions with the words, "I had a bad dream."

His nightmare had been so terrible that he refused to speak of it, and the Grand Vizier proposed that they should visit the baths together. Because of their many cares and anxieties they had both drunk too much and so become a prey to nightmares and even waking il-

375

lusions. But the Sultan was plunged in his own thoughts; his eyes were lowered and he would not look the Grand Vizier in the face.

The execution of Iskender-*tseleb,* which had caused such an uproar in Bagdad, nevertheless cleared the air and made plain to everyone who was master. One of its results was to bring about a shuffle of appointments by which some found themselves a rung higher in the hierarchy. These had every reason to feel grateful to the Grand Vizier. Moreover the newly conquered provinces in Persia offered new and profitable posts. By means of these and other measures superficial order was restored, and there were even cheers to be heard when the Sultan and the Grand Vizier together rode to the mosque or to the holy tombs in the neighborhood of the city.

In the course of these devotional exercises the Sultan was always greatly saddened by the fact that Shiites had long since destroyed the tomb of the founder of Sunna, the wise Abu-Hanif, and in their heretic frenzy had even burned his holy bones, so that no orthodox Sunnite had since then been able to pay homage to the greatest saint of the true path.

Though discontent in the army was temporarily allayed, the Grand Vizier thought with some uneasiness of the coming spring and the renewed campaigns against Persia. He engaged a learned historian to chronicle the course of events, and having thus ensured a fair and impartial record he questioned the learned man as to previous campaigns, constantly reverting to the story of Eiup, the Prophet's standard-bearer, and demanding to know every detail of his life. Eiup had died a hero's death before the impregnable walls of Constantinople, and hundreds of years later his sacred bones were mysteriously found in the forgotten grave—a discovery that fired the janissaries of Muhammed the Conqueror at the final victorious assault on Constantinople. There was a strange light in Ibrahim's eyes as he said to me, "Such another find would be very welcome just now, to inspire the troops with courage and enthusiasm. Yet I fear the days of miracles are past."

I am resolved to express no opinion about what followed. According to a secret tradition handed down among the descendants of one of the guards of Abu-Hanif's tomb, this guard rejected the Shiite heresy, rescued the saint's remains, and buried them elsewhere, replacing them by those of a heretic. These false bones had afterward

376

been burned, but the sacred relics of the great teacher were in safe-keeping somewhere within the walls of Bagdad.

This story was told, for a consideration, to one of the Sultan's attendants by a direct descendant of the watchman. The attendant related it to the Grand Vizier, who commanded a certain devout and learned man named Tashkun to seek out the resting place of the bones.

After much research and diligent peering among the ruins, Tashkun ordered his men to dig up the floor of a certain dilapidated house. An ancient vault was revealed, through one of whose walls came a heavenly fragrance of musk. Hearing of this discovery, the Grand Vizier at once hastened to the spot and with his own hands pulled away a few stones, leaving a gap large enough to crawl through. Thus the resting place of the great Imam was discovered and its sanctity vouched for by the mysterious fragrance. An express messenger was sent to the Sultan, who came in haste and descended into the tomb. The army could now see for themselves that by the grace of Allah, Ibrahim and Suleiman had rediscovered the long-lost but miraculously preserved remains. The Sultan spent nearly a day and a night at the tomb in prayer and fasting, and his fervor infected the troops; even the dullest could see that Abu-Hanif hoped for the uprooting of the Shiite heresy, so that the path of Sunna, which he had founded, might take the place of honor in every country of Islam.

I naturally visited the tomb myself and saw the yellow-brown skull and the skeleton in its rotting shroud, and I was able to satisfy myself that these remains gave out the same scent that I remembered from my boyhood when, as a reward for scholarship, I was allowed to help at the enshrining of holy Hemming's bones in Åbo cathedral. Nevertheless this strange and timely discovery caused me some distress of mind, and at a convenient moment I inquired of the Grand Vizier how it had come about. He was far from being a devout man. Was it deliberate deception, I asked him, or some diabolical illusion?

Grand Vizier Ibrahim looked upon me with shining eyes, and his whole being seemed purified by his prayer and fasting as in a firm and convincing tone he replied, "Believe me or not, Michael, the discovery of those bones was the greatest surprise of my life. I had planned to deceive and with the help of my most faithful dervishes I buried some bones of suitable holiness for pious, credulous old Tashkun to find. No doubt they lie hidden to this day. I was far more

377

amazed than Tashkun when thanks to his dreams and other visions he actually found Abu-Hanif's tomb. Surely if such things can befall me, the star of my fortune cannot fail to reach the zenith."

But the suspicions of the Seraglio had poisoned my mind, and his words did not convince me.

The discovery of Abu-Hanif's holy bones eclipsed all unpleasant or troublesome memories, and the army spent the remainder of the winter in feasting and merrymaking. With the coming of spring the Grand Vizier grew more serene. His despair melted away and gave place to an exhilarated, joyful mood. Nothing seemed impossible, and the whole world witnessed his triumphs. He had sent word to Venice and Vienna of the capture of Bagdad, and even now the French ambassador with a brilliant retinue was on his way with felicitations and proposals for an alliance. Ibrahim seemed to have attained the climax of his fame and glory; nevertheless he was not blinded by it, and before I left that beautiful city he sent for me to give me my final instructions.

"I've had enough of treachery and in future I will show no mercy to any who plot against me. You must go to Khaireddin in Tunis, and if you value your head keep him from succumbing to the blandishments of either the Seraglio or the Emperor; let him remember his debt to me. It was not to help him extend his own kingdom that I made him Kapudan-pasha, and he must now keep Doria and the Emperor busy at sea so that I need not give a thought to what goes on behind my back while I'm waging war in Persia. Impress this on him, or he may lose his horsehair switches as suddenly as he came by them."

In proof of his favor and his continued trust he bestowed such princely gifts upon me as to surpass my wildest hopes. From them I gained some notion of the sums the Bagdad merchants must have paid him for protection; from them also I glimpsed the glorious future awaiting me if fortune continued to smile upon him and I proved myself worthy of his trust.

I came home to find Giulia in a state of agitation.

"The Seraglio is in an uproar over the murder of Iskender-*tseleb*, and Ibrahim has not a single friend left. He has shown that neither fortune, birth, merit, nor the most tested fidelity in the Sultan's service can protect a man from his mad lust for blood."

This and much more she said, but I paid little heed, being still full of the wonder of Bagdad, and I had not the smallest doubt that despite

378

all intrigues the Grand Vizier's star of fortune was now rising to its zenith.

Soon after my return a wealthy Jewish dealer in precious stones called upon me, honored me with many fine presents, and by way of introduction brought me greetings from Aaron in Vienna. After mutual expressions of esteem he said, "You're the friend of the great Khaireddin, Michael el-Hakim, and it seems that last summer when Khaireddin attacked Tunis, Sultan Muley-Hassan was forced to flee from his kasbah. In his fright he left behind him a red velvet bag containing two hundred selected diamonds of considerable size. In the list of presents sent by Khaireddin to the Sultan there is no mention of these stones, and no trace of their sale has been found either in Istanbul, Aleppo, or Cairo. I have made many inquiries about the matter among my colleagues in different cities, for as you may fancy, so considerable a treasure aroused my curiosity. You need not regret speaking openly to me, Michael el-Hakim, and telling me all you know of this. I would offer you the highest possible prices and assure you of my silence. If necessary I can sell these diamonds in India and even China without anything becoming known of the matter. I am accustomed to such traffic, and if as I suppose the Grand Vizier is concerned in it—for it represents a vast fortune—he need feel no uneasiness about the consequences."

"Allah is Allah!" I exclaimed in some indignation. "Where did you hear all this nonsense? And how dare you insult the Grand Vizier by mentioning his name in the same breath with such an affair? I have never even heard of these diamonds."

But the Jew swore to the truth of what he said and in an attempt to convince me he went on, "Muley-Hassan himself laments his loss in a letter to the Emperor—a letter actually seen by a colleague of mine. The Tunisian Sultan's ambassador to the Imperial Court has openly boasted of it, to draw attention to his lord's wealth."

Aghast, I seized the Jew by the beard, and shaking his head by it I cried, "Wretch, what are you saying? What is Muley-Hassan's ambassador doing at the Emperor's Court?"

The honest Jew freed his beard and said reproachfully, "Are you a stranger in the city? The news is in every man's mouth. The Knights of St. John and the Pope himself have besought the Emperor to drive Khaireddin from Tunis. Sultan Muley-Hassan has appealed to the Emperor; he declares that all his misfortunes have resulted from his

379

loyalty to Charles, and so for his own sake Charles must at least try to help him."

If all this was true it was indeed high time for me to hasten to Tunis, carry out my task there, and hurry away before the Emperor's attack. I ought to have relied more on Ibrahim's foresight and not dallied so long on the way. I therefore hastily dismissed the Jew with renewed assurances that I knew nothing of his diamonds, and with promises to inquire secretly into the matter. This I did merely to be rid of him, for I had other things to think of now.

Fair winds and a swift galley brought me to the yellow Tunisian coast and within sight of the Fortress of La Goletta, from whose tower floated Khaireddin's green and red standard with its silver crescent. Great activity prevailed. Trenches were being dug, barricades erected, and thousands of half-naked, sunburned Spanish and Italian slaves were widening the canal to Tunis. This city is situated on the shores of a shallow salt lake and is separated from the sea by swamps. The sight of Khaireddin's war galleys anchored in long rows in the harbor greatly relieved and cheered me, but not until I approached the city itself did I realize the true significance of Khaireddin's latest capture. I had indeed heard much of the wealth and might of Tunis, but discounted much of it as flights of fancy on the part of Khaireddin and Sinan the Jew. Within the city walls there were, besides the kasbah and the great mosque, about twenty thousand houses, or at least two hundred thousand people; Tunis could thus compare with the great cities of Europe. Not even Khaireddin knew the number of Christian slaves, but I fancy their number did not exceed twenty thousand.

To my great delight I saw that the reconquest of Tunis for Muley-Hassan would be no easy task even for the Emperor. Only by cunning and the incitement of the inhabitants to revolt had Khaireddin contrived to enter it, and even after Muley-Hassan's flight there had been long and bloody street fighting before the people laid down their arms. The sturdy, defiant towers of La Goletta appeared impregnable and blocked the road that ran along the canal into the city, while numberless little lakes and poisonous swamps on either side of this canal made encirclement almost impossible.

Khaireddin received me with every sign of delight, embracing me like a long-lost son and entertaining me so lavishly that I began to fear the worst. He gave me no opportunity of speaking, but boasted

380

loudly of his defenses and the savage lesson he would give the Emperor and Doria if they came too near Tunis. When I inquired how it was that his proud ships lay at anchor instead of sailing forth to engage Doria in open combat, he turned very sulky and asked for the latest news of the war in Persia and of Iskender-*tseleb's* execution, of which he had heard only the mendacious rumors of the Seraglio. Was it indeed true that Grand Vizier Ibrahim had gone out of his mind and ran about on all fours foaming at the mouth and chewing the carpets? To this I replied sharply that such a tale was nothing but malicious invention. Khaireddin listened attentively, stroking his beard, and I fancied I saw a guilty look in those prominent eyes of his, as of a child caught out in some misdeed. My misgivings increased.

The same evening, therefore, I sought out Abu el-Kasim, since Andy was outside the city directing the fortifications. Abu had bought himself a pleasant house with a walled garden and had so far overcome his avarice as to furnish it richly and buy a flock of slaves to wait upon his wife and son. Looking at him now it was easy to forget that he was nothing but a petty merchant who had made his fortune by adulterating drugs and inventing new names for age-old ointments.

Like a proud father he led the splendidly dressed Kasim forward to greet me, and seemed to imagine I had forgotten that the boy was not his son. Contrary to Moslem custom he allowed his Russian wife to approach me with only a thin veil over her face, hoping to elicit my admiration for her gorgeous clothes and jewels, beside which he looked like a gray spider.

Having sent wife and son back to the harem, Abu el-Kasim offered me wine and said in a worried tone, "Khaireddin's janissaries and renegades are perhaps not the best shepherds in the world, and their manner of fleecing their sheep has aroused much discontent among the inhabitants of Tunis—above all among the old Arab families who under Tunisian sultans were members of the Divan and could manage the city as they pleased. A month or so ago a Spanish merchant arrived here. He seems to have no notion of the nature or value of his wares, and sells the most precious of them to chosen customers for a mere song in the hope of winning their favor. He sells spices and even perfumes without the least reference to the prices agreed upon among the merchants here, so you may judge of my indignation when I heard of him."

381

Abu el-Kasim assumed an injured air and looked sideways at me as he sipped his wine.

"This Spaniard has in his service a Christian Moor who is far too much inclined to wander about after dark—not with sighs and a rose in his hand, but on visits to Muley-Hassan's warmest adherents and other malcontents. From sheer curiosity I have had these two men shadowed and several times the Spaniard has openly visited the kasbah and offered merchandise to no less a man than Khaireddin. Not only that, but Khaireddin has had lengthy conversations with him in private. I'm prepared to wager that the foreigner is an Imperial agent and probably a Spanish nobleman, since he behaves so foolishly and has a Christian Moor for a servant."

We talked far into the night, and next morning I betook myself to the harbor and went aboard the Spaniard's ship on the pretext of buying a good Venetian hand mirror. When the Moorish servant informed his master that a wealthy and distinguished customer had arrived, the Spaniard hurried up on deck and greeted me with marked respect. From his features, hands, and bearing I saw at once that he had never grown up among drugs. He soon led the conversation round to world affairs, and when I told him that I had just arrived from the Seraglio in Istanbul to enter Khaireddin's service, he displayed great eagerness to learn the latest news. I told him truthfully of the unrest in the Seraglio and of the suspicions concerning Grand Vizier Ibrahim, and of how, despite the capture of Bagdad, no one believed in a happy outcome to the war in Persia.

At this point in my narrative I abandoned truth for fiction and remarked that I had felt the time ripe for seeking a new master since no man, however perfect his integrity, could hope to escape the Grand Vizier's morbid suspicions. From my complaints the Spaniard judged me to have committed some misdemeanor and escaped to Tunis beyond the reach of Ibrahim's wrath. He at once invited me into his luxuriously appointed stateroom and asked me where I was born and how I had come to take the turban. As if in passing he mentioned that the Pope, on the Emperor's recommendation, had recently permitted certain eminent renegades to be received again into the bosom of the Church. Because of the great services they had rendered the Emperor he had even pardoned them their falling away, without asking too many awkward questions.

Few words were needed, therefore, to bring us into perfect understanding, and the Spaniard now confided that his name was Luis de Presandes, that he had been born in Genoa, belonged to Charles's personal suite, and enjoyed his full confidence in all the complicated affairs that were commonly placed in his hands. Charles was shortly to sail for Tunis with the mightiest navy ever seen. The patriotic inhabitants were ready to rise when the time came and support the Emperor, having had enough of the Turkish reign of terror; they longed for the noble Muley-Hassan, their rightful sultan. The wise man must trim his sails to the veering wind, and all the world knew the Emperor to be a just ruler; he would not forget any man who sincerely repented of past errors and now did his part for the good cause. But fearful would be the punishment for any renegade who persisted in denying his faith and serving the Turks.

In such words as these he sought both to lure and to frighten me, and in the name of Christ and His mother he exhorted me to recall the faith of my childhood, return to the Christian fellowship, and so win pardon for my grievous sin. He wept as he spoke and I too shed tears, being tenderhearted and ever susceptible to beautiful words. Nevertheless I would make no promises, nor would I accept the earnest money he offered me, for through Andy I had conceived the greatest respect for the articles of war and the binding nature of such payments. Yet we parted like bosom friends, and I promised to think over his proposal. I furthermore swore by Cross and Koran never to breathe a word of what he had said.

This oath put me in an awkward position, but his own missionary zeal inspired me with an idea. After only two days Abu el-Kasim succeeded in persuading Master Presandes's Moorish servant to remember with a contrite heart the Moslem faith of his forefathers and, in terror of the hideous punishment that awaited apostates, disclose his master's plots. Without breaking my promise I could thus confront Khaireddin and say, "What has the Kapudan-pasha of the High Porte to do with the secret emissary of the Emperor? What is in your mind, Khaireddin? Do you really believe the Grand Vizier's arm is too short to reach you, even from Persia?"

Khaireddin was much startled and began hastily to defend himself. "The noble Presandes is the Emperor's plenipotentiary and thus enjoys diplomatic immunity. I've kept him dangling only to gain time for completing the defenses of Tunis, and could not receive him openly without arousing suspicion among the Grand Vizier's agents.

That is the whole truth, Michael, and I beg you won't misinterpret my perfectly innocent actions."

He stroked his beard uneasily, and his whole appearance betrayed fear and a guilty conscience. But I disclosed the Spaniard's secret plan for inciting the inhabitants of Tunis to armed revolt, to coincide with the Emperor's arrival, and also handed him a list, given me by the Moor, of dependable sheiks and merchants recommended to Presandes by Muley-Hassan's envoy in Madrid. Khaireddin's face darkened; he tore his beard in rage, and with a roar that shook the walls of the kasbah he said, "That hound of an unbeliever has betrayed me! He showed me the Emperor's written instructions by which he was authorized to offer me the independent sovereignty of Algeria, Tunis, and other cities, on condition I left the Sultan's service. I have not the smallest intention of leaving the Sultan, to whose favor I owe my high position. But all favors are precarious. Therefore I thought I should lose nothing by conversing with Presandes and profiting by the Emperor's generous terms. But the Emperor is clearly falser than I could have believed, and never again will I put my faith in Christian oaths."

I realized from this agitated confession that the Spaniard was not quite so simple and inexperienced as I had thought. On the contrary, he had secured his position and fancied that Khaireddin would let him go even were someone to denounce him. Khaireddin, he thought, would laugh up his sleeve at such a denunciation, believing himself to know more of the Spaniard's business in Tunis than anyone. Now, however, Khaireddin had him arrested at once. In a secret hiding place aboard his vessel another of the Emperor's instructions was found, clearly demonstrating the deceit and treachery of his negotiations. Despite Master de Presandes's loudly repeated claims to diplomatic immunity, the sword fell; his protests were silenced forever.

Being now fully aware of Khaireddin's irresolute and vacillating nature I made ready to leave Tunis, as I had a dislike of violence and bloodshed. But precious time slipped away unnoticed, storms and bad weather hindered my departure, Abu el-Kasim's hospitality enticed me evening after evening, and above all I hoped to see Andy before my departure, to persuade him to return with me to Istanbul. Not until I met him barefoot, ragged, and dirty in the courtyard of the kasbah did I learn that Khaireddin had never told him of my coming, and indeed had sought on various pretexts to keep us apart. This was understandable enough, for like a prudent general Khaireddin was unwilling to lose a good master gunner just before the outbreak of war. We embraced one another joyfully and Andy exclaimed, "I've had enough of this place. Khaireddin made me a laughingstock in the eyes of all decent gunners last winter, when we were fighting Berbers and Arabs in the desert. He made me rig sails to our cannon, and of course they were of some help on level ground with a following wind. But when I saw my honest guns flying along like so many drabs with lifted petticoats I was ashamed. But Khaireddin just laughed and bent on larger sails, and I can never quite forgive him for the disgrace. I much doubt whether he is capable of land fighting. And then the savage treatment of Christian slaves has cut me to the heart, so I shall be more than glad to come back with you to Istanbul."

Andy now looked like a Greek monk or some pious dervish. He had let his beard grow till it stood out round his face like a jungle, and I felt it was time to take him in hand before he turned quite queer in the head. But he said, "At heart I've always been a good-natured fellow. My losses and sorrows have led me to understand people better than before, and I cannot see why we must be forever hurting one another. If you had seen how the renegades and janissaries treated the captive Italian boys and women—I can't believe that the purpose of this life is witless destruction and slaughter. Brooding over these things has given me headaches that the African sun does nothing to cure. So now I punish my body for all its misdeeds by fasting, and letting the sun scorch my back."

I seized him by the arm to lead him quickly to the baths and thence to Abu el-Kasim's house to dress him in proper clothes. But at the gate of the kasbah Andy remembered something, and with a strange look at me he said, "I have something to show you."

He led me past the stables to the middens, and there gave a whistle. A ragged seven-year-old boy crept from his hiding place and greeted him with a yelp of pleasure, just as a dog welcomes its master. The boy had a red velvet cap upon his head but his eyes were almost closed, so swollen were they by the bites of flies. His arms and legs were thin and crooked, and his dull expression showed him to be feeble minded. Nevertheless Andy took him and tossed him into the air until he howled with delight, then gave him a piece of bread and a bunch of onions from the wallet at his girdle. At length he said to me, "Give him an asper! But it must be newly minted and shiny."

I did so, in the name of the Compassionate. The boy looked at Andy, who nodded, then disappeared behind the heaps of garbage. He soon returned and after another glance at Andy he gave me in return a dirty pebble. I took it to please him, and pretended to put it in my purse. Then wearying of the game I urged Andy to come away. He patted the boy on the head, nodded to him, and came. As we walked he spoke in a low voice as if to himself, telling how he had rescued the boy from the janissaries at the time of the capture of the kasbah, and given him into the care of the grooms. Thrusting his hand into his wallet he drew out a handful of dirty little pebbles like the one the boy had given me. They were about the size of a finger tip. Showing them to me he remarked, "He's not ungrateful. Every time I bring him food he gives me one of these, and he will give me as many as I like for really shiny aspers."

I now began to feel grave fears for Andy's reason, and said, "Dear Andy, you must have a touch of the sun! You don't mean you exchange silver aspers for the rubbish that boy gives you, and keep it in your purse?"

I was about to throw away the stone that I'd been given, as the fowl droppings that stuck to it dirtied my fingers. But Andy held my arm urgently and said, "Spit on the stone and rub it on your sleeve!"

I had no wish to soil my fine kaftan, yet I did as he asked, and when I had rubbed the stone it began to shine like a piece of polished glass. A queer thrill ran through me, though I dared not believe I held a jewel in my hand. One of that size would have been worth many thousand ducats.

"Just a piece of glass," I said doubtfully.

"So I thought. But I happened to show the smallest of these stones to a trustworthy Jew in the bazaar, and he at once offered me fifty ducats for it. This showed me that it was worth at least five hundred, and I put it away again. I laugh sometimes to think what an enormous fortune is rattling about in my purse."

I still found it hard to believe him until suddenly I remembered the boy's red velvet cap. I clapped my hand to my forehead and cried, "Allah is indeed merciful! That idiot boy no doubt had time to ransack the empty rooms of the kasbah before it was captured, and found Muley-Hassan's velvet bag which he left behind in his haste."

I told Andy what the Jewish merchant in Istanbul had confided to me, and suggested that we should return to the boy at once and get the rest of the two hundred from him. Andy said, "It won't do, for the boy never parts with more than one or two at a time. He's as cunning as a fox, for all his idiocy, and though I've spied upon him once or twice I have never been able to find his hiding place."

"The matter is somewhat complicated," I said, "and must be carefully considered. The diamonds being Muley-Hassan's property form part of Khaireddin's spoils of war; that's to say they belong to the Sultan. We should get little reward for finding them; indeed they would only seek to extort the rest of the two hundred stones and suspect us of dishonesty if we were simple enough to hand over no more than those that by the grace of Allah have fallen into our hands. Yet we should be mad to leave the rest of this great fortune lying in the dirt."

Such was also Andy's opinion. We dared not breathe a word to anyone of our discovery, but postponed our journey from day to day. Every time we visited the boy he gave us two or three stones, for which we dared not offer more than one asper each, lest the sums he received should attract attention. However, I spoke to the Imam of Jamin's mosque and left with him a sum sufficient for the support and schooling of the boy. If his intellect proved inadequate for reading and writing he was to be trained in some handicraft by which he could earn his living.

At the end of June, when we had collected one hundred and ninety-seven stones, the boy sadly showed us his empty hands, and though we visited him several times afterward, pleading and threatening, it was clear that either he had lost the three remaining stones or that Muley-Hassan had counted them wrongly. We then washed the boy, dressed him in good clothes, and led him to the Imam of the mosque, though he struggled and resisted with all his strength and would not be quieted even by Andy's kindly words. Having thus salved our consciences we bade a hasty farewell to Abu el-Kasim, meaning to make for the harbor and take ship for Istanbul.

A distant boom froze us to the spot, and soon flocks of terrified fugitives were streaming into the city shrieking that the Emperor's fleet had appeared before the fortress of La Goletta. The harbor was thus blockaded, and under cover of the unceasing cannonade the Spaniards landed many troops. My own greed had trapped me. I blamed myself bitterly for not having been content with fewer stones, so that I might have sailed from Tunis while there was yet time.

It was small comfort to learn that the Emperor had arrived at least

387

a fortnight before he was expected, and now held the greater part of Khaireddin's fleet trapped and helpless within the blockaded harbor. Only fifteen of his lightest galleys were able to seek shelter at other points along the coast.

We hastened to La Goletta to discover how true these reports were, and whether we might yet run the blockade in one of Khaireddin's vessels. But from the tower we beheld the enemy fleet of not less than three hundred sail spread over the waters as far as the eye could see. Only a cannon-shot away, a large group of German pikemen were pouring ashore, and these at once began to throw up ramparts and palisades to protect their beachhead. To prevent Khaireddin's fleet from breaking out, the great galleys of the Knights of St. John lay in the forefront; behind them I beheld the terrible carrack that like a floating hill rose high above the other vessels. From its four rows of gaping gun ports protruded the dark mouth of cannon. Doria's slender war galleys, the sturdy caravels of Portugal, and Neapolitan galleasses covered the calm surface of the sea, and in the midst of them all rode the Emperor's mighty flagship with its four banks of oars and its gilded pavilion gleaming on the high poop deck.

To Khaireddin's credit be it said that the hour of danger brought out the best in him. Forgotten was his empty boasting; his bearing was assured, he drew in his belly, and in thunderous tones issued the necessary orders. The command of the Goletta fortress he entrusted to Sinan the Jew with six thousand picked janissaries—almost too large a garrison to be crammed into tower and fortifications. He sent Arabian and Moorish cavalry to oppose the landings and gain time. They could not prevent them, but they could at least keep the Imperial troops on the defensive both day and night.

Not until the camp had been strongly fortified did the invaders mount their guns and open the bombardment of La Goletta, and after this the cavalry dared not venture within range. And now the incessant, appalling din of artillery fire made life within the fort so unendurable that I left Andy on the battlements to watch with joyful wonder the progress of the conflict, and returned in deep dejection to Tunis.

Retreat by land was unthinkable, for the wild Berbers, whose hostility Khaireddin had aroused, controlled the roads and robbed all who sought to flee from the city. Muley-Hassan himself was not far away, though like a cautious man he had not yet joined the Imperial troops,

388

despite his promises. But Charles had no need of his help, for his own army consisted of thirty thousand seasoned German, Spanish, and Italian mercenaries, and his artillery kept the area about La Goletta under continuous and accurate fire, so that many of Sinan's Turkish janissaries were daily carried up the short way to Paradise. And every day fresh vessels brought warriors from all over Christendom to join the Emperor and in his sight win imperishable glory in the fight against the infidel.

Three weeks of savage warfare ensued, and despite the courage and religious zeal of the Moslem defenders only Abu el-Kasim refused to believe that Allah would give Christians the victory and through them bring Muley-Hassan back to power. And so I saw how even a shrewd, cunning man like Abu could be so blinded by happiness that for the sake of his wife and son he believed to the last only what he wished to believe.

La Goletta held out for a month, and this in itself was a miracle. Then the walls began to crumble, and the towers fell. When at last the Emperor ordered the general assault, Doria's vessels rowed past the fortress in line, firing off their pieces as they went. The huge carrack of the Knights of St. John anchored near the shore and fired unceasingly over the galleys. Then Sinan the Jew submitted to the will of Allah and blew all Khaireddin's irreplaceable fleet out of the water, sending a vast column of smoke into the air and setting crockery clattering in the distant city.

The assault was launched from two directions at once. The Knights of St. John charged in from the sea, up to the waist in water, and when they and the Spaniards took possession of the fortress Sinan the Jew issued his last command—each man for himself! To set a good example he flung himself out across the salt marsh that surrounded the stronghold, having already prospected and marked a safe path across the swamps by which the survivors could reach the shelter of the city.

The muddy, bleeding little party staggered up to the gates of Tunis that evening, but at the tips of the staves to which the horsehair switches were attached Khaireddin's silver crescents still gleamed, in token of the deathless honor won that day by the defenders of La Goletta.

Panic now seized the inhabitants of Tunis. All roads leading from the city were soon packed with fugitives carrying bundles and dragging loads in a blind rush to get as far away as possible. I would of course have joined them had not common sense told me that all would soon fall a prey to Muley-Hassan's roving horsemen. Fortunately the Imperial troops had suffered so severely that for many days they rested in their camp to lick their wounds, and meanwhile Khaireddin with flattery, prayers, and threats contrived to calm the worst of the panic before summoning his captains, the most eminent men of Tunis, and also the leaders of his Arab allies to a ceremonial Divan in the great hall of the kasbah.

He spoke to them like a father, and as only he could speak when occasion demanded. His plan was to march out of the city and in the time-honored Moslem fashion offer the Emperor a pitched battle in the open. And indeed this scheme was less crazy than I at first believed, though I admit I listened in openmouthed wonder at his valor. So persuasively did he speak that Abu first among them all rolled up his sleeves, brandished his scimitar, and yelled that for the sake of his wife and son he meant to seek the road to Paradise. It is even possible that this behavior was not prearranged, for Khaireddin himself looked surprised. The eminent Tunisian gentlemen joined a little dubiously in the bloodthirsty shouts, and a spark of hope was kindled in my own dejected heart, since I am prone to believe whatever is told me with sufficient emphasis—especially if it is something I hope for.

But when the greater number of the audience left the kasbah, Khaireddin gathered about him the trustiest of his raises for a nocturnal conference. Not even Abu el-Kasim was invited, though Andy and I were allowed to attend on condition of secrecy. This time Khaireddin spoke in a different tone. He stroked his beard vigorously, his face was grave, and he did not even feign confidence in the outcome.

"Only a miracle from Allah can save us," he said, "and experience has taught me not to expect miracles in warfare. We must seek a pitched battle, for the ruinous city walls would collapse under bombardment and the treacherous inhabitants would sooner stab us in the back than fight against the Emperor. At the same time we must keep an eye upon the Christian slaves packed in the cellars beneath our feet. Nor do I trust the Arab horsemen, for as soon as they're fired on with cannon and harquebus they will scatter like chaff before the wind. Allah's will be done. Let us try our luck in pitched battle rather than seek safety in shameful flight, which in any case presents its own difficulties."

390

He shook his head, glanced about him sourly, and went on, "The first essential is to get rid of the Christian prisoners. Many are fit to bear arms—even to ride—and one traitor among us is enough to prevent our return to the city. I am no cruel man, as you know, but these prisoners number eighteen or twenty thousand, and for the sake of our own lives we must set to work immediately if all are to be strangled before sundown. Let us console ourselves for the financial loss involved by the thought that when Allah turns the leaves of his great book on the Last Day, the slaying of these unbelievers will be accounted to us for merit."

But at this even the most loyal captains looked askance at one another, and Sinan, who had invested his whole fortune in Christian slaves and made good money by hiring them out, fingered his sparse beard and exclaimed, "Not my worst enemy could call me sentimental, but so cruel a deed would forever sully our name and fame in every country in the world. The Christians would avenge their death on those Moslems who sigh in their dungeons, and my stomach turns over at the thought of the loss that would be caused us by so hasty an action. Let us rather stack powder barrels beneath the vaults so that if the worst happens we can blow up the whole kasbah; for if Allah should give us the victory, how damped would our rejoicings be by any needless loss!"

His cautious plan prevailed. When early next morning the Emperor's forces marched from their camp, we left the city to resume our battle with the most experienced and seasoned troops of Christendom. In this Khaireddin acted more courageously than did the Sultan and Grand Vizier in Hungary, though it must be admitted that he had no choice.

Once drawn up in order of battle on the plains, our numbers seemed far from contemptible. The white-clad Arab horsemen covered the slopes of the low hills and the brave inhabitants of Tunis, driven from the city with whips, had armed themselves with cleavers and carving knives, since Khaireddin after the loss of his arsenal in La Goletta could give them nothing better. In numbers, at least, we were nearly equal to the Imperial troops, though not quite ninety thousand as the Emperor's historians afterward reported to enhance their sovereign's glory.

I followed Andy's cannon, armed with a light musket and a scimitar. It was not from ambition or love of fighting that I marched with the rest, but simply because I felt safer among Khaireddin's janissaries and renegades than in the turbulent city. But the battle lasted little longer than the prayer of one girt for a journey. When the Imperial infantry advanced in squares, the Arab riders poured down the slopes in scattered groups and with wild howls discharged a rain of arrows into the enemy ranks. But the answering artillery fire veiled the yellow battlefield in clouds of smoke, and with even wilder yells the Arabs scattered like chaff. They caught up in their flight the bold defenders of Tunis and swept back into the city more swiftly than they had come. Meanwhile we discharged our cannon. Khaireddin, mounted on his champing steed, noticed that he was now somewhat solitary on that wide field; there were but four hundred or so renegades about him, while thirty thousand well-trained Imperial soldiers were steadily advancing, to say nothing of cannon and muskets.

In this most perilous moment of his life the lord of the sea kept his wits about him. Calling to Allah for help in a voice of thunder, he then exhorted his men to deserve Paradise and hold up the enemy by resolute fighting, while he sought to persuade the fugitives to return. He then set spurs to his horse and galloped so speedily back to the city that many of those he pursued fell beneath his horse's hoofs.

To us who remained fell the honor of gallantly engaging the whole Imperial army, firing off our cannon once more and shoulder to shoulder defending ourselves against the advancing Germans and Spaniards. Our only hope of safety lay in keeping close order and retiring step by step on the city, since unlike Khaireddin we had no horses at our disposal.

When at last, bleeding and exhausted, we reached the city we found battle raging in the streets. The inhabitants hurled themselves upon the Turks and renegades and from the housetops showered down stones, pots, cauldrons, and whatever else they could lay hands on. They screeched that they would throw off the yoke of the High Porte and greet Muley-Hassan with rejoicing as their deliverer. Then the white flag was run up on the kasbah, and when Khaireddin sought to enter it and save his treasure he found the gates barred, while the Christian slaves who had freed themselves of their shackles greeted him with a hail of stones from the walls, wounding him in head and jaw.

What wonder then that before the gates of the kasbah Khaireddin lost all control of himself, ground his teeth, and yelled between foaming lips, "All is lost! The dogs of unbelievers have captured the citadel and stolen my treasure!"

Terror overwhelmed me when I saw that all was indeed lost. I tried to run after Khaireddin's horse and hang onto its tail, but my only reward was a kick in the stomach. With a howl of agony I writhed on the ground clutching my belly until Andy dragged me to my feet and led me away, cutting a path through the mob with his sword.

When the Arab horsemen saw that the battle was lost and that Khaireddin had fled, they quickly tore up their treaty with him and galloped off toward the Imperial army, each striving to be the first to pay homage to Muley-Hussan and seek the Emperor's protection. Their eager yells of peace so alarmed the Spaniards that they drove their rests into the ground again and fired their harquebuses into the advancing hordes. Many hundred Arabs lost their lives, or at least their splendid horses, before the unfortunate mistake was discovered. Was this perhaps the judgment of Allah upon them for their treachery?

Meanwhile, the inhabitants broke off palm branches and stripped the trees in their gardens so as to hail in time-honored fashion the victorious Muley-Hassan and the Emperor, who entered Tunis in his company. They were therefore utterly dismayed when Germans, Italians, and Spaniards with sword in hand poured in to win salvation by murdering every Moslem they could lay hands on, and to plunder the city.

The sack of Tunis continued for three days, and I have been told that in the course of it no fewer than one hundred thousand Moslems were slain, whether they belonged to Muley-Hassan's party or to Khaireddin's.

But I have run ahead of events, and must relate what happened after Khaireddin had fled from the gates of the kasbah. Loyally followed by Sinan the Jew and other bold captains, he made off so swiftly as to abandon the horsetail switches in the street. Here it was that Andy seized an Arab horse by the bridle, threw off the rider, and pushed me up in his place, so that I found myself very suddenly clinging to the saddle of a shying steed and fumbling frantically for the reins. Andy roared at me to ride to Abu el-Kasim's house where he would join me as soon as he had collected enough horses. As I left I saw him snatch up Khaireddin's standard, roaring to janissaries and Mussulmans to rally to the Crescent.

I rode to Abu el-Kasim's house, protecting my head as best I might from the missiles hurled from the roofs. But when at last I arrived I found Abu lying naked and senseless before his gate. His forehead was smashed in and his beard bloody. Round about him lay a quantity of valuables that had fallen from his bundle, and men were kicking and spitting on his body and reviling him as one of Khaireddin's spies. I rode straight at them being unable to control my horse, calling upon all the faithful to help me, and they scattered like hens, in the belief that Khaireddin's mamelukes were at my heels.

I threw myself from the saddle and tethered my quivering, lathered steed. In the courtyard I saw Abu el-Kasim's wife lying ripped up in her own blood, but even in death she strove to protect her child in her broad bosom. His head was so battered as to be unrecognizable. I knelt quickly beside my friend Abu el-Kasim and poured a little water over his waxen face. He opened his weary monkey eyes for the last time and said in a broken voice, "Ah, Michael! Life is nothing but one great dunghill. This thought is all I can bequeath you in the hour of my death, for the rabble have stolen my purse."

The veil dropped over his eyes and on dark wings came that One who severs the bonds of friendship, silences song, and reveals the vanity of human happiness and grief.

I sat on the ground beside his dead body and wept bitterly. Just then Andy rode into the courtyard, followed by a few men who had remained loyal to Khaireddin. Rising hastily I shouted, "Dear brother Andy, we're lost! Nothing is left but to seek the Emperor's protection, and if the worst comes to the worst we can deny our Moslem faith, since fortunately we were never circumcised. My faith in the Prophet has today suffered so hard a blow that it can scarcely recover."

But Andy brandished Khaireddin's horsetail standard above his head and in a loud voice cursed all unbelievers. Then quietly he said to me, "Do you really fancy that the Spaniards and Germans would show mercy to renegades? Jump into your saddle, Michael, and fight like a man so that we may catch up with Khaireddin at Bona, before he has time to hoist sail and escape to sea without us! Believe me, this is our only hope."

He was battle mad, and his gray eyes rolled so wildly in his powder-blackened face that I could not oppose him. We rode into the street and thanks to the disorder wrought by the Christian slaves we were able to leave the city without violence. We passed countless plundered fugitives who wrung their hands and blindly sought refuge in the desert where the best they could hope for was death from thirst, for the hottest season of the year was now upon us.

At length our exhausted horses brought us to Tagaste where Augustine, the great Father of the Church, was born. At that time, however, I did not stop the meditate upon this, but with sun-dazzled eyes looked eagerly for Khaireddin's galleys in the harbor. They were just rowing out to sea, but our musket shots and despairing cries induced Khaireddin to send back a boat for us. He greeted us with tears and embraced us like a father, assuring us of his uneasiness on our account. But I slid senseless to the deck, worn out with my exertions. Next morning the skin peeled from my face, and my limbs felt as if they had been crushed. But Khaireddin comforted me, saying, "Allah's will be done! I dare not return to the Sultan with the fragments of the greatest Ottoman fleet that ever sailed the sea. I shall therefore make for Algiers and remain there until he has had time to calm himself. I'm a poor man now and must begin again from the beginning. I see that my proper place is at sea, not ashore. My friends must speak for me at the Divan, if I still have any friends there. I will be prudent and stay away from the High Porte, and this time gladly leave the talking to others."

Thus the irrepressible Khaireddin began already to form new plans, though we were not yet out of danger and the Emperor had sent his swiftest galleys in pursuit of us. Khaireddin's escape threatened to snatch the fruits of victory from Charles's hands, for dominion of the sea was the Emperor's main object; the restoration of Muley-Hassan to the throne of Tunis was a matter of complete indifference to him. But Khaireddin easily shook off his pursuers and we arrived safely in Algiers, whence he instantly dispatched every seaworthy craft to capture unprotected Christian merchantmen and at the same time to spread fire and devastation along the Italian and Sardinian coasts. These raids were well timed, for victory peals were ringing in every village, and Christian congregations flocked into the churches to sing the *Te Deum* in thanksgiving for Khaireddin's defeat.

On the third day the Emperor commanded that the looting of Tunis should cease and order be restored in the ravaged city, to allow Muley-Hassan to ascend to the throne of his fathers. In this way the Emperor sought to show how selfless had been his part in the war, which he had embarked upon merely as a favor to a prince who had begged his help.

I have felt it necessary to record the events of this Tunisian crusade, which historians and poets have celebrated and eminent painters immortalized in many pictures. By leading the enterprise in person and exposing himself to countless dangers, the Emperor won the admiration of all Christendom. Poets referred to him as the first chevalier of Europe, to the fury of King Francis I. Yet the true object was never attained, for the summer had not ended before Khaireddin and his captains had given convincing proof of their continued life and vigor. The Emperor's efforts to annihilate Moslem sea power had been in vain and exceedingly expensive—a circumstance passed over in silence by the historians.

I willingly confess that I was in no hurry to return to Istanbul, and stayed for some time in Algiers as the guest of Khaireddin. Not until just before the onset of the winter gales did I venture upon the long voyage home. The arsenal guns fired no acknowledgment of our salute. The Sultan and the Grand Vizier had not yet returned from the Persian campaign, which was of course a great relief to me, and having handed Khaireddin's letter to a court official who hurried to meet us at the quay, Andy and I took a boat straight to my house, where I might hide my shame away from the gloating stares of the Seraglio.

Giulia received me with a pale face and swollen eyes, and reproached me bitterly for neither writing to her nor sending her money. Yet when she perceived my exhaustion and grief she let me be. It is no easy thing even for a mature and hardened man to watch high hopes go up in smoke and to witness the death of a good friend.

She promised to forgive me, therefore, and spoke with malicious pleasure of the Sultan's army, which after three months of campaigning had recaptured Tabriz and remained there for weeks in the vain attempt to lure Shah Tahmasp into decisive conflict. The Sultan had liberally distributed provinces and cities to distinguished Persians who made submission to him, and when his forces began to run short of food he had started on the homeward march. But as they left first one and then another of the Persian lands behind them, the Shah's forces recaptured them and inflicted severe losses on the Ottoman rear guard. The Shiite heretics rejoiced and purified their mosques from Sunnite pollution; so the great Persian campaign petered out.

"But," said Giulia, "the Sultan is in no way to blame for the defeat. The culprits are the bad advisers who enticed him on this questionable enterprise. It is high time the Sultan realized Ibrahim's uselessness as a general. The Mufti is enraged because he protected the Shiite heretics and forbade the plundering of Persian cities, despite the *fatwa* prepared for the purpose."

I answered sorrowfully, "While the cat's away the mice will play. I shall not abate my loyalty to the Grand Vizier just because he has suffered defeat. Now more than ever does he need a friend's support, and I'll merely remind you of the old proverb, he laughs best who laughs last."

"I shall laugh, never fear! Expect no sympathy from me if you choose to ruin yourself. But there's still time. I have spoken to Khurrem on your behalf and she is willing to forgive you, for the sake of Prince Jehangir. I may tell you in confidence that she does not blame Khaireddin for his defeat and is ready to put in a word for him too if you humbly ask it of her. Such is the honesty of this good and devout lady."

I suspected deceit, having learned to mistrust everyone and especially Giulia. But next day Sultana Khurrem sent her pleasure barge to fetch me to the Seraglio, where she received me in her own porphyry chamber in the Court of Bliss. At first she spoke from behind a curtain, but later she drew it aside and revealed her face to me. Her immodest behavior showed how customs here had changed in a few years. At the time when I became the Sultan's slave certain death awaited every man who beheld a woman of the harem unveiled, even by accident.

The Sultana spoke to me in a playful, teasing tone and gurgled with laughter as if someone were tickling her. Yet her eyes were cold and hard, and at length she ordered me to tell her openly and without reserve all that I had seen and done in Tunis and what had happened afterward. I at once admitted Khaireddin's reverses, but in his defense went on to speak of his success in the later part of the summer, and assured her that with my own eyes I had seen eighteen big galleys under construction at Algiers, so that by the spring Khaireddin's fleet would be ready to rule the seas once more.

Khurrem held her head a little sideways as she listened, and a smile played continually over her beautiful lips. It seemed to me that she was paying more attention to my appearance than to what I was saying, and at last she remarked absently, "Khaireddin Barbarossa is a devout and valiant man and a faithful servant of the Sultan. The Prophet himself appears to him in dreams and when he shakes his long beard he looks like a lion with a luxuriant mane. He needs no one to speak in his defense, for I know best how to win my lord's favor for him. But still you have not told me everything, Michael el-Hakim. Why did you go to Tunis in the first place? And what message was it that the malignant Grand Vizier sent by you to Khaireddin and dared not put into writing?"

I stared at her, disconcerted, unable to guess at her meaning. Then I licked my lips and mumbled something. She encouraged me laughingly, "Michael el-Hakim, you're a great rogue. Confess honestly that Seraskier Ibrahim sent you to Tunis to inquire secretly whether Khaireddin would acknowledge the Grand Vizier's title of Seraskier-sultan. If he said yes, you were to bid him to take his fleet to the Sea of Marmara and await further orders. But the Emperor's unexpected attack foiled these ugly schemes and Khaireddin was saved from making a negative reply, which would have brought down upon him the Grand Vizier's wrath."

"Allah is Allah!" I exclaimed in dismay. "That is nonsense—base lies from beginning to end. The Grand Vizier sent me to warn Khaireddin against the Emperor's false promises, for Charles had offered to make him king of Africa."

"Quite so," assented Khurrem hastily. "Then the Grand Vizier ordered you to tell Khaireddin that it lay in *his* power to make him king of Africa with the right to appoint his own heirs. Then with the Emperor as ruler of Europe and the Seraskier-sultan as ruler of Asia, Khaireddin would take his place as the third of the world's sovereigns."

"What do you mean by that foolish title Seraskier-sultan?" I demanded, so exasperated that I forgot my lowly position. "You turn everything upsidedown. I had no such mission and my only object has been to serve the Sultan loyally. Neither Khaireddin nor I can be blamed for the defeat and I have nothing to add, since you will persist in distorting the truth."

The smile faded from the Sultana's lips and her plump face became a chalky mask. Her eyes took on an icy blue glint, and for a moment I seemed to be face to face with a monster in human form. Yet this singular expression vanished so quickly that I fancied I must have dreamed it or been bewitched by her look.

Presently she said in her usual cooing tones, "Perhaps you are speaking the truth and my informant was mistaken. I can only rejoice that

398

all serve the Sultan so loyally and faithfully. You have greatly relieved my mind, Michael el-Hakim; you deserve liberal reward, and I shall not forget to put in a good word for you with the Sultan. Perhaps I am foolish to imagine that so gifted a man as the Grand Vizier would do anything behind his lord's back. We must wait and see. All will turn out for the best and you and I will be silent about the whole distressing affair."

She smiled at me again in her bewitching manner, but the cold glint remained in her eye as she repeated the words that seemed to veil a stern warning: "All will turn out for the best, and you and I will be silent about the whole distressing affair."

With this she made a sign with her plump hand and a slave girl dropped the curtain between us.

As I returned through the splendid courtyards of the Seraglio I was overcome by a sense of unreality. This was like a story, or a dream, and I seemed to have been through it all before. I looked at the countless slaves who from the highest to the lowest turned their backs on me, and they no longer appeared to me as living people. It was as if they had no faces of their own, and only by their clothes, headdresses, sticks, whips, ladles, and other tokens of rank could I tell their position and occupation. They looked like nothing so much as brilliant beetles. Any one of them could have changed places with any other without altering the pattern. All would go on in the same empty way and with the same senseless and outmoded customs as before.

I seemed to stand outside. I no longer brooded over myself or my fate. I felt only an unspeakable weariness and depression, and the vanity of it all was like a raw December day in my heart.

At the beginning of January, 1536, Sultan Suleiman arrived at Scutari on the opposite shore of the Marmara, and allowed members of the Divan to help him from the saddle as a sign that the Persian campaign was at an end. The Grand Vizier had secretly ordered the building of a splendid barge, well able to compare with the fabled "Bucentoro" of the Doge of Venice, so that in a manner worthy of the conquerer of Persia the Sultan might glide over to Istanbul amid the thunder of salutes.

Once more the names of captured fortresses and cities were proclaimed to the populace. Once more the bonfires blazed for nights on end and the people roared their acclamations of the returning spahis and janissaries. But this time the joy was forced, as if evil forebodings

399

had poisoned the mood of triumph. Moreover, the army had suffered very severe losses on the retreat, on account of both the Persian cavalry attacks and the bad weather, and many wives bitterly mourned their dead husbands, though they might do this only in solitude and within the four walls of their homes.

After the days of jubilation, life in the capital resumed its normal course, and no foreigner would have noticed any change. King Francis I's representative, who had attended the Sultan from Bagdad to Tabriz and back to Istanbul, was rewarded for his trouble by the Sultan's consent to a commercial treaty with France. Slaves of French birth in the Sultan's dominions were given their freedom and all things pointed to the fact that King Francis, having learned nothing from former failures, was preparing for another war against the Emperor. Khaireddin did not fall into disgrace as many had hoped; on the contrary, the treaty was drawn up in his name and he was designated therein as king of Algeria. Without this, ill feeling would have been aroused among both Moslems and Christians. As it was, many otherwise shrewd Moslems blamed the Grand Vizier for secretly favoring the Christians, just as he had been blamed for protecting the Shiite heretics at the Ottoman army's expense. But by this time all evil that occurred was laid at his door, to blacken his face and undermine his position, while all good was credited to the Sultan.

In the course of that spring the people's senseless and unreasoning hatred for the Grand Vizier became so evident that he preferred not to appear in public, and remained either in his palace beyond the Atmeidan or among the buildings of the third courtyard of the Seraglio. Janissaries exercising on the Atmeidan would yell insults and make faces at his palace, and one night some drunken wrestlers broke into it, tore the trophies from the walls and smashed them, and befouled the corners of his rooms. Yet to avoid all troublesome publicity the Grand Vizier made no inquiry and summoned none of the culprits to answer for the outrage.

After his return from Persia the Grand Vizier was compelled first of all to deal with matters that had arisen during his absence and that the pashas had refused to handle for fear of making mistakes. Negotiations in preparation for the French treaty also occupied his time, so that with the best will in the world he could not receive me. The winter days went by without hope of a personal interview, although I longed to warn him of dangers that I did not dare to hint at in a letter. Now and then he sent me word that he would attend to me all in good time.

In response to my continual pestering, the Grand Vizier sent me two hundred gold pieces in a silken bag. This was intended as a proof of his favor, but never did a present sadden and hurt me so much. It showed that in his heart he despised me and believed that I served him only for money—and how could I blame him for that? The fault was mine. Too long I had thought only of presents and rewards. But now as I stood idly among the slender pillars of the Grand Vizier's entrance hall with that embroidered purse in my hand, I perceived with agonizing clarity that not all the gold in the world could deaden the pain now gnawing at my heart.

Yet I will not seek to appear better than I am, for my object in writing this story is to be as honest as it is possible for imperfect human nature to be. Therefore I admit freely that since sharing the Tunisian diamonds with Andy I felt—though without any great pleasure—that my future was financially secure.

On my return Giulia laid her white arms about my neck and said coaxingly, "Dear Michael, while you were out I searched your medicine chest for a remedy for stomach trouble. The Greek gardener is ill. But I dared not take the African drug that you brought from Tunis, for you told me that an overdose might be dangerous. I don't want to harm the man through ignorance."

I disliked her habit of ransacking my chests while I was out, and I told her so. But my mind was on other things and I gave her a drug that Abu el-Kasim had warmly recommended, warning her against administering too much at a time. The same evening I was attacked by pains in the stomach after eating fruit, and Giulia told me that besides the gardener, one of the boatmen had also fallen sick. Such disorders were common in Istanbul and I paid no heed to my own pains. I took a dose of aloes and opium before going to bed and in the morning was fully recovered.

Next day I learned that the Sultan had suffered the same thing after an evening meal taken with the Grand Vizier. Suleiman at once succumbed to a mood of depression—a common enough thing among those suffering from stomach disorders.

As a result of the Sultan's sickness the Grand Vizier at last had his evenings to himself, and at sunset after the prayer he sent for me. I hastened at once to his palace, but that lovely building, usually brilliant

401

with countless lamps and surrounded by crowds, now stood dark, empty, and silent, like a house of mourning. Only a few pale slaves stood idly in the great hall, which was lit by a few faintly burning lamps, but between the slender columns of the audience chamber the German clockmaker came hurrying toward me. With him, to my surprise, was the Sultan's French clockmaker, whom King Francis had sent to Suleiman after hearing of his weakness for clocks. Both these masters were examining with solemn physicians' airs the unevenly ticking clock, made by Nürnberg's most famous horologist, that should have indicated unerringly the hour, date, month, year, and even the position of the planets. The German fell on his knees, kissed my hand, and said, "Ah, Master Michael, I am lost—I have forgotten my cunning. Thanks to my skilled repairs this unlucky timepiece has gone perfectly for six years, and now it has begun to lose. I cannot find what is wrong, and have had to beg the excellent Master François to help me."

The clock ticked heavily, its hand pointed to seven, and the little figure of the smith came out and began jerkily striking the silver bell. But he managed only three feeble strokes, the clock resumed its uneven ticking and the smith, his hammer still raised to strike, turned and disappeared. I looked searchingly at the two men and noted that the Frenchman guiltily thrust a wine jar behind the clock with his foot. Both men averted their eyes in some embarrassment, and then Master François said boastfully, "All clocks have their little ways, or we clockmakers would be out of work. I know this one inside out and to take apart so complicated a mechanism would be laborious and risky. So we have been content to refresh our memories and compare our pre-eminent knowledge, and so perhaps discover what the fault may be. It is not worth dismantling so costly a toy without good reason. The Grand Vizier is—forgive my candor—somewhat eccentric to regard this little irregularity as a bad omen."

In his drunkenness he continued to speak so slightingly of the Grand Vizier that I grew angry and raised my hand to strike him—though I doubt whether I would have done so as he held a hammer in his hand and had the look of a testy man. But the German flung himself between us and said, "If the clock is sick, the noble Grand Vizier is more so. No man in his senses keeps his eyes constantly on a clock and loses sleep because of it. At night he often gets up to look at it and in the daytime he will break off in the middle of a sentence before

402

the assembled Divan and stand staring at the dial. Each time he holds his head in his hand and says, 'My clock is losing. Allah be gracious to me, my clock runs slow.' Is that the talk of a sensible man?"

I left the fellow and hurried to the brightly lit chamber where the Grand Vizier was sitting cross legged on a triple cushion with a reading stand before him. I am not sure whether he was really reading or pretending to do so; at any rate, he turned a page calmly before raising his eyes to mine. I prostrated myself to kiss the ground before him, stammering for joy and calling down blessings upon him on his happy return from the war. He silenced me with a gesture of his thin hand and looked me straight in the eyes, while a shadow of ineffable sorrow stole over his face. His skin had lost its youthful glow and the roses of his cheeks were faded. His soft black beard made his face seem ghostly pale in the lamplight, and as he had removed his turban no diamonds sparkled over his brow. He had grown so thin that the rings hung loose upon his fingers and seemed too heavy for them.

"What do you want, Michael el-Hakim?" he asked. "I am Ibrahim, lord of the nations and steward of the Sultan's power. I can make you vizier if it pleases me. I can transform beggars into defterdars and boatmen to admirals. But though I hold the Sultan's own seal I cannot help myself."

He showed me the Sultan's square seal hanging on a gold chain about his neck under the flowered kaftan. I uttered a cry of amazement and pressed my face to the ground once more in veneration for this most precious object that no one but the Sultan might use. The Grand Vizier hid it beneath his kaftan once more and said in a tone of indifference, "With your own eyes you have seen the boundless trust reposed in me. This seal exacts unconditional obedience from high and low in all the Sultan's dominions. Perhaps you knew that?"

He smiled a queer smile, stared before him with a twitching face, and went on, "Perhaps you know too that the Sultan's square seal opens even the doors of the harem. There is nothing I cannot do as easily as if I were Suleiman himself. Do you understand what that means, Michael el-Hakim?"

I could only kneel before him, shake my head, and stammer, "No, no—I understand nothing—nothing!"

"You see how I pass the time in my solitude. I read—I tell the chaplet of words. On the golden shelves of my treasury stands the assembled wisdom of all lands and all ages. I read and let the words

403

flow past my eyes. On lonely evenings I can hear the sages speak together—famous generals, great rulers, cunning architects, and inspired poets, besides all the holy men who in their way are as possessed and inspired as the poets. All this wisdom is at my disposal—but how can it profit me now? I am Ibrahim the fortunate. My eyes have been opened and I see through all human prejudice. All this wisdom—hear what I say, Michael—all this wisdom is but words beautifully strung together. Chosen with taste, no doubt, but words only—strings of words and nothing more. I, Ibrahim, alone of all men, have in my possession the personal seal of the Ruler of the World. And what do I do, Michael el-Hakim? You see me. In my lonely room I read words that have been beautifully strung together."

He drew off the magnificent rings, irked by their looseness.

"He knows me and I know him. Twins could not divine one another's thoughts more swiftly and completely. Last night when he fell sick he handed me his seal, thereby delivering himself and his power into my hands. Perhaps it was to show me his unshaken trust. But I know him no longer and cannot read his thoughts as I used to do. Then he was a mirror, but another has breathed upon that mirror and I cannot see what is in his mind. I can do nothing—I cannot save myself. His trust has stolen my strength and my will."

Though he strove to master himself I saw his tremulous hands and twitching face, and as a physician I knew how sick must be his heart. I said soothingly, "Noble lord, the month of Ramadan has begun—a month as trying for rulers as for slaves. When the fast is over you will see all with other eyes and laugh at your hallucinations. You would do well to eat and drink your fill, visit your harem, and linger there until the new day of fasting and it is light enough to distinguish a black thread from a white. Experience had shown that pious vigil among the women of the harem has a soothing effect on the mind during Ramadan, and is prescribed by the Prophet himself."

He looked at me from out of his despair. "How can I eat or drink when because of his sickness my lord must fast? He is not my lord, he is my heart's brother, and I have never felt it so strongly as at the beginning of this Ramadan. My heart's brother and my only true friend on earth. For years I forgot this, arrogantly enjoying his gifts and his infinite favor. While his cruel father Selim lived we rode side by side and the dark wings of death hovered over our heads. He trusted me then—he knew I was ready at any moment to die for him.

404

But now his trust is gone. Were it not so he would not have given me this seal. He did it only to convince himself. He is a singular man, Michael. But why speak of that? It is all too late. My clock loses more and more and I have nothing to do but read words that have been beautifully strung together. For my eyes are still alive—"

He could sit still no longer, but rose to pace back and forth restlessly, the sound of his steps muffled by the gorgeous Oriental rugs. He cried out in despair, "My clock is losing! It has been slow from the first hour. The clocks of Europe tick more quickly than the best clocks of the East. Whatever I dreamed, desired, hoped, and even achieved, I heard only the answer of my dragging clock—'Too late, too late.' It was too late before Vienna. Too late in Bagdad, too late in Tabriz. Khaireddin came too late. Whatever I have done or decided— all has been too late."

Blood was mounting to his head and his eyes were suffused with it as he stared at me. "Allah, what can one man do! What armies of prejudice have I not had to fight, every moment! Everything I have achieved, every law I have made, has been met with hatred and ridicule. Yet when at length all opposition was vanquished the answer was the same—'Too late!' Only yesterday in my foolish conceit I could fancy no greater bitterness than this. But now at the beginning of Ramadan, as I sit reading words, I no longer care to defy my destiny."

His arms fell limply and his face, beautiful in its pallor, became calm and peaceful. An almost mischievous smile played over his lips as he said, "One of the Roman emperors sighed, when he was at the point of death, 'What an actor the world loses in me!' But I can hardly call myself even an actor. For the sake of our friendship I have so renounced myself that I hardly know when I'm acting and when I'm in earnest. Too much power turns a man into an actor—above all if that power is dependent on the will and favor of another, though that other be the most excellent man in the world. Yet I know that it is the same with him and perhaps even worse, for after all that has happened he will never be entirely sincere with anyone. He must choose every word and control every change of expression. Michael, Michael, he will suffer worse than I, and he will never know which is truth and which is falsehood in his own heart. And so I shudder for him, knowing how hideously alone he will be in the world. God, Allah, unknown tempter! Whoever You be, You cannot deny our friendship."

He fell silent and listened, shocked, to the echo of his voice. Then he whispered, "No man can trust his neighbor. That is the only enduring truth; there is none other in the world."

"Noble lord," I said, "too great mistrust is as bad as overconfidence. Both are disastrous in their effects. We should in all things seek the golden mean."

The Grand Vizier looked at me scornfully and asked, "Is that unpleasant woman seeking, through you, to lull me once more into a false sense of security before the blow falls? What do women know of friendship? Listen carefully, Michael—if there is on earth a devil in human shape it is that woman. But she has only a woman's understanding; she judges the world by herself and therefore could never see why the Sultan gave me the seal and its sovereign powers. Take her this greeting from me, Michael. To her life's end she will never succeed in cracking that nut, and nothing angers a woman more than the discovery that in the relationship between man and man there are things that women can never understand."

He surveyed me proudly with his brilliant eyes and seemed to me at that moment as beautiful as a fallen angel. With a gesture that waved away my attempts at contradiction, he said, "Perhaps you know that last night I dined with the Sultan. The more poison is dropped into his ear the more eager is he to keep me by him, to watch my thoughts and scrutinize my face. I chose for him as is fitting the best fruit in the dish. He peeled and ate it, and a quarter of an hour had barely passed when he felt a burning in his stomach and fancied he was going to die on the spot. He thought I had poisoned him. Exhausted by the emetics of the physicians he nevertheless realized that he would live, and looking me straight in the eye he handed me his personal seal. In this way he thought to bind me to him and prevent me from doing him harm. No stranger could understand his action, but ever since our boyhood I have shared his meals, slept beneath the same roof, and been his closest friend, until that fatal woman induced him to shut his heart from me. You spoke of too great mistrust, and I have reproached myself for it. But when with the sweat of terror on my brow I saw him poisoned I knew that the Russian woman had bewitched the fruit in my hand to cast suspicion upon me. Roxelana is no fool. I ate of the fruit—I ordered the slaves to eat the rest. Neither I nor they sickened. Only in the fruit I chose for him was there poison. Can you imagine anything more devilish than that?"

I shook my head compassionately.

"You are ill, lord. Your poisoned fancy has given you these notions. An infectious stomach disorder is rife in the city, and I myself fell sick the day before yesterday after eating apples. I beg you, lord, to drink this soothing medicine that I have brought. You need sleep—you need to forget your clock."

"So, you would give me a soothing drink, Michael el-Hakim! That, then, was the object of your visit. When you denied your Christ you did it to save your own miserable life. This time no doubt you have been offered more than thirty pieces of silver. You see, I know the Christian Scriptures."

Looking him in the eyes I answered, "Grand Vizier Ibrahim, I'm a poor man indeed, for I suppose I have neither God nor holy book on which I may swear a binding oath. But you I have never betrayed, and never shall. Not for your sake, but for mine—though I cannot hope you will understand that, since I hardly understand it myself. Perhaps to prove to myself that I, renegade and backslider, can be loyal to at least one person in the world and stand by his side in time of need."

Despite the conflict within him I believe my words made their impression, and when he had sat for some time gazing searchingly into my eyes he rose, walked over to a chest with a golden lid, threw it open and tossed out onto the floor a number of purses so stuffed with coin that the thin leather split and the pieces rolled over the floor. On the heap of purses he threw handfuls of pearls, rubies, sapphires, emeralds, and other stones; not even at Khaireddin's arrival had I beheld so much gold and so many sparkling jewels gathered together in one place.

"Michael el-Hakim! As sure as I am that there was poison in the fruit the Sultan ate, so sure am I that you are a betrayer. I ask only to know the truth. Not even the Russian can pay you so princely a sum as I can. Tell me the whole truth, Michael, and you shall take all this treasure away. This time no mutes stand behind the curtain. Truth alone can bring some relief to my burdened mind. The swiftest galley and a hundred sea janissaries shall take you to what country you please. Only have pity, Michael, and tell me the truth."

I stared as if bewitched at the dazzling heap, but soon with a bitter taste in my mouth I said, "My lord Ibrahim, if I were to tell you that I am a betrayer you would believe it because you want to believe it.

407

But I cannot confess to what is not true. Let me kiss your hand in farewell and go, and no longer plague you with my presence."

"If indeed you are loyal to me you're simpler than I thought. In the world of statecraft, loyalty is a form of idiocy."

I found the word of release and said smiling, "Then let us be two blockheads in the same boat. You are even more foolish than I, for you wear the Sultan's personal seal and yet refuse to use it to save yourself."

The Grand Vizier stared at me, and his eyes were weary with the struggle that rent his soul. His face was ashy pale and a dull film seemed to veil his eyes. In a lifeless voice he said, "Why, why do you stay by me? Are you bound to me by gratitude? It cannot be true. There is no more thankless creature than man, for unlike the beasts man hates his benefactor. Tell me why you will not desert me."

I kissed his hand with veneration, sat cross legged on the floor before him with my head in my hand, and thought about myself and my life, and about him and his.

For a long time we sat in silence, and then I said, "The question is not easy to answer. It must be because of the love I bear you, noble lord. Not for your gifts to me, but because you have sometimes spoken to me and treated me as if I were a reasoning being. I love you for your beauty, your intelligence, your pride, your doubts, and your wisdom. Your like has hardly been seen upon this earth. It is true that you have your faults. You're jealous of your power—you're a spendthrift, a blasphemer, and many other things that people blame you for. But none of this affects my feelings for you. No one hates you for your human failings, Grand Vizier Ibrahim, though they like to talk of them and magnify them, to justify to themselves and to their fellows the malice they bear you. They detest you only because you stand so high above other men, and that is something that mediocre souls can never endure. And yet in each one of us lies the latent faculty of surpassing others. Of that I am sure.

"Perhaps I love you best for your high aims and motives and for never behaving with deliberate cruelty to anyone. Thanks to you no one in the Sultan's dominions is persecuted for his faith, be he Christian or Jew. Do you wonder that men hate you, Grand Vizier Ibrahim? But because of these things I love you."

He listened with a tired smile, as if mocking himself and admiring my talent for stringing words so pleasantly together. I tiptoed from the room and fetched the tray of covered dishes that servants had prepared, setting it beside him, lifting the silver lids and tasting a little of all the food to reassure him. Abstractedly he began to eat, and when I gave him the sleeping draught he took it without demur. I held his hand until he slept, kissed it once more respectfully, and then replaced all the money and jewels in the chest so as not to expose the servants to too great temptation. I called these men and ordered them to undress their lord and carry him to bed, and they obeyed me with gladness, having felt deep concern for the sleeplessness that the Grand Vizier had so long suffered.

Three days afterward Mustafa ben-Nakir appeared, unexpectedly, as was his custom. I feared the worst, for he seemed to bring with him a breath of cold menace. The silver bells at his knees rang as pleasantly as ever, but he was less carefully dressed and less clean than he was wont to be. He had even forgotten the Persian book. I asked where he had been and what he had been doing, and he said, "Let us go down to your marble quay and watch the stars come out. A poem is about to be born in my heart and I do not want your servants or even your wife to be present at this solemn moment."

When we had made our way down to the water's edge, Mustafa ben-Nakir looked about him and asked, "Where is your brother Antar the wrestler?"

I replied impatiently that I knew little of his movements, because since our return from Tunis he had gone barefoot, let his hair grow, and spent days together among the dervishes, watching their magic arts and listening to the shameless tales with which they beguiled credulous women into giving them money. Yet I called him and he emerged reluctantly from the boathouse, gnawing a bone.

"Ah, Antar, do you think to join our brotherhood?" asked Mustafa ben-Nakir in wonder at his appearance. Andy stared at him oafishly with his round gray eyes and said, "You see I have no lionskin over my shoulders. But my aim has indeed been to seek God upon the mountaintops and in the desert. How could you guess my thoughts, when I have not hinted them even to the dervishes?"

Mustafa ben-Nakir was so greatly astonished that he touched brow and ground with his finger tips at Andy's feet.

"In truth," he said, "Allah is great and marvelous are his ways. This is the last thing I should have expected. Tell me what has led you to seek the holy path."

409

Andy seated himself on the edge of the landing stage and dipped his weary feet into the water, gnawing meanwhile at his bone.

"How am I to explain to you what I hardly understand myself? While I had my friend Michael's little dog beside me I felt a better creature. Rael hated no one and at once forgave all wrongs. If when I was drunk I happened to tread on his paws and make him yelp with pain, he'd come up to me at once to lick me as if asking forgiveness for having got in the way. He took the blame for my mistake, though over and over again I tried to explain the foolishness of this. On cold nights Rael would keep me warm. But who rightly values happiness and friendship before they're gone? Not until that good dog found his well-deserved reward in the Seraglio did I see how much Michael and I had lost."

He wiped away a few tears and went on, "Now that sorrow has found me I can see that the little dog was wiser than I; I see at last that I bear the guilt of the world's evil. Whenever I see a man do an evil or a cruel deed I say to myself, the fault is yours! Alas, I'm a simple man and would do best to betake myself to a mountaintop or a desert, for these new thoughts of mine seem greatly to irritate other people, and I think I shall never again go to war. If I do it must be for some good and righteous cause."

"I can offer you a good cause at this moment," said Mustafa ben-Nakir eagerly. "Move away out of earshot and guard us against eavesdroppers; make short work of them if they appear. A poem is about to be born in my heart."

Andy answered good naturedly, "I'm an ignorant fellow, yet I understand the anguish of such a birth. But I've noticed too that wine can allay much of it, and I will fetch Michael's largest wine jar from the cellar."

When he had gone, Mustafa ben-Nakir at once began, "I've been in the city to perform certain devotional exercises, and at the same time I heard news. There was also a story being told which I shall now repeat to you."

In vain I protested that I was in no mood for stories and would prefer to hear his errand in plain language. He insisted in injured tones that ill tidings must be wrapped in silk, and in the name of the Compassionate he went on, "There was once a rich and respected lord whose falconer was a handsome youth of the same age as himself. The master became exceedingly fond of his servant and believed him as honorable as he was handsome, but when he would have entrusted him with the stewardship of his household, the guileful servant protested, saying, 'It is not easy to govern so large a household. What surety have I that one day my lord will not be wroth with me and take off my head?' The honorable master laughed and said, 'I, wroth with thee? Thy friendship is more to me than the sight of my eyes. Yet, since neither of us can see into the future, I swear by the Prophet and the Koran that I will never dismiss or punish thee for any error. Rather I will protect and shield thee with all the power that Allah has given me, all the days of my life.'

"Not many years had passed before the slave squandered his master's substance and endangered his house by forming connections in the teeth of law and custom. All too late the noble lord perceived his mistake and would have punished the slave who had so basely abused his trust, but he was a devout man and could not break his oath. The slave, who after the manner of slaves hated and envied his master because of his noble nature, crept to his bedside one night, strangled him, and sold his house and possessions to the unbeliever, thus doing not only his master but all Islam irreparable harm."

Mustafa ben-Nakir fell silent, and in the blue darkness I saw the glitter of his eyes. He added coolly, "Is not that a strange story? What would you have done, Michael, in that noble master's place?"

"Allah, what a foolish question! I would have hastened to the Mufti and asked him for a *fatwa* to release me from my rash oath. That is what a mufti is for."

"Exactly!" whispered Mustafa. "This very morning the story has been told to the Mufti. He has been asked to prepare a *fatwa,* in return for which Sultan Suleiman has promised to build the most splendid mosque ever seen, at the highest point of the city. The *fatwa* frees him from the sacred oath that he swore in the folly of his youth, and he can now act without offending against the laws of the Koran."

I was silent, for the significance of the story had already dawned upon me. The Grand Vizier's fate was irrevocably sealed, and no one in the world could help him now. Mustafa ben-Nakir covertly watched my face in the blue twilight and became impatient.

"Why don't you speak, Michael? Are you as simple as your brother Antar? The opportunity will slip through our fingers. The Mufti has been given until tomorrow evening to consider. Tomorrow is the Ides of March, according to the Christian calendar, when all notable events are wont to take place. The time for action has come. The Ides of March favor the bold man, but crush the weak and vacillating beneath an iron heel."

"If by action you mean that we must fly, it is too late. In any case I will not desert the Grand Vizier in his most desperate hour, however foolish this may seem in the eyes of the prudent."

Mustafa ben-Nakir cried impatiently, "Are you asleep, Michael? Sultan Suleiman is unfit to be lord of the world. The Grand Vizier carries the Sultan's personal seal, and the Seraglio knows that Suleiman has been sick for some days. The janissaries love Prince Mustafa. The Young Moor is wintering here with his ships, and all we need is a large enough sum to distribute among the janissaries, rosy promises for the people, and larger farms for the spahis. Then the Seraglio would joyfully proclaim Prince Mustafa sultan. Michael, Michael! Destiny unaided has prepared all things for tomorrow."

"But," I asked in amazement, "what do you mean to do with Sultan Suleiman?"

"He must die, of course," said Mustafa in surprise. "One of those two must die, as you must see for yourself. When the Sultan has obtained his *fatwa* he will invite the Grand Vizier to an evening meal with him, but this time the meal will end with the coming of the mutes. Before this, however, will be the Grand Vizier's moment—the only moment and the last. They eat together; then poison, dagger, or noose will speak. The Sultan's face can be painted to conceal all signs of violence. And in any event, after his death the people will be thinking more about young Mustafa than about him."

My thoughts took a bold flight, and after my long depression and apathy I was fired with enthusiasm; for reason told me that Mustafa's plan was excellent. Once the deed was done neither janissaries nor eunuchs would ask needless questions; they would quickly submit to the will of Allah and hasten forward to receive from the heir the gifts to be expected at the beginning of a new reign. Meanwhile the cannon of the Young Moor would command the city. Should any pasha of the Divan be foolish enough to demand an inquiry, his colleagues would hasten to suppress him in the hope of seizing his appointment. I myself would lose nothing by the altered regime, whereas if the Grand Vizier were to die a traitor's death at the hands of the mutes, my own head would soon roll into the vaults beneath the Gateway of

412

Peace. Tradition would require the distribution of a large number of black kaftans among the Grand Vizier's adherents and servants.

We had already drunk deeply of the wine that Andy had set down within reach, and now I said, "Your health, Mustafa ben-Nakir! Your plan is excellent but you have not yet told me all. Be honest for once and say why you're risking your neck. I know you and your philosophy well enough to be sure that you wouldn't lift a finger for the Grand Vizier alone."

By the light of the rising moon I saw him incline his head toward mine. He seized the wine jar and drank, then said rapidly, "Ah, Michael my friend! Though I sought solace among the fair daughters of Bagdad how could I find it, when in *her* I had learned to adore the unattainable? I must be freed from this phantom, for reason tells me that she is but a woman like other women. But I can only win to this release in her arms, which is possible only if Sultan Suleiman dies and I can claim her as my reward. It is as simple as that. For the sake of a woman's rippling laugh the goddess of history will tomorrow turn a fresh page in her great book."

He hid his face in his hands and his whole body shook with passion, pain, and the sorcery that wine and the cool spring night had wrought. Andy approached, commiserated with him on the birth pangs of his poem, and helped him to his feet, though he too was so unsteady that they nearly tumbled into the water together. When Mustafa had released himself from Andy's arms he seized me by the shoulders and muttered thickly, "You know enough, Michael el-Hakim! Hasten now to him who is in both our thoughts. When he has promised to do his part we will make all ready for tomorrow."

Andy helped Mustafa away to bed and then at my orders put on a clean kaftan to attend me, for I dared not set forth alone on so perilous an errand. While the sleepy slaves were preparing the boat, Giulia came hurrying down to the landing stage, wringing her hands and weeping.

"Don't leave me alone, Michael! What has happened and what did Mustafa ben-Nakir want of you? And whither are you bound? You would not hide anything from me?"

I told her that Mustafa ben-Nakir had drunk himself insensible while composing a poem in honor of a certain exalted lady, but that I, being unable to sleep, was on my way to the great mosque to watch and pray. She told me that she too was sleepless and begged me to take her with me, that she might seek the company of the harem ladies. I could not refuse, yet it was without pleasure than I took my place beside her beneath the stern awning; indeed, I was surprised at my own sudden antipathy to her presence. Chancing to brush against her I felt that she was trembling.

"Are you cold, Giulia?" I asked in wonder. Then as she drew away from me, I turned my eyes to Alberto's dark, expressionless face. I remembered Giulia's cat, and many other things, until I too began to tremble.

"That Tunisian drug," I said in a low voice. "Why did you put it in the fruit you gave me some days ago? I had no need of it; I was quite well."

My calm tones lured her into the trap, for scheming though her nature was she often saw no farther than the end of her nose.

"Ah, Michael, you're not angry with me? It was for your good. You looked unwell and I feared you might have caught the boatman's sickness. I could not guess it would make you so ill."

After this admission I knew for certain that Sultana Khurrem had heard of the drug and begged her to obtain some of it. But Giulia had wanted first to try it out on me. It was clear that in such a matter the Sultana could not approach the Seraglio physicians. But Giulia was her confidante, and the very next evening the drug was in Khurrem's hands, to be skillfully introduced into the finest of the fruits destined for the Sultan's dessert. Courtesy, of course, required the Grand Vizier to offer the Sultan this very fruit.

Despite this new evidence of Giulia's treachery I felt no particular anger. Perhaps it had consumed itself. Indeed the certainty brought me something approaching relief. No more was said, and when we came alongside the Seraglio quay I set her and Alberto ashore before proceeding further to the end of the street leading to the great mosque. From here Andy and I could walk unnoticed uphill toward the Atmeidan and then follow the high wall surrounding the forbidden gardens. While I entered the Grand Vizier's palace by a back entrance, Andy remained on guard in the street.

I was taken straight to the Grand Vizier, who was sitting in his library on a plain leather cushion, holding a Greek parchment in his hand. He smiled pleasantly and said, "My clock is slow, and so I am not at all surprised to see you at so late an hour."

This time he was singularly well and carefully dressed. His hair was oiled and his hands and nails colored. He had even put red on his lips and wore earrings set with sparkling diamonds, and seemed to have regained his usual serenity. Wasting no time on preliminary courtesies I said, "Noble lord, your clock is not slow. I fancy that someone has bribed your clockmaker or the Sultan's to put it deliberately out of order, for you to take it as a bad omen. But your clock is not slow, happy Ibrahim. Indeed, it gains upon that of your enemies."

I told him rapidly of all I had learned—of the poison in the fruit, of the *fatwa,* of Mustafa ben-Nakir's plan, and of his brotherhood that stood ready to give Ibrahim the Grand Master their support.

"All is in readiness and nothing remains for you to do but to grasp the rudder of events. Strike first! Remember that where you are concerned the Sultan is nothing but an assassin. You eat alone together, and you are certainly stronger than he. You can take no weapon with you, but you can strangle him with the chain of the square seal. No one will suspect that of being the means of death, however carefully they search your clothes. But first strike him a heavy blow on the temple to keep him quiet. Be swift and bold and all will go well. Dominion of the empire awaits you—dominion perhaps of the whole world!"

He listened to me quietly and as if I were telling him some familiar tale. When I had finished, he said softly, "So, Michael el-Hakim, you're a traitor after all. But why did you not poison me, when you had so good an opportunity, or at least rob me? But I have had the money counted and none is missing. Truly Allah's creatures are strange in their diversity. There, do not weep! I would not for the world distress my only friend."

He patted me lightly on the cheek with his warm hand and invited me to sit at his right side; he poured wine for me into a golden goblet and chose for me the best pieces from a dish before him, as if I had been an honored guest. Having calmed me he went on, "You may be my friend, yet you do not know me. I have long considered all you suggest, and the plan in itself is excellent. Yet there is one drawback. Myself. No one knows this but the Sultan, and he showed his knowledge of it in giving me his seal. In his heart he knows that our friendship binds me closer than iron fetters. No, I shall not murder him. Since his youth he has been a melancholy man, and sorrow will keep him even closer company when I am gone. Henceforth terror will rule

415

the Seraglio—and all because of the Russian. Deeply, deeply do I pity him. He will be the loneliest man in all the Empire.

"You once said that a man must be loyal to at least one creature on earth. If you, then why not I? Man is greater than statecraft, honor, wealth, and power, though many will not see this. But let us be honest and admit that just as your loyalty to me is no more than loyalty to yourself, so is my loyalty to the Sultan nothing but loyalty to a certain poor Ibrahim who sits at his side, trying to persuade himself that he is a true man. The hour of parting is at hand, and we may doff our masks."

For a long time we sat in silence until no doubt he wearied of my company, for he said politely, "If indeed you do not mean to run away, do me one last service and have my body buried decently, after the Moslem fashion."

I suspect that he made me this last request from sheer courtesy, to show his faith in me, for he can have cared little what became of his remains. But I promised to do as he asked and kissed his hand and shoulder in farewell. Thus I parted forever from the most notable and singular of all the men I have met, a greater man than either the Emperor or the Sultan.

When I emerged from the servants' entrance I found Andy sitting in the street in the moonlight, singing a scurrilous German song. I said, "This is Ramadan, my dear Andy. Let us go to the great mosque to pray."

As with slippers in hand we stepped through the great copper gates and in among the porphyry pillars, peace entered my heart as softly and gently as my bare feet sank into the rich carpets on the floor. Only a few lamps were burning, and above them the vast dome soared up like the night sky.

The mosque was empty, but soon the feast of Bairam would come, when on the last night of Ramadan the hundred lamps would burn, the gilded texts would gleam from the giant medallions, and tens of thousands of Moslems would crowd under the great dome to hear the Koran read aloud from the throne of the Imams. Sultan Suleiman himself would be present, and behind the golden grille the ladies of the harem would follow the ceremonial, among them the devout Sultana Khurrem with Giulia at her side. But I should not share in the rejoicing. Along subterranean conduits my headless body would be sluggishly moving toward the Marmara.

416

Beneath a solitary lamp I pressed my forehead to the soft rug, rose, and once more prostrated myself before the face of Allah. But above all I directed my prayers to the incorruptible judge within myself, begging for strength to leave my imprisoning body without fear.

The crescent moon was dipping into cloud as the boat touched our landing stage and we stepped ashore. Giulia had not returned, nor was the skulking Alberto to be seen. Mustafa ben-Nakir still lay in profound slumber on my bed. I resolved to take advantage of the moment and said to Andy, "I want to speak to you seriously, so don't interrupt me with foolish questions. Tomorrow, the next day, or at latest in three days' time I shall be a dead man. As I am a slave of the Sultan's, my house and possessions revert to him, though through the favor she enjoys Giulia may be able to secure a lawful settlement. She is a free woman. And you, Andy, are a free man; I have seen to that. Your share of Muley-Hassan's diamonds is in my care and after my death you're to have my share, too. No one knows of these stones. Now is our chance to bury them in the garden. After my death, after the auction that will be held here, and when I have been quite forgotten—that will be at most a week, if I know the Seraglio—you can dig them up and sell the smallest of them to a reliable Jew for your journey money. I will give you his name later. The wisest thing you can do is to go to Egypt and seek the protection of the good eunuch Suleiman. You can either sail with him to India or, if he advises it, return to Venice and the Christian countries. You would do best to leave this house early tomorrow and stay for the time with the dervishes, for Moslems treat their holy men and other eccentrics well and do not persecute them."

Andy stared at me with an expressionless face. Then sighing deeply he said, "Allah truly is the one God, though at times I have doubted his sanity, peace be with him. I hear and I obey, and will pack up and go to Egypt if need be. But there's a time for everything and I shall not give up until I have seen your head fall with my own eyes. No, I shall not leave you, though they should crack my skull for it—if they can."

I rebuked him; I sought with both harsh and gentle words to persuade him. But he was obdurate, and I could do nothing but thank him irritably for his friendship and then hurry down with him to bury the diamonds.

By the time we returned from this task, one could distinguish a

417

black thread from a white, and a new day in Ramadan was beginning. Regardless of the sacred laws we went at once to rest, and with the peace of renunciation in my heart I sank into a profound slumber. I lay thus until roused by Mustafa ben-Nakir, who hung over me with tousled hair and his lionskin askew over his shoulders. Rising quickly I washed and dressed without a word, and at the sight of my face he too held his peace. Then unwilling to keep him longer in suspense I told him of what had passed.

As I spoke his face grew ever darker, though like a wise man he allowed no needless ejaculation to escape his lips—a circumstance greatly to his credit, for who else could have listened without cursing to the story of the crazed obstinacy with which the Grand Vizier had thrust aside our helping hands? When I had ended, Mustafa ben-Nakir began in his turn to wash himself, dye his hands, and anoint his head.

"Grand Vizier Ibrahim has condemned himself," he said at last. "It is easy to be mistaken in people. But now both your neck and mine are in danger, and no one will thank us for following Ibrahim to his death like sheep. Let us save our skins and cleanse ourselves from blame by testifying against him. No further harm can come to him through that, since the Sultan has already pronounced his doom by appealing to the Mufti."

"Allah, Allah!" I cried aghast. "May your name be accursed if ever you do such a thing."

He looked at me in wonder and said coldly, "I have my position and my work to do in the world, and the cornerstone of statesmanship is realism. The wise man abstains from vain struggle and joins the victor, so as to claim his share in the spoils. The turncoat is often in a better position than the conqueror, for he knows more and can sell his knowledge at a higher price."

I gazed into his shining eyes and beautiful face.

"No," I said softly. "I follow you no longer, Mustafa ben-Nakir. I have had enough of your doctrines."

"Then you're a simpleton, Michael el-Hakim, and I've been mistaken in you. Remember that only stupidity is punished. Not lechery, nor greed, nor betrayal, nor apostasy, but stupidity alone. And truth is the worst stupidity, for only the feeble-minded thinks he has found truth. But we will speak no more of this, and I will not seek to persuade a man as simple as you."

418

"You're right, son of the angel of death," I answered. "All you have told me I have found out for myself. And so it is high time for me to prove that there is something greater in man than I used to think. This concerns only me, and you must forgive me if I now ask you to go. I'm weak and easily led, and should hate to betray myself at the last moment."

A seductive smile overspread Mustafa ben-Nakir's face, like sunlight on a shroud.

"How can you be so sure that I am evil? How can you know that I am not the incorruptible judge within you, Michael el-Hakim?"

His bright eyes seemed to pierce me through. How he came to speak of that incorruptible judge I could not understand, and his words filled me with such horror that I sank to my knees trembling.

"Get thee behind me, Satan!" my lips murmured. But my heart was silent.

Giulia swept into the room, having just returned from the Seraglio. She drew the thin veil from her face, revealing cheeks glowing with excitement and eyes lit with secret triumph.

"Oh, Mustafa ben-Nakir!" she exclaimed. "How fortunate that you're still here. What will you give me for bringing you good tidings?"

"Torment me not, merciless Giulia, but tell me at once what you have to say. My heart is a leaf in the wind and my hands are ice."

Giulia tittered and said, "A certain exalted person has heard of the poems you have carved in the bark of the plane trees in the janissaries' courtyard, and those you sent with the merchants from Basra. She laughs at your poems, but is flattered by your attention, and it may be that she is curious to see your face once more. Tonight favors a meeting of which none need know. Perhaps she will allow you to read your poems to her, for it's said that during the nights of Ramadan women are full of whims. Hasten to the baths, Mustafa ben-Nakir, and let the attendants rub you with fragrant oils. At sunset, immediately after the hour of prayer, the forbidden door will open to you, and who knows what a night in Ramadan may hold in store?"

"Don't believe her!" I cried, deeply agitated. "This is nothing but a plot to get you out of the way. Fly to the monastery of your brotherhood, where none will dare to raise a hand against you."

Giulia stamped and her eyes shot lightnings of rage as she screamed, "Hold your tongue, Michael! You have nothing to say in this matter."

419

Mustafa ben-Nakir said, "Though it should mean death, yet she is and must ever be the only woman in the world for me. Perhaps it is a plot, but when she has heard what I have to say she may change her mind. Ah, Michael! I should be mad not to take the opportunity so freely offered. An hour or so ago I was ready to overturn the Empire —nay, the world—only to touch her. If I must die I will do so gladly, once I have dispelled the illusion that the unattainable is worth striving for."

When I went down to the landing stage with Mustafa ben-Nakir I saw to my surprise two blue-clad janissaries, who came in through the gate and began to follow me. Then as I looked about me I beheld armed janissaries on guard at every entrance, in the garden, and down on the marble quay. By this I saw that Khurrem meant to leave nothing to chance. I lingered to watch Giulia glide away in my beautifully carved boat, Alberto standing beside her with folded arms and a sneer on his dark face. A cold hand seemed to clutch at my heart, and as I stood staring at the hazy roofs of the Seraglio across the water the onbash of the janissaries came up to me and bowed respectfully. The crossed ladles on his white felt cap glinted in the sun. Touching brow and ground with his finger tips he said, "I have been ordered by the Aga to accompany you everywhere and protect you against all evil. I am to answer for your safety with my head; therefore, do not be angered by my constant attendance. For this service the ambassadors of unbelievers pay three aspers a day to the janissaries and six to me— but such things vary with means and position and I have no doubt that you are greatly superior to the ambassadors of unbelievers."

With a hopeful smile he twisted the ends of his long mustaches and looked admiringly at my turban, my earrings, and the buttons of my kaftan. There was nothing for it but to call down blessings on him and his men and to hand him a purse filled with aspers.

Few days in my life have seemed so long and heavy as that brilliant Ides of March, but after an eternity I watched the sun sink toward the Seraglio and tinge the billows of the Bosphorus with red. I sought out Abu el-Kasim's deaf-mute under the boatmen's shed on the shore, explained to him by signs what I wanted, and bade him betake himself as usual to the janissaries' courtyard by the Gateway of Peace.

I slept not a wink all that night, and at dawn I ordered the sentries to wake the sleeping janissaries, with whom Andy and I then made the journey to the Seraglio. At the Gateway of Peace I found my faithful deaf-mute keeping watch. At my coming he stepped forward and told me with eager signs that the Grand Vizier had come to the Seraglio the evening before, dismissed his followers, and passed through the Gateway of Peace. He had not returned. A further gesture told me that my lord and friend was no more, and regardless of rank and dignity I sat down upon the ground to await the moment when the body of the murdered man would be thrown out into the courtyard. My attendant janissaries sat down also at a respectful distance. In the slowly growing light I saw the shrewd eyes of the onbash fixed upon me, but he asked no questions, knowing that our least actions are written in Allah's great book long before our birth. Foolish curiosity was thus inconsistent with human dignity and self-respect.

The morning star faded, the cocks in the Seraglio forecourt began to crow, and soon the distant voice of the muezzin from the minaret of the great mosque reminded us that prayer is better than sleep. The onbash roused the janissaries, and we moved off in single file to the tiled fountain, where we proclaimed our intention and in turn performed our ablutions. Then turning our faces toward the Holy City we said our prayers. Soon the sun rose over the spring landscape and the great gates swung wide open. The porter, yawning and scratching his back, replied to our wordless query by pointing at a bier that stood under the archway for relatives to fetch away. But I alone, the renegade, with Andy and the deaf-mute, came to take Grand Vizier Ibrahim on his last journey.

Lying on that shabby bier he was less handsome than in life. His body was full of gaping wounds, and the green silk noose about his neck was drawn so tight that his face was black. His costly garments had been tossed pell mell over his naked body and the porter was even now removing them as his traditional perquisites. Nevertheless he willingly sold me a black cloth in which to swathe the body.

But it was too late. The janissaries who guarded me had already recognized him and could not restrain their cries of amazement and delight, though as a rule these men do not easily forget themselves and make it a point of honor to preserve impassive silence at all times. A crowd of others came to see what had happened, and soon the court resounded to excited chattering. I quickly gave the onbash the order to march and after only momentary hesitation he bowed, ordered four of his men to lift the bier, and took up his position in front of it, sending the other five on ahead to clear the way. Moslems have great respect for the One who severs all the bonds of friendship, and once we had left the courtyard we could make our way in peace, unmolested by passers-by.

We crossed the deserted Atmeidan and entered the Grand Vizier's palace, where we laid the bier down before the famous clock in the great audience chamber. I was not at all surprised to see that the clock had at last stopped during the evening of the fatal Ides of March. Only a few frightened servants obeyed my angry summons and crept from their hiding places with bent heads. To them and to the eunuchs I gave orders that the Grand Vizier's body should be arrayed in clean clothes and the face treated and colored to simulate the hues of life. Andy, meanwhile, went to find a hearse and a pair of horses.

While he was gone a dignitary sent by the Mufti arrived to announce in formal terms that burial in any of the Moslem graveyards of a protector of unbelievers and grand master of a heretic sect could on no account be permitted. This was an unforeseen difficulty, but while I was pondering what to do the young poet Baki arrived at the palace in tears, careless of the danger he ran by displaying grief for the death of a man disgraced. He told me that the dervishes would gladly allow the body to be laid at their sacred meeting place at Pera, if only to annoy the Mufti. I therefore sent him forward to arrange the matter with Murad-*tseleb*.

Andy returned from the coach houses where he had found only a hay wagon, as all the Grand Vizier's state carriages had been removed for fear of the Sultan's wrath. With curses and threats he had forced the terrified grooms to harness to this a pair of night-black horses that had been used at the funeral of the Sultan's mother a year or two before. Then I chose the finest carpets and silken covers in the house and with Andy's help transformed the wagon into a splendid hearse. When I had laid the body of the Grand Vizier upon it—leaving his face uncovered for all to see, for the skillful eunuch had given it back its former proud look—I sprinkled over it many flasks of rose water and also a pot of musk.

Having nothing to lose but my head, and that only once, I resolved to be thorough in my defiance of the Sultan's wrath. Therefore I ordered plumes to be fastened to the horses' heads and fine pepper to be sprinkled in their eyes until the poor beasts wept copious tears, as at the funerals of sultans. Encouraged by my boldness, two Negro grooms put on mourning and offered to lead the animals. So, by our resolute action, the procession soon moved off from the courtyard, headed by the onbash. His eyebrows were drawn fiercely together, his mustaches stood out stiffly, and he strutted and swung his staff of office as if he were a subash, at least. Andy and I walked with slow steps immediately behind the wagon, and we were followed by a few of Ibrahim's faithful old retainers.

In the meantime a crowd of silent onlookers had filled the Atmeidan, and had any ill-wisher taken it into his head to send agitators among them it might have gone badly with us. But all was deathly still; none dared molest us, and reverence for the dark, hovering wings held all decent Moslems motionless. Thus we crossed the Atmeidan unhindered, and the crowds fell in behind us until it seemed as if all Istanbul in deep, wordless grief meant to follow Grand Vizier Ibrahim to his grave.

At last we reached the great wall near the Adrianople Gate, where we turned our steps toward the shore and crossed the Arsenal Bridge to the Pera quarter, on the opposite side of the Golden Horn. The silent crowds halted at the bridge, but at the other end of it the dervishes were already waiting, led by Murad-*tseleb,* and beneath the sacred if somewhat notorious banner of their brotherhood they escorted us to their monastery at the top of the hill. Some of them whirled in wild mourning dances, while those with the shrillest voices sang laments. The professional mourning women who had long led the procession were now filled with emulous rivalry, scratching their faces till the blood flowed and tearing their hair as they uttered fiercer and fiercer howls.

Thus it was that contrary to all expectation the Grand Vizier's funeral procession proved an effective spectacle and one worthy of his standing, despite the short time at our disposal. I fancy that Sultana Khurrem never bargained for such a thing, but rather hoped that the janissaries would desecrate the hated body in the forecourt and rend it in pieces, as had been known to happen before.

When the grave was dug and lined with the costly rugs and silks from the hay wagon, I took my lord Ibrahim's body in my arms and laid him down for his last sleep, with his face toward the Holy City and his right hand under his cheek, that all requirements for a decent burial might be fulfilled. We then quickly filled in the grave, and to my delight the fragrance of musk floated up through the soil. Here on the mound I planted a young plane tree. Such trees live to be many hundreds of years old, and I hoped that this one would stand as a memorial to the Grand Vizier long after the capricious dervishes had abandoned the place.

With this I felt that my task was fully accomplished. I therefore took a tender leave of Murad-*tseleb,* thanking him for his friendship and calling down many blessings upon his head. My deaf-mute slave, who had followed the procession as inconspicuously as possible so as not to bring shame and ridicule upon it by his appearance, now approached and signed to me to hasten home. I began to suspect that his fellow mutes were awaiting me there, and turning to Andy I said, "Dear brother Andy, you must stay here among the dervishes and under the protection of the pious Murad-*tseleb.* This is my express order. Remember what I said to you last night. From now on your presence would be more trouble to me than it's worth."

Only such cold words as these could have kept him away from me and from danger. Crimson in the face he replied, "You could have taken leave of me in a kindlier way than that. But you were always headstrong, and I have always forgiven you your harshness. Go in peace, then, before I start to howl."

When I came home, the janissaries still in attendance, it was not yet midday. The house was empty and silent and the slaves had fled. Only the Indian who tended the fish sat cross legged by the pool, seemingly plunged in meditation. I walked quietly upstairs and to my astonishment found Mirmah busily engaged in pouring ink over page after page of my half-finished translation of the Koran. My most precious books she had torn in pieces so that the floor was white with their leaves. She started when she saw me, then put her hands behind her and stared at me in defiance. I had never struck her, and perhaps she thought I would not do so now. I asked, "Why have you done this, Mirmah? I don't think I ever did you any harm."

She stared at me with a strange leer. Then, unable to contain herself any longer, she screamed with laughter and cried, "Down on the landing stage you'll find a present that someone has thrown to you. That's why everyone has run away. Go down and look."

Full of forebodings I hurried down to the quay with the delighted Mirmah at my heels. But the janissaries had already found the body and the onbash was just turning the head with his foot to see the face. The body was naked, and so completely covered with blood that I thought at first the flayed carcass of an animal lay before me on the ground. The face was hard to recognize, as ears and nose had been cut away, the eyes put out, and the tongue gone from the gaping mouth. I had seen much in my life but never so gruesome and appalling a sight as this. I have no wish to describe all that had been done to the body. It would serve no purpose but to chase sleep from my eyes, though some years have passed since it happened. Nevertheless I summoned up all my resolution and bent down, and bit by bit I seemed to recognize familiar lines in that mutilated face. I noted the henna color of those soft hands and their well-cared-for, polished nails. My heart stood still and the blood turned to ice in my veins, for I saw that this was Mustafa ben-Nakir returned from his visit to the Seraglio. The eunuchs of the harem had thrown him on to my landing stage, having dealt with him as with all who are caught in the forbidden rooms.

Mirmah bent down, stuck her finger in Mustafa ben-Nakir's mouth and felt his pearly teeth. I snatched her up, thrust her into the arms of the onbash, and ordered him to take her out of my sight. Mirmah shrieked, scratched, and kicked, but the men took her away by force and locked her into Giulia's room. For a time she screamed and kicked at the door and smashed her mother's valuable ornaments to pieces; then I think she fell asleep on Giulia's bed, for presently we heard no more.

I left the janissaries to bury the ravaged body of my friend Mustafa ben-Nakir, rewarding them with the last gold pieces in my purse. The sight had filled me with such nausea that I could not stay to help them, but was compelled to go in and lie upon my bed.

After lying there for some hours and staring motionless at the ceiling I broke the fast of Ramadan, drank a cup of wine, and tried to eat, but found I could not swallow a mouthful. Soon I saw a magnificently ornamented boat gliding in toward the shore, and feeling strengthened by the wine I went down to receive my guests. The grateful janissaries had scrubbed the marble clean of all the blood. I fancy Mustafa ben-Nakir had been alive when he was thrown there and had bled copiously before he died. But now all was clean and neat and fit to receive the Seraglio barge with its silken awning. So incurably vain is human nature that I could not help feeling flattered as I beheld, besides the three red-clad deaf-mutes, the Kislar-Aga himself comfortably reclining in the stern. This mark of honor was enough to make me feel a man of consequence in the Ottoman Empire.

425

With him was Giulia and her inseparable Alberto, but without so much as a glance at them I bowed low before the Kislar-Aga and touched brow and ground with my finger tips. Then I helped my distinguished guest from the boat. The deaf-mutes followed him on noiseless feet. When all were ashore I made a becoming speech of welcome and acknowledgment of the high honor he did me in coming to supervise the execution of the Sultan's commands, and regretted that because of Ramadan I could not offer him so much as a cup of water.

In his gracious reply he begged me to bear him no malice for the melancholy task with which he had been entrusted, and to express any wishes I might have before this task was carried out. I replied that I would gladly speak with my wife in private on certain household affairs. To this he assented, and when I had quietly placed a bowl of sherbet and a dish of sweetmeats beside him—leaving it to him and Allah between them to determine his attitude to the fast—I walked upstairs. Giulia followed me hesitantly, and close behind her as a shadow came the yellow-clad Alberto, who narrowly watched my every movement. Having assured herself that Mirmah was safely sleeping she turned to me. Inquisitive even at the last I asked her, "Has anything unusual happened at the Seraglio?"

"The Sultan woke late," she answered absently, "and after very many prayers he commanded that all gold and silver plate be taken to the treasury and turned into minted coin. Henceforth he means to eat from platters of copper and drink from earthenware mugs. The whole city is to live by the law of the Koran, he says. All the afternoon he has been studying Sinan the Builder's plans for the greatest mosque ever designed. It is to have ten minarets and the Sultan will build his tomb there."

She paused and looked at me with those eyes of different colors; then with an air of innocence she asked, "Have you not seen your friend Mustafa ben-Nakir? He could tell you more than I can of the secrets of the Seraglio."

"So that was why they tore his tongue out," I said coolly. "You may be easy about him, Giulia. He is at rest in his grave. Have you no more news?"

Giulia, enraged at my seeming indifference, sneered, "Are you so inquisitive? Well, it was to tell you everything that I returned. It may amuse you to know that your friend Mustafa ben-Nakir revealed Ibra-

426

him's plans to murder the Sultan and seize power by bribing the janissaries. Suleiman no longer dared be alone with his dear friend; the mutes stood hidden behind the curtain while Sultana Khurrem and I watched through a hidden opening in the wall. They had little to say to one another, those two old friends. The Grand Vizier played his violin with unusual fire, and immediately after the meal the Sultan took a strong sleeping draught. No sooner was he asleep than Sultana Khurrem began taunting Ibrahim from behind the lattice and telling him of what Mustafa ben-Nakir had done. The Grand Vizier flew into a passion and told her his innermost thoughts about her. To put an end to this she beckoned the mutes to do their work. But he was so strong that contrary to custom the mutes had to inflict many deep wounds before they could master him enough to get the noose about his neck. We both saw how the blood splashed the walls of the room. The Sultan was carried elsewhere to have his sleep out undisturbed. Sultana Khurrem took the square seal from Ibrahim's neck and had his body carried out to the Gateway of Peace. But the door of that bloody room was sealed at Khurrem's orders by the Sultan's seal, to remain forever a reminder of what can happen to an overambitious man."

"And Mustafa ben-Nakir?"

Giulia's face flushed deeply; she quivered almost voluptuously and pressed against Alberto as she replied, "Sultana Khurrem is capricious and becomes much excited by the sight of blood. I may not speak of all that happened, but I fancy that Mustafa was not entirely disappointed. He remained long alone with her, but in the morning when a black thread could once more be distinguished from a white she sent him away lest he compromise her good name. But the trusty eunuchs found him in the forbidden garden and castrated him at once. They did a great deal more to him by means of short, keen knives, as is customary in the harem, and I believe that not even at Ibrahim's death did Sultana Khurrem laugh so cooing a laugh as when she witnessed Mustafa's fate. He heard it and raised his face to look upon her once more before they put out his eyes."

"I know, I know. You need say no more of that. But dusk is falling and it is time to tell me of yourself, dear Giulia. Tell me what sort of woman you are and why I have never pleased you—why it is you bear me so bitter a hatred."

Giulia's voice sank to a whisper and her whole body shook as she

427

replied, "Last night I learned something new, Michael, though I thought I knew it all. It is for that alone that I've returned, for I know now—though you can never understand—what exquisite pleasure I shall find in watching the silken noose drawn tight about your throat. I hope you will do me one last service and struggle hard against the mutes, weakling though you are. If sleep is death's brother, then for a chosen few voluptuous pleasure is its twin! This the Sultana has taught me, and my only regret is that I did not know it sooner; though at times when Alberto thrashed me I seemed to guess at something of the kind."

"What do I care about Alberto? I have long known that Mirmah is not my daughter, though I never cared to think of that too often. Also I loved you very dearly, desperately though I fought against my love when once I knew what you were. Answer me one question. Have you ever, even for a short time, truly loved me? That is all I want to hear from you now, Giulia—only that."

Giulia hesitated and turned a frightened glance toward Alberto's expressionless face. Then she said quickly, "No, I have never really loved you—never. At least not after I found the man who could master me. This you never understood, though often I angered you to make you behave like a man and beat me. Ah, Michael, as a husband you've been worse than a eunuch."

She was now such a stranger to me that I did not even hate her. This strangeness terrified me more than all else, and I could not conceive how I had ever kissed her limbs and her false lips, and with tears. At last in a tremulous voice I said, "The sun is setting and soon the stars will come out. Forgive me then, Giulia, for having spoiled your life and wearied you so long. No doubt it is partly my fault that during our life together you have been turned into a witch—a wild beast incapable of mercy. In my madness I fancied that deep love meant warmth and kindness between two people, and some mutual solace in the hideous loneliness that is the lot of each one of us. I don't blame you, Giulia. The mistake was mine and I blame only myself."

Giulia stared at me without grasping a word of what I was saying. I might have been speaking an unknown language. As I had no wish to delight her by displaying my terror of death, I straightened my trembling body and with head erect descended the stairs without giving her a glance. I believe I never even stammered as in the name of the Merciful and Compassionate I begged the Kislar-Aga respectfully to

428

be prompt in the execution of his task. He started from his pleasant snooze, regarded me benignly, and clapped his fat hands. The three mutes at once entered the room, the first of them bearing beneath his arm a bundle that I supposed to contain the necessary black kaftan. I could not but feel some curiosity as to the color of the silken noose. For the green I could not dare to hope, but even the red would have been a mark of high favor, for the salary I received entitled me to no more than the modest yellow cord.

But when the mute unfolded the bundle I was surprised to see only a large leather sack which he spread out upon the floor. At a sign from the Kislar-Aga he took out a hempen rope and while the other two seized Alberto firmly by the arms, he slipped the loop over the slave's head from behind and strangled him so swiftly and deftly that he had no time to realize what was happening. Alberto had fallen lifeless with a swollen and distorted face before Giulia had taken it in. Then she sprang on the kneeling eunuch like a cat, but his comrades knew their business. They caught her arms and twisted them behind her, holding her fast. She kicked, howled, and tossed her head from side to side, her eyes bloodshot with fury. The Kislar-Aga surveyed her with his head on one side, as if deriving pleasure from her anguish.

To me he said courteously, "Forgive me, slave Michael. By command of my sovereign lady I am to see that your wife is strangled, after which she will be sewn into a leather sack and thrown into the Marmara. Sultana Khurrem is as you know a devout lady and abominates the indecencies of which your wife Giulia has so repeatedly been guilty. Only recently did she learn how criminally Giulia abused her confidence by disguising her lover as a eunuch so as to take him with her into the forbidden apartments of the Seraglio. Naturally you are guiltless of this and I share your deep sorrow, but so shameful an offense must be punished and I can assure you that in future the noble Sultana Khurrem will be more discriminating in her choice of company."

Giulia had ceased her outcry and was now listening incredulously to his quiet speech. Froth appeared at the corners of her mouth as she screamed, "Are you out of your mind, Kislar-Aga? You shall pay for this with your head. I know too much about you and your secret dealings with the Seraglio physicians."

"Quite so," said the Kislar-Aga, and his fat, pale face was stony. "You know too much, you foolish woman. It is for that reason that

429

Sultana Khurrem has resolved to render you harmless. You should have understood that long ago—you should have seen it in the sand!"

With that he had had enough of words. Once more he gave a sign, the noose was slipped about Giulia's throat and drawn tight, so that her wild shriek was cut short. Trembling all over I turned away my head, unwilling to see those eyes fade in death. Her body was then lashed to Alberto's and both were pushed into the sack, which was quickly sewn up. When at last the mutes had departed with their burden I said in astonishment, "How dare they leave us alone together? I might have a weapon upon me and in my terror of death do you an injury. And why put off the inevitable any longer, for I suppose that my fate at your hands was preordained before my birth, noble Kislar-Aga."

He stroked his bulging chin and his eyes were cold as steel as he replied, "I have executed the Sultana's orders as confirmed by the Sultan. You also were to have been strangled, but here matters took an unexpected turn. The Sultan, noble man, greatly admires loyalty and daring, though he does not care to speak his mind to the Sultana. Perhaps too he stands just now in special need of acquiring merit. Therefore he commanded me secretly, without Sultana Khurrem's knowledge, to spare you, because you risked your life to give Grand Vizier Ibrahim an honorable burial. The city was in so disturbed a state that you might have been torn in pieces for it. I may tell you in confidence that your action has greatly healed and solaced his heart. Yet, as you will understand, he is compelled to banish you from the city, that the Sultana may never learn of your reprieve. He is once more a prey to profound melancholy and needs the consolation of white arms and a soft embrace. But you have placed me in a grave dilemma, Michael el-Hakim. I am bound to obey the Sultan's express command, yet I greatly fear the wrath of Sultana Khurrem. Whither will you go, Michael?"

"What do you say to Egypt, noble Kislar-Aga?" I asked meekly. "I fancy that that land is far enough away, and I believe I could find refuge there if you allow it."

While I was speaking there entered on noiseless feet a little eunuch who was also a mute; he closely scrutinized my appearance and with a gesture invited me to be seated. He then began to shave me, and afterward set out many materials and pots of color.

"Egypt will do very well," the Kislar-Aga assented. "You must forget

430

your former life and assume a new name. You must also alter your appearance. My barber is now shaving you and will next dye your skin brown. Don't be afraid at the wrinkles that will appear on your face as a result—they will disappear in a few weeks. Tomorrow the Sultan is to proclaim the dissolution of the brotherhood of whom Ibrahim was grand master. Countless dervishes will be fleeing for fear of the Mufti, and if you disguise yourself as one of them you need not fear detection. Remember only to talk as little as possible—and try in every way to behave yourself, or Sultana Khurrem will never forgive me."

The queer tone in which he said this made me suddenly suspicious, and I leaned forward to look more closely at the inscrutable face of a man trained in the Seraglio.

"Noble Kislar-Aga! Only the mutes have seen us and the Sultan need know nothing of what happens. How comes it that you're willing to spare me, when in general I know you to be a shrewd man?"

"I am a Moslem," he replied piously, "and the Sultan is Allah's shadow on earth. It is he alone whom I must obey, though it should cost me my head." He stroked his fat chin, coughed, and added casually, "Of course I expect a present worthy of you, and I fancy I shall not be disappointed. No doubt you will allow me to glance into the sack that you'll be taking with you to Egypt."

"Alas, what are you saying? Through my wife's extravagance I'm a poor man, as you must know. I own nothing but my house and furniture, and these I freely give you."

He shook his head reproachfully.

"Remember you are dead. Your wife also is dead, therefore your fair daughter Mirmah is your only lawful heir. How can you be so base as to seek to deceive the man who has saved your life?"

"Mirmah!" I cried with a start. "What is to become of her?"

The Kislar-Aga, resentful of my ingratitude, nevertheless answered patiently, "Sultana Khurrem is a pious woman and out of compassion for your unprotected daughter will take her into the harem and give her a suitable upbringing. She will also take over the stewardship of her property. The Defterdar's clerk will shortly appear here to make an inventory and to seal the house with the Sultana's personal seal. It would be well for you to make haste and bring out your treasure chest, or I may be tempted to follow your good advice."

I found myself in very great perplexity, for I knew that if I showed

431

him Muley-Hassan's diamonds I should never see a sign of them again, and he would certainly not allow me to dig up the bag alone.

While we were conversing the little barber had completely altered my appearance and now stood admiring the results of his work. He gave me a set of ragged garments, such as dervishes wear, and an evil-smelling goatskin to throw over my shoulders. He had even provided me with an old staff. I could not recognize myself when I looked at my reflection in the mirror.

I was still anxiously debating with myself how to satisfy the rapacious Kislar-Aga when my own deaf-mute entered the room. With flickering fingers he begged my pardon for entering unsummoned, then signed to me to accompany him to the cellars. The Kislar-Aga would not let me out of his sight for an instant, so we took a lantern and went down together. I seldom went to the cellar save to fetch up a jar of wine, and the deaf-mute led us to a room whose existence I had never suspected, since Giulia alone had instructed Sinan how the house was to be built. Clothes belonging to Alberto lay scattered about, and there was also a richly covered bed where Giulia must often have been when I fancied her at the Seraglio. Remains of food, already moldy, a jar of wine, and a lithe cane showed how diligently they had refreshed and revived themselves. The deaf-mute raised one of the flagstones and from the hole thus exposed came the blaze of gold and precious stones. The Kislar-Aga, forgetful of his dignity, fell on his knees and buried his arms to the elbows in coin, then brought out some magnificent ornaments that he inspected with the air of a connoisseur. Only now did I understand what had become of my wealth during all these years.

"Michael el-Hakim," said the Kislar-Aga, "your slave is more intelligent than you and deserves recompense. He will be raised to a position undreamed-of for one of his quality, for the mutes have chosen him to be their seventh man, now that his predecessor has disgraced himself by the wounds he inflicted on the Grand Vizier. They have already taught him how to handle the noose and he will soon be entirely competent for his merciful function. It was no doubt to win my favor that he showed us this hidden treasure."

He glanced with benevolent condescension at the deaf-mute and even patted him on the back. But the slave fell upon his knees to me, kissed my feet, watered my hands with his tears, and looked at me with so intelligent and human an expression that with a flash of insight I

432

realized that he knew more about me than I had ever suspected. My repugnance melted away and with my finger tips I touched his brow, eyes, and cheeks as a sign that I understood him. At the same time I felt greatly relieved not to be burdened with him on my journey to Egypt. The Kislar-Aga grew impatient and said, "Michael, you know me for an honest man. Take ten gold pieces from this heap; that's a great sum for a poor dervish. You may also give a gold piece to your slave."

Without further delay he took off his costly kaftan and spread it upon the ground, then with both hands heaped gold and jewels upon it. He had just tied sleeves and hem together to make a bundle when there was a fearful explosion. The floor shook, and plaster poured from the ceiling. The portly Kislar-Aga shook like a jelly and cried, "Allah means to punish the city! This is an earthquake. Let us hurry out before we're trapped like rats beneath the tumbling walls."

I too was frightened, but as I listened I could distinguish thunderous shots and understood that a cannon ball had struck the house. The janissaries in the garden were yelling at the tops of their voices and guessing at once what had happened I cursed Andy from the bottom of my heart because he would not even let me die in peace, but at the last moment must come meddling in my affairs. I ran swiftly upstairs and out into the garden, to see flames bursting from the janissaries' muskets. The din of the shooting deafened me, and it was then that I became aware of a dozen wine- and opium-maddened dervishes howling and whirling and brandishing scimitars all over my flowerbeds. I roared to Andy to call off this nonsense, the Kislar-Aga standing behind me meanwhile, trembling and holding me convulsively by the sleeves. Like most eunuchs he was afraid of noise and shooting. Andy obeyed and staggered forward, yet his eyes passed me by and he said inquiringly, "The voice is Jacob's, but where is Esau's hairy breast? I seemed to hear my brother Michael's bleating voice, though I came only to take charge of his corpse."

The Kislar-Aga, much to the onbash's relief, dismissed the janissaries, who had not dared fire directly on the holy men. These now whirled about the garden in their wild dances, calling on the name of Allah, reciting verses from the Koran, and gashing one another with their swords until their blood ran down in streams. To my delight not even the onbash had recognized me after my treatment at the barber's hands.

It was long before I could persuade Andy of my identity, but at last we attended the Kislar-Aga to his boat with all honor, and even helped him with his bundle, which was too heavy for a man of his years to carry alone. Then, when Andy and I were by ourselves, we dug up our buried diamonds, left the dervishes to their sacred dances, and slipped away in silence and without regret. That same night a fishing boat took us across the straits to Scutari, whence we were to embark upon our long voyage.

These nine books of my life I have written in the course of two years, at the dervish monastery near Cairo. For when after innumerable difficulties and sufferings I stood at last before Suleiman the eunuch he would not believe my story. He robbed me of my diamonds and locked me up in this cloister. The purpose of these books has been to prove to the noble Suleiman that after Grand Vizier Ibrahim's death I did not steal his diamonds. Ill-natured persons have even declared that I arranged his funeral solely in order to come at the treasure he had amassed in the course of years, since as his confidential friend I alone knew of their secret hiding place in the palace. Yet it is not my fault if the incompetent Defterdar's clerks have not been able to find that hiding place, and if they fancy I had time to conceal the treasure before the mutes strangled me in my house.

I wrote these nine books also to bring peace to my heart and to free myself from the oppressive memories of my former existence, for only thus can I begin a new life, having now—at least in my own eyes—matured as a human being. To attain this I have had to undergo many hard trials, of which my wife Giulia with her strange eyes was by no means the least. But now I believe I have found the right path, and I believe also that I am able to lead the life of an ordinary man, if only I may be given the opportunity to do so.

Openly and finally I mean to abstain from good resolutions, having found that where others are concerned they are apt to do more harm than good.

Epilogue

THE Nile had twice overflowed its banks before the unhappy dervish Michael reached the end of his long story. He wrote at night, and each morning presented himself at Suleiman the eunuch's palace to read aloud to him what he had written. And when at last he made an end, the thin and ragged dervish prostrated himself before Suleiman shedding bitter tears, and raising his hands in supplication he said, "Hear my prayer, noble Suleiman! Release me from these intolerable devotional exercises of the dervishes and above all restore to me my lawful property. Through this long story of mine I have shown conclusively that I came by it in what amounts to an honest manner, and now need it to begin the life of an ordinary man. It would be foolish indeed to start again as a beggar, and I would rather submit to the grim necessity of remaining for the rest of my days in this monastery."

Suleiman the eunuch stroked his many chins and his eyes were like slits as he surveyed the weeping dervish. Then a smile overspread his moonlike face, as he said, "Ah, Michael el-Hakim! Strange indeed are the shapes into which Allah molds his clay! Sometimes he fashions men of such honesty as to bring about their own downfall, and with the same earth he makes such cunning liars that even the wise man's head is turned by them and his reason fails. Of his grace Allah has favored me with a long life, and the profound knowledge of human nature that I have gathered in the course of it tells me that you are the greatest and most loquacious liar I have ever met. Nevertheless I must believe in your sincerity as a man, and by diverting me during many a heavy morning you have deserved the diamonds that you stole.

437

I will keep only two for myself—one in memory of you and the other as a reward for my patience in listening. You may now return to the world a free man, Michael el-Hakim, and begin life anew if such a task be in your power. But should you weary of it, return to me, for while Allah leaves me life and health you may count on my favor. Go therefore, Michael el-Hakim, and peace be with you!"

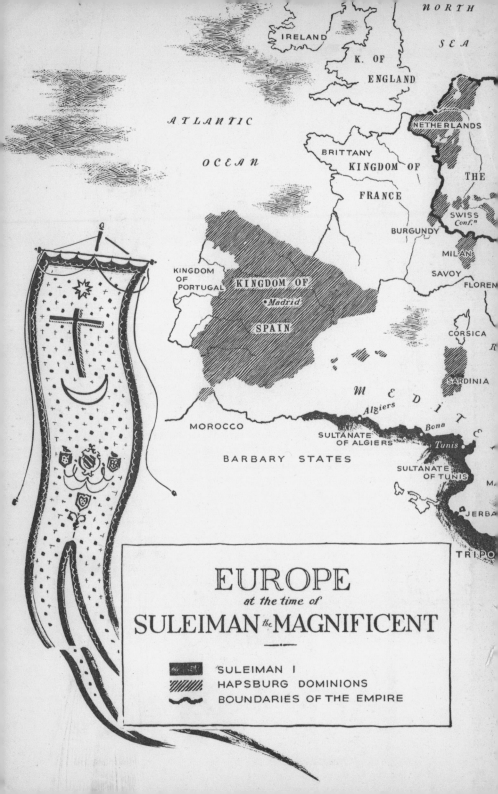

EUROPE
at the time of
SULEIMAN *the* MAGNIFICENT

SULEIMAN I
HAPSBURG DOMINIONS
BOUNDARIES OF THE EMPIRE